Close To Death

Also by Anthony Horowitz

The House of Silk
Moriarty
Trigger Mortis
Magpie Murders
The Word is Murder
Forever and a Day
The Sentence is Death
Moonflower Murders
A Line to Kill
With a Mind to Kill
The Twist of a Knife

ANTHONY
HOROWITZ

Close To
Death

CENTURY

1 3 5 7 9 10 8 6 4 2

Century
20 Vauxhall Bridge Road
London S W 1V 2SA

Century is part of the Penguin Random House group of companies
whose addresses can be found at global.penguinrandomhouse.com.

 Penguin
Random House
UK

First published by Century in 2024

www.penguin.co.uk

A CIP catalogue record for this book is available from the British Library.

ISBN 9781529904239 (hardback)
ISBN 9781529904246 (trade paperback)

Map © Darren Bennett at DKB Creative Ltd (www.dkbcreative.com)

Typeset in 13.5/17pt Fournier MT Std by Jouve (UK), Milton Keynes

Printed and bound in Great Britain by Clays Ltd, Elcograf S.p.A.

The authorised representative in the EEA is Penguin Random House Ireland,
Morrison Chambers, 32 Nassau Street, Dublin D02 YH68

In memory of Peter Wilson
12 January 1951 – 4 September 2023

The end is where we start from.

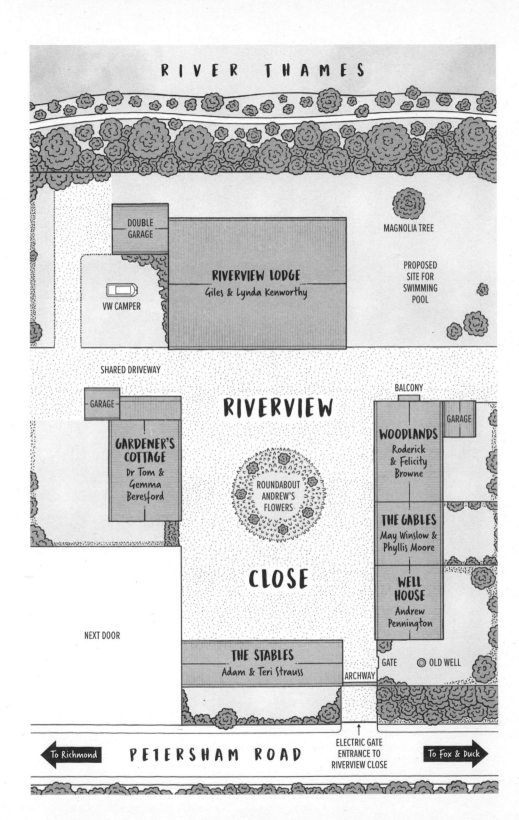

ONE
RIVERVIEW CLOSE

1

It was four o'clock in the morning, that strange interval between night and morning when both seem to be fighting each other for control of the day ahead. Riverview Close was perfectly silent, nothing moving, not a single light showing behind any of the windows – which was exactly how Adam Strauss liked it. He could imagine the entire world hanging in outer space, undecided, catching its breath while the mechanism of the universe ticked slowly round, preparing for the business of the next twenty-four hours, the start of another week. He alone was awake. Even the birds hadn't begun their infernal dawn chorus and the road, invisible on the other side of the brick wall that enclosed his garden, was delightfully empty of traffic.

It had been two hours since he had climbed out of bed and dressed himself in the smoking jacket, crisp white shirt and bow tie that his wife had left out for him. In the world he inhabited, what he chose to wear was not just a choice, it was a strategy, and it made no difference if, as now, his audience was unable to see him. He could see himself and, more importantly, his self-image, carefully created over several decades. His one deviation was the velvet slippers he had put on at the last minute, leaving the freshly polished shoes by the door. Slippers would be more comfortable and they were quieter, ensuring that Teri wouldn't be woken up as he made his way downstairs.

He was sitting, alone, in the long room that occupied almost the entire ground floor of The Stables, an open-plan kitchen at one end and a library/television area with its comfortable arrangement of sofas and chairs at the other. His seat was on castors, allowing him to slide up and down, alongside the eighteenth-century oak refectory table that had been rescued from a French monastery and which could easily have seated a dozen *frères*. The table drew a straight line from one end of the room to the other.

Six laptop computers had been placed side by side on the wooden surface and, apart from a single lamp in one corner, the only illumination in the room came from the glow of their screens. They sat in a sprawl of wires with an extension lead and plug connecting each one to the mains. The laptops could easily have operated on their own batteries for the required four hours, but Adam would have been aware of the power running down, of the battery symbols at the top of the screens diminishing, and even the faintest concern that one of them might blink out would have been enough to put him off his stride. He needed total focus. Everything had to be exactly right.

Adam Strauss, a grandmaster, had already played twenty-two games of simultaneous chess, connected over the internet to clubs in San Francisco, Los Angeles, Santa Barbara and Palm Springs. There were two sessions: he was well into the second, with twenty-four games, four to a screen, in front of him. The tournament had begun at six o'clock in the evening, Californian time – which was why he'd had to get up so early and continue through the night. In fact, it made little difference to him. Whether he was involved in a single game or a tournament, when he was playing chess he might as well have been on the moon. He wouldn't even notice the lack of gravity – or air.

Adam had won all twenty-two games in the first round and so far had seen off seventeen of his opponents in the second, although he had been pleasantly surprised by the abilities of these American amateurs. One of them – a man called Frank (no surnames were being used) – had managed to shatter his kingside pawn structure and he had been lucky to engineer a passed pawn for the endgame. Moving now to the next screen, he saw that Frank had pulled back a bishop, only making his position worse. Surely he could see that there were five moves to mate against any defence? The other contests were also drawing to a close and, at the current rate of play, he calculated that in eighteen minutes it would all be over. Theoretically, it

5

didn't matter if he lost or drew; the fee he was being paid would stay the same. But Adam had decided that he wanted to make a clean sweep: forty-six games, forty-six wins. However well they had played, these people were amateurs. They should have expected nothing less.

He advanced a rook on one screen (leaving it en prise . . . would Dean be unwise enough to take the bait?), put Charmaine in check (mate in three) and was just focusing on the next game, about to make his move, when he heard the gate opening outside his house.

Riverview Close was set back from the main road, connected to it by a narrow drive that ran through an archway with an electronic gate controlling who came in and out. Adam Strauss's house was right next to this entrance and although he couldn't hear the gate from his bedroom, which was on the other side, he was quite close to it here. Even as the mechanism whirred into action, it was accompanied by a blast of pop music cutting through the air like a blade through grey silk. '*So we danced all night to the best song ever . . .*' The lyrics were so loud they were echoing in the room and, for a brief moment, Strauss froze, his index finger hanging over the trackpad. He knew the car. He knew the driver. It was so typical. Only one man could be as gauche, as inconsiderate as this.

He looked up at the screen and even as he felt the cool touch of the plastic against his finger, he saw to his dismay that he had allowed his hand to fall. He had accidentally pressed the key and selected the wrong piece! The next move had been clear in his head: ♘xf2. It was so obvious, it could have been signposted in neon. But somehow he had managed to highlight the king standing next to the knight and the rules dictated that there could be no going back. He had to reposition the king on a legal square, although he saw at once that any move involving that piece would destroy his game. In that tiny second of non-concentration, he had ruined everything. It was over!

And so it proved. A tiny part of him had hoped that his opponent – Wayne – unable to believe his good luck, would come to the conclusion that Adam had laid some deep and impenetrable trap and would make a mistake of his own. Wayne was not a strong player. His opening had been standard, his middle game confused and he had stumbled into an endgame that should have been over in no more than six moves. But when, after completing another circuit, Adam returned to the game, he saw that Wayne had advanced his rook (♖d4), closing in for the kill. With a flicker of annoyance, he resigned.

Forty-five wins. One defeat. Somewhere in Santa Barbara he could imagine a schoolteacher or an accountant, or worse still a teenager, whooping it up. Wayne Nobody had just outmanoeuvred the man who had once beaten Kasparov and Spassky. On the thirty-eighth move. In a game that had been Adam's for the taking.

Fifteen minutes later, sitting there, utterly still, he heard a movement behind him. Teri, his wife, had come into the room, making no sound, her bare feet soft on the carpet. She laid a gentle hand on his shoulder but didn't speak until he looked up and she knew that the tournament had ended.

'How did it go?' she asked.

'Did you hear the car?' he asked back.

She nodded. 'It woke me up.' She glanced at the blank screens. 'What happened?'

'I lost focus. I threw a game away.'

Teri walked over to the front window and looked out. She saw that lights had come on in the big house on the far side of the close. A bright green sports car was parked outside the front door, its roof still down. For a moment, she didn't speak. She knew exactly what was going on inside her husband's head. She also knew that it was twenty past four and time to get back to bed. 'Just one game?' she asked.

'Yes.'

'You won all the others . . .'

'Yes.' He sounded irritable. Far from victorious.

'Of course it's annoying, Adam.' She was talking quickly, not allowing him to interrupt. 'But it's not important at all. It wasn't over the board and it won't be reported.' She smiled and held out a hand. 'Why don't you come up and get some sleep? You'll have forgotten the whole thing by tomorrow.'

Adam stood up and put his arms around her. She was wearing an ivory-coloured nightie which hung loosely off her shoulders and her skin had the wonderful warmth that is only generated beneath the covers of a bed. There was a faint muskiness about her. He would have recognised that scent anywhere. Teri was his second wife. His first marriage had been a hopeless mistake, but with her he had found the love of his life. He allowed the memory of forty-five of the games he had just played to slip away from him.

But one still remained.

Suddenly tired, Adam Strauss followed his wife upstairs. At the far end of the close, the lights in the big house blinked off.

2

Tom Beresford also heard his neighbour arrive, but in his case it was the slam of the car door rather than the strains of One Direction at full volume that jerked him out of his shallow sleep. Even without looking, he could tell exactly where the emerald-green Porsche Boxster (number plate COK 999) had parked. The sound of the tyres on the gravel and the crunch of footsteps heading towards the front door of the big house had given him a perfect mental image. It was going to happen again. When he tried to drive to work in about three hours' time, the car would be on the drive, perhaps with an inch either side allowing him to squeeze his way through, although it was more likely that he would have to ring the doorbell, engage in another pointless confrontation and quite probably end up walking or taking the bus to his surgery in Richmond.

He glanced sideways, searching for the silhouette of his

wife in the darkness. Gemma was lying on her back, quite still apart from the almost imperceptible rise and fall of her chest. He was glad she hadn't been woken up, although if there had been the slightest sound from the twins next door, she would have been out of bed in an instant. Forget the fact that there was a live-in nanny upstairs, fast asleep in her cosy room built into the eaves. Gemma had been connected to the girls from the day they had been born. If one of them fell over and hurt herself in a playground a mile away, she would somehow know.

Lying on his back next to his sleeping wife, alone but not alone, Dr Beresford had that familiar sense of a life no longer in his control. He had never wanted to come to Riverview Close, even if the house had seemed perfect when the estate agent had shown them round. A study for him, a garden for the children, the river, a golf club and the deer park all nearby. Richmond was regularly voted one of the happiest places in London, but he still missed the terraced house in Notting Hill Gate where he and Gemma had first lived together and where he'd had his own parking spot with no arguments, nobody blocking the way.

He also missed his old surgery. What was it that had changed, moving just seven miles west? He liked the other GPs he was working with in Richmond, although he saw very little of them. He was busier than he'd ever been, tired when he arrived at his consulting room and worn out by the time he left. He thought about the day ahead. Monday . . .

always the worst day of the week. He could expect twenty patients in his morning surgery, as many as twenty-five in the afternoon. There would be the usual backlog from the weekend. He could already see the letters piled up on his desk: clinic letters, lab reports, referrals, hospital discharge letters demanding one action or another. QOF indicators, CCG prescribing initiatives, CQE assessments. This was something that had become ever more apparent in the years since he had left Notting Hill. He had to wade through a slurry of different acronyms before he could actually start doing his job.

There was an unpleasant taste in his mouth and he remembered the whiskies he had thrown back before he'd gone to bed — but after he'd cleaned his teeth. The mixture of mint, fluoride and single malt had left an indelible coating on his tongue. If he had thought it would help him sleep, it had done exactly the opposite.

He was aware of a movement in the corner of his vision, as if someone or something had entered the room. But there was nobody there. The lights had gone out in the big house, allowing the night to leap up, filling in the corners. He closed his eyes. Go back to sleep, he told himself. Count sheep! Think about chapter six of *Fishburne and Grove: Workforce Planning and Development in the NHS*. Sink into the pillows and forget everything else. He should have taken a sleeping pill. He had prescribed zolpidem for himself. The 5 mg sleeping pills worked quickly and caused no residual cognitive impairment. Nor were they addictive. He took them once or maybe twice a week but never more than that. He had the situation under control. He was tempted to swallow one now, but even half a pill at this time of the morning would be disastrous. The one thing he couldn't do today was oversleep.

Quite apart from all the paperwork and the half-dozen home visits he would have to fit in (although he wondered if Mrs Leigh, with her enlarging aortic aneurism, would have survived the weekend), he had been asked to interview another candidate for the nurse vacancy that the practice had been unable to fill for the past three months. There was a young man due to arrive once the surgery closed – if he remembered to turn up. Just thinking about it all made his head hurt. If he was lucky, he would be home by seven for a quick dinner with Gemma before the meeting that had been called half an hour later at The Stables, the home of Adam Strauss.

That was the only thing that was keeping him going.

There was no point lying here trying to get back to a sleep that would never come. Dr Beresford gently slid out of the covers on his side of the bed, got up and padded out of the bedroom, dragging his dressing gown with him but leaving his slippers behind. Gemma always left the door ajar for the twins, so there was no need to turn the handle, no click from the spring mechanism inside the lock.

He padded down to the kitchen and it was only when he was there that he turned on the light. A half-empty bottle of single malt and a glass with an inch of water from melted ice stood on the counter, accusing him. He had let Gemma go to bed ahead of him, saying he had wanted to catch up with his emails – which was true. But it had also been an excuse to squeeze a few last drops of pleasure out of the weekend. If he were one of his patients, he would interrogate himself as to how much he was drinking. And like most of his patients, he would lie.

He flicked the kettle on and set about making himself a cup of coffee. If he turned on the grinder, he would only wake up the entire house. He would have to make do with instant. It didn't matter. Was it too early for a cigarette? He hadn't told Gemma that he was smoking again, but he wasn't going outside, barefoot, in his pyjamas. He waited for the kettle to boil. Forget the endless paperwork, the patients and his room at the surgery that backed on to the A316 with the traffic rushing past and the smell of exhaust fumes. Don't worry about Mrs Leigh. What mattered right now was the driveway used by all the residents of Riverview Close. Think about the meeting! It was happening tonight: a chance to come face to face with Giles Kenworthy and settle all the grievances that had been mounting up from the day their new neighbour had arrived. The noise, the parties, the ugly camper van, the smoke from the BBQs – but worse than all of these, the shared driveway. It had become an obsession with him. He knew it was ridiculous, but he was sure the challenge of getting in and out of it was the real reason why Richmond felt so alien to him.

Everything had been fine when he bought Gardener's Cottage, the second-largest house in the close. Or rather, when Gemma had bought it. It was her money that had made it possible, her success as a jewellery designer running an international business with boutiques in London, Paris, New York and Dubai. The three-storey house stood on the side furthest away from the entrance. To reach it, you drove through the automatic gate, past a line of terraced cottages and then round the top of a circle of grass and flower beds in the centre of the courtyard: effectively a roundabout with its own one-way system. Everyone travelled anticlockwise.

Things became more complicated, though, as Dr Beresford approached his own home. There were three garages in Riverview Close and, perhaps sensibly, the architects had built them out of sight, round the backs of the houses to which they belonged. The problem for Dr Beresford was that he shared a narrow driveway which led off from the round-about and ran a short distance between the side of Gardener's Cottage and the garden wall that belonged to Riverview Lodge before coming to a fork at the end: left for the Beresfords, right for the Kenworthys. Both families used this same stretch of gravel to reach their garages, but if Giles Kenworthy parked outside his own garage, it made it almost impossible for Dr Beresford to drive past and enter his.

The Kenworthys, who had come to Riverview Lodge seven months ago, had a two-car garage of their own. Unfortunately, they owned four cars. As well as the Porsche, there was a Mercedes, a Mini Cooper driven by Lynda Kenworthy and a Pontiac LeMans cabriolet, an absurd (and wide) classic car from the seventies. They had also parked a white VW camper van in the space next to their garage. It had never moved from the day it had arrived and for Dr Beresford it had become a skulking monster that he couldn't help noticing every time he went into his bathroom.

Giles Kenworthy worked in finance, of course. He was one of those people who made money out of money but did nothing for anybody around them. He didn't save lives, for example, or go into schools to lecture children on healthy eating. But that wasn't what bothered Tom Beresford. It was the man's extraordinary sense of entitlement, his utter lack of kindness or empathy. How many times had Tom explained he needed to get in and out whenever he wanted, that he might have to reach his surgery for an emergency? Kenworthy always had an excuse. *It was late. I was in a hurry. I was only there for half an hour. You could have got past.* But he never listened.

Tom Beresford had taken legal advice. As it happened, one of his neighbours – Andrew Pennington – was a retired barrister and he had examined the management contract they had all signed. The entire driveway, including the section that led to the two garages, belonged to all six houses in the close, meaning that any costs for its maintenance and repair were divided between them. Burrow into the small print and you would discover that everyone was legally obliged 'to be considerate and not block the driveway from other users'. But what did that mean, exactly? How did you prove a lack of consideration? And if one person was being wilfully obstructive, what could you do about it? Andrew Pennington had advised patience and negotiation.

But it was driving Tom Beresford mad.

He went over to the kitchen window and pressed his face against the glass, looking obliquely out. He saw it at once, exactly where he had expected it to be: facing his garage, its bright green backside visible where the front wall ended, jutting into the middle of the drive. The rage he felt at that moment was almost physical, a wave of nausea and tiredness that shuddered through him. Much of it was caused by his work, the twins, Mrs Leigh, the form-filling, the hours, the bills, the complete helplessness, the sense of being adrift in his own life. But above all it was Giles Kenworthy's car. It wasn't fair. He had spent his entire life helping other people. How could one man treat him with such contempt?

They were going to meet tonight. Everyone who lived in Riverview Close. There was to be a reckoning.

For Tom Beresford, it couldn't come soon enough.

3

Despite its name, Riverview Close had no view of the River Thames.

It stood in the grounds of a former royal residence, Rievaulx Hall, built in 1758 for Jane Rievaulx, a less well-known mistress of King George II. According to contemporary reports, the original house was something of a rarity: a Palladian villa that managed to be asymmetrical and ugly. It was perhaps no surprise that its architect, William de Quincey, eventually died in a prison that, by coincidence, he had also designed. Nothing remained of the old house. It had been damaged by fire in the early nineteenth century, left abandoned for almost a hundred and fifty years and finally bombed in 1941 by the Luftwaffe, who had done the entire neighbourhood a favour by getting rid of what had become a well-known eyesore. At some time during all this, Rievaulx had been distorted into Riverview, either because the locals had no time for fancy French names or simply because they were unable to spell it properly.

What had been left of the estate was an irregular patch of land just off the Petersham Road, separated from the River Thames by a thick ribbon of woodland, with the towpath on the other side and no glimpse of the water, not even in winter when the branches were bare. Even so, the misnomer had stuck and when the area was finally developed with six new houses, the largest of them standing in the footprint of the original villa and two others built where the gardener's cottage and the stables had been, Riverview Close was what it was called.

The architects had decided on a deliberately picturesque design using traditional stock brick that might have characterised an English village, along with Dutch gables, sash windows and plenty of flowers and shrubbery to help the new owners forget that they were on the edge of a major city and, indeed, in the modern world. Once the gate swung shut, the close lived up to its name in every respect. It was a tightly knit community. In fact, it was almost hermetically sealed. Yes, you could still hear the traffic crawling up and down Richmond Hill – particularly in the morning and evening rush hours. But the sound was counterbalanced by birdsong, the whirr of weekend lawnmowers, the occasional snatch of Bach or Sidney Bechet through an open window. Everyone knew each other. Everyone got on.

At least, they had until the Kenworthys arrived.

Andrew Pennington had been at home that day and had watched the removal men drive in, the pantechnicons only just scraping under the archway directly outside his house. He wasn't sure what the procession resembled more: a royal pageant or a funeral. One after another they had pulled up outside Riverview Lodge, a dozen young men bursting out and then scurrying around with boxes, crates and different pieces of furniture shrouded in what must have been a mile of bubble wrap. Andrew had already spoken to Adam Strauss, who had sold the property and then moved into The Stables, on the other side of the entranceway from him. He had learned that Giles Kenworthy was some sort of hedge fund manager, with offices in Liverpool Street. His wife, Lynda, was a retired flight attendant. They had two children – Hugo, twelve, and Tristram, nine – both of them at a local prep school, on their way to Eton. They had a ski chalet in Les Trois Vallées. They had been living in Guildford but wanted to be closer to London.

The family had arrived a few days after their furnishings. Andrew knew the moment they were there. They had announced their presence with pop music pounding out from somewhere upstairs, followed shortly by the snarl of buzz saws as two English yews that had been planted a few years back were chopped down to make way for a patio extension. A day later, he had spotted two boys chasing each other round the close on skateboards, armed with plastic *Star Wars* light-sabres. Two cars had already driven (the wrong way) round the roundabout and taken a tight right turn into the garage. A third, a Mercedes-Benz M-Class, took its place on the drive. All of this might have set him against his new neighbours, but Andrew preferred to give them the benefit of the doubt. It was perhaps a paradox that forty years as a criminal barrister had persuaded him to see the best in the worst of people, but then again he had always worked in defence and had learned that although everyone had the capacity to commit murder, even the most cold-blooded killers had a grain of goodness buried somewhere inside them, if you just looked hard enough. Fear, guilt, remorse . . . It took many forms, but he had never met anyone with no humanity at all.

His career was behind him now. He had retired at about the same time his wife had been diagnosed with the cancer that would eventually take her from him. With the encouragement of his neighbours, he had planted the flowers in the courtyard roundabout, each one of them a small celebration of her life. There were white peonies, which she had carried in her wedding bouquet, and lavender, a perfume she had often worn. *Argyranthemum* 'Jamaica Primrose', because that was where she had been born and where the two of them had met. And sweet iris, which recalled her name. Riverview Close employed a full-time gardener and handyman – in fact a woman – but she never touched the flower display. Andrew insisted on doing all the work himself.

His first meeting with Giles Kenworthy had been nothing short of a disaster.

On the first Sunday afternoon following their arrival, Andrew had walked round with a ginger cake he had baked that morning and which he thought might be a nice way to introduce himself. It was the last week in November and surprisingly warm, one of those days that the British weather occasionally throws out to take everyone by surprise. He had nearly always done the cooking when Iris was alive and his ginger cake with cinnamon and black treacle had been one of her favourites.

Carrying the cake in a plastic box, Andrew had crossed the close and rung the doorbell of Riverview Lodge. He had often been in the house when Adam Strauss had lived there – there had been regular suppers and drinks parties in each other's homes – and he resisted the temptation to peer into the windows on either side to see what changes had been made. After a long wait, just when he was tempted to ring a second time, the door suddenly jerked open and Andrew was given his first close-up view of his new neighbour.

Giles Kenworthy did not look very friendly, as if he had been disturbed in the middle of something important. He was a short man with very dark, beady eyes and neatly combed hair that was so jet black it might have been dyed. His cheeks were round and well polished, and this, along with his upturned nose and the white cricket jersey he was wearing, suggested something of the schoolboy about him, although he must have been in his forties. He was smiling but in an unpleasant way. It was the way a child might smile whilst pulling the legs of a spider.

'Yes?' he said. He had a high-pitched voice. A single word was enough to reveal his public-school background. Andrew hesitated, and in that moment, Kenworthy took control of the situation. 'It's going round the back,' he said. 'You can use the garden gate.'

'I'm sorry?'

'You're delivering the barbecue?' It was as much a statement as a question. Kenworthy looked past him. 'Where's your van?'

'No. I'm your neighbour. I just wanted to welcome you to the close.' Andrew lifted the Tupperware box. 'I made this for you.'

Kenworthy's face fell. 'God! What a stupid bloody mistake. I'm terribly sorry. We've bought a new gas barbecue and it's meant to be delivered around now.' He reached out and took the box. 'That's very kind of you . . . but you're going to have to forgive me. I can't invite you in right now. We're both at sixes and sevens and one of the boys seems to have got whooping cough. Will you think me very rude if I take a rain check?'

'No. I'm sorry if I've called at a bad time.'

'Not at all. It's a very kind thought. You didn't tell me your name.'

'Andrew Pennington.'

'Well, Andy, it's a pleasure to meet you. I'm sure we'll be having a housewarming party in due course and that'll give us a chance to get to know each other better. Which is your place?'

23

'I'm over by the entrance.' Andrew pointed. 'Well House. You may have noticed the old well next to the archway. They say it dates back to the fifteenth century.' He wasn't quite sure why he had volunteered this information. 'You should keep your boys away from it,' he added. 'You wouldn't want one of them to fall in.'

'I'm sure they're more sensible than that, but I'll have a word. And if you see the chaps with the barbecue, maybe you can point them in the right direction.'

'I'll do that.'

'Thank you.'

The door closed. Andrew was almost surprised to find that the cake was no longer in his hand. He turned round and walked home.

It was only later that the doubts came clouding in.

It was true that he hadn't looked his best. He had spent the morning doing odd jobs and he was still wearing his old corduroy trousers and a loose-fitting shirt. He should have taken a shower first and changed into something a little smarter. But could Kenworthy have possibly mistaken him for a delivery man when there was no van in sight – and didn't most delivery people wear uniforms? And there had definitely been something a little fake, a little knowing about that opening statement. *'It's going round the back. You can use the garden gate.'* Giles Kenworthy had delivered it with a curl of the lip that had been dismissive in every sense, as if he were deliberately making a point.

Casual racism had been a part of Andrew Pennington's life for as long as he could remember. He knew that he had been fortunate. His father had made a great deal of money in tele-communications, which had unlocked a private education and, when he announced that he wanted a career in law, entry into a big-name chambers in Lincoln's Inn. Not for him the so-called 'black ghetto chambers' that would have seen him working with local solicitors on pedestrian cases funded by legal aid. First as a pupil and then as a tenant, he had worked tirelessly. He had never allowed himself a margin of error. There could be no mistakes. Twice as hard to get half as far – that was the old adage.

Nobody ever said anything. Nobody was offensive. But he could feel it the moment he walked into a room, the sense that he was different, because of his colour. And there was that strange lack of progress. He got on well with the clerks, but his name was never put forward for the more high-profile cases. He was still trawling through stacks of documents late into the night when he should have been, at the very least, a junior junior.

Even in the latter part of his career, when he had become a QC, it had continued. How many times had he been stopped on his way into court, mistaken for a clerk, for a journalist or – worse still – for a defendant? *'Excuse me, sir. Can I have your name so I can mark you as here for your case?'* The security guards were always polite and apologetic, but he sometimes felt that they were all part of the same conspiracy against him.

And then there were the judges who patronised him or dis-
missed him – at least, until he began his cross-examination.

He had never complained. Iris had always insisted that if
he was going to advance in a world where black barristers
made up only one per cent of the workforce, he should play
the game, keep his head down.

'But what about those who follow?' he had asked her.
'Don't I owe it to them to speak out, to make a noise? I spend
my entire life talking about justice – but how can I do that
when there's no justice for me?'

'You are a successful man, Andrew,' she had replied. 'I'm
proud of you. And you being so successful . . . that will lead
the way for others.'

Lying alone in the bed that they had shared for thirty-five
years, Andrew remembered her voice. It was half past five in
the morning and already light. He had been woken up by the
Porsche, just like Adam Strauss and Tom Beresford. Where
had Giles Kenworthy been, out all night until four in the
morning? Didn't he ever sleep?

Was Giles a racist?

There was something else Andrew had noticed while
standing there with the cake. A flyer had been placed in one
of the windows – quite unnecessarily, as the only people who
could see it lived in the close. It was a bright red square with
the words BELIEVE IN BRITAIN printed in white. He
had recognised the slogan of the UK Independence Party,
none of whose members were racist, of course, but whose

candidates had so far managed to offend just about every ethnic group in the country, including his own. Every time he walked home, Andrew saw the poster and couldn't escape the feeling that it was aimed, directly, at him.

And although there had been half a dozen parties at Riverview Lodge, including a New Year's Eve special that had managed to extend itself until midnight on 1 January, Andrew's invitation had somehow never materialised. Seven months later, he had never been inside the house.

He got out of bed and went downstairs to make himself some tea. There were photographs of Iris all around him and he wondered what she would say. Would she have come with him to the meeting that was being held that evening, a chance for everyone to air their grievances, or would she have warned him not to go? He opened the fridge and sniffed the milk, and at the same time he heard her voice.

'No good will come of it, Andrew. You know that. How many times have you seen it? Little grudges that get out of control and turn into fights, and fights that somehow become violent and end up with you standing there in court? You stay away!'

He closed the fridge door. He knew what she would have said, but this time he wasn't going to listen to her. It was only much later that he would wish he had.

4

At exactly eight o'clock that morning, May Winslow and Phyllis Moore sat down to breakfast together in their tiny, perfectly arranged kitchen. They each had an organic free-range egg boiled for three and a half minutes, a square of white toast without the crusts and a glass of freshly squeezed orange juice, along with a shared pot of tea. They faced each other across a small kitchen table with a gingham cloth, two plates, two spoons, two egg cups and two porcelain mugs. Upstairs, there were two small bedrooms with single beds. Both women had been married and both of them were widows. May had a son who had moved abroad, and outside the close they had few friends. They were quite happy to live the single life but preferred to do so together.

They had moved into The Gables in February 2000, fourteen years ago.

In keeping with the village ethos of the place, the architects had created a terrace of three cottages that stretched out along the eastern side. The Gables was in the middle, between Well House and Woodlands; with narrow corridors and a garden that seemed to struggle for space, it was the smallest home in the close and also the least expensive. But May, who had found the house, was determined to move into a smart neighbourhood. She had been born in Richmond and her parents had been what she would have called 'respectable people'. In her last years, she was determined to live like them.

The new development had sold very quickly, although it had still been six months before everyone arrived, and once the dust had settled, May could see that she had made the right decision. Her immediate neighbours – Andrew and Iris Pennington on one side and Roderick and Felicity Browne on the other – were delightful. The Beresfords had arrived next, moving into Gardener's Cottage, exactly opposite them.

That just left two properties.

Adam Strauss, a very famous chess player and a minor celebrity with his own game show on television, had originally moved into Riverview Lodge, the largest and by far the most expensive property in the close. At the same time, The Stables, backing on to the Petersham Road, became the home of a businessman called Jon Emin, who had moved in with his wife, two very polite children and a black Labrador called Doris. He was the last to arrive and, as things turned out, would be the first to go.

From the very start, everyone had got on perfectly, the way

that neighbours used to long ago, when May was a girl. They were friendly but not obtrusive, helping each other when needed, swapping local information, stopping for a chat whenever the occasion demanded. Occasionally, they had lunches or dinners in each other's houses. Andrew and Iris played bridge with Roderick and Felicity. The Beresfords and the Emins were close. Adam Strauss and his first wife, Wendy, threw a garden party every summer and everyone came.

Inevitably, over the years, things had changed. Life is seldom perfect and even when it is, it's not for ever. May and Phyllis had largely kept themselves to themselves, part of the little community but not dependent on it. However, as they drifted into and then out of their seventies, they both found themselves having to adapt to new circumstances.

The women who lived on either side of them – Felicity Browne and Iris Pennington – both became sick. Despite her relatively young age, Felicity was soon confined to her bed and rarely left the house. Iris's illness was worse. She was diagnosed with pancreatic cancer and died a few years later. Death was followed by new life. Gemma Beresford in Gardener's Cottage gave birth to twin girls. At around the same time, Adam and Wendy Strauss got divorced. Wendy had never fitted into the close and it was no secret that she had been unhappy for some time. Adam remarried a year later, but he and his new wife, Teri, never took to the Lodge: it was too big for them – and too expensive. Adam's earnings had shrunk. His TV quiz show, *It's Your Move*, had been cancelled, and he had been hit by a series of poor investments. Although the couple would remain where they were for another three years, they both knew they had no choice and began looking for somewhere else to live, outside Richmond.

But then, at exactly the right moment, Jon Emin announced that he was relocating his family to Suffolk. He had made a fortune out of his business, arranging private and business loans, and wanted somewhere bigger to bring up his children, preferably in the countryside. May Winslow was particularly sorry to see the family go. Like them, she had a pet — a French bulldog — and they'd often met walking along the river. However, their departure brought an unexpected bonus. Adam spoke to Jon Emin and the two men agreed a private sale. The week the Emins left, Adam and Teri Strauss moved across to The Stables, keeping the Riverview community intact.

The only question was, who would be the new owner of Riverview Lodge — and more importantly, would they fit in?

'Did you hear him last night?' Phyllis asked, as she sliced the top off her egg with a decisive swing of the knife. She was the smaller of the two women, with tightly permed white hair and a thin frame. Her face had folded itself into so many creases that if she had been mummified, no one would have noticed. Certainly, it was almost impossible to imagine her as a young woman. Her seventy-nine years had her in their grip and she had long ago given up caring. Even her clothes could have been deliberately chosen to date her. Today she was wearing a floral-patterned dress that hung as loosely on her

31

as if it had still been in the wardrobe and brown derby shoes that took her all the way back to World War Two.

'Do you mean, Mr Kenworthy?' May asked.

'He got home at twenty past four. I saw the time on my alarm clock. And he had the music playing full on in his motor car.'

'I wonder where he'd been?'

'At a party, from the sound of it.' Phyllis pursed her lips in disapproval. 'He was blasting out music as if he wanted the whole world to hear it. I'm sure everyone will have been woken up!'

The two elderly women seemed to fit together perfectly. They were seldom apart and had known each other so long they had the awareness and the timing of a comedy double act, although without the jokes. They did everything in sync. The hoovering and the dusting. The cooking and the laying of the table. While one reached for the tea leaves, the other would be warming the pot. They watched the same programmes on television and went upstairs to bed at the same time. They never argued. People assumed they were sisters, which quite amused them because, as they explained, for almost thirty years they had been nuns, living together in the same convent in Leeds.

In fact, May very much controlled the relationship. For a start, the house belonged entirely to her. She had bought The Gables off-plan, without even visiting it, using money she had inherited. Phyllis lived with her rent-free as a sort of unpaid companion. May came from the south of England, enunciating her words with the care and exactitude of a Norland nanny, whereas Phyllis had never lost her Birmingham accent. May's large physique also gave her the edge. She had recently put on weight, which made her breathless and inclined to become red in the face if she did anything too quickly, although this somehow suited her. With her bright clothes, her chunky jewellery and the glasses hanging on a cord around her neck, she had the optimistic look of old age – the round, satisfied, homely cheerfulness of a fairy godmother.

'Well, I didn't hear him.' May spread a pat of Cornish butter onto a triangle of toast and then bit into it with very white teeth that were, perhaps surprisingly, her own. 'Did he wake you up?' she asked.

'No. I wasn't asleep. I never sleep well any more. I don't know what's wrong with me.'

'Maybe you should talk to Dr Beresford.'

'I think Dr Beresford should see a doctor himself. I bumped into him yesterday in the High Street.'

'You told me, dear.' May quickly became irritated when Phyllis repeated herself.

Phyllis blinked apologetically. 'He didn't look at all well, poor man.'

There was a whine from underneath the table and a brown face with bulging eyes, oversized ears and a look of permanent dissatisfaction peered up at the two women. This was Ellery, the French bulldog they had bought a few years after they had moved into Riverview Close. Ellery was a small, bulky creature who only took on the shape of a dog when he was walking. Lying on the bed or in his basket, he was more like an overfilled sack of potatoes.

'Little Ellery!' Without even thinking, May leaned down and fed the animal a corner of her toast. The dog wasn't hungry, but he liked to be included. 'Who's a good boy, then? Who's a good boy?'

This cooing might have gone on for several minutes more, but just then the doorbell rang. May glanced at Phyllis and something flashed in her eyes: nervousness, perhaps, or annoyance. It couldn't be the postman. It was only half past eight and he wouldn't come until mid-morning – not that either of them received very much mail. Nor were they expecting any deliveries. Somehow, they both knew who it was. At this time of the day, who else could it be?

'I'll go,' Phyllis said.

'No.' May had taken charge. 'I'll see to it.'

Wiping her hands on a tea towel (printed with the slogan *Stolen from Bertram's Hotel*), she walked stiffly out into the hall and over to the front door. She didn't have far to go. She could make out a figure on the other side of the smoked glass, and two pinpricks of red appeared in her cheeks as she reached down, slid the security lock to one side and opened the door.

A woman was standing on the doorstep, wearing designer jeans that hugged her a little too tightly, a loose blouse and no make-up. Her hair, ash blonde with an undertone of silver, tumbled down her neck. In one hand, she was pinching a small plastic bag between her index finger and thumb, emphasising the fact that it had something unpleasant inside. She held it out.

'I think this is yours,' she said in a voice that was at once cultivated and coarse, as if she had spent years with an elocution teacher but one who had let her down badly.

'Good morning, Mrs Kenworthy,' May replied, standing her ground and refusing to play along.

'I found this on our lawn this morning,' Lynda Kenworthy continued. She was struggling to keep her temper. 'It's the second one I've had to pick up this week.'

'I'm sorry? I don't understand . . .'

'You know perfectly well what I'm talking about, Mrs Winslow. Your bleeding dog is completely out of control. It comes in under the fence and digs up the grass around our magnolia tree. You should see the damage! And then if that isn't enough, it does its poops in the flower beds. It's disgusting!'

'Please can I ask you to not to use that language with me, Mrs Kenworthy? And I've said this to you many times. The fence belongs to Mr Browne. It's got nothing to do with us.'

'But your dog goes into Mr Browne's garden and then comes through the fence into ours.'

'I think you need to talk to Mr Browne.'

'No, Mrs Winslow. I'm talking to you. I really don't think I'm being unreasonable, asking you to keep your animal under control.'

Lynda Kenworthy was still holding out the green plastic

bag, but May was reluctant to take it. 'Did you see Ellery do that?' she enquired.

'I didn't need to see him, did I? There's only one dog in these houses.'

'It could have been a dog from outside. How do you know it's even a dog?'

'I'm not going to argue with you, Mrs Winslow.' Lynda sniffed. 'But I'm warning you. I've spoken to my husband and he wants you to understand something.' She jabbed at the older woman with a finger topped by a long and brilliantly coloured nail. 'If your animal strays into our garden one more time, I'm going to ask him to deal with it.'

May scowled and two spots of red appeared in her cheeks. 'I'm not going to be bullied by you or your husband, Mrs Kenworthy!'

But the other woman was already leaving. As she turned, she dropped the bag so that it landed at May's feet. May stood still for a moment, then leaned down, picked it up and went back into the house.

Phyllis was standing on the other side of the door, cradling the French bulldog in her arms. She had heard the entire exchange. 'What a horrible woman!' she exclaimed.

The dog gazed mournfully at the door, as if in agreement.

'I really don't think we need to worry about her,' May said. 'We can talk about it this evening. That's the whole point of the meeting. To clear the air. The trouble with the Kenworthys is that even though they've been here for more than six months, they're still behaving as if they're new to the close and haven't learned how to fit in with our ways.'

'It's been seven months,' Phyllis scowled.

'You've been counting! Well, I'm sure it will all sort itself out somehow.' May walked purposefully into the kitchen and added the bag to the general rubbish. 'We ought to be on our way,' she said, reaching for the bright red beret she liked to wear when she went out and positioning it carefully on her head. 'Could you bring the almond slices, dear? We don't want to be late!'

Ten minutes later, the two women were standing at the bus stop, waiting for the number 65, which would take them into Richmond. Despite their age, they were still working, running a small business that May also owned.

The Tea Cosy was a bookshop with a café attached, although given that the space was divided fifty-fifty between the two, it could just as easily have been the other way round. It specialised in detective stories – but only those that belonged to the so-called Golden Age of Crime or modern novels that reimagined it. So, in conversation, the two women would fondly refer to 'Peter' or 'Adela' or 'Albert' in such a way that an eavesdropper might think they were referring to a friend or a regular customer when in fact they meant Lord Peter Wimsey, Mrs Bradley or Albert Campion, all fictional detectives whose adventures they sold either in antiquarian editions or in new, retro paperbacks put out by British Library Crime Classics. They did not stock any modern, violent crime novels, especially ones that contained bad language. A casual reader looking for Harlan Coben, Stieg Larsson, Ian Rankin or even James M. Cain (*The Postman Always Rings Twice*) would have to continue down the hill to Waterstones at the corner. What they specialised in – exclusively – was cosy crime.

They also stocked a range of gifts that were all crime-related, including the Agatha Christie tea towel May had used to wipe her hands. Other novelties included a Sherlock Holmes magnifying glass, *Midsomer Murders* mugs and T-shirts, Cluedo jigsaw puzzles and a box of assorted chocolates marked 'POISONED', a tribute to the great novel by Anthony Berkeley.

They should have gone bankrupt long ago, but for some reason they continued to scrape by. The books were at the back, packed into floor-to-ceiling oak shelves with the different authors and categories divided by potted plants. The gift section was at the front of the shop on half a dozen tables close to the entrance. There were several different varieties of tea and coffee on offer, along with an assortment of cakes and pastries that Phyllis cooked fresh every day. Her blood orange sponge was probably the most violent object in the entire place.

Ellery went with them. He seldom left their side. And that was how they would spend the rest of the day, May and Phyllis bustling about, chatting to whichever customers happened to look in, Ellery asleep in his special basket, surrounded by books.

An English Murder. The Nursing Home Murder. Murder Must Advertise. Sleeping Murder.

Murder was all around them.

5

Standing in his bedroom on the first floor of Woodlands, Roderick Browne had heard the entire exchange between May Winslow and Lynda Kenworthy. It was a warm summer morning in early June and the window was open. If he had leaned out, he would have been able to see them, albeit at an oblique angle, but he would never have considered doing such a thing. Lynda Kenworthy made him feel nervous. She reminded him of the matron at the prep school where he had spent five unhappy years, racked by a sense of inferiority and relentlessly teased by the other boys. Unlike Brenda Forbes (who had exhibited a textbook case of diastema, an unsightly gap between her two front teeth – an open invitation to plaque and quite possibly an indication of serious gum disease), Lynda had a perfect smile. But the two women were equally menacing, one patrolling the corridors after lights out, the other casting a malign presence over day-to-day life in Riverview Close.

May Winslow and Phyllis Moore were quite different. Although twice its size, Roderick's house was attached to theirs, the two front doors only a few steps apart, so they encountered each other often. They had a friendly, smiling, easy relationship, although they weren't what he would have called friends. The only time he ever went into The Gables was when something was wrong: once when all the lights had inexplicably fused, once to help relight the Aga, and again to remove a quite remarkably large spider from their bath. On all these occasions, the ladies had reciprocated with home-made jars of lemon curd or jam, paperback novels and crime-related souvenirs, left on his doorstep with a ribbon and a handwritten thank-you card.

It wasn't just that they were so much older than him. They seemed to be quite nervous of the outside world. Roderick couldn't help noticing that they seldom received any post and what letters did come their way, he suspected, were bills or circulars. He had never seen any visitors arrive at their door. He knew that they ran their weird little bookshop in Richmond, although he had never shopped there. He had no interest in crime fiction and tried not to eat sugar or carbohy-drates, since why would he want to give *Treponema denticola* or *Streptococcus mutans* a free lunch? There were occasions, however, when he had picked up the two ladies in his Skoda Octavia because it was raining, pausing at the bus stop and taking them where they wanted to go.

He had tried to learn a little more about them on these brief journeys, but, as grateful as they were, they were also quite reluctant to talk too much about themselves. He knew they had both been married, that they weren't related, that May had a son living in the USA and that Phyllis was childless. May had grown up less than half a mile away. Phyllis had come from Stourbridge, on the edge of Birmingham. The most remarkable thing about them was that they had both taken holy orders, which was how they had met. They had been Franciscan sisters in the Convent of St Clare in Leeds but had left when May inherited money from a distant relative. That was when they had moved to Riverview Close. The Gables had been the first house to be sold.

Riverview Lodge had been the last to change hands. Making sure he couldn't be seen from the other side of the glass, Roderick Browne watched Lynda Kenworthy disappear through her front door, then he stepped away and continued getting dressed. He always wore a suit to work, even though he would change into white scrubs as soon as he arrived at the clinic in Cadogan Square. He owned the practice and it was important to make a good impression on his staff: the two receptionists, the oral hygienists, the assistant dentists. He was, after all, 'the Dentist to the Stars'. That was what he had been called in the *Evening Standard* diary and he still liked to play the part. He did indeed have several well-known actors, a major pop singer and two bestselling authors among his clients, and although many people might not find anything particularly glamorous about dental medicine, he strongly disagreed. He loved his work, helping people and making them healthier. It was all he had ever wanted to do.

He picked out a wide, patterned Versace silk tie and tightened it around his neck. The tie was pink and worked very well against the pale blue Gieves & Hawkes suit. Looking at himself in the mirror, Roderick was not ashamed by what he saw. For a man approaching fifty, he was in good shape, with a head of hair that was still thick and lustrous even if it had already turned white, bright eyes, ruddy cheeks and, of course, superb teeth. He had put on a little weight recently. He would have to watch that. He tilted his head, wondering if the flesh around his neck was beginning to sag – or was it just the line of his collar? The trouble was, it had been years since he had played squash or tennis, and he had stopped jogging too.

No. It was the collar. He looked fine.

Everything in their lives had changed shortly after they had moved into the close. If Roderick had been a philosophical man, he might have considered more seriously the randomness of what had happened, the toss of a coin or the throw of a dice that could derail two careers, two lifestyles, a successful marriage. Felicity had been a senior associate in a leading firm of chartered accountants, on the edge of becoming a partner, but then she had become ill. It had started with tiredness. She couldn't sleep. Then there had been the lack of focus, the memory loss, the headaches, more and more days spent in bed. Glandular fever, hormone imbalance, anaemia . . . all of these had been suggested by the various doctors they had consulted. In a strange way, the real diagnosis, which was much worse, had almost come as a relief. At least they both knew what they had to fight.

Myalgic encephalomyelitis. ME for short. A condition whose main symptom was chronic fatigue.

In truth, there was no fight to be had. Painkillers and antidepressants helped a little, but the doctors could offer no hope of a cure. Felicity seldom left the house now. Sometimes, when the weather was warm, Roderick might persuade her to come out into the garden, but she found the stairs a challenge and too much sunlight hurt her eyes. She listened to books as it was easier than reading. She also liked classical music, opera, choirs. Roderick had adapted the largest bedroom, making it comfortable for her. French windows on the side of the house opened onto a narrow balcony with a view over the garden of Riverview Lodge, a blazing magnolia tree and a lawn running down all the way to the strip of woodland after which the Brownes' own home had been named.

This was where Roderick left her every morning. His own life had been heavily circumscribed by the need to look after his wife. When he had first come to Richmond, he had enjoyed sports. He had regularly played bridge with Andrew and Iris Pennington in Well House. He had been a keen member of the Royal Mid-Surrey Golf Club, the Richmond Bridge Boat Club and the London School of Archery, the last of these a hangover from his university days. They were all behind him now, and the garage, tucked away behind his house, contained a sad collection of his forgotten pursuits: sagging golf clubs, dusty tennis rackets, a useless life jacket, the Barnett Wildcat crossbow he had been given by his parents as a graduation present, back in the eighties.

He made one last adjustment to his tie, then left the room and crossed the landing to what had originally been the master bedroom, which Felicity now occupied alone. She was lying in bed, gazing out of the window.

'I'm just leaving,' he said.

'Did you see?' Felicity could have been somewhere else. 'There are so many parakeets today.'

'I haven't looked . . .'

'They're everywhere.'

The bright green parakeets were all over Richmond. Nobody was quite sure how they had arrived. Some said that Humphrey Bogart was responsible, that they had escaped from a film he was shooting at Isleworth Studios. Others had claimed it was the American guitarist Jimi Hendrix who had released the first pair deliberately. Historians insisted that they had been around for hundreds of years, originally kept in a menagerie belonging to King Henry VIII. Whatever their origins, Roderick knew they had become a source of comfort to his wife and he was grateful to them.

'I won't be home late,' he said. 'But I've got a meeting over at The Stables.'

'You never told me that.'

He had told her the evening before. 'Oh. I'm sorry,' he said. 'I thought I'd mentioned it. We're just having a general chat about things in the close.'

'Would you like me to come?'

'Well, let's see how you're feeling.'

It was often Felicity's way. She would suggest joining him for a cup of tea in the kitchen, a walk around the garden or even a drink at the Fox and Duck, but when the time came, she would usually change her mind.

Roderick heard the front door opening. 'Damien's here,' he said. 'Is there anything you want?'

'I can ask him when he comes up.'

'I'll see you tonight.' He leaned over and kissed her on the forehead. She smiled at him but in the same way that she might have smiled at a memory.

He went downstairs just as Damien was closing the door behind him. A tall, slender young man with black, curly hair, he was dressed in jeans and a lilac polo shirt with a Whole Foods tote bag over his arm. He had been Felicity's carer for two years now, coming in three days a week, and although Roderick was paying him — or rather, his agency — a fortune, it was money well spent. Damien was reliable and endlessly cheerful. Felicity felt comfortable when he was there. It was impossible to imagine life without him.

'Good morning, Roderick!' Damien had been informal from the very start.

'Hello, Damien.'

'I got some of that soft cheese Felicity likes.' He raised the arm with the tote bag, then reached in and took something out. 'And this was on the doormat.'

He handed over an official-looking brown envelope, addressed to the owners of Woodlands. Roderick tore it open with his thumb and took out a letter, which he saw at once had come from Richmond Council. His first thought was that it was probably a change to the rubbish collection. Or perhaps they were finally going to do something about the traffic on the Petersham Road. But glancing at the single sheet of paper, he saw the headline and the details that followed.

NOTICE OF APPLICATION

Town and County Planning (Development Management Procedure) (England) Order 2010
Town and Country Planning Act 1990
Planning (Listed Buildings and Conservation Areas Act) 1990

Riverview Lodge, Riverview Close, Petersham Road, Richmond, Surrey.

Ref No: J. 05/041955/RIV – Outline Planning Permission

FOR: Residential development of a swimming pool and pavilion and the creation of a new patio area on the eastern lawn of the property . . .

'What is it?' Damien asked.

He sounded concerned and Roderick realised that he hadn't spoken for some time. Nor had he taken a breath. The letter seemed to have broken into different pieces in front of his eyes and it took an effort of concentration to put it back together again. In fact, it was simple. Giles and Lynda Kenworthy had applied to build a swimming pool and some sort of changing area, bar and Jacuzzi in their garden. The eastern lawn. That was the strip of land that ran towards his own house, directly in front of Felicity's bedroom. Roderick read the application a second time and then a third.

The Kenworthys wanted to take away the one thing that still mattered to Felicity. They were going to replace the lawn and the magnolia tree, the flower beds and the simple, uncluttered view with . . .

A swimming pool! A Jacuzzi!

Standing in the hallway, Roderick heard the screams of children, the splash of water, the chatter of the invited guests, the explosion of champagne corks. He saw steam billowing out of the hot tub and smelled the chlorine in the air. And this changing room! The application didn't say how tall it was or in what style it was going to be built. It could be anything from a Scandinavian log cabin to a Japanese pagoda! What was he supposed to do? Could he move Felicity to another part of the house? Why should he?

They wouldn't get away with it. They couldn't. Richmond Council was famous when it came to planning applications like this. They would do anything to preserve the historical and environmental value of the area. Roderick would protest. Everyone in the close would do the same. There was no way this was going through.

But even as he stood there, crumpling the single page in his hand, with Damien staring at him and asking him questions he couldn't hear, he knew that the first volley in a war had just been fired. Giles Kenworthy would have lawyers. He might have friends in the council. He was the sort of man who always got what he wanted and he wouldn't have applied for planning permission if he didn't think there was a good chance of success. But Roderick was going to stop him.

He remembered the meeting at The Stables. It couldn't have been better timed. Everyone in Riverview Close would have received the same letter.

It was a fight to the death and it was starting now.

6

That evening, from half past seven onwards, the residents of Riverview Close gathered at The Stables, the home of Adam and Teri Strauss, who were hosting the event.

As punctual as he had always been during his time as a barrister, Andrew Pennington was the first to arrive, wearing slacks and a V-neck jersey, carrying a small bunch of flowers and a bottle of wine. He was followed, a few minutes later, by Tom Beresford and his wife, who came empty-handed. Dr Beresford, having been held up at work, had wolfed down a quick supper and had come without changing his clothes. His wife, Gemma, looked more demure in a black suit and one of her own creations, a silver serpent necklace curving around her throat. Neither of them was in a good mood. May Winslow and Phyllis Moore were the next to appear, bringing with them a box of chocolate bullets, part of a consignment that had arrived at The Tea Cosy that afternoon. Their neighbour, Roderick Browne, was right behind them, accompanied by – to everyone's surprise – his wife, Felicity, who had decided that the meeting was important enough to be worth what was, for her, a challenging journey.

There were nine of them, standing and sitting in the main living space where, just fifteen hours earlier, the single chess game had been lost. The room looked beautiful, with low lighting, fresh flowers in porcelain vases and piano music by Chopin playing out of hidden speakers. The many shelves of books also displayed some of the awards Adam Strauss had won throughout his career. The laptop computers had been cleared away, but there were still half a dozen chessboards on display, beautiful sets that Strauss had been given as prizes: wood, ivory, porcelain and glass. Spread out on the long table were different plates of food that Teri had prepared, including the bao buns, egg tarts and pineapple bread that connected her with her childhood. There were bottles of wine and spirits in the kitchen, a fruit salad, a cheese board – everything you would expect at a party, apart from, that is, the atmosphere. As the various guests waited, there was an unmistakable feeling of suspense.

Giles and Lynda Kenworthy had not yet arrived. It wasn't surprising that they had chosen to be late, but there was one question on everyone's mind. Would they arrive at all? The Kenworthys knew only too well that the evening had been designed to address some of the problems that had arisen in Riverview Close, but perhaps they had realised that *they* were the problems and so had decided to stay away. That said, it was only a quarter to eight. The doorbell would surely ring at any moment.

Adam Strauss had joined Andrew Pennington, who was examining one of the chessboards, cradling a G&T in his other hand.

'This one is my favourite,' Strauss said, moving down the table. He delicately picked up a bishop kneeling with his hands clasped in prayer and held it in the light. The set it had come from was inspired by *The Lord of the Rings*. Sauron and Saruman ruled over the black side, facing Gandalf and Galadriel in white. Orcs fought it out against hobbits. Frodo and Sam Gamgee were knights. 'It was handmade in Prague and there are only half a dozen of them in the world,' he explained. 'It's very valuable – but that's not the reason why it's so precious to me. It was given to me as a fortieth-birthday present by Sheikh Mohammed bin Rashid Al Maktoum, the ruler of Dubai.'

Andrew couldn't help smiling. Adam Strauss was a terrible name-dropper . . . it was something of a joke in Riverview Close. The chess grandmaster was not an imposing man, with his black-framed glasses and a triangle of beard that sat rather too precisely on his chin. He dressed neatly and expensively. Appearances evidently mattered to him, from his well-oiled hair to his shoes, both of which gleamed. Everyone knew that he had been rather humiliated by having to move out of the Lodge. Now on the wrong side of fifty, he was a man of diminished stature in every sense, and the name-dropping, the endless anecdotes about famous people he had met, was obviously his way of asserting himself.

'I was invited to a chess tournament over there,' Strauss went on. 'The Sheikh took a liking to me, and as a matter of fact, I gave one of his sons a few lessons. A very handsome lad and quite adept at the game.' He handed the bishop over to the barrister. 'I didn't really know the books at the time, but I read them afterwards. I rather liked them. Tolkien played chess, you know. I think he would have approved.'

'This looks just like Orlando Bloom,' Andrew said.

'There is a resemblance.'

'Is it ivory?'

Strauss shook his head. 'No. Porcelain. I do have one set made of ivory.' He pointed. 'That one over there. Of course, you're not meant to have anything made of ivory any more, but I won that one when I was just twenty-one – my first major tournament – so I suppose it's all right to hang on to it.'

He took back the bishop and delicately placed it in its correct position.

A few steps away, in the kitchen, Teri Strauss was holding out a plate of cheese straws for May Winslow and Phyllis Moore. The elderly ladies had managed to squeeze themselves onto two of the high stools next to the central island. They both had fruit cocktails laced with vodka. It was well known that they would never say no to a good slug of alcohol, possibly making up for years of abstinence at the Convent of St Clare.

'Not for me, thank you.' Phyllis held up two hands in a gesture of surrender, refusing the cheese straws. 'We ate before we came out. But this cocktail is very nice. What's in it?'

'Mangosteen,' Teri said.

'Oh.' Phyllis smiled, none the wiser. She drained her glass. 'Can I have another?'

'Perhaps not, Phyllis,' May suggested. She looked at her watch. 'I wonder what's happened to Mr and Mrs Kenworthy?'

It was so typical of her to use surnames. Both women seemed to have modelled themselves on the Jane Marple novels they sold in their bookshop. It was as if the last six decades had never happened.

'I'm sure they're on their way,' Teri said.

'It's not very far to drive!' This was a penitent Phyllis, nursing her empty glass, trying her hand at a joke.

'Let's give them the benefit of the doubt.' Andrew Pennington had overheard the conversation and joined them. 'I knew a barrister who always insisted on arriving late in court. He said it made more of an impression.'

'I'll have one of those, if you don't mind.' Gemma Beresford leaned over and lazily plucked out a cheese straw.

'We were just wondering if the Kenworthys were going to grace us with their presence,' May remarked. There was an edge of sarcasm in her voice.

'I do hope so.' Gemma glanced briefly at her husband, who

53

was pouring himself a second whisky. 'Tom is very much hoping to meet them.'

'Well, I'm glad to have you all here, anyway,' Teri said. 'We don't get together half as often as we used to. It's important we stay close.'

Teri was Hong Kong Chinese, a very striking, elegant woman. Her parents – who ran a successful clothing business – had predicted what would happen to the city they had always loved when the Chinese authorities took control of it and had emigrated to the UK before the handover in 1997. They now lived in Manchester. The fact that both Adam Strauss's wives shared the same ethnicity had, of course, been noted in Riverview Close. He was attracted to Asian women, but this was entirely a matter of personal taste and something that none of them would have dreamed of mentioning.

Gemma took her cheese straw and went over to her husband. 'Are you all right, darling?' she asked.

Tom slid the bottle away, as if he been caught trying to steal it. 'The bastard's not going to come, is he!' he said.

She looked at her watch. 'It doesn't look like it,' she admitted.

'He's laughing at us!'

Gemma frowned. 'Maybe you should just try to relax,' she said, keeping her voice low. 'You can't keep letting him drag you down. It's not good for you.'

Tom ignored her. 'He woke me up in the middle of the

night last night. And this morning, when I tried to get to the surgery, his bloody car was blocking the way. Again!'

'How did you get in?' She had left before him, taking the tube into the centre of town.

'I walked.'

'He can be very inconsiderate.'

'He does it on purpose.' Tom drank half the whisky in his glass. 'Like not coming here tonight. I don't know why he moved into the close. He clearly holds all of us in contempt.'

Gemma was becoming increasingly worried about her husband. It wasn't just the drinking, the secret smoking or even the anger that she could see welling up inside him. It was the distance that was growing between them. There were times when she barely recognised the happy, easy-going man she had married. Tall and slim, with tumbling, sand-coloured hair, there had always been a boyish quality about him. But now he was being pulled in different directions – by life, by work, above all by Giles Kenworthy and his wretched cars – and it was beginning to show. He was going to be forty next year, but he looked much older. Unhappiness was etched into every part of his face. She regretted bringing him here. How could she save him? How could she save both of them?

'Try not to get too stressed,' she said, gently touching his arm and then moving away before he could protest.

She went over to the other side of the room where Roderick Browne was standing protectively behind his wife, who was in an armchair, almost folded into it. Gemma remembered

Felicity when they had first arrived. Their houses faced each other across the courtyard, on either side of Riverview Lodge, and the two of them had often met. Felicity ('Fee') had been so different then: socially and politically active, campaigning for the Liberal Democrats, supporting the Orange Tree Theatre, dragging Roderick off to her beloved archery club – she was a much better shot than him, she said – and occasionally throwing gourmet dinners.

And then this wretched illness had not so much crept up on her as pounced, draining all her energy and vitality and turning her into the casualty who had somehow made it here tonight. Gemma had been surprised to see her. She knew that Felicity spent most of her time in bed.

'How lovely to see you, Felicity,' she said now. 'I'm so glad you came.'

'We have to talk about the swimming pool,' Felicity replied. Even speaking was a struggle for her, the words falling heavily from her lips.

'Oh, yes.' Like everyone else in Riverview Close, Gemma had received the planning application, which had been waiting for her in the kitchen when she got home. It didn't bother her too much if the Kenworthys wanted to vandalise their own garden: the pool would be situated on the other side of the house, some distance from Gardener's Cottage. But of course it would be directly in Felicity's line of vision, along with the Jacuzzi and the changing room.

'We're not going to let them get away with it,' Roderick

exclaimed. 'Someone should do something about him! Someone should . . . I don't know! Ever since he came here, he's been nothing but trouble.'

'I'm sure the council won't allow it,' Andrew Pennington said, although it was clear from his voice that he had misgivings. All the houses in the close were modern and the garden was out of sight of the main road. It was quite possible that the Kenworthys would be allowed to do whatever they wanted.

'We might have to move if it goes ahead,' Roderick added, glumly.

'I'm not moving.' Suddenly Felicity was fearsome, her hands clutching the arms of her chair. 'Why should I? It's not fair. This is my home!'

There was the sound of a fork hitting the side of a glass. Adam Strauss was standing in front of a gold-framed mirror next to the front door. 'Excuse me, everyone,' he called out. He put down the fork and picked up his telephone. Everyone knew there was bad news coming. They could see it on his face. 'I'm afraid I've just had a text from Giles Kenworthy. He and his wife won't be joining us after all.'

The announcement was met with a profound silence. Nobody in the room moved, as if they were waiting for the person next to them to react.

It was Tom Beresford who spoke first. 'Why not?' he demanded.

'He doesn't really say.' Adam read from the screen. ' "*Sorry.*

57

Can't be with you tonight. Trouble at work. Maybe next time."'
He lowered the phone. 'I suppose I'm not surprised.'

'He sounds quite cheerful about it,' Tom said.

'It's very rude of him!' Teri Strauss blinked, her eyes bright with anger. She waved a delicate hand over the refectory table. 'I go to all this effort to make it a nice evening.' She remembered that she was not the only one who had been put out. 'And Felicity! I know how very, very hard it was for you coming here. It's not fair!'

'It's wrong of them.' Felicity looked defeated.

'It's not just rude, it's extremely inconsiderate,' Gemma Beresford weighed in. 'We've had to pay Kylie extra to baby-sit tonight.'

'I thought Kylie lived with you,' Teri said. Kylie was the nanny, originally from Australia, who looked after the Beresfords' twin daughters.

'She does. But we still have to pay her if she works over-time.' Gemma went over to her husband. 'Tom s exhausted. He was woken up at four o'clock this morning . . .'

'By Giles Kenworthy,' Adam muttered, sourly. 'I heard him too.'

'The only reason we're here is because we wanted to have it out with them,' Gemma said. 'I don't mean to insult you, Teri. It's a lovely spread. But it's just too bad . . .'

'I did want to talk to them about the fence,' May said. 'I know it's not our fence, but they won't stop going on about it.'

'That woman won't leave us alone,' Phyllis added. 'She was around this morning – making threats.'

'The swimming pool!' Felicity insisted. 'We have to stop them. You have no idea. It will be awful!'

Adam held up a hand for silence. 'My friends,' he began, 'I feel terrible about all this. After all, I was the one who sold them Riverview Lodge in the first place. It certainly wasn't my intention, but I was the one who brought all this trouble into our lives. Even now, I ask myself if I should have asked more questions when I met them, or perhaps explained things better.'

He paused, his face full of regret.

'I met both the Kenworthys,' he continued, 'and it never occurred to me that they would be so . . . complicated. They seemed very pleasant to deal with, although it's true that Giles Kenworthy did behave badly. I've made no secret of the fact that he reduced his offer one day before exchanging, knowing that I'd have no choice but to go along with it. But then, he's a financier. I assumed that's how these people behaved – and to be fair, quite a few issues had shown up in the survey. I would have sold the house to someone else if I could have, but there were no other serious buyers.'

'Nobody blames you,' Teri said. Her face challenged anyone in the room to disagree.

'The question is . . . what are we going to do? What can we do?'

'Maybe we should give them a taste of their own medicine,' Tom Beresford suggested. 'Let's see how they feel when they find their own cars barricaded in.'

'We could have a few parties of our own,' Gemma added. 'Blast music at them in the middle of the night and litter their front drive with champagne bottles the next day, like they do. I think Tom's right. We've all been far too polite about this.'

'Could I have a drop more vodka?' Phyllis asked. 'But this time without the mango juice?'

Andrew Pennington had stepped forward. He was a quiet man, but he had a way of commanding a room that came from years spent in court. He waited for everyone to stop talking. Then he began.

'If I may advise you,' he said, 'the one thing we shouldn't do is engage in a war of attrition. The sort of neighbourhood disputes that we have been experiencing are terribly common, I'm afraid, and they have a nasty way of escalating. It's always better to discuss things in a civilised manner.'

'We can't do that if they don't show up,' Roderick Browne pointed out.

'We can write to them. I'd be happy to draft a letter setting out our concerns.'

'What makes you think they'll even read it?' Gemma asked.

'We'll cross that bridge when we come to it. But in the meantime, we must take things one step at a time – and whatever we do, we must remain within the law. We should record everything that happens from this moment on. Tom, if the drive is blocked, make a note of the time, and if Giles Kenworthy is offensive to you, try to record it on your iPhone. The same when they have parties or allow their bottles to litter the close.'

'What about their children?' May asked. 'I don't like the way they go whizzing around on their skateboards. One of them nearly crashed into me the other day.'

'I called out to him and he gave me the finger,' Phyllis said.

'Language, dear!'

'Well, he did.'

'There is a code of conduct that we all signed when we moved into the close,' Andrew Pennington reminded them. 'It precludes ball games and the use of bicycles, although I'm not sure if there is any mention of skateboards.'

'And cricket!' Gemma added. 'They whack the ball around like nobody's business. They almost hit Kylie once. What if it had been one of the girls? It could have been a nasty accident.'

'They need to move that bloody camper van,' Tom Beresford said. 'Surely they can't just leave it sitting there the whole year round.' He turned to Andrew Pennington. 'Can't we sue them or something?'

'There's very little we can do,' the barrister replied, regretfully. 'I suppose we could write to them and threaten them with legal action, but once you start hiring outside lawyers that can become an extremely expensive proposition — and there can be no doubt that Mr Kenworthy will have deeper pockets than any of us. Are you sure you want to take him on?'

'What about the swimming pool?' Felicity demanded, struggling to express the anger she felt. It was the third time she had raised the subject.

Her husband immediately took her side. 'It may not be so important to the rest of you,' Roderick said, 'but it's going right underneath Fee's window.' He looked to Andrew Pennington. 'We must be able to stop it.'

'Well, as I said, the council hasn't given permission yet and there's every chance that they'll refuse.'

'It will ruin my view!'

'Unfortunately, the loss of a view is never a consideration in planning law,' Andrew continued. 'However, there are plenty of other objections we can legitimately make. Noise is one. It will most certainly affect the character of the close. This is a conservation area and the threat to the environment, from chlorine and other chemicals, must be relevant. They may decide to cut down trees—'

'They already cut down my two yews and no one paid a blind bit of notice,' Adam remarked.

'Well, we'll need to see the architectural plans. What is this changing facility they're hoping to build? If it blocks a significant amount of daylight for Roderick and Felicity, that's definitely grounds for dismissal.'

'The pool could be dangerous for Ellery!' Phyllis blurted out the words as if the thought had just occurred to her.

Suddenly, she was the centre of attention. 'He goes into the Kenworthys' garden sometimes. He doesn't do any harm. He just likes sniffing around. If there's a swimming pool there, he could fall in.'

'You might like to put that in your letter,' Andrew said kindly. 'It's another consideration, and the more the merrier. We should all write letters to the council,' he went on, 'setting out our objections. And it would be a good idea if these were coordinated. Again, I'll be happy to help. But it's essential that we're restrained. It won't do any good being vindictive.'

There was a pause while everyone took this in.

'So that's it, then?' Roderick said. 'We write letters – and we wait.'

'That's my advice, yes.' Andrew took a sip of his gin and tonic as if to signal that he had said enough

'I agree absolutely,' May said. 'There's absolutely no point getting into a fight with this man, and I'm certainly not interested in hiring lawyers. I say we just ignore him and hope he goes away. That's the only way to treat bullies. Pretend they're not there!'

'I agree with May.' Phyllis tried a wobbly smile. 'Live and let live. That's what I say. But since we're all here, why don't we have another drink?'

The party, if that's what it was, continued for another thirty minutes, but the Kenworthys' non-appearance had made the whole thing pointless. Adam Strauss, supported by

63

May Winslow and Andrew Pennington, tried to keep everyone's spirits up, but the evening quickly fizzled out. Roderick and Felicity Browne were the first to leave and the others drifted away soon after, leaving the bao buns and the custard tarts uneaten on the refectory table.

It would be another six weeks before death came to Riverview Close and everyone who had attended the party would find their lives turned upside down. And throughout the police investigation, with its mutual suspicion and alternative truths, there was one thing on which they would all agree.

Giles Kenworthy really should have been there.

TWO

THE FIFTH BOOK

1

Anyone who has read the four books I have written about my adventures with ex-Detective Inspector Daniel Hawthorne, may be surprised by this one. Where is Hawthorne? Where am I? What's going on with the third-person narrative?

None of this was exactly my choice.

More than a year had passed since my play, *Mindgame*, had been produced, largely trashed by the critics and tucked away in that file marked 'Unlikely to be revived by the National Theatre'. Was I depressed by what had happened? Not really. If you're going to spend your entire life writing, you have to accept the possibility of failure and live with it when it arrives. There's an old saying 'You're only as good as your last script', but that's not true. You're only as good as your next one. Writing is all about looking ahead. The worst thing that had happened to me as a result of *Mindgame* was being arrested for the violent murder of Harriet Throsby, the critic who had given the play its most venomous review. Frankly, of the two of us, I think she came out of it worse.

My agent, Hilda Starke, knew nothing of this. I hadn't sent her the novel yet and she'd only seen a brief synopsis of *Murder at the Vaudeville Theatre*, which was my working title. She would certainly be delighted that I had cleared my name, if only because it wouldn't have been easy to get books out of me if I'd been banged up in Wormwood Scrubs. I've never been quite sure if literary agents work for their writers or the other way round. Hilda had already twisted my arm into signing a four-book deal with Penguin Random House, arranging delivery dates that even an AI-powered neural network machine would have had difficulty meeting. Either I'm too weak or I like writing too much, but I always seem to be locked in a room with a ream of A4 while other writers are out and about having a good time.

There had, however, been a development that even Hilda could not have foreseen.

I couldn't write another murder story for the simple reason that nobody had been murdered. I hadn't heard from Hawthorne for months.

That's the trouble with writing what I suppose I must call true crime. When I was working on the television programme *Midsomer Murders*, nobody so much as blinked if there were four or five homicides in a single episode. Hercule Poirot investigated no fewer than eighty-five mysterious deaths (starting with the one at Styles) during his career. Real life is not like that. There are seven or eight hundred murders a year in the United Kingdom, but most of them aren't mysteries at all. A fight in a pub. A domestic argument that turns violent. Knife crime. These are all horrible, but nobody wants to read about them. Even journalists find them pedestrian. The police don't need to call Hawthorne when the killer is sitting in the kitchen with a meat tenderiser in one hand, a bottle of whisky in the other and blood all over the walls.

None of this had occurred to Hilda when she called me unexpectedly, around noon. I was, as usual, in my office in Clerkenwell, listening to the thud of jackhammers and the endless whine of huge industrial drills as the new Crossrail underground was constructed just across the road. Everywhere I looked, there were cranes circling one another like prehistoric beasts deep in conversation. All the activity, the sense of London reinventing itself, only made me feel more isolated, which was one of the reasons I never failed to answer my phone.

'How are you getting on with the next book?' the familiar voice barked into my ear.

'Hello, Hilda,' I said. 'Which book are you talking about?'

'The new Hawthorne. We need the fifth in the series.'

She always called them the Hawthorne books. Everyone did. It was strange the way I did all the work but never got a mention.

'Why are you asking? We've got plenty of time. And I still haven't finished *Murder at the Vaudeville Theatre.*'

'I really don't like that title. It's too old-fashioned. Hawthorne has a much better one . . .'

'When did you see him?' I had that strange sense of unreality that seemed to have taken over my life from the day I'd met Hawthorne.

'He called in last week. They want him to appear on the *Today* programme.'

'Talking about what, exactly?'

'Working with you, I suppose.'

Shouldn't it have been the other way round? I decided not to go there. 'Why are you asking me about a book I haven't even started writing?' I demanded.

'Because you've got to deliver it by Christmas.'

'Who said that?'

'Didn't you read your contract?'

'I never read my contracts. That's your job.'

'Well, I agreed to a December delivery. It's ahead of the game, but it shows how much confidence they have in you. They want to publish in time for spring.' I heard a bump and a rustling sound at Hilda's end, and her voice became distant as she lowered her mobile into her lap. 'I'll have a tuna fish baguette, a flat white and a peppermint Aero.'

'Hilda? Are you ordering lunch?'

She either didn't hear what I said or ignored it. 'So when are you going to get started?' she demanded.

'I don't know. I haven't seen Hawthorne in months. And unless he told you something different, he hasn't investigated any new cases.'

There was a pause as she digested this.

'Well, you'll have to write about an old one,' she said. 'Talk to Hawthorne. He must have solved half a dozen murders before he met you. Give it a think, Tony, and get back to me.'

Tony! Was she really calling me that too? I opened my mouth to protest, but she had already hung up.

Several thoughts went through my head.

I had always liked the security of a multiple book deal. It effectively meant that I was being paid for four bites of the cherry. Even if my next book was a disaster, I'd be guaranteed three more. Most writers live with what is known as 'imposter syndrome', a chronic fear that at any moment they'll be found out and their books will be unceremoniously taken off the shelves and pulped, reduced to a milky white substance that will then be reconstituted into new paper and used for somebody else's book. My deal pushed that possibility further into the future.

The downside was that it tied me to my publisher, making me almost a full-time employee. It committed me to another lorry-load of words, three hundred thousand of them, or maybe even five hundred thousand by the time I'd done second drafts and edits. It was a mountain to climb, and given that Hawthorne hadn't so much as sent me an email or a text since Harriet Throsby's killer had been arrested (life in jail with a minimum of twenty-three years), I couldn't so much as take the first step. It was as if I was suffering from somebody else's writer's block.

I flicked on the kettle and considered what Hilda had

suggested. An old case . . . a murder that Hawthorne had solved before he had forced his way into my life. It did have some attractions.

It would be much easier to write. All the facts would have been set out, the clues assembled, the killer already known. This would be, for me, a huge relief. I wouldn't have to follow half a dozen steps behind Hawthorne for several weeks, desperately hoping he would find the solution so that I'd be able to finish the book. I wouldn't get everything wrong like a real-life Watson or Hastings and nor would I get stabbed . . . as had happened on two occasions. All I would have to do was sit down with Hawthorne, listen to him set out the main beats of the story, examine any case notes he might have, maybe visit the crime scene to get the atmosphere and physical description, and then sit down quietly and write the whole thing in the comfort of my own home.

The timing could hardly be better. Eleventh Hour Films, the television production company run by wife, had just started developing *Alex Rider* for Amazon TV, but I'd decided not to write the scripts. There were two reasons for this. The first was that I was writing a new book, *Nightshade*. But I was also thinking of *Stormbreaker*, the feature film that had been made sixteen years earlier in 2003. The experience of working with a certain Harvey Weinstein, our American producer, had not been an altogether happy one and I thought it might be more sensible to let someone else have a crack of the whip. We'd found a great writer who was about twenty years younger than me: he'd bring his own vision to the character, and although I'd help shape some of the episodes, I would be free to focus on other things.

One of these was a new James Bond novel. *Trigger Mortis* had come out and had done well, and to my surprise, the Ian Fleming estate had offered me the chance to write a second. My first instinct had been to say no. Bond novels demanded an enormous amount of work: doing the research, getting the language right, avoiding the obvious pitfalls of bringing a 1950s character to life for a twenty-first-century audience with a whole new set of values. I wasn't even sure I had a second story in me.

Then something had happened. A first line fell into my head. I have no idea where it came from. I sometimes think that all writers are like radio receivers, picking up signals from . . . who knows where? *'So, 007 is dead.'* It was M talking. One of his agents had been killed, but it wasn't Bond. This would be an origin story, predating *Casino Royale*, telling how Bond got his licence to kill, inherited the number and was sent on his first mission. I'm not saying it's the most brilliant idea anyone's ever had, but that's how it works for me. I knew I had to write it.

I was thinking about setting it in the South of France. It would involve the CIA and the true scandal of American involvement with heroin traffickers back in the fifties. I already had some thoughts about the main villain, Jean-Paul Scipio. Fleming had a penchant for physical peculiarities, from Dr No's contact lenses to Scaramanga's third nipple. Scipio would be massively, unnaturally obese and that would also play a part in the way he died.

I wasn't writing it yet, although I was thinking about it all the time. This meant my desk was clear and there might just be time to get Hilda off my back.

There was something else I remembered. When Hawthorne and I visited Alderney for the literary festival that had led to the first murder on that island for a thousand years, he had mentioned something that had taken place in a close or a crescent of houses in Richmond, on the edge of London. It was one of the first cases he had solved as a private detective after he had been thrown out of the police force following an 'accident' that had led to the hospitalisation of a suspect he'd been questioning. Those inverted commas are well deserved. The man in question was a vile human being dealing in child pornography and Hawthorne had been right behind him on a steep flight of stairs when the man had somehow tripped and fallen.

I hadn't seen Hawthorne for some time and it occurred to me that in a strange way I was missing him. I wouldn't have described him as a friend, but after four outings together we were becoming something that vaguely resembled a team. It was also true that but for him, I would have been writing this from inside a prison cell. Even while I'd been talking to Hilda, I'd been thinking how good it would be to see him again.

I picked up the phone and called.

2

We met, as usual, in one of those coffee bars that have managed to get a stranglehold on the streets of London, each one of them not just identical to each other but, perversely, to the coffee bars owned by their competitors. Hawthorne's flat was only a fifteen-minute walk from where I lived, but it was equally uninviting: perhaps one of the reasons why he seldom invited me there. We ended up at a Starbucks – or was it a Costa? – nearby, sitting outside in the not very fresh air so that he could smoke.

I've described Hawthorne's London home often enough: the emptiness and lack of any personal touches apart from his extensive model collection – the planes, tanks, battleships and transport vehicles from two world wars that he had painstakingly assembled there. Hawthorne was so reluctant to tell me anything about himself that I had taken an almost unhealthy interest in where – and how – he lived, hoping it might provide me with a few clues. Take his hobby, for example. Was it a throwback to a childhood that had been damaged in some way or just an enjoyable way to pass the time?

And what about his book club, the weird group of people who met every month in a flat one floor below? I had been introduced to a vet, a retired concert pianist and a psychiatrist who had taken an almost perverse pleasure in dismantling the work of my literary hero, Sir Arthur Conan Doyle. After just a short while in their company, I wondered if any of them were quite what they seemed. It was as if they were united by some ghastly secret, like the cast of *Rosemary's Baby*. Not one of the people I met there had been straightforward.

Take Kevin Chakraborty, Lisa's son. He was Hawthorne's teenaged friend, confined to a wheelchair with Duchenne muscular dystrophy and quite possibly one of the most dangerous young men in the world. He regularly helped Hawthorne by hacking into computer systems and, when necessary, causing them to crash. He had access to the entire UK CCTV camera network and could find anyone, anywhere, with a single twitch of his mouse. I had no doubt that he could bring the whole country to a standstill or cause planes to drop out of the sky if he was so minded, and it was fortunate that the two of them were, at least to an extent, on the side of the angels. Hawthorne solved murders. He believed in justice. The only trouble was that he didn't care how he achieved it.

When I was a fugitive from the police, I had spent a night at his flat, tucked into William Hawthorne's bed. Or as much of me as would fit. William was Hawthorne's fourteen-year-old son and his bed was about a metre too short for me. That was something else I didn't understand. Hawthorne was still married. He clearly saw a lot of his son. But he was on his own. How did that work?

And how did he come to be living in that architecturally incongruous, vaguely brutalist apartment block on the edge of the River Thames, close to Blackfriars Bridge? His flat didn't belong to him. He had told me that he was living there as a caretaker, working for his half-brother who was an estate agent, but neither of these statements was true. It was all quite complicated, but as far as I could see, the facts were as follows:

- Roland Hawthorne was not an estate agent.
- Roland worked for some sort of shadowy security organisation that owned flats throughout the building.
- The organisation was run by a man called Morton who also employed Hawthorne as an investigator whenever he wasn't working for the police.
- Roland was not Hawthorne's half-brother. His father, a police officer, had adopted Hawthorne after his parents died in mysterious circumstances.

The more I learned about Hawthorne, the less I knew him. He was a brilliant detective. Four times, I'd watched him pluck solutions out of the air, knitting together clues I hadn't noticed even as I'd described them. But his private life, in so far as he had one, was peculiar, quite possibly dangerous, and I'd be perfectly happy if I never went anywhere near Hawthorne's flat again.

I could have invited him over to my own home in Farringdon, but I wasn't too keen to do that either. For a start, my wife, Jill Green, had a television production company just around the corner and she could have walked in on us at any time. I didn't want them to meet. Jill had never really approved of Hawthorne – not since he had first tricked his way into my life. She had read *The Word is Murder* and *The Sentence is Death* and said she'd enjoyed them, but she had serious reservations about my appearing in them and certainly didn't want to do so herself. I was still worrying about what I was going to do when the fourth novel, *Murder at the Vaudeville Theatre*, came out. I had never told her everything that had happened and I wondered how she'd react when she read that I'd had been arrested by the police on suspicion of the murder of Harriet Throsby and had spent twenty-four hours being interrogated under caution.

Also, Hawthorne was the only person I knew who still smoked, although he never seemed to enjoy cigarettes. He smoked mechanically: an idiosyncrasy rather than an addiction. If I have one abiding memory of him, it's watching him hunched over a black coffee in his trademark suit, white shirt and tie, his shoulders hunched, gazing at me with those softly menacing brown eyes whilst tapping ash into the lid of his polystyrene cup. At those moments, he could have walked out of one of those films shot in the forties: a reborn Cagney or Bogart. Nothing about him was black and white. It was all various shades of grey.

So that was where we found ourselves, sitting outside a Starbucks on the Clerkenwell Road. It was the first week in August and I had just five months to produce a book which, at that moment, had no title, no plot, no characters. In fact, I didn't have the faintest idea what it was going to be about. Hawthorne had agreed to meet me, but I still didn't know if he was going to help.

'How are you?' I began.

He shrugged non-committally, as unwilling as ever to provide any information about himself. I wondered what would happen if he ever got ill. A doctor would have to tie him to a chair to get so much as a blood sample. 'I'm OK,' he said, at length.

'How was Radio 4?' I was still a little put out that he'd been invited and not me, but did my best not to show it.

He shook his head. 'I turned them down. I'm not interested in publicity.'

'Publicity sells books.'

'Not my job, mate. I should have kept my name out of the books to start with.' He pulled out a cigarette. 'Too late now.'

'So what have you been working on?'

'Not a lot.' He looked at me suspiciously. 'Why are you asking?'

I explained that Hilda had called me and that we needed to start a new book straight away.

Hawthorne already knew. 'Yeah. She told me she was going to call you,' he said.

Of course she had told him. He wouldn't have met me if it was just for coffee and a general chat. I didn't feel comfortable that he was now represented by my agent, particularly as she seemed rather more invested in him than in me. I bet she hadn't ordered lunch while she was talking to him. 'So what do you think?' I asked.

'You want to write about a murder that happened before we met?'

'Well, you said it would be a good idea. When we were at the Alderney Book Festival, you mentioned a case you'd solved in Richmond. Somewhere called Riverside Close.'

He lit the cigarette and took in his first lungful of smoke. 'It wasn't Riverside. It was Riverview.'

'You told me someone was hammered to death.'

'They were shot with a crossbow.'

I glared at him. 'Hawthorne! Do you know how many tweets and emails I get when I make mistakes?'

He shrugged. 'I don't like people knowing too much about me.'

'That doesn't mean you can deliberately lie to them.'

He frowned and tapped ash. 'Things have changed,' he explained. 'I never expected we'd get all this attention. Radio 4 and all the rest of it. There are people I know who would prefer me to keep a low profile. And this business in Richmond – if you want the truth, I'm not too happy about the way it all worked out.'

'But you solved the case . . .'

He was offended. 'Of course I did.'

'Would you be prepared to tell me about it?'

'I don't know.' He seemed genuinely pained. I had seen the same look on his face when I had asked him about Reeth, the village in Yorkshire where he had lived as a child. 'It all happened five years ago. And how can you even write it if you weren't there?'

'I've just been writing about Alex Rider in outer space . . .'

'But that's not real.'

'So what happened in Riverside . . . or Riverview Close?' I waited while he smoked in silence. I was actually getting quite annoyed. 'Who was murdered?'

'A man called Giles Kenworthy. He wasn't very nice . . . some sort of hedge fund manager. Old Etonian. Right-wing, borderline racist. He had a wife and a couple of kids, though, and they weren't too happy about him dying.'

'It sounds like a great start,' I said. 'Why was he killed?'

'He didn't get on with his neighbours.'

I wondered if Hawthorne was being sarcastic. 'Did you keep your notes from the case?' I asked. 'Can you remember all the details?'

'I had an assistant. He took notes. And he recorded the interviews.'

Hawthorne said this in a way that was completely matter-of-fact and didn't seem to notice how much it affected me. I'd spent weeks with him, following in his footsteps, and then months writing about him. He'd never once mentioned or even hinted that he'd had a different sidekick before he met me.

'What was his name?' I asked.

'Why do you want to know?'

'Because if we go ahead with this, I suppose I might just end up writing about him.'

'John Dudley,' Hawthorne said, reluctantly. 'He helped me with the case. He did the same job as you. Not the writing, though. He was more . . . professional.'

'Thanks a lot,' I muttered. 'Where is he now?' I asked.

'We haven't seen each other for a while.'

'Why did he stop working with you?'

Hawthorne shrugged. 'He had other things to do.'

That was a non-answer if ever I'd heard one.

'Well, I don't think we have any choice,' I went on, repeating what Hilda had told me. 'We've only got five months to deliver because the publishers want the next book out at the end of next year. Of course, we could sit back and wait for another murder, but it sounds as if things have been quiet for you recently, and even if someone does get killed, there's no saying it'll be interesting enough for book five.'

'Can't you make something up?'

'And put you in it? I don't think that would work. Look,

82

what we've got here is a case you've already investigated – and solved. Why can't you just tell me what happened?'

Hawthorne thought for a few moments as he finished smoking. 'I suppose I could describe it for you,' he said eventually. He ground out the cigarette and dropped it into the plastic lid. 'But I'd want to see what you were writing.'

'You mean . . . while I was writing it?'

'Yes.'

The thought horrified me. I wasn't sure I could work with Hawthorne peering over my shoulder. I'd have to censor half the things I said about him. Worse than that, he would have the upper hand. He had met all the suspects. He'd been there, whereas, to some extent, I would be groping in the dark. Inevitably, I'd have to make a lot of it up and I could see us arguing about every word, every description. It might take years to complete. 'Why would you want to do that?' I asked. 'Don't you trust me?'

'I trust you so much, I don't even read you. But this time I'd have to make sure you got it right. We'd be writing it together.'

'That's not how I work . . .'

'But this is different!'

He had a point. I could look at photographs, read police reports, listen to recordings, get Hawthorne to describe everything he'd seen . . . but I'd still be writing from a distance. The book would be in the third person (he/they) and not the first (I). As every writer knows, this would completely change the way the story was presented. It would have a universality, a sense of disconnection. It would not be *my* story, *my* arrival on the scene, *my* first impressions. Everything would have to be channelled through Hawthorne and he was right to say that it would be, to some extent, a collaboration.

I still didn't like the idea.

'We're not writing it together,' I said. 'You're supplying the basic information, but I'm the one doing the writing. It's my style. My descriptions. And,' I added, 'my name on the cover.'

He looked at me innocently. 'I know that, Tony.'

'No shared credit.'

'Whatever you say, mate.'

'And you'll give me everything you have.'

'You can have it all.' He paused. 'One step at a time.'

My cappuccino had gone cold. 'I'm sorry?'

'I just think it'll be easier that way. I'll give you everything you need – but in instalments. You write two or three chapters. I read them. Then we talk about them. If you get anything wrong, I can steer you back on the right track. Like – you know – fact-checking.'

'But you will give me the solution!'

'No. I won't.'

'Why not?'

'You never know the solution, mate. That's what makes your writing so special. You don't have a clue.'

Had any compliment ever been more backhanded? I thought about what he was offering and came to a decision. Like it or not, there was no other way of delivering a book to my publishers in time. I reached down and opened my work-bag. I took out a notepad and a pen.

'All right,' I said. 'Where do we begin?'

3

Hawthorne and I spent a couple more hours sitting outside the coffee shop, making us the least profitable customers that particular branch must have ever entertained. The first thing he told me was the location of the private road where the murder had taken place – Riverview Close. He said it was a turning off the Petersham Road, near a pub I vaguely remembered, the Fox and Duck. I was sure I'd gone there for a drink a couple of times when I was living in west London and used to take my dog for walks in Richmond Park. I'd never noticed the close, though.

He described the layout of the buildings, the history of the place, Petersham Road and the immediate surroundings. For the first time, he gave me the names of the people I was going to be living with for the next few months. Tom and Gemma Beresford. Roderick Browne, dentist to the stars, with his invalid wife. Chess mastermind Adam Strauss . . . and so on.

He also introduced me to some of the minor characters who would appear later: the lady gardener, the Australian nanny who also looked after an old lady in Hampton Wick, the detective superintendent in charge of the case and a detective constable who worked with him but who just seemed like one officer too many and would barely make it into my second draft.

He was only reticent about one character and that, not surprisingly, was John Dudley. Even a physical description seemed to challenge him. 'Same age as me. Dark hair. Ordinary-looking.' That was all he gave me. As we talked, I got the sense that the two of them had parted acrimoniously, or at least that something had come between them, and in a way I found this quite gratifying. Perhaps I hadn't been such a useless assistant after all.

Hawthorne promised he would dig out more information for me and it arrived the next day by courier: a neatly wrapped parcel that opened to reveal about twenty black-and-white photographs, police reports, typescripts and handwritten notes made by his erstwhile assistant. More surprising was a plastic box full of old-fashioned memory sticks that turned out to contain the recordings of entire conversations. One way and another, I had more than enough material to imagine myself in Riverview Close and even in The Tea Cosy bookshop, which Hawthorne would only visit later.

What's important is that everything I have written so far (Part One: Riverview Close) is based on fact, with just a few extra flourishes from me. It's worth remembering, though, that even as I set it all down, I was as much in the dark as I had been when I followed Hawthorne around London after the death of Diana Cowper, or when I travelled to Yorkshire to discover the truth about a potholing accident, or when my visit to the Alderney Literary Festival was rudely interrupted by the main sponsor being tied to a chair and stabbed. This was exactly what Hawthorne wanted. He was still in charge.

And despite my earlier misgivings, I was also quite pleased with what I had written, following the investigation from different perspectives, finishing with the non-appearance of Giles and Lynda Kenworthy at the drinks party and generally making the murder an inevitable consequence. It felt solid to me and entirely accurate. Once I'd got to the end of the section, I sent it off to Hawthorne with a degree of confidence and when it came to our second meeting, I broke my own rules by inviting him over to my flat. Jill was on the set of *Safe House*, a drama she was making for ITV. I was home alone.

He didn't like what I'd done.

'You've made half of it up!' That was the first thing he said. He had printed up the thirty-two pages and spread them in front of me. We were sitting in my office.

'What do you mean?'

'That chess game in the first chapter. I never told you about players called Frank or Charmaine. How do you know what May and Phyllis had for breakfast? That business about

Roderick Browne's matron when he was at prep school . . . ?
You say she had a gap in her teeth. Where did that come
from?'

'Come on, Hawthorne. I can't just write the information
you gave me. First of all, the whole book would only be thirty
pages long and it would be boring! Nobody would read it.
I've taken what you've given me and I've added a bit of
colour, that's all.'

'I get that. But you don't think people are going to get a bit
fed up with it? I mean, there's even a paragraph about bloody
parakeets! You've written all these pages and nobody's been
killed.'

'I have to set the scene! And anyway, you know perfectly
well that there's more to a novel – even a crime novel – than
violent death. It's all about character and atmosphere and
language. Why do you think people read Jane Austen? She
wrote thousands of pages and she never felt the need to
murder anyone.'

'Actually, that's not true. Anna Parker murdered both her
parents and she was planning to do the same to her sister.'

'And she's a character in Jane Austen?' My head swam. 'I
suppose you came across that in your book club.'

'*Juvenilia and Short Stories*.' Hawthorne was toying with a
cigarette, but he'd had the good grace not to light it. 'Anyway,
there are things you've left out that are important.'

'Such as?'

'The Union Jack in Giles Kenworthy's garden. The

lighting in Roderick Browne's house. The state of May Winslow's flower beds.'

'Why are any of them relevant?'

'They're all clues.'

'Well, how can I possibly know that when you haven't even arrived on the scene? And the sooner you arrive the better, by the way. So far, we've got a murder mystery with no murder and no one to solve the mystery. Graham's not going to like it.' Graham was Graham Lucas, my editor at Penguin Random House. If he'd had his way, Giles Kenworthy would have died in the first paragraph.

'And why do you say there was a life jacket in Roderick Browne's garage?' Hawthorne asked.

'It's reasonable enough. He'd been a member of the Richmond Bridge Boat Club. He said so!'

'There were a lot of things in that garage that really mattered. But he didn't have a life jacket. Not one that I saw.'

'I put it in there so people wouldn't focus on the crossbow.'

'I'm sorry?'

I sighed. 'It's the narrative principle known as Chekhov's gun. If I simply mention there's a crossbow in Roderick's garage, it'll be obvious that it's going to be used as the murder weapon.'

'So why mention it at all?'

'Because it would be unfair not to! What I've done, though, is I've disguised it by adding the life jacket and the golf clubs. That way, it might still come as a surprise.' I watched the cigarette Hawthorne was still twisting between his fingers. 'Go ahead and light the bloody thing,' I snapped. I got up and opened a window. 'Aren't you worried about your health?'

'I'm more worried about your prose style, mate.' Hawthorne flicked his lighter and drew in a lungful of smoke. 'I mean, reading this, do you really get the position of the houses and what you could see from one to the other? You've got to get that right.'

'We could put a map in at the beginning. Would that make you happy?'

'It would certainly cheer up some of your readers. I'm not saying it's confusing, but going through this, I'm not sure I could deliver the mail.'

All my life I've been getting notes. I get them from producers in London and New York, from directors, from Jill, from lead actors . . . even, on occasions, from their partners. My books are scrutinised by editors and copy editors and (more recently) sensitivity readers. I sometimes feel that I'm surrounded by notes, like a cloud of midges. But I never lose my temper. I always try to see the alternative point of view.

It wasn't easy with Hawthorne.

'I'll ask Graham to put a map in,' I said. 'But he won't like it.'

'Why not?'

'Because it's an extra cost. Is there anything else?'

'Yes. There is one thing. You say that the barrister – Andrew Pennington – played bridge with the Brownes.'

'He did.'

'But he also played with friends who lived outside Riverview Close.'

That was one note too many. 'Are you really telling me that was relevant to the murder?' I exploded.

'That meeting you describe, when all the neighbours got together, which took place on a Monday. Andrew Pennington played bridge every Monday and Wednesday and he had to cancel a game to be there.'

'So he killed Giles Kenworthy for not showing up? He was upset he'd cancelled his game for no good reason?'

Hawthorne looked at me sadly. 'Of course not. You're missing the point.'

'Well, since I don't know exactly how or when Giles Kenworthy died, I'm not sure what the point is.'

I stopped. There was one thing Hawthorne had said that worried me slightly. It might be true that the book needed some action. I didn't want to spend another ten thousand words describing the joys of suburban life.

'When did he die?' I asked.

'You know the answer to that,' Hawthorne said. 'You've already written it.'

'Six weeks later.'

'Yes.'

'Six weeks after the meeting at The Stables.'

'Exactly.' Hawthorne looked around him for an ashtray and found a hollow silver acorn that he used to deposit his ash. It was a children's book award I'd been given about twenty years before. 'I got a call from the investigating officer – DS Khan.'

'Why did he think he needed you?'

Hawthorne gazed at me. 'Tony, mate! A multimillionaire was found dead in a posh London suburb with a crossbow bolt stuck in his throat. Every single one of his neighbours wanted him dead. It was pretty obvious this wasn't an ordinary case. It was a sticker if ever there was one, and frankly, the local plod had as much chance of solving it as . . . well, you!'

'Thanks.'

'I got the call the same day the body was found. Me and John Dudley.'

'So what happened next?'

THREE
SIX WEEKS LATER

1

Detective Superintendent Tariq Khan had realised straight away that the murder of Giles Kenworthy would be like nothing he had ever investigated and that it might threaten what had so far been an unblemished career.

The dead man had been waiting for him in the hallway of his home, covered with a sheet, and it wasn't so much the multiple bloodstains – on the carpet, the walls, even a few specks on the ceiling – as the sheer incongruousness of it that struck Khan first. The white linen was clinging to the hips and shoulders so that most of the body was clearly visible in silhouette. But when it reached the neck, it rose up like a miniature tent. The effect was grotesque, almost comical. Khan had drawn the sheet back and looked at the crossbow bolt, still lodged in Giles Kenworthy's throat. The deceased would have been unrecognisable even to his nearest and dearest. His eyes were still open in shock, his mouth twisted in a scream that death had turned into a grimace. The bolt had entered directly under his chin. If he had been wearing a tie, it would have gone through the knot.

Everything had been wrong from the start, and as the day progressed it only got worse.

First of all, there was the murder weapon: a crossbow, for heaven's sake! Khan had never heard of anyone being the target of a crossbow, not since William Tell's son – and that hadn't hit him. The killer hadn't even tried to get rid of it, simply leaving it on the gravel in front of the house as if he – or she – didn't even care about being caught. The weapon had already been identified as the property of one Roderick Browne, the middle-aged dentist who lived next door. Then there was Riverview Close itself, an unlikely murder scene with its perfectly attractive houses and Alan Ayckbourn collection of characters: a GP, a jewellery designer and their twin daughters, a chess grandmaster, two little old ladies, a retired barrister, and the dentist.

He wouldn't normally have thought of them as suspects, but he had to take the facts into consideration. First and foremost, they all had a motive. It was clear that they had disliked or even hated Giles Kenworthy, who, from the sound of it, had been one of those 'neighbours from hell', the sort who frequently turned up in sensationalist television documentaries. He had only arrived with his family eight months before, but he seemed to have gone out of his way to annoy everyone around him. Any one of them could have killed him — and for exactly the same reason. They wanted him out.

And then there was the physicality of Riverview Close itself: the electronic gate that automatically locked itself at seven o'clock in the evening, sealing them all in, and the crossbow stored in a garage that was locked and bolted and which nobody from the outside world could possibly have known was there. Khan was sure that other suspects would show up; you didn't get to be as rich as Giles Kenworthy without making enemies. But he had been killed in the middle of the night. The gate hadn't been forced and it would have been hard to climb over without leaving some sort of evidence. The entire set-up screamed 'inside job'.

There was something else going on. Khan had spent most of the day talking to the residents, who had all been asked to stay at home. He was trying to keep things casual: not so much a formal interview as a general chat. It should have been easy. A nice neighbourhood like this, everyone would be eager to help the police with their inquiries. If nothing else, it would be a new experience, a break from routine, something to talk about at their next dinner party. But all along he had sensed there was something wrong. Each one of them had been evasive, reticent . . . even afraid.

The dentist, Roderick Browne, had been the worst of all, his eyes blinking as he spoke, his tongue darting across his lips. 'Yes. I heard. I couldn't believe it. Giles Kenworthy! Of course, he wasn't an easy man to get on with, but none of us would ever have done such a thing. Certainly not me! I'm a dentist. I look after people. I mean, I know it was my cross-bow. Tom Beresford called me and I went straight to the garage. It's gone! I have no idea when it was taken. To be honest with you, I'd almost forgotten it was there. I haven't fired it in years. Years and years. I hope you don't think . . . My wife is upstairs. She's not at all well. But she'll tell you. I was asleep last night. We don't share the same room any more . . . because of her illness. But she'd have heard . . .'

The words tumbled out of him almost incoherently, made worse by the idiotic smile he had pinned to his lips. There was a sheen of sweat on his forehead. In Khan's opinion, all that was missing was the billboard mounted on his shoulders with GUILTY written on it and a hand with an outstretched finger pointing down.

The others were just as bad. The two old ladies had to be persuaded to let him into the house, preferring to address him from the other side of a half-open door. The barrister, Andrew Pennington, was so circumspect that he tied himself in knots, talking as much as he could without actually saying anything. By contrast, Adam Strauss, whom Khan remem-bered from a terrible quiz show his grandmother had liked to watch, was monosyllabic. Gemma Beresford, the doctor's wife, was openly hostile.

Detective Superintendent Tariq Khan was something of a poster boy for the Metropolitan Police – and knew it. He was young, good-looking, Oxford-educated, a great communicator from a working-class background. His father had been employed as a hospital porter. With his prematurely silver hair, his slim physique, his Bollywood good looks and his easy manner, Khan was admired by everyone who knew him and was regularly put forward for press briefings and evening news slots. This was the first time he had ever felt out of his depth. He'd found himself in drug-ridden sink estates in the worst parts of south London that had been more open and accommodating than Riverview Close. So far, they hadn't given him so much as a Mr Kipling cake.

Late in the afternoon, he stood in the sunlight, comparing notes with DC Ruth Goodwin, who had worked with him for the last five years. The two of them got on well even though they came from different worlds – in her case, Hampstead Garden Suburb and a well-to-do Jewish family who wouldn't have objected if she'd married a police officer but were surprised when she announced she was going to become one. Short and dark, with a round face and close-cropped hair, she had recently given up smoking, much to Khan's satisfaction. Unfortunately, she had replaced cigarettes with a series of brightly coloured vapes, each one with a more unlikely flavour. Today it was lemon and mint. Khan thought she looked ridiculous, like a child sucking a sweet.

'What do you think's going on here?' he asked. They were both leaning against the car that had brought them here.

'I don't know, sir. They're all hiding something. That much is obvious.'

'Do you think one of them killed Giles Kenworthy?'

It seems unlikely. They're all friends, living in each other's back gardens. But this is murder and they don't seem like the sort of people who would cover up anything as serious as that.'

'Unless they were somehow involved.'

'Well, they can't all have done it.'

Khan nodded. 'He'd have had nine crossbow bolts in him if they had.' He watched as a cloud of steam from the vape formed in the air and then disappeared. 'I've got a bad feeling about this, Ruth. If they're covering for each other, it's going to be hard to untangle.'

'And they've all got the same motive. The neighbour from hell. That doesn't make it any easier.'

There was a long silence. The police and forensic officers were moving around them like pieces on one of Adam Strauss's chessboards.

'I wonder if we could use some outside help?' DC Goodwin suggested at length.

'What are you talking about?'

'Well, don't shout at me, but I was thinking. Maybe . . . Hawthorne?'

'Are you serious?'

'It can't do any harm and this might be right up his street . . .'

Neither of them had met Hawthorne, but they both knew who he was: the detective inspector who had lost his job when a suspect he'd been interrogating had sustained life-changing injuries – although he'd had a reputation long before that. He was a hard-working, solitary, difficult man who somehow always managed to pull the guilty rabbit out of the blood-soaked hat. After he'd been thrown out, his reputation had grown. They had both heard DI Cara Grunshaw talking about him. She had come across him on two occasions and had a deep loathing for him, but even she admitted that he had helped her. He also had plenty of friends inside the force. DCI Ian Rutherford had been his superior officer and wouldn't hear a word said against him.

'We could bring him in as an outside consultant,' DC Goodwin went on. 'If you think this one is a special case.'

'I don't know.' Khan shook his head doubtfully.

'It's a crossbow, sir. In a private close in Richmond. We've already got the local hacks outside. They're going to lap it up.'

'But how do we even reach him? And who authorises payment?'

'I can ask DCI Rutherford.' Goodwin inhaled on her bright yellow vape. The light at the end blinked on. A smell of something like candyfloss shimmered in the air between them. 'From what I hear, Hawthorne never takes any of the credit.'

This mattered to Khan. He didn't want anyone to think that he was already giving up on such a shocking crime.

'All right,' he said. 'Why don't we give him a call?'

2

Hawthorne arrived the following morning, a Wednesday.

A taxi pulled up at the archway just after nine o'clock and two men got out. Khan was waiting on the other side, holding a cardboard file. He was glad to see that the press people had disappeared. There was still something about getting outside help that troubled him, as did the sight of the taxi. Was that going to be charged to expenses? Khan had called Hawthorne the night before and had been surprised how cheerful he had sounded at his end of the line, as if he had been expecting the call. Khan had quickly gone through what had happened in Riverview Close. In broad strokes, he had described the various residents: age, profession, ethnicity, what they had told him, what he believed. So far, it didn't add up to very much. Now that Hawthorne was here, would he be able to do any better?

Quickly, he made his assessment of the man he'd called in to help.

Hawthorne was a diminutive figure, oddly dressed in a suit and a loose raincoat despite the warm July weather, looking around him with eyes that seemed to absorb and analyse every detail, a face that gave nothing away. His hair was short, neatly brushed, of no particular colour. He was in his mid- to late thirties, although it was difficult to be sure as there was something childlike about his appearance. Khan had begun his career as a juvenile protection officer and in some strange way Hawthorne reminded him of some of the victims he had met.

The person he had brought with him was equally puzzling. He seemed an unlikely partner for Hawthorne, keeping his distance and taking less interest in his surroundings – as if he was bored by it all. He was about the same age, with sloping shoulders and long, lank hair, untidily dressed in ill-fitting corduroy trousers, a jacket with patches on the elbows and scuffed shoes. He hadn't shaved that morning and the lower part of his pale, oblong face was covered with stubble. Everything about him had an air of carelessness. He had the appearance of a man who didn't know how to look after himself or who couldn't be bothered, and Khan thought that if he hadn't been in the company of Hawthorne, he wouldn't have allowed him anywhere near a crime scene.

Hawthorne saw the detective superintendent and walked

over, his companion a few steps behind. Already, Khan was wondering if he hadn't made a mistake. He took Hawthorne's outstretched hand and shook it. 'Thank you for coming,' he said.

'Thank you for inviting me. This is John Dudley.'

The other man nodded vaguely.

'I take it that's the house where Giles Kenworthy lived.' Hawthorne pointed at Riverview Lodge.

'Yes. That's right.' For a brief moment, Khan allowed his irritation to get the better of him. 'I need to get one thing straight before we go in,' he said. 'You're working for me. I hope you understand. The moment you find anything, I want to know. And you're to hold nothing back.'

'Don't worry, mate. That's my job – to tell you what you've missed.'

'I don't think I've missed anything so far. And I'd prefer it if you addressed me as Detective Superintendent.'

They began to walk towards the house.

'Mr Kenworthy was killed on Monday night at around eleven o'clock,' Khan began. 'I'll send you a copy of the pathologist's report. A single crossbow bolt, fired at close range, penetrated his cricoid cartilage and buried itself in his throat. They took the body yesterday, but I've got some of the photographs here. Death was caused by haemorrhagic shock.'

'Were the cricothyroid or cricotracheal ligaments severed?' Dudley asked.

'No.'

'Then it wasn't his kids who killed him!'

Khan wondered if he was joking. 'How do you work that one out?'

'The bolt didn't slant up or down. It must have been fired by someone of about his own height.'

'The kids aren't suspects.' Khan scowled. 'In fact, they've got a rock-solid alibi. They're at a local prep school which does a couple of nights' boarding each week. They weren't at home. Probably just as well.'

'Was Kenworthy on his own?' Hawthorne asked.

'Yes. His wife was having dinner with a friend. She was the one who discovered the body. She's upstairs now . . . and not in a good way. They also have a Filipino housekeeper, but she's on annual leave, in her own country. She's not expected back for another week. Then there's a part-time chauffeur. We're talking to him and we'll let you know if he's got anything to say.'

'When did the wife get in?'

'Twenty past eleven on Monday night. The door was half-open, which puzzled her. Her husband was on the other side, blood everywhere. She screamed the house down and that woke up the neighbours. Must have made a change from the parties and the car stereo and all the other things they were complaining about.'

They had reached the front door, where a uniformed policeman stood to one side. But before they went in, Khan stopped. 'We haven't talked money,' he said.

Hawthorne looked offended. 'We don't need to, Detective Superintendent.'

John Dudley drew an envelope out of his jacket pocket and offered it to Khan. 'Terms and conditions,' he explained. 'I take it you got clearance from Special Grant Funding?'

'I spoke to them yesterday.' Khan took the envelope and folded it away without looking at it. 'Someone will get back to you,' he said.

They went in. As they entered the hallway, Dudley took out his iPhone, found the Voice Memos app in the Utilities folder and turned it on. At the end of the day he would save the file, transfer it to his laptop and share it with Hawthorne. He also took several photographs, focusing on the extensive bloodstain on the once beige carpet and the splatter on the walls.

'What was Giles Kenworthy wearing when he answered the door?' Hawthorne asked.

'He hadn't got ready for bed, if that's what you mean. He had a white shirt, suit trousers. The jacket and tie were in his office.' Khan pointed towards an open door. 'He had his slippers on. Prada – mauve cashmere. And he'd drunk a couple of glasses of Hakushu single malt whisky. Expensive stuff and not small measures.'

'So he was working late. The doorbell rang. He answered and the weapon was fired over the threshold.'

'It looks that way.'

'Where did you find it?'

'It was just dropped on the ground, outside. Mrs Kenworthy didn't notice it in the darkness. The crossbow belongs to Roderick Browne, who lives next door in the house at the end of the terrace . . . Woodlands, it's called. No fingerprints – apart from his. It's always possible that the killer wore gloves.'

'They just left it?' Dudley was surprised. 'You'd have thought they'd have got rid of it. Chucked it in the Thames.'

'Funnily enough, it was pointing at Roderick Browne's home. It was almost as if the killer wanted us to know who it belonged to.'

Khan opened the file he had been carrying and took out several photographs, which he handed to Hawthorne. They had been taken from different angles and showed Giles Kenworthy's body as it had been found. Half of them were in black and white. The ones in colour were more horrible. Hawthorne stopped on a close-up shot of the dead man's head. He said nothing and his face gave nothing away, but somehow Khan was aware of an extraordinary intensity, a sense that at that moment nothing else in the world mattered.

'It's a standard bolt,' Khan explained. 'Twenty inches long, aluminium shaft, plastic vanes. We found five more, identical, in the Brownes' garage.'

'Has Browne confessed to the killing?' Dudley asked.

The question took Khan by surprise. 'No. Why do you ask?'

'If he'd used his own weapon and his own bolt and he just left it all there for you to find, you'd think maybe he didn't care if he was caught.'

'Well, he's a nervous wreck,' Khan said. 'But he hasn't confessed to anything. Quite the contrary. The first time I met him, all he would say was how shocked he was, how upset, how it couldn't have had anything to do with him because he was asleep, in bed, with his wife in the next room . . . I wasn't even accusing him!'

Hawthorne handed the photographs back. 'You said we could talk to Mr Kenworthy's widow.'

'She's upstairs.'

The Kenworthys' home was expensive and wanted you to know it. The furniture was Scandinavian, the lights ultra-modern, the carpets ankle-deep and the paintings straight out of some smart auction-house catalogue. Two young boys lived here with their parents, but there was no mess, no scattered clothes or toys, as if their very existence had been wiped away. A plate-glass window at the back, rising almost the full height of the stairs, looked out over the new patio with a Union Jack fluttering on the other side of a chrome-plated beast of a gas barbecue.

Lynda Kenworthy was lying on a bed so large that her entire family could have joined her with room to spare. She seemed to be sinking into the duvet and pillows, her blonde hair hanging loose, her silk dressing gown rising and falling over the folds of her body, her face, with its once perfect make-up, streaked by tears. The room smelled of cigarette smoke. There was an ashtray next to her filled with cigarette butts, each one signed off with a smear of bright red lipstick.

None of the windows was open and even if they had been they'd have been helpless behind the great swathes of silk curtains, pelmets, gold cords and tassels.

'How are you feeling, love?' Hawthorne asked. From the way he spoke, she could have been recovering from a bad cold.

'Who are you?' Lynda asked – her voice little more than a whisper.

'We're helping the police,' Dudley said. 'We want to find out who killed your husband.'

'They all hated him!' Fresh tears followed in the tracks of the old ones. 'I told him it was a mistake, the moment we came here. They were stuck-up and snobby, the whole lot of them.'

'So you didn't get on with the neighbours,' Dudley remarked.

'It wasn't our fault!' She reached for a tissue, pulling it out of a box embroidered with a gondola on a Venetian canal. 'We never did anything wrong. They were always trying to find fault. Everything we did! Nothing was ever right.'

Hawthorne and Dudley waited until she had calmed down.

'Would you say there was anyone in Riverview Close who had a particular animus towards your husband?' Hawthorne asked.

'I've just told you. They were all the same. They'd made up their minds about us before we even moved in.'

'Had there been any recent incidents that you might want to tell us about?'

111

Lynda used the tissue to dry her eyes, at the same time wiping away some of the blusher on her cheekbones. 'I don't know what you mean,' she said.

'Had anyone threatened your husband with violence?'

'Well . . .' She thought for a moment. 'Giles was always fighting with Dr Beresford,' she said. 'He and his wife live next door and they never stopped complaining about our cars. Why *can't* we park our cars outside? It's our drive, our house, and it wasn't as if we were deliberately blocking the way. If Dr Beresford hadn't been such a bad driver, he could easily have got past.' She stopped herself as she remembered what had happened. 'The two of them had a proper set-to about a week ago and Dr Beresford threatened to kill Giles!' Her eyes widened. 'He used those very words!'

'What did he say, exactly?'

'I'm going to kill you!'

'You heard him?'

'No. Giles told me.'

Hawthorne and Dudley exchanged glances. They both knew that a lot of people argued about parking rights; it was one of the things that always came close to the top of neigh-bourhood disputes. But even if Dr Beresford had made the threat, a parking dispute would be an unusual motive for murder. 'Anything else?' Dudley asked.

Lynda gazed into the distance. 'I already told him all this,' she said, referring to Detective Superintendent Khan, who had been listening to the conversation from a distance.

'Tell us.'

She swallowed. 'Well, he had a falling-out with Sarah.'

'Who's Sarah?'

'She's the gardener. That was on Friday,' she added.

'And what happened on Friday?'

'Giles went into his study and there she was, standing in front of his desk. She had no right to be there. She'd come in through the French windows. And she was looking at his computers. Giles was very sensitive about that. He'd had a hack at his office just a few weeks before – someone trying to get into his database. It was the reason we couldn't go to that drinks do at The Stables. It hadn't worked that time, but he didn't have the same security at home so he had every right to ask her what she was doing. Sarah was just horrible and abusive and he fired her on the spot – and quite right too. I said he ought to report her to the police.'

'What for, exactly?'

'What do you think?' It was remarkable how quickly Lynda could switch between desolation, indignation and malice. 'Do you know how much information there was on those screens about money markets and investments and all that stuff? She could have been working for someone!' Lynda drew herself up against the pillows. 'Giles wouldn't even let me into his office because of all the sensitive stuff he had in there and I wouldn't have understood a word of it if he had. So what did Sarah think she was doing in there?'

'You think your gardener was involved in . . . what? Financial espionage?'

'She might have been. She was certainly a thief. All sorts of things had gone missing. Giles lost a Rolex watch. I'd bought it for him myself when we were in Dubai. And I had fifty pounds taken from my bag. Giles said I left it at the hairdresser, but I know it was Sarah. We only gave her the job in the first place because she was doing the gardens for everyone else in the close. I always said she was trouble. We should have found someone of our own.'

She fell silent, dabbing her eyes.

'Is there anyone else you employ in the house?' Dudley asked. 'I understand you've got a Filipino cleaner. I bet she's a treasure!'

'She's lazy and she's never there when you need her. In fact, she's away right now. Every summer we have to give her the whole month off so she can see her family, but getting any sort of help is so difficult these days. Jasmine hardly speaks a word of English and getting her to do anything is always an uphill struggle.' She paused. 'And there's Gary. He's Giles's driver, but he's only part-time. He doesn't live here.'

'How did you meet your husband?' Dudley had changed the subject, perhaps hoping the question would cheer her up.

Instead, it brought fresh tears. 'On a British Airways flight to New York. He was in first class. I was one of the cabin crew. I served him a mai tai and we hit it off immediately. He was so kind to me. He invited me to his hotel next to Central Park. We had so many laughs!'

'So where were you last night?' Hawthorne cut in.

That stopped her. 'I was seeing a friend.'

'Can we have his name?' Dudley had produced a small notebook, which he was holding in front of him. He had somehow assumed that the friend was male and Lynda didn't disappoint him.

'What's that got to do with you?'

'You're going to have to tell us sooner or later, love.' It was always a mistake taking on Hawthorne. When he was at his sweetest and most reasonable, that was when he was most dangerous. 'You got back after eleven o'clock. That's time for a lot of laughs.'

'It was horrible! The door was open. And he was lying there . . . !'

'Who were you with?' Hawthorne insisted.

Lynda reached for another tissue. 'His name is Jean-François. He's my French teacher.'

'You're learning French?'

'Giles was talking about buying a place in Antibes.'

'*Mais malhereusement, cela n'arrivera pas*,' Dudley muttered.

Lynda stared at him. 'What?'

3

Khan was unimpressed with the interrogation he had just witnessed. It seemed to him that Hawthorne had been unnecessarily hostile and had learned very little that Khan didn't already know.

'I've got things to do, so I'm going to let you get on with it,' he said as they left the Kenworthys' house. 'We allowed Dr Beresford to leave for work . . . NHS doctor and all that. And the two old ladies – May Winslow and Phyllis Moore – own some sort of gift shop in Richmond. I thought they were better off out of it too.'

'Not on your suspect list?' Hawthorne asked.

Khan ignored him. 'All the others are at home and you can talk to the whole lot of them, but I think it would be better if you didn't mention you're freelance. Just say you're part of my support team or something. And maybe you could try to be a little more sympathetic? These people are in shock.'

'One of them may not be,' Dudley said.

But Khan was already walking away, catching up with DC Goodwin, who had just arrived in a police car.

Dudley watched him go. 'Where do you want to start?' he asked.

'The murder weapon belonged to Roderick Browne,' Hawthorne replied.

'I don't like dentists,' Dudley sighed.

They walked the short distance across the courtyard and rang the bell of Woodlands, the last house in the terrace of three. The door opened almost at once, as if Roderick Browne had been waiting for them on the other side. He looked ill. He clearly wasn't going into work today and had forsaken his morning routine, not shaving, not picking out the right tie, not even flossing. He had pulled on a crumpled shirt that ballooned over his trousers. Looking at him, with his pink face and cloud of white hair, Dudley was reminded of something you might win at a funfair. At the same time, the way he was gazing at them, he could have just stepped off the ghost train.

He had been expecting Khan and looked at Hawthorne with bewilderment. 'Yes?'

'Mr Browne?'

'Yes. Yes . . . That's me.'

'My name's Hawthorne. I'm helping the police with this inquiry. This is my assistant, John Dudley. Can we come in?'

'Of course you can. I spoke to the police yesterday, but if there's anything I can do to help . . .'

He stood back and allowed them to enter a hallway which had an elegance and formality that might have mirrored the reception area of his clinic in Cadogan Square. Everything was very neat. A faux-antique chest of drawers stood against the back wall, with a small pile of magazines next to an art deco lamp. A photograph in a silver frame had been carefully placed to one side so that it was hard to miss. It showed Roderick standing next to Ewan McGregor, presumably one of his celebrity clients. Two wooden chairs had been positioned symmetrically, one on either side of the front door, and Hawthorne noticed a suitcase perched on one of them, with a woman's light raincoat draped over the top. Roderick led them into the kitchen, which provided a complete contrast to the entrance: everything modern, white and silver, too brightly lit, and so clean it might never have been used. A true dentist's kitchen. There was a window at the far end with views towards the Kenworthys' garden.

'Has anyone said anything?' Roderick asked before they had even sat down. He hadn't offered either of them a coffee. He didn't look in any fit state to make it.

'Are you talking about your neighbours?' Hawthorne took a seat at the head of the table that stretched out in front of the window.

'Yes.'

'That seems a very strange question to ask, Mr Browne.'

'Do you think so? I was just wondering if you'd talked to any of them and if they'd said anything . . .'

'About you?'

'No! About Giles Kenworthy. You'll have to forgive me, Mr Hawthorne. For something like this to happen, not just in the close but right next door to me . . . and with my cross-bow! As you can imagine, the whole thing is a complete nightmare and I find it hard to know what to think. Do you have any suspects?'

'I would say that everyone who lives here is a suspect, Mr Browne.' Hawthorne paused. 'Including you.'

'Well, that's ridiculous. I'm a highly respected dental prac-titioner. I've never had so much as a speeding ticket in my life. Do I really look like a murderer to you?'

'Well, actually . . .' Dudley began.

'It's outrageous. We certainly had our issues with Giles Kenworthy. I'm not making any secret of that. But to come here, into my house, asking me all these questions . . .'

'We haven't asked you very much yet,' Hawthorne said reasonably. 'And we will be talking to everyone in Riverview Close.'

'I'm sure you know who lives in this community. We're very respectable people. A doctor. A barrister. Two ladies who used to be nuns. This is Richmond, for heaven's sake! I feel as if I've woken up in Mexico City.'

Hawthorne waited for him to finish. 'Why don't you start by telling us when you came here?' he suggested. 'You and your wife?'

'You haven't told us her name,' Dudley said.

'Felicity. She's upstairs in bed. She has ME.' He leaned forward, confidentially. 'That's why this business with the swimming pool mattered so much to us. If you take away the view from her, you take away everything. And the noise! Their children are bad enough anyway, but with all their friends, shouting and screaming . . . We'd have had to move. And that's not fair. We love it here.'

'So when did you move in?' Hawthorne repeated the question he'd asked earlier.

'Fourteen years ago, just after the close had been developed. We arrived about a month after our neighbours, May Winslow and Phyllis Moore. They're next door.'

'Like most neighbours,' Dudley said.

'Yes. They're quite elderly and they have a bookshop in the town centre. They sell crime novels. Then there's Andrew Pennington next to them, Adam Strauss and his wife in The Stables and Dr Beresford and his family across the way. We're all good friends – in a neighbourly sort of way. We like to have a drink together now and then. Nothing wrong with that! We look out for each other.'

'When did the Kenworthys arrive?'

'At the end of last year.' Roderick Browne was speaking more confidently now. 'Jon Emin and his wife were living in The Stables . . . a very nice couple. At that time, Adam was living in Riverview Lodge with his second wife, Teri, but she persuaded him that they would be more comfortable with something smaller. So they moved into The Stables when the Emins sold and that was when Giles Kenworthy bought the Lodge. We were all looking forward to meeting him. We really were. We're not stand-offish here. Don't let anyone tell you that.'

'So what went wrong?'

'Everything!' Roderick Browne shook his head in dismay. 'Nobody liked him,' he went on. 'Nobody! It wasn't just me. Mr Kenworthy was a horrible man – not that he deserved what happened to him. He didn't deserve that at all, and whatever I may have said in the heat of the moment, I never wished him any harm. None of us did. The fact is, he seemed to take a delight in putting our noses out of joint. He and his wife and his children. There were so many incidents, and they just got worse and worse until they were making all our lives unbearable.'

'What sort of incidents?'

'Well . . .' Roderick already seemed to be regretting that he had volunteered so much, but now that he had started it was hard to stop. 'There were lots of things. They may seem petty, describing them to you now, but they added up. The parking, the loud music, cricket and skateboards . . . The children were out of control. I said to Felicity things were going from bad to worse when he just dumped his Christmas tree in the drive as if it was up to us to get rid of it. No consideration! And then there were the parties. He never stopped having parties, although he never invited any of us. The swimming pool was the final straw. We never thought the council would give them permission, but it did and maybe

121

that's something you should look into. I wouldn't be surprised if there wasn't some sort of backhander involved. I
mean . . . see for yourself.' He pointed out of the window.
'He was going to rip up the lawn – right there! You see that
lovely magnolia? It attracts so many wild birds. Adam planted
it, but they were going to chop it down . . . just like they did
his yew trees when they moved in.'

Hawthorne glanced at John Dudley. 'You put all that
together, it does sound like a motive for murder,' he said.

'I agree.' Dudley nodded. 'If it was me, once the pool was
finished, I'd have drowned him in it.'

'No, no, no. You're deliberately misunderstanding me.'
Roderick got up and grabbed a roll of paper towel. 'It was
just very upsetting. I've already told you. Fee and I might
have had to move. We weren't going to stay here with the
noise, the chemicals, the disruption. And everyone agreed.
We had a meeting!' Something close to panic flitted across his
eyes, as if he had inadvertently told Hawthorne something he
had meant to keep back. 'It was a while ago. Six weeks! A
Monday evening. We all of us had complaints – not just about
the pool. We invited Giles Kenworthy to meet us, to try and
iron out our differences in a civilised way.'

'Did he come?' Hawthorne asked.

Roderick shook his head. 'He was coming. He said he was
coming. But at the last minute, he sent a text saying he was
too busy.' He paused. 'It was absolutely bloody typical of
him – and it was after that that things got really bad.'

'In what way?'

'Well . . .' Roderick was sweating. He used the paper towel to wipe his face. 'Ask May and Phyllis about their dog. Adam Strauss lost a beautiful chess set, smashed by a cricket ball. That was the two boys' fault – Hugo and Tristram Kenworthy. They also ruined the flowers in the courtyard. That really upset Andrew. But the worst thing – by far the worst thing – was what happened to Tom.'

'Tom?'

'Dr Beresford. Giles Kenworthy blocked his driveway.'

'What was so bad about that?' Dudley asked.

'He wasn't able to get to his surgery and as a result, a patient died. He was extremely upset about it. You should talk to him.'

'What can you tell us about the crossbow?'

'I already told the police. I wish I hadn't kept the bloody thing. I hadn't fired it in years.' Roderick sat down heavily. Perhaps he had been hoping that Hawthorne might have forgotten about the murder weapon.

'Where did you get it?'

'I was given it when I was at university. A Barnett Wildcat recurve. It's quite old now. I'm surprised it was even working.'

'It certainly worked two nights ago,' Dudley observed.

'Well, obviously, yes. But I wasn't to know.' From the look of him, Roderick was almost begging them to believe him. 'For a short while, after I moved to Richmond, I belonged to the London School of Archery. We both did. But when

123

Felicity became ill, it was one of the first things she had to give up, and as for me, I had less and less time. Fee has a carer now. Damien comes in three times a week but he's not here today, so, if you don't mind, I'm afraid I'll have to go upstairs in a minute. Fee may need help getting dressed.'

'Where did you keep the crossbow?' Hawthorne wasn't interested in Felicity's needs.

'In the garage.'

'Locked?' Dudley asked.

'The garage is usually kept locked. Not because of the crossbow. Fee insists. If a burglar broke in, the garage is connected directly to the house and they could easily come through to us.'

'How many keys do you have?'

Roderick had to think for a moment. 'Three,' he announced. 'There's one in the door, which I suppose is mine. Fee has a spare on her keyring. And our neighbour, May Winslow, keeps a set in case of emergencies.'

'What about the carer?'

'He has a key to the front door. Not to the garage.'

'Can we see inside?' Hawthorne made it sound like a question but he was only expecting one response.

'Of course.'

Roderick got up and the two detectives followed him out of the kitchen, through an archway and into a narrow corridor with a solid-looking door at the end. Just as he said, there was a key in the lock and Roderick turned it and opened the door, leading them into a small garage that jutted out of the back of the house. Much of the space was taken up by a navy-blue Skoda Octavia Mark 3. It was Roderick's pride and joy and he had loaded it with enough extras to make it top of the range: tinted windows, rain sensors, satnav and more besides. An up-and-over door – manual, not electric – closed off the far end of the garage, with metal bolts on either side locking into the framework. The sun was streaming in through a square skylight set in the roof and they could see the upper floor of the house and what looked like a bathroom window. A single shelf ran down both of the long walls, with an array of tools, paint pots and brushes, gardening equipment and bits of old machinery that might have been there for years. There was an electric mower plugged into a socket and, on the opposite wall, a tap with water dripping into a plastic bucket. A spade, a fork and a rake hung on hooks, with a sack of compost slumped beneath. That hardly left enough room to reach the car.

Roderick pointed at an empty space in the middle of a shelf. 'That's where it was kept,' he said.

'The crossbow?'

'And the bolts. The police took them all.'

'You said you weren't using it any more, so why *did* you keep it?' Dudley asked.

Roderick shrugged. 'I couldn't sell it and why would I want to throw it away?'

'Who apart from you came into this garage?' This time it was Hawthorne who had posed the question.

'Well, Sarah, I suppose. She does all the gardens in the close and she's also a general handyman – or handywoman, I should say. She's a fine young woman, very hard-working and always helpful. I suppose Damien could have come in if he'd wanted to. He has his key to the house and we trust him one hundred per cent. Felicity will come through the kitchen when I'm driving her to a doctor's appointment or whatever. Look, I really have told the police everything I know. To be honest with you, a complete stranger could have taken the crossbow when I was upstairs and I'm not sure I'd have noticed. They could have come through the house or through the garden. I leave the garage open sometimes when I drive to work.' He looked exhausted. 'I don't think I can help you any more.'

'I have one more question,' Hawthorne said. 'Are you planning on going somewhere?'

'I'm sorry?'

'I noticed a suitcase in your hall.'

'That's for Felicity. We've spoken about it and I just don't think it's good for her being here. I have to think of her. All my life, that's all I've ever done.' Roderick blinked, as if holding back tears. 'I'm sending her off to her sister in Woking . . . just for a few days. I've already told Superintendent Khan.' He had seemed more at ease in the garage, but mentioning the suitcase had upset him again. 'You have no idea what it's

126

like for her,' he continued. 'It's very upsetting. She has no part in this terrible murder and I want to get her far away. I have to protect her!'

As he finished speaking, his phone rang. Roderick fished it out and glanced at the screen, tilting it away from Dudley, who was standing behind him. Quickly, he flicked it off and slid it back into his pocket.

'Anyone important?' Hawthorne asked.

'No. Nothing at all.'

'Well, we've seen enough. Can we leave this way?'

'Of course. I'll open the door for you.'

The bolts on the garage door didn't need keys. They simply drew back. Roderick pulled the door up and the two men stepped out into the fresh air. Roderick looked at them as if trying to find one last thing to say to persuade them of his innocence. Then he slid the door back down.

Hawthorne and Dudley found themselves standing in the driveway that led back to the main courtyard. But Hawthorne hadn't quite finished. There was a gate beside the garage, opening into the Brownes' garden, and he walked through it, pulling out a cigarette and lighting it as he went. He stopped on the other side, taking in his surroundings.

The garden was long and rectangular, with a fence on one side and a line of shrubs at the end. It hadn't rained for a while and the lawn was covered with brown patches. Many of the flowers were wilting in their beds. At the same time, the fruit trees had been left to look after themselves and the branches were spreading out, fighting each other for space. Looking over the shrubs, Hawthorne could see that the garden belonging to the Brownes' elderly neighbours was in much the same state.

'Did you get the caller's number?' Hawthorne asked.

Dudley nodded. 'The name came up on the screen. Sarah Baines.'

'Sarah the gardener?'

'Must be. He didn't want me to see.'

Hawthorne examined the garden. 'Funny, isn't it. He described her as hard-working and helpful . . .'

'Yeah. I thought that. It doesn't look as if she's done anything hard or helpful here!'

Meanwhile, on the other side of the folding garage door, Roderick Browne had taken his phone out again. He listened carefully to make sure that Hawthorne was nowhere close.

Then he opened his phone to see what he had missed.

4

The Tea Cosy bookshop was open for business, but neither May Winslow nor Phyllis Moore was in any mood to sell books.

They were sitting at one of the empty tables close to the main door. In fact, all the tables were empty. Nobody had come in yet and although they often passed the time reading, knitting or playing gin rummy together when they had no business, today they were just sitting in silence. They had already given full statements to Detective Superintendent Khan and, after they had been forced to take the whole of Tuesday off, he had allowed them to leave for work – so long as they promised not to discuss the murder with any of their customers. Well, there was no chance of that today.

Phyllis had been agitated all morning. 'I need a burner!' she announced, suddenly.

May stared at her. 'A cigarette?'

'I can't just sit here thinking about it all. I'm going out-side.' She reached down for her handbag, then rummaged in it for a pouch of Golden Virginia tobacco.

But before she could get up, May reached out and laid a hand on her companion's arm. 'I think we should talk,' she said.

'Why?'

'You know very well.'

'You've been sitting here all morning. You haven't said a word.'

It wasn't very often that there was any friction between the two women, but just for a moment they glared at each other like old enemies. May released her grip. 'We have to be very careful,' she said. 'We've got the police all over Riverview Close and my guess is they'll be there for quite a while.'

'We've got nothing to be afraid of.'

'We have everything to be afraid of. You know the way it works. They'll be investigating us even now. Do you want to stay in Richmond?'

'I like it here.'

'So do I. But we won't be able to. Not if they start digging.'

There was another silence. Phyllis opened the packet and began to roll herself a cigarette. 'We should tell them about what happened,' she said.

'What do you mean?'

'The night before the murder! When Roderick told us what he was going to do. He said it in front of us all.'

'He'd been drinking.'

'It doesn't mean it wasn't true . . .'

May thought for a moment. 'We could tell the police. But what good do you think it would do?'

'If they arrest him, they'll leave the rest of us alone.'

'I only wish that was the case.' May was breathing heavily. 'We were all there, Phyllis. We were all part of it. And we've all agreed to keep our mouths shut. You know what that is? That's conspiracy.' She paused, forcing herself to calm down. 'I wish the whole thing had never happened. It was stupid. Madness!' She drew a breath. 'You go to the police, you could find yourself under arrest. And me with you.'

Phyllis had finished making her roll-up. It contained so little tobacco that when she lit it, she would mainly be inhaling burnt paper. 'We could send the police a note,' she said. 'Anonymously.'

May shook her head. 'It won't do any good. There's no proof Roderick killed Mr Kenworthy. Do you really think he had it in him? I've met women older than us who've been more violent than him. And anyway, what was his motive?'

'The swimming pool.'

'We were all against the swimming pool. And you must remember, dear, that the police are dreadfully unimaginative. They're unlikely to conclude that Mr Browne committed murder because the Kenworthys were going to spoil his view, even if that's exactly what we want them to think!'

The shop door opened and a customer came in, a

middle-aged man with a bag of groceries hanging from his arm. 'Hello,' he said. 'Do you by any chance have any Jo Nesbø?'

'Try Waterstones!' May snapped, not even looking at him.

'Oh . . . All right.'

He left. The door closed.

'And since we're talking about motives . . .' May continued as if the interruption had never happened. 'Detective Superintendent Khan could well come to the conclusion that you and I are much more likely suspects than Mr Browne.'

Phyllis knew exactly what she meant. She glanced at the corner of the room where Ellery's basket had always been, at the far end of the non-fiction section. It was no longer there. Her eyes filled with tears and for a moment she couldn't speak.

They had loved that dog since he was a puppy and now he was gone. In the past two weeks, the two women's lives had changed irrevocably for the worse. As far as they were concerned, the death of Giles Kenworthy had been by far the lesser of two evils.

They both knew who was responsible. Lynda Kenworthy had threatened them. She couldn't have been clearer. *'If your animal strays into our garden one more time, I'm going to ask my husband to deal with it.'* May and Phyllis hadn't really listened to her at the time. Now they dearly wished they had.

For it seemed that Ellery had done exactly that, slipping out of the house and once again burrowing under the Brownes' fence. Worse than that, he had left behind evidence of his visit. They'd had no idea what had happened until they were leaving to catch the bus into Richmond and had discovered another plastic bag of dog waste clipped into the letter box of their front door. There was no message. No further warning. Of course, both women knew perfectly well what Lynda had said, but they weren't entirely sure what she'd meant by 'dealing' with it and so once again they'd put the whole thing out of their minds. Neither of them believed for a moment that she or her husband would do anything vindictive.

That evening, they'd got home from the shop in time for supper, fed Ellery and let him out to make himself comfortable before bed. Meanwhile, they'd settled down to watch an episode of *Bergerac* on television (they had all nine seasons on DVD). It was only when they realised it had grown dark and Ellery hadn't returned that they went out looking for him.

He wasn't in the garden. They went past the Brownes' house and called out for him, but he didn't seem to have wandered into the grounds of Riverview Lodge either. By now, both of them were getting nervous. Ellery had never been out so late and for so long on his own. May walked round the entire close, calling out his name. Then she knocked on the door of Woodlands. If Ellery had strayed back into the grounds of Riverview Lodge, he would have had to pass through the next-door garden and there was always a chance that Roderick Browne might have seen him. A light came on in the hall, visible on the other side of the window, and the dentist appeared a few moments later, wearing a red striped apron. He had just done the washing-up and was taking a cup of camomile tea up to Felicity.

'I'm so sorry to trouble you, Mr Browne. Ellery seems to have gone missing and we were wondering if you'd seen him.'

'No. I'm afraid not. How long has he been gone?'

'We don't really know. He came home with us, then went out while we were watching TV.'

'Well, I haven't seen anything, but I'll keep an eye out for him. I'm sure he'll turn up . . .'

May already had a knotted feeling in her stomach. Ellery had never done this before. It was true that he treated the entire close as his personal domain, but he was still a nervous creature and never strayed for very long.

'Maybe you should ask at the Lodge,' Roderick suggested.

'Yes. I'll do that.'

May didn't want to go anywhere near the Kenworthys' home, not on her own, not even with Phyllis beside her. She hated the idea of prostrating herself before them, asking for their help. Not that they'd listen anyway. *I'm going to ask my husband to deal with it.'* The words were drumming themselves over and over in her ears.

Phyllis knew what her companion was thinking. 'Maybe Mr Pennington has seen Ellery,' she suggested.

They went back towards Well House and it was as they approached the front door that they heard it: the unmistakable sound of an animal in pain . . . a faint whimpering. Could it be

Ellery? It didn't sound like him. And the cries were coming from somewhere further away, perhaps behind the house.

May was really panicking now. Forgetting the bell, she rapped on the door so hard that she would feel the pain in her knuckles for days to come. The whimpering had stopped. Had she imagined it? She hoped so. There were plenty of foxes in Richmond, semi-domesticated, prowling the streets in search of open dustbins. It must have been one of them.

The door opened. Andrew Pennington peered out at them. He had been reading Anthony Trollope in bed when he heard the knocking on the door.

'Please, Mr Pennington. Can you help us? We've been looking for Ellery. He's disappeared. And just now we thought we heard something in your garden.' The words poured out. May's chest was rising and falling. She had been wearing her glasses when she was watching television. They were still hanging around her neck and rose and fell as if they too were trying to join in the search.

Andrew stepped outside and listened. 'I can't hear anything,' he said.

All three of them fell silent and for a brief moment it seemed to be true. Perhaps they had imagined it after all. But then it came again from behind the house, or from somewhere nearby. It was a sound that carried with it all the pain in the world and May knew for certain that it was not a fox.

'He's in your garden,' Phyllis said.

'I don't think so.' Pennington cocked his head, trying to

work out where the sound was coming from. 'The sound's coming from over there,' he said. And then, with a sense of dread, 'In the well.'

He was pointing towards the medieval well that stood between the house and the archway. It was one of the unique features of Riverview Close. His home was named after it. On the day that he and Iris moved in, they had both tossed a coin in for good luck.

'Wait a minute. I'll get some light,' he said.

It was dark by now. Andrew's night vision had deteriorated in recent years and he always kept a torch close to the front door. He went in and retrieved it, then led the two women round the side of the house. As they approached the well, the whimpering began again, more forlorn, more desperate.

Andrew directed the beam of the torch into the circular opening.

Ellery was about five metres down, curled up at the bottom, straining with his neck as if searching for salvation. He struggled to get to his feet, but it was clear he could no longer stand. Andrew heard May let out a moan beside him. Phyllis called out the dog's name.

'Don't worry!' Andrew found himself saying. 'We'll get him out of there. We'll get help.'

But what sort of help were they going to find at ten o'clock at night and how long would it take to get there? It wasn't important enough to trouble the police. The RSPCA, perhaps? Did they even have an office anywhere near Richmond?

'Can you do anything? Can you get him out?' Phyllis asked, tears streaming down her cheeks.

'I don't know . . .'

It was impossible. The shaft of the well was too narrow and he wasn't sure he would be able to climb back out again. A ladder was needed and someone thin enough to fit inside.

'I'll call the RSPCA,' he said.

'Oh, Ellery! Poor Ellery!' May was also crying.

Ellery had fallen silent. He was no longer moving. Later on, May would say he had heard their voices, had known they were there, and that perhaps there was some crumb of comfort in the knowledge that he had not died alone.

'He must have fallen in,' Pennington said. But he knew it wasn't true. Ellery wouldn't have been able to jump in. The brick well head was far too high for the little French bulldog with its stubby legs, and why would he even have tried? There was only one solution. Ellery must have been picked up and deliberately dropped in. Pennington knew it, but he didn't say it. His years at the bar had taught him never to make an accusation without proper evidence, and anyway, what would be the point? He flicked off the torch, sparing the two women the sight of their dead pet.

May had reached the same conclusion. Her face was set in stone. 'This was them!' she whispered. 'They did it!'

'What do you mean, Mrs Winslow?'

'You know what I mean. Giles Kenworthy. She asked him to do something – to sort it out – and this is what happened.

He was responsible and I'll never forgive him. I'm not going to allow him to get away with it . . .'

May and Phyllis were still sitting at the table in The Tea Cosy, Phyllis rolling her cigarette between her fingers like a very old pianist warming up before a performance. They were both haunted by the empty space where Ellery's basket had been. They knew they would never have another dog. Even if they had wanted one, it was too late for them.

It had been Sarah, the gardener, who had retrieved Ellery's body from the well in the end. They'd had to wait until the next day for it to happen and once again the sun had been shining. Sarah was wearing a sleeveless T-shirt and as she had lowered a ladder into the opening, they had both seen it.

Fresh, livid scratches on both her arms.

5

After they had left Roderick Browne's garden, Hawthorne and Dudley walked back round to the close and stood in the centre, enjoying the sunshine and the smell of the flowers. If it hadn't been for the parked police vehicles, it could have been just another pleasant July day.

'Look at it!' Hawthorne muttered. 'A private close in one of the nicest suburbs in London. Designer houses. What do you think they're worth? Millions! And yet all these people at each other's throats . . .'

'Quite literally in the case of Giles Kenworthy,' Dudley agreed. He had a strange sense of humour, a way of joking that always made him sound sad. 'Although, I suppose it could have been an outsider,' he added.

'I doubt it,' Hawthorne said. He pointed to the archway. 'First of all, there's the automatic gate. Closed at night and you need an electronic key to get in. The crossbow was tucked away in Roderick Browne's garage. Someone must have known it was there. And then there's the opportunity. Kenworthy on his own in the house, his wife having it away with her French teacher, the kids at boarding school, the Filipino cleaner out of the country. It had to be someone close by.'

'Nightmare neighbours,' Dudley agreed. 'When I was in Bristol, we were always getting called out to local estates. Loud music, parties, dustbins and parking. It was the most miserable part of the job, the sheer futility of it all. Makes it a bit tricky, though, when you add murder into the mix. I mean, basically they've all got the same motive. They all hated Giles Kenworthy. That's all it comes down to.'

'Parking . . .' Hawthorne said.

A woman had appeared in the doorway of Gardener's Cottage and was leaning forward, examining the driveway as if she was afraid of what she was going to find. From a distance, she presented herself as healthy and attractive, dressed in a loose shirt, designer jeans and sandals, with a silver necklace and earrings. She had jet-black hair, parted in the centre, framing a serious face. However, as Hawthorne and Dudley walked towards her, it was as if the sky had clouded over and a shadow had fallen. The woman hadn't slept. There were dark worry lines tugging at the corners of her eyes and lips. She had put on too much make-up, trying to disguise her malaise. It was striking that all the jewellery she was wearing seemed to have been inspired by poisonous creatures.

Hawthorne stopped in front of her. 'Mrs Beresford?'

'Yes?'

'Can we talk to you?'

'Now?'

'Do you mind?'

'Are you journalists?'

'What makes you think that?'

So far it had been a conversation made up entirely of questions. 'You don't look like police officers,' she said.

'As a matter of fact, we're helping the police with their inquiries.'

Gemma Beresford examined Hawthorne with suspicion. She seemed even more undecided about his assistant. 'You could be anyone,' she said. 'Why should I believe you?'

'Well, you could ask DS Khan. He's got to be somewhere around – or maybe you can call him.' Hawthorne tried to look sympathetic. 'We've already spoken to Lynda Kenworthy and to your neighbour, Roderick Browne.'

Hawthorne had mentioned enough names to persuade her. 'I can only give you ten minutes,' she said. 'I have to pick up my children from playgroup at two.'

'We won't need any more time with you than that,' Hawthorne assured her.

Gardener's Cottage was misnamed. There might have been a cottage here in the eighteenth century when a gardener had been employed to look after the extensive grounds of Rievaulx Hall, but what had replaced it was hardly a cottage, more a sizeable family house. The front door opened into a hallway that had almost too much space, with a high ceiling and a can-tilevered staircase leading up to a galleried landing. The style was a tasteful mix of modern and traditional: glass panels hemming in the stairs, exposed beams in the walls. Everything seemed neat and ordered until she led them into the kitchen, which told the real story of the Beresfords' home with its piles of unwashed dishes, the toys, dolls and children's clothes everywhere, the Marks & Spencer ready meals defrosting on the counter, the unwatered plants flopping in their pots and unpaid bills stacked up beside the toaster.

Gemma Beresford waved them both to a solid farmhouse table. Dudley rested his elbows in front of him, then removed them when he realised they had lightly stuck themselves to the surface.

'You'll have to forgive the mess,' she said. Her voice was low and husky. 'This has been quite a week and I'm not even talking about the murder. Our cleaning lady hasn't been in. She says she's depressed. Honestly! You're not allowed to question mental health issues these days, but it's getting beyond a joke. And we don't have our nanny either.'

'What's happened to her?' Dudley asked.

'Nothing. Kylie's a wonderful girl and she keeps the whole ship running. That's what the children call her. Captain Kylie! Her room's at the top of the house . . . like a crow's-nest.' She looked at the mess all around her. 'You can see for yourself what it's like when she's not here. She was called away at the weekend.'

'What happened?'

'When she joined us – that was two years ago – she was doing part-time work for a charity and she didn't want to leave it. Age UK.'

'Old people,' Hawthorne muttered helpfully.

'Yes. She's one of their volunteers and she's befriended a very elderly lady in Hampton Wick. That's just a few miles from here. Anyway – would you believe it – on Sunday evening, Marsha was attacked. That's her name. Marsha Clarke. It's absolutely shocking. She's eighty-five years old, but someone was waiting outside her house and hit her with a cosh or something and now she's in Kingston Hospital. But the thing is, she has three cats and absolutely nobody to support her. Social services were no use, so Kylie agreed to stay in her house and look after the animals until Marsha is well enough to come home. Goodness knows how long that will be. But that's typical of Kylie. She's from Australia and has no relatives over here. I suppose she sees Marsha as a sort of grandmother figure.'

All of this had come out in a rush, as if Gemma had been desperately waiting to tell someone – anyone – about her misfortunes.

'That's why I have to collect the children,' she added, glancing at her watch. 'They hate it when we're late.'

'How old are your kids?' Dudley asked.

'They're twins. Claire and Lucy. They're four.'

'Did Marsha Clarke have money on her when she was attacked?' Hawthorne asked.

'I don't know.' Gemma was puzzled by the question.

'I was just wondering about the motive.'

'I don't think she had any money taken from her. The police think it may have been racially motivated. Marsha is a woman of colour.'

Dudley scribbled the information into his notebook. 'So right now you're on your own,' he said.

'Well, my husband, Tom, will be back this evening. He's a GP. He works in Richmond.'

'How is your husband?' Hawthorne asked. He sounded genuinely concerned.

'He's very tired. He's overworked. But he's well. He's fine.'

'I understand he often argued with Giles Kenworthy. In fact, I've been told that just a short while ago, he threatened to kill him.'

Gemma Beresford blushed, the colour visible even under her make-up. 'Who told you that?' she demanded.

'Is it true?' Hawthorne countered.

'It's true about the parking. Giles Kenworthy was extraordinarily inconsiderate. Quite apart from his camper van, which is an eyesore and never goes anywhere, he had four cars: a Porsche, a Mercedes, some sort of American thing and a Mini Cooper. Who needs four cars in this day and age? His garage only had space for two of them, so he often parked outside, blocking us in. When I came out just now, I was checking to make sure the driveway was clear. He may not be here any more, but I've got into the habit.'

'Did it make your husband very angry?'

'If you're asking me if Tom killed Giles Kenworthy, that's ridiculous. Of course not. Tom's not like that. He saves lives, and you have no idea the pressure he's under, Mr Hawthorne – like everyone in the NHS. In fact, if you really want to know, that was what the argument was about two weeks ago. A man died. It was Giles Kenworthy's fault.'

'How did that happen?'

Gemma Beresford was still angry. She had one eye on the clock. She had to pick up her children. But she wasn't going to leave without telling Hawthorne the truth about what had occurred.

'Tom was leaving for work. It was just another day, but he had to get in on time because the surgery was short-staffed. Also, he had a patient coming in at nine o'clock, a man he'd been treating for several months. His name was Raymond Shaw. He wasn't particularly old – in his forties, I think – but he was overweight, with high cholesterol, high blood pressure . . . a heart attack waiting to happen. And it did happen that morning. Tom got held up because the drive-way was blocked and Mr Shaw was waiting for him in the surgery. He waited twenty minutes and he kept asking the receptionist when Tom was going to arrive and he got more and more angry and then it happened. He had what's called an SCA. A sudden cardiac arrest. By the time Tom arrived, he was already dead. Of course, the surgery had done every-thing they could to revive him. Nobody blamed Tom, and as

I said, Mr Shaw could have had the heart attack at any time. Anyone can be held up in traffic or whatever, and twenty minutes late is hardly negligence.

'But Tom blamed himself. That's the sort of man he is. And that's why he lost his temper and may have said some stupid things to Giles Kenworthy. We all say stupid things from time to time, things we don't mean. The idea that he crept out, stole a crossbow and put a bolt into him is out of the question. You don't know Tom! Anyway, it's impossible. He was here all night in bed, next to me, so if you've got him on your list of suspects, you'll have to add me to it too.'

She took another look at her watch.

'And now I really have to go.'

'Just one last thing,' Hawthorne said. 'If your husband didn't kill Giles Kenworthy, who do you think did?'

'How can I possibly answer that?'

'The police seem to think that it may have been one of the residents living in Riverview Close,' Dudley chipped in. 'You probably know them as well as anyone.'

'I know them well enough to know that none of them would be capable of such a thing.'

'You'd be surprised who's capable of murder, Mrs Beresford,' Hawthorne said. 'Is there someone you're trying to protect?'

Her eyes flared. 'Why would I want to do that?'

'You live with these people. Maybe you've seen something. I understand! You want to play nice neighbours. But you all hated Giles Kenworthy.'

'I didn't hate him.'

'There was something about a dog . . .'

Gemma looked scornful. 'That was dreadful. Poor May and Phyllis! Their dog fell into the well and they blamed him. But they're both in their eighties. They're completely harmless! I certainly can't see them creeping around with a crossbow in the middle of the night.'

'Did you ever hear anyone else talking about killing Giles Kenworthy, Mrs Beresford?' Dudley asked.

For just a brief moment, Gemma was unsure of herself. 'No. Of course not. When would anyone ever say something like that? I never heard anything!' She stopped herself. 'You won't turn me against my neighbours,' she went on. 'Just as you'll never turn them against Tom and me.'

'Is that what you've all agreed?'

'It's how we are.'

She stood up, signalling that she wanted Hawthorne and Dudley to leave.

'I like the jewellery,' Dudley said. 'Is that a snake around your neck?'

'As a matter of fact, I designed it. I have a jewellery business. And it's part of my Rare Poison collection.'

'Sounds unusual.'

'The necklace is shaped like the butterfly viper that lives in Central Africa. The creature is really quite wonderful with its brilliant blue-green markings and bright red triangles. It's also venomous. The earrings are inspired by the webs of the orb-weaver spider from Madagascar, which turn gold in sunlight. I'm exploring the correlation between beauty and death in nature.'

'They look lovely but they kill you,' Hawthorne said.

Gemma Beresford smiled for the first time. 'Exactly.'

6

'Well, she was nice,' Dudley said as they watched Gemma Beresford drive out of the close, on her way to her children's playgroup.

'Interesting woman,' Hawthorne agreed. 'What's she hiding?'

Dudley raised his eyebrows. 'The truth? She'd certainly heard someone talking about the death of Mr Kenworthy. Before it happened.'

There were fewer police around, but this was the second day of their inquiry and they had things wrapped up – quite literally in the case of the forensic teams, who were carrying out the last pieces of evidence concealed in white plastic. Everything else would have gone the day before: clothing, computers, documents and files, anything that might have a story to tell. Hawthorne and Dudley had both been in this world once, following the procedures set out in *Blackstone's Police Investigators' Manual*, volumes 1–4. Now, for different reasons, they had been cast adrift, unnoticed on the edge of the crime scene.

Dudley watched the slightly listless activity in silence. With the afternoon sun shining and everything so perfect, surrounded by designer houses with their stock-brick chimneys, Dutch gables and flowering jasmine, there was an unreality to the scene.

'Look at them,' he muttered. 'This has got to be the unlike-liest place in the world for a murder. When you think about it, the worst crime you could imagine happening here would be someone borrowing someone else's lawnmower without asking permission.'

Detective Superintendent Khan appeared, coming out of the long, narrow building that stretched across the bottom end of the close. He was accompanied by a man who was sup-porting himself on a walking stick, limping badly. The man, dressed rather too warmly for the summer weather, was short, neatly bearded, vaguely professorial, with thinning hair and spectacles. He seemed unusually relaxed, as if the two of them had been discussing the cricket season rather than the violent death of a local resident. Khan waved them over.

'This is Daniel Hawthorne and John Dudley,' he said, once they'd arrived. 'They're colleagues of mine. Helping us with our inquiries.' He must have had a successful morning, Haw-thorne thought. He was almost friendly. 'How's it going?' Khan asked.

'Swimmingly,' Dudley said.

Khan scowled. 'Let me introduce you to Mr Adam Strauss.

He lives in The Stables. He knows quite a bit about the neighbourhood.'

'You played a brilliant game against Kramnik in the World Chess Championship last year,' Hawthorne said. 'Move seventy-two. A rook manoeuvre when you were two pawns down. Nobody could have seen that coming.'

Strauss beamed. 'In a game at that level, you have to look ten moves ahead, Mr Hawthorne. Kramnik helped me, sacrificing his bishop on move sixty. Do you play chess?'

'No. But my son's crazy about it. He's only fourteen, but he likes to read magazines with me.'

'Maybe you have a chess prodigy on your hands.'

'I doubt it. It's chess one week, BMX bikes the next.'

Khan had been listening to this conversation with a sense of disbelief. He didn't even know Hawthorne had a child. 'Mr Hawthorne is asking some follow-up questions,' he interrupted. 'You've been very helpful to me, Mr Strauss, but would you mind having a chat with him too? A second perspective always helps.'

Strauss didn't hesitate. 'It would be my pleasure, Mr Hawthorne. Come in and have a cup of tea. I'm sure my wife will be delighted to meet you.'

Leaning heavily on his stick, he led the way into the main room, which stretched the full length of the building. A woman was sitting demurely on a sofa with an iPad on her lap, but she stood up as they came in. She was wearing a tight-fitting dress and leather thong sandals, a necklace of black

151

pearls and gold clip-on earrings. Khan had already told Hawthorne that she was Hong Kong Chinese. He would have been less able to describe the steeliness behind her smile, the way she quickly weighed up the new visitors and came to a conclusion that she seemed determined to keep to herself.

'This is my wife, Teri.'

'More police officers?' Teri was not pleased.

'Daniel Hawthorne and John Dudley.' Strauss was more convivial. 'They're helping the police. I've spoken to Mr Khan, and we should give them any help we can. This is an awful business – but the worst of it is that, like it or not, the shadow of suspicion has fallen on all of us. It's clear the police believe someone living in the close may have been responsible, and as absurd as it sounds, that's an intolerable situation. I just want to get back to normal.' Strauss limped over to a sofa and sat down. 'Let's have some tea.'

'Thank you.'

'Jasmine or English breakfast?' Taking her cue from her husband, Teri had risen – almost levitated – to her feet. Now she was the smiling hostess.

'Builder's will be fine,' Dudley said.

Teri glided into the kitchen. She could still take part in the conversation as she set about making the tea, filling the pot with one of those taps providing instant boiling water.

'Have you worked with Superintendent Khan before?' Strauss asked.

'First time,' Hawthorne said.

'So you are . . . what? Private detectives?'

'You could say that.'

'How wonderful. I used to know Trevor Eve quite well. That was in the days when I was working in television. He appeared as Shoestring – do you remember? He was a private detective, but I didn't know they existed in real life.'

'When did you come to the UK?' Hawthorne asked. As well as the surname, he had noticed Strauss's faint German accent.

'I arrived here when I was seven years old. My father was in the diplomatic service and he was posted here in the late sixties. I was taught in Richmond. There's a famous international German school just down the road, which is where I completed my Abitur. It was also where I found my love of chess. They had a club and I joined.' He smiled sadly. 'That's why I'm so upset about what's happened. Richmond has always been my true home.'

The statement was accompanied by the sound of a tune beaten out on a xylophone: the classic marimba ringtone. Strauss pulled an iPhone from his pocket and glanced at the screen. 'Do you mind if I take this? It's my manager . . .' Without waiting for an answer, he got up and, moving as quickly as he could, disappeared into his office, which led off from the library area.

Teri came over with the tea. She had also arranged a plate of home-made butter cookies. 'Milk and sugar?' she asked.

'Both, thanks. Two sugars.' Dudley reached for a biscuit. 'So how long have you been married?' he asked.

153

'Four years.' Teri smiled. 'I'm his second wife. Adam is divorced.'

'Where did you meet?'

'I know his first wife, Wendy. In fact, she's my cousin.' She sounded only a little apologetic. 'We grew up together. Her mother and my mother were sisters.'

'Where is she now?'

'She went back to Hong Kong, although the two of us have stayed in touch. All the time she was in England, she was never happy. She didn't like Richmond. She said it was too quiet. She wanted to live in town. And she wasn't interested in chess either. How can you marry a chess grandmaster if you don't have any interest in chess? That was what broke up the marriage. She was stupid.'

'Do you like the game?' Hawthorne asked.

'It's more than a game, Mr Hawthorne. It's a way of life.' She paused. 'I cannot follow all the moves. I do not understand the strategy. But I watch my husband play and it is like seeing God at work in the human brain. He is one of the greatest chess players who ever lived. You know, he played Deep Blue twelve times in a row and twelve times the computer lost. At the very end, the motherboard crashed. It suffered a complete meltdown. They say that the computer pulled the plug on itself to end the shame.'

'Do you always travel with him?' Dudley asked.

'Always. My husband must have complete rest, isolation

before every game. If I were not there, he would not even eat. He needs someone to look after him.'

Adam Strauss came back into the room. 'It's good news,' he said. 'I can go to Chennai after all. They've arranged a wheelchair for me at Heathrow Airport if I still can't walk properly and the same at the other end. There'll be someone to look after me at the Sheraton and they're giving me a room close to the elevator.'

'And your wife's coming with you?' Dudley asked.

Strauss nodded. 'Teri always comes with me when I'm playing abroad. I couldn't do it without her.' He accepted a cup of jasmine tea and sat down again. 'What do you want to know, Mr Hawthorne?'

'Let's start with that injury of yours, if you don't mind. How did you hurt yourself?'

'I had an accident a few days ago – last Friday. I was on my way to meet my manager to talk about the tournament in Chennai, as a matter of fact. I never got there. Somebody pushed into me on the steps at Richmond station and I fell quite badly.' He stretched out his ankle, showing it to Hawthorne. 'It's not broken, but it's a bad sprain. I was quite worried I wouldn't be able to go.'

'When exactly was this?' Hawthorne asked.

'It was during the morning rush hour. About nine a.m.'

Hawthorne nodded at Dudley, who made a note of the time. 'You used to live in Riverview Lodge,' he went on.

155

'Yes. That's right. I have to say, I feel personally responsible for everything that's happened here. If I hadn't sold the house, none of us would ever have heard of Giles Kenworthy.'

'Why did you move?'

'Teri thought it was too big for us – and she was right. I didn't need all that space.' There was another reason, which he was less willing to put into words. 'My income isn't what it used to be either. You know I used to have my own show on TV?'

'*It's Your Move*,' said Dudley.

'That's the one. It was a chess-based quiz. Very popular in its time . . . It was co-hosted by Debbie McGee! I was also a commentator at some of the major tournaments, but they're not covered so much these days. And if I'm going to be honest with you, I'm getting too old for the major ones. Magnus Carlsen, the current world champion, is twenty-four. Levon Aronian is only a few years older. He became a grandmaster at seventeen. Anyway, Teri was never very comfortable at Riverview Lodge. It wasn't a home we'd made together. So when The Stables suddenly became available, it felt like a no-brainer.'

'I never liked the house,' Teri agreed. 'It's better here.'

'I still don't understand why Giles Kenworthy and his family couldn't fit in more,' Strauss continued. 'You don't buy a house in a place like this if you're not going to get on with your neighbours. I'm sure he wasn't a bad person, but he did manage to annoy the hell out of us. The parking, the noise, the camper van, the children. We invited them to a

156

meeting here about six weeks ago. We thought it might be an opportunity to sort things out – but at the last minute they didn't show up. That was typical of them. Maybe they were just thoughtless, but they came over as rude.'

'Everything got worse after that,' Teri said.

'That's true, my love. Yes.' He took a sip of his tea. 'First there was the dog belonging to those two dear ladies in The Gables.'

'How well do you know them?'

'Oh – we're very close. The Gables and The Stables! They had a French bulldog, which was found at the bottom of the well. They were quite sure the Kenworthys were responsible. Then Andrew Pennington – he's a retired barrister and our neighbour across the way in Well House – he had his flower display ruined by the children. They drove through it on skateboards, would you believe? Not a motive for murder, I'm sure, but he was very upset.'

'And also there was your chess set,' Teri reminded him.

'Oh, yes.' For a moment, Strauss lost his cheerful composure. 'That was extremely annoying.'

'What happened exactly?' Hawthorne asked.

Strauss put his cup down. 'I was in town, having lunch with a journalist friend of mine. This was the week before my accident. Teri was also out. When I got back, I noticed that one of the windows had been broken, and my first thought was that we had been burgled. In fact, it was simpler than that. The two Kenworthy boys – Hugo and Tristram – had taken to playing cricket in the courtyard, even though there's supposed to be a rule about no ball games. There had been quite a few complaints about it. I remember that the Beresfords were particularly worried – but then they've got small children.'

'They said it was dangerous,' Teri agreed.

'Well, I could see at once what had happened. They had hit their ball through my window. I found it on the floor. That would have been bad enough, but it had also smashed one of my most treasured chess sets, a gift from Sheikh Mohammed bin Rashid Al Maktoum, the ruler of Dubai.'

'Did you complain to the parents?' Dudley asked.

'Of course I did. I telephoned Giles Kenworthy and spoke to him at length.' He sighed. 'He refused to accept responsibility. He said that he talked to the boys and they had denied it and suggested that it might have been one of their friends. He promised he would look into it, but I have a feeling he couldn't really have cared less.'

'Do you still have the chess set?' Dudley asked. 'There's a model-maker I know. Brilliant at putting stuff together.'

'I'm not sure it's possible,' Adam said.

'I wouldn't say that,' Hawthorne cut in. 'A tube of Revell Contacta Professional and a handful of fast clamps . . .'

Teri had already got to her feet. 'It's here!' she said. She went to a low cupboard, reached inside and took out a chessboard, holding it carefully so that the pieces wouldn't fall off. She brought it over for Hawthorne to examine. It was a set modelled on *The Lord of the Rings*, but the white king and queen and bishops were badly smashed. Several of the pawns were broken.

'It looks a bit hopeless,' Hawthorne admitted. 'You wouldn't have thought that a cricket ball could do so much damage.'

'Well, the pieces were extremely fragile,' Adam muttered tetchily. 'There were only six sets ever made,' he went on. 'Put it away, dear. I can't bear looking at it.'

Teri returned it to the cupboard.

'So Kenworthy refused to accept responsibility,' Dudley said. 'He lied to you. And a few days later, he was dead . . .' He sounded surprised by the force of his own logic. 'Where were you on Monday night?' he asked.

'I was playing chess until well after midnight. Then I went to bed. And before you ask, my opponent was in Warsaw. We were playing online. His name is Grzegorz Gajewski and, like me, he's a grandmaster.' Strauss waited until Teri had sat down again. 'I hope you're not suggesting that I killed Giles Kenworthy out of revenge,' he went on. 'If every parent was responsible for their children's misdemeanours, the entire country would be strewn with corpses! Anyway, I've already told you. Everyone in the close had a reason to dislike the Kenworthys. A man died because of them! Tom Beresford's patient. That's rather more important than a smashed chess set.'

'Even a very valuable one.'

'Yes.'

There was a brief silence.

'It seems to me you're in pole position, Mr Strauss,'

Hawthorne observed. 'You used to live in the big house. Now you're right beside the entrance. This meeting you had, when the Kenworthys were no-shows, that was your idea?'

'Actually, I think it was Andrew Pennington who suggested it. He's on his own now. His wife died of cancer a few years ago and he's become something of a counsellor to all of us. He thought an informal drinks do might help. Teri and I were happy to host it.'

'So tell me – if Giles Kenworthy was killed by someone in Riverview Close, who do you think it was most likely to be?'

Adam Strauss leaned forward, his palms touching and his fingers resting just beneath his chin, as if he was contemplating a move in an invisible chess game. 'I'm not sure I accept your premise that the killer was one of us, Mr Hawthorne. Giles Kenworthy was a wealthy man, a hedge fund manager. I'd have said you should be looking for someone who lost money. An unhappy client. That makes much more sense to me.'

'But how many of his clients would have been able to get through the gate or would have known that Roderick Browne kept a crossbow inside his locked garage?' Hawthorne countered.

'That's a fair point – although the garage was frequently left open. Sarah, our gardener, was in and out all the time.'

'Are you pointing the finger at her?'

'I'm not pointing the finger at anyone. That's exactly the point I'm trying to make. You're asking me to turn against people whom I have always considered to be my friends. I'm not prepared to do that.'

'How about Roderick Browne himself?'

Strauss let out a sniff of exasperation. 'I'm probably closer to Roderick than to anyone else. For a start, he's my dentist.'

'He didn't mention that.'

'I'm glad to hear it. Frankly, it's none of your business. But since you ask, I was going to his clinic before he even moved into Riverview Close. He was recommended to me because he has quite a few celebrity clients. I actually met Ewan McGregor in his waiting room. A very charming man. Roderick has had the most appalling difficulties, what with Felicity's illness and everything, and Teri and I have both been trying to offer him our support.'

'He was upset about the swimming pool.'

'And the Jacuzzi! I can understand that. They're going to be right underneath Felicity's window and there's no doubt that they will make a huge impact on her life. I'm astonished Kenworthy even got planning permission.' Strauss smiled a little mournfully. 'With Kenworthy dead, the rest of the family may move,' he said, as if the idea had only just occurred to him. 'I suppose it's quite possible there won't be a Jacuzzi, a swimming pool or anything.'

'Perhaps that's exactly what he wanted.'

'And that's a motive for murder, I agree. But take it from me. Roderick couldn't hurt a fly.'

'Flies don't have teeth,' Dudley pointed out.

'I can tell you this.' Strauss ignored Dudley's remark. 'Roderick is more upset than anyone about what's happened. I spoke to him yesterday after Detective Superintendent Khan interviewed him and he was in considerable distress. I know him very well and I would urge you to leave him alone.' Strauss drew himself to his feet. 'And now, if you gentlemen have no other questions, I really don't think there's anything more to say.'

Strauss had clearly forgotten Hawthorne's chess-loving son. The attack on Roderick Browne had been one step too far and the two investigators found themselves being shown rapidly out of the door.

'That went well!' Dudley said.

'It's interesting.' Hawthorne didn't seem at all put out. 'Two random attacks in a matter of days.'

Dudley nodded. 'I noticed that. An old lady being looked after by the Beresfords' nanny is hit with a cosh in Hampton Wick . . .'

'And Adam Strauss is pushed down the stairs.'

'Seems a bit random. I can't see a connection.'

'It still bothers me.' Hawthorne made his decision. 'Ask DS Khan for any CCTV footage from Richmond station last Friday morning – or nip round yourself. It might be interesting to see what really happened . . .'

7

There was a pub, the Fox and Duck, on the other side of the Petersham Road and after they left The Stables, Hawthorne and Dudley walked over there and found a table outside for a late lunch. The two of them had met very early that morning and had travelled to Richmond together. Neither of them had had time to eat. Dudley ordered a pie and chips with a glass of lemonade and didn't seem aware of Hawthorne watching him over a black coffee and a cigarette. They sat in silence, each lost in their own thoughts, until the food had been served. Then Hawthorne leaned forward.

'Thoughts?' he asked.

'Not a bad pie,' Dudley replied.

'That's not what I meant, mate.'

'Well, of course, they're all lying . . . the whole lot of them. I agree with you that Lynda Kenworthy was shagging the French teacher. Roderick Browne is in meltdown either because he committed the murder or because he knows who did. The wicked witch with the silver jewellery thinks her husband did it, and she's certainly talked about killing Giles Kenworthy at some time, even if she wasn't being completely serious. And I wouldn't have thought anything happens in Riverview Close without Adam Strauss and his wife knowing about it. I hated that bloody chess set, by the way, but then I never much liked *The Lord of the Rings* either. Hobbits and talking trees? Not for me, thanks.'

Hawthorne examined his assistant with both curiosity and concern. 'So, how are things going with you?' he asked.

'I'm all right.'

'How's the flat working out?'

'It's great. I'm very grateful to you.' Dudley paused. 'How much longer am I going to be able to live there?'

Hawthorne shrugged. 'As long as you like.'

'And rent-free? How does that work?'

'The people who own it aren't short of cash.'

'Well, it's very handy. And if I ever need a cup of sugar, I know where to go.'

'I don't have any sugar.'

'I was talking about the Waitrose round the corner.'

Dudley continued to eat, almost mechanically. There could have been anything on his plate. Hawthorne finished his cigarette. He was very rarely ill at ease, but he hesitated before asking: 'Are you still seeing Suzmann?'

Dudley stopped, the fork halfway to his mouth. 'Now and then,' he said.

'Do you want to talk about it?'

'Not really.'

'Do you mind me asking?'

'I'd prefer it if you didn't.' Dudley put down his knife and fork, making sure they were parallel on the plate. 'It's been a year now since it happened. Bristol courthouse and all the rest of it. But I've got things under control, largely thanks to Dr Suzmann. And thanks to you, Danny. I like doing this job and I'm grateful to you. I'm getting things together in my own way, one day at a time. All the rest of it's behind me, so I'd appreciate it if you'd leave it alone.'

'I only asked,' Hawthorne said, stubbing out his cigarette.

'I appreciate it.'

'So what do you suggest we do next?'

'It would be nice to get hold of the barrister – Pennington. He arranged the big get-together everyone's been talking about. And there was something about his flowers getting trashed.'

'And Sarah Baines.'

'Oh yeah. The gardener.' Dudley took out his notebook and turned to a page. 'Accused of theft and some sort of financial espionage. She had access to Roderick Browne's house and she was in and out all the time. She's also sending text messages to Mr Browne and it may have been her who threw that poor bloody dog down the well.' Dudley snapped the book shut. 'Yes. I'd definitely like to speak to her.'

8

There was a single policeman standing guard at the entrance to Riverview Close, keeping away any sightseers, but otherwise the whole place was eerily empty by mid-afternoon, when Hawthorne and Dudley returned. All the investigating officers, including Khan, had disappeared, as if, just a couple of days after a particularly violent and unusual murder, they had decided there was nothing more for them to do.

'Have they made any arrests?' Hawthorne asked the young constable – who at least knew who he was.

'No, sir. Not that I heard.'

They walked through, into the close.

'You think they've pulled Roderick Browne in?' Dudley asked.

Hawthorne nodded. Dudley could have been reading his mind. 'I'm not sure he murdered Giles Kenworthy – although he did his best to convince us otherwise. But I don't think DS

Khan will be able to resist it. Pull him in. Give him a night in police custody. Hope to terrify him enough into talking.'

The door of Well House was the first they came to and Dudley rang the bell. It was opened by Andrew Pennington, who seemed to know exactly who they were and had been expecting them. 'Adam called me after you spoke to him,' he explained. 'He said you might want to speak to me.' He leaned out and looked around the close. 'It looks as if everyone else is out.'

'Do you talk to each other a lot?' Dudley asked.

'I'm sorry?'

'You and Mr Strauss. It seems to me that the whole lot of you are pretty tight. You keep each other informed of what's going on.'

'We're all friends, if that's what you mean. At least, we were until the Kenworthys arrived. Please, come in . . .'

Andrew Pennington's home was neat, comfortable, old-fashioned. The sitting room had a desk in one corner, a matching three-piece suite, bookshelves filled with mainly nineteenth-century English, French and Russian classics. The colour scheme tended towards the dark – walls painted in shades of green and mauve, with oak and mahogany furniture, thick carpets and curtains. Triple French windows at the back looked out into the garden, but only allowed a little afternoon sun to trickle in.

It was immediately obvious that he lived alone. The house had a sense of emptiness. It felt stuck in time, as if nothing had changed, but it was immediately obvious what was missing. There were photographs on every surface, mounted in a variety of frames, but all of them showing the same subject: a beautiful woman, always smiling, her face filled with life. Iris Pennington at work, Iris on the beach, Iris and Andrew arm in arm on a swing chair, Iris and Andrew dancing, Iris making a heart sign with both hands, Iris in bed, ill and wasted but still smiling for the camera. Well House spoke equally of her death and her surviving husband's life.

Andrew was in his early sixties, a handsome, softly spoken black man with hair that was tinged with white around his ears. It would be easy to imagine him in court. He would be courteous, precise . . . but he would miss nothing. Those grey eyes of his would pick up the slightest nuance and when he sensed a weak spot he would strike with lethal accuracy. Of course, all of that was far behind him now. He had not so much embraced retirement as allowed it to engulf him. The slippers he was wearing, the cardigan pushed out of shape by the bulge of his stomach, the glasses, the tiredness in his face . . . He was tumbling into old age.

'Can I get you tea or coffee?' he asked as he showed them to a seat.

'No, thank you. We just had lunch.' Hawthorne picked up on what Dudley had been asking. 'We've been told that you and your friends had a meeting,' he said. 'You were going to confront your new neighbours about their behaviour.'

'You're referring to the meeting we had six weeks ago at

Adam Strauss's house. But I don't think "confront" is the right word.'

'What word would you use?'

The barrister shrugged. 'I haven't quite put my finger on what it was about the Kenworthys that annoyed so many of us. I'm not convinced it was the issues – the noise and all the rest of it. I think it was the people themselves. There was something about them that was deeply off-putting. I've seen it in court, many a time. A jury takes against a defendant for no clear reason and it's almost impossible to make them see sense, no matter how many facts you have at your fingertips.

'For what it's worth, I would have said the meeting was more about conciliation than confrontation. It seemed a good idea to discuss the issues before they got out of hand.'

'They got out of hand – big time,' Dudley muttered.

'It was unfortunate that the Kenworthys decided not to come. They sent a text while we were together, after we'd arrived. It didn't go down well.'

'The meeting was your idea?' Hawthorne asked.

'The idea presented itself when I was talking to Adam. It's long been my experience that it's all too easy to get a false impression of someone if you don't talk to them. You imagine the worst and that's what they become. There's a poem by William Blake.' He closed his eyes, recalling the words. ' "*I was angry with my friend; I told my wrath, my wrath did end. I was angry with my foe: I told it not, my wrath did grow.*" ' He

169

smiled. 'The poem is called "A Poison Tree". I suppose we met to avoid cultivating one.'

'There must have been a lot of anger in the room,' Hawthorne said.

'Wrath,' Dudley corrected him.

'Again, that's not the case. Tom was probably more annoyed than anyone because of the parking situation – quite rightly, as it turned out. A man died in his surgery when he couldn't get there to save him. Roderick and Felicity were determined to fight the swimming pool. They'd just received notice of the planning application. We all had. If it went through, they would lose their view – not at all helpful when you're bed-ridden. But nobody said anything particularly aggressive and certainly nothing that might be deemed illegal. Adam didn't complain at all, as far as I can recall, although of course his most precious chess set hadn't been smashed at the time. That happened later. May actually said what a lot of us were thinking, which was that we should do everything by the book. The important thing was not to let the situation escalate. In the end, it was quite a pleasant evening, albeit a short one. There was no point hanging around if they weren't going to show up.'

'But then things got worse,' Dudley said.

'It's true. The next six weeks were very trying.'

'Mrs Winslow lost her dog.'

'The dog belonged to both her and her companion. I was with them when they found him. He was at the bottom of the old well in the corner of my garden and in considerable pain, poor thing. They'd had a long dispute with the Kenworthys – I'm afraid the dog had a habit of burrowing into their garden – but there's absolutely no evidence that either Giles or Lynda had anything to do with it.'

'What did it do, then? Commit suicide?' Dudley was unimpressed.

'May and Phyllis believe that Giles Kenworthy ordered Sarah Baines to do away with it. It's true she had scratches on her arms the following day, but I've spoken to her and I believe her when she says she would never have done anything like that. For that matter, I'm not sure that the Kenworthys would have given the order.'

'You mentioned Adam Strauss's chess set,' Hawthorne said.

'That was the children playing cricket. No doubt about that.'

'They also rode their skateboards over some of your flowers.'

For the first time, Andrew Pennington was taken aback, losing some of his poise. When he spoke again, his voice was low. 'Yes. That was Hugo and Tristram Kenworthy again. They're very young and I'm sure they meant no harm, but we have repeatedly asked their parents to keep them under control.'

He wanted to stop there, but Hawthorne and Dudley waited in silence, expecting more.

'You may have noticed the roundabout in the centre of the close. With the permission – indeed, with the encouragement – of the other residents, I had planted it with shrubs and flowers that had a special significance for my late wife, Iris. She died of cancer just as I retired and I have to tell you, I miss her

171

terribly. I try to keep myself busy. I've joined a bridge club and I play twice a week – Mondays and Wednesdays. In fact, I'm playing tonight. There's a walking group. Swimming in the summer. But it's not easy without her, which is perhaps why the display means so much to me.

'Anyway, I came home one evening to discover wheel marks from two skateboards cutting right through the beds. A lot of the flowers were severed. In fact, the whole bed was decimated. I would say "profaned", but perhaps that's going too far.' He tried to make light of it. 'It's not hugely import-ant. I can always plant more. But I was upset because it happened to be the fifth anniversary of her death.' His eyes met Hawthorne's. 'Perhaps that leads you to think that I had a motive to kill their father. He didn't even apologise. The boys still race around on their skateboards.'

'It might do.'

'Well, I'll give you a much better motive if it will help you with your inquiries, Mr Hawthorne. Giles Kenworthy was a card-carrying member of the UK Independence Party.'

'What of it?'

'I think it informed the way he treated me.'

'And how was that, Mr Pennington?' Hawthorne asked.

'With disdain.'

'Are you saying he was a racist?'

'I'm asking what sort of man puts jingoistic slogans in his front window and flies a Union Jack in his back garden?'

'A patriot?'

'I'm afraid it's been a very long time since the Union Jack was associated with patriotism, Mr Dudley,' Andrew replied.

'The UK Independence Party wouldn't call itself racist,' Dudley said.

'Their leader said he wouldn't want to live next to a Romanian. One of their councillors was recorded admitting she had a problem with "Negroes". The Prime Minister himself has referred to them as "closet racists". Maybe the view is different when you're seeing it from your side of the fence, Mr Dudley. But as I understand it, the police are even looking into a possible political connection in the attack on Marsha Clarke. You won't have heard of her, but there have been quite a few stories about her in the local press.'

'She was the old lady being looked after by the Beresfords' nanny.'

'That's right. Apparently, an Independence Party leaflet has been found in her letter box. It may have been a calling card.'

Hawthorne and Dudley took this in. Marsha Clarke, a woman living in Hampton Wick, had been the victim of what might have been a racist attack. Her assailant might have belonged to a right-wing political party. Giles Kenworthy supported the same party. And he happened to have lived next door to the young woman who had been caring for Marsha.

There might be a connection, but it was definitely an oblique one.

'Giles Kenworthy never spoke to me,' Andrew went on. 'He never invited me into the house. He always looked at me with a sense of superiority, almost contempt. I used to think that he deliberately revved the engine of his car outside my house to wake me up.'

'Why are you telling us all this, Mr Pennington?' Hawthorne asked.

'Because I think you're focusing on the wrong angle. All the trivia of a suburban close means nothing at all. Nobody ever murdered anyone because they played their music too loud. It may be that Kenworthy was a racist and a deeply unpleasant man who deserved to die.'

'Did you kill him?'

'No. I did not.'

Before either of them could say anything more, there was a movement outside the window and a young woman walked past, dressed in a vest top and jeans, pushing a wheelbarrow.

'Is that Sarah Baines?' Hawthorne asked.

'Yes.'

'She works here?'

'She does all the gardens.'

'Not the Kenworthys',' Dudley said. 'They fired her.'

'Would you mind if we had a word with her?' Hawthorne asked.

'There's nothing more you want to ask me?'

'Not for the moment, thanks.'

Andrew Pennington got up and opened the French windows. 'Then be my guest . . .'

9

Sarah Baines had been mowing. As Hawthorne and Dudley walked up to her, she was unloading the wheelbarrow onto a compost heap.

She was a statuesque woman, tall and muscular, with auburn hair brushing over her eyes, twisting around her neck and plunging down to her ample breast. Her clothes, especially her heavy black gardening gloves, did her no favours – but when she turned and smiled, she was strikingly attractive: formidable, certainly, but with something of the magnetism of a movie star, perhaps in a superhero film. Her vest top revealed bare arms with tattoos on both biceps: a pair of dice on the left and a spider's web on the right. The wheelbarrow was old and heavy, but she had no trouble man-ouevring it, spilling weeds and grass cuttings – along with a number of undeserving flowers – onto the pile.

Andrew Pennington's garden was surprisingly large,

almost twice the size of its neighbours. It was L-shaped, starting with a York stone patio, a wooden table and six chairs. Beyond this, the lawn stretched all the way round the side of the house, bordered by a long line of flower beds that stretched from one end to the other. Climbing roses and jasmine had been planted against a brick wall that separated the property from the main road. They provided a colourful background for the medieval well that had been the cause of so much misery and which stood on its own with a gravel surround. Ellery would have had no trouble coming through the shrubs that separated the garden from May Winslow's. He could have been carried just as easily.

The scratches were no longer showing on Sarah Baines's arms.

'Ms Baines?' Dudley was the first to reach her. 'Can we have a word?'

'I've already spoken with the police. I'm busy.'

'But less busy than you were, or so I understand.'

Sarah stopped what she was doing and set the wheelbarrow down. She looked at them with sullen hostility, as if she was only looking for an excuse to start a fight. 'What's that meant to mean?'

'Well, you got fired by Giles Kenworthy, didn't you? The same weekend he got murdered!' Dudley made it sound as if the two events were an extraordinary coincidence.

Sarah sneered at him. 'You think I had something to do with it?' Her voice was hard-edged, pitiless.

'You knew about the crossbow in Roderick Browne's garage. You were in and out all the time.'

'Doesn't mean I killed him.' A wasp buzzed briefly around her head and she flicked it away. 'Yes, I knew about the crossbow. Yes, I had access. But you think I'm stupid? You think I'd kill someone just because they gave me the push? I've got plenty of work here and I'm doing very nicely, thank you very much.' It was warm out in the sun and she pulled off her gloves, revealing jagged nails stained with earth and nicotine. 'Anyway, he wouldn't have booted me out if it hadn't been for his wife. The two of us got on all right, but she never liked me.'

'She found you in his office.'

'Did she tell you that?'

'What were you doing there?'

'I was in and out of that house all the time. I didn't just do their garden. I was their electrician, their painter, their bloody cleaner when Miss Ping-Pong couldn't be bothered to do it herself.'

'That's a bit racist,' Dudley said.

'That's what Kenworthy called her. He didn't even know her real name.'

'You also killed dogs for them,' Hawthorne remarked, speaking for the first time.

Baines gave Hawthorne an ugly look, taking it as a personal insult. 'That's a lie,' she said. 'I never touched Mrs Winslow's dog. Why would I have done that? I'd never have hurt any animal, even if Giles Kenworthy told me to. And he didn't. Who are you, anyway? What gives you the right to ask me questions?'

'Giles Kenworthy lost a Rolex,' Dudley said.

'He was careless. But he was rich enough. He could buy another.'

'How long were you in prison?' Hawthorne asked.

The question had come out of nowhere, but it was a blow that landed. Sarah looked around her as if she was afraid someone might have heard. 'Who told you that?' she demanded.

'You did, Sarah, with those tattoos of yours. That's not ink under your skin, is it? There's no proper ink in the nick. I'd say it's soot from burnt hair grease or maybe burnt plastic mixed with water and alcohol. And those designs you've chosen! A lot of inmates have a dice on their arm. It means they're prepared to take risks. And the spider's web . . . it's the prison that traps the spider. Out of interest, how long were you in for?'

Sarah reached into her jeans pocket, took out a packet of cigarettes and lit one. She was wondering whether to answer. 'I was stitched up,' she said, at length. 'I did six months at Feltham. Burglary.'

'And?'

'Two years at New Hall, Wakefield. I hurt someone in a pub.'

'Hurt?'

'I put a glass in his face. He deserved it.'

Hawthorne sighed. 'They always do.'

'That was three years ago.' Sarah scowled. 'What's it got to do with you?'

'Well, someone has just been shot with a crossbow,' Dudley said. 'So it might be a tiny bit relevant.'

'I've already spoken to Khan.'

'Detective Superintendent Khan to you, I think.'

'He knows who I am, what I've done. I didn't murder anyone and if he thought I had, why would I still be free?'

'Why did May Winslow recommend you for the job?' Hawthorne asked.

'Because she's a decent sort – not a hard bastard like you.' She took a breath. 'I was looking for work,' she went on. 'I was knocking on doors all over Richmond, but nobody trusts anybody any more. She was the only one who listened to me. She took me in, and one after another all the others followed.'

'Why Richmond?'

'Richmond is full of rich people – or haven't you noticed? I did an Open College Network course in farms and gardens at New Hall and I've always been good with my hands. I'm doing all right here. I don't need to steal Rolexes and if you think otherwise, you're as stupid as Giles Kenworthy.'

'You sent Roderick Browne a text this morning,' Dudley said. 'What was that about?'

'His petunias need watering.'

'You really know anything about petunias?' He pointed to the flowers on the compost heap. 'You've cut half of them down.'

179

She shrugged. 'The lawnmower's twenty years out of date. It's got a mind of its own.'

Sarah Baines had decided that the interview was over. She put her gloves back on, picked up the wheelbarrow and headed towards the other side of the garden. The cigarette was still in her mouth.

'Benson and Hedges at eight quid a pack,' Dudley muttered. 'She's doing all right for herself.'

The two of them walked round past the well. Hawthorne briefly peered into the tunnel of ancient brickwork but said nothing. They continued through a gate that led back to the close.

'You want to wait for the two old ladies?' Dudley asked. 'And Dr Beresford?'

Hawthorne shook his head. 'I think we've done enough for one day. How do we get a taxi out of here?'

'The station's five minutes away.'

'I don't like tube trains.'

They set off, walking up the hill towards the town centre. It was late afternoon and the close was empty and silent, the shadows lengthening. At that moment, with no cars parked, no police officers present and everything bathed in golden light, it could have inspired the cover of one of the books sold at The Tea Cosy. One murder had already taken place, but now there was a hushed expectancy, a feeling of evil in the air, and it would be easy to imagine that the stage had been set for another.

FOUR
FENCHURCH
INTERNATIONAL

1

Hawthorne was as unhappy with the second instalment as he had been with the first . . . and I hadn't even shown him the whole thing. I had deliberately kept back one or two sections that I knew he wouldn't like and there were some parts I hadn't written yet. I would add them later.

Our next session was particularly awkward. The weather didn't help. It was another one of those uncomfortably warm days that occasionally take hold of London, a city that was never really built to handle intense weather, so we had met on the balcony of my Clerkenwell flat, where a line of olive trees separated us from the traffic and there was at least a hint of a breeze. A fountain that had looked good in the catalogue but in fact resembled an oversized latrine tinkled to one side, providing an illusion of coolness.

Hawthorne didn't like the way I was writing the story. Perhaps neither of us had quite understood the power of the

ANTHONY HOROWITZ

third person. I was describing what people were saying, thinking, where they had come from, how other people saw them – even though, unlike Hawthorne, I had never met them. I was using the notes, pictures and recordings that he had given me, but I was interpreting them my own way and he was insisting that was a departure from the truth. So which one of us was actually in control? We were beginning to see that neither of us was. It was as if the characters themselves had taken control.

I still had absolutely no idea who had committed the murder.

The material he'd given me did not include the arrest report and I'd probably need to meet him three or four more times to get to the end of the book. At this stage, I couldn't even be certain that the story would be worth telling. For example, I was very much hoping that Sarah Baines wasn't going to be revealed as the killer. With her prison record, her tattoos and her possible involvement in the death of Ellery, she was frankly too obvious a suspect and if it did turn out to be her, the solution would be much less of a surprise than if it was, say, Andrew Pennington who was revealed. Unfortunately, things seemed to be pointing that way. She had access to the garage. She knew about the crossbow. She had just lost her job. I also wondered how she had managed to sweet-talk an old lady who was also an ex-nun into giving her the job in the first place.

Sitting on my terrace, Hawthorne poured himself a black coffee and lit his first cigarette. Curiously, what upset him most was the way I'd described John Dudley. He still hadn't answered any of the questions about the man I had effectively replaced and he was as reluctant to talk about him as he was to tell me anything about himself. I'd scribbled a series of questions on a sheet of paper. How long had they known each other? Where did they meet? Where was he now? What had happened to Dudley in Bristol? I was still waiting for the opportunity to ask them.

'You've got him all wrong, mate,' Hawthorne said.

'What do you mean?'

'Well . . . the description. Scruffy, sloping shoulders, lank hair. What does "lank" mean, anyway?'

'It means limp. Lifeless.'

'That's wrong for a start. There was nothing wrong with his hair. And why do you say he wore scuffed shoes? John always wore trainers.'

'Well, I may have just imagined the shoes, but I think the general picture is accurate.' I searched around all the documents spread out on the table in front of us and pulled out a photograph. It was the only picture of Dudley I had found in the bundle he had given me. It must have been taken by a police photographer and showed Hawthorne and Dudley standing outside Riverview Lodge. Khan was in the background too, slightly out of focus.

'His hair definitely looks a bit lank,' I said. 'Those trousers of his are shapeless. And I've heard his voice on the recordings. I think my description fits him pretty well.'

'You keep trying to make him seem stupid. Yes, he had a strange sense of humour. But I'm telling you, he was sharp as a knife. In fact, I'd never have solved the case without him.'

'So you did solve it!'

'Of course I solved it. You think I'd be sitting here talking about it if I hadn't? But Dudley was always on the money. He was the one who saw the packed suitcase in the hallway of the dentist's house, for example. Not me. That turned out to be important. And he also worked out that Sarah Baines had been in prison.' He paused. 'I know you've been out with me a few times and you've never noticed a thing. In fact, you've helped the killers more than you've helped me. But he's not the same.'

'So what happened?' I asked. I refused to rise to the bait. 'If he's so brilliant, how come he's not working with you any more? Why did you have to come to me?'

'I came to you because Peter James turned me down.'

'Only Peter James? I thought you approached half the crime writers in London!'

'I approached a few of them.'

'That's not the point. What I'm asking is – where is he?'

'I already told you. I haven't seen him for a while.' He looked at me angrily. 'Maybe this is a mistake.' He contemplated his cigarette. 'But it's not too late to stop.'

'What are you talking about?' I exclaimed. 'It's about forty thousand words too late! I'm not stopping now.' I forced myself to calm down. 'Why can't I meet him?' I asked.

'Why would you want to?'

'To get his side of the story.'

Hawthorne shook his head. 'You don't need it. You've got mine.' His voice was bleak. He was warning me not to argue.

'Well, at least tell me this. How did you meet him?'

'It's not relevant.'

'I'm the one writing the book, Hawthorne. Maybe I should decide what's relevant or not.'

'He'd been a police officer, but he was on sick leave. He came to London. We met.'

'That's not good enough.'

'That's all I'm going to tell you.'

'Then maybe you should go back to Peter James.'

We had never argued like this before. There was a brief silence while we glowered at each other. I decided to change the subject.

'All right, then,' I said. 'If you won't talk about John Dudley, let's talk about you and what was going on in your head.' I took out another page of notes. 'Khan had telephoned you. You went round to Riverview Close. You talked to Lynda Kenworthy, Roderick Browne, Gemma Beresford, Andrew Pennington, Adam Strauss and his wife. You didn't meet May Winslow and Phyllis Moore because they were at their bookshop . . . but I'm not sure they were suspects anyway. So here's the question. At this stage, on the first day of your investigation, had you guessed who did it?'

'I never guess!'

'You know what I mean . . .'

It's the one thing nobody ever tells you in a detective story. At what point does the detective solve the crime? It's a remarkable coincidence that he or she only seems to arrive at the solution in the last couple of chapters, but it's always made clear that the main clues, the ones that gave the whole thing away, turned up long before. Sitting there on the balcony of my flat, with the water trickling down the wall, it quite amused me to put Hawthorne on the spot. At this point, how much had he worked out?

'I didn't know who killed Giles Kenworthy,' he admitted. 'It's not like that. You don't just meet someone and say, "Oh – he's the killer!" You've got to talk to everyone, see how they fit together, and at the point you've reached, there were people we hadn't even spoken to. May Winslow and Phyllis Moore, for a start – and they were just as much suspects as everyone else. Dr Beresford. Kylie the nanny. Damien the carer. Jean-François the French teacher. The picture's not complete. But I'll tell you this, Tony. By the end of that first day, the finger was definitely pointing in one direction.'

'Who?'

He shook his head. 'I didn't have a name. I just had an idea of what might have happened.'

'Tell me!' He didn't answer. 'Hawthorne! It's great if the readers don't guess who did it. It's not so brilliant if the author doesn't know either.'

He took pity on me.

'Look, mate. I've told you everything that happened and you've written it down. And if you just read it all again, there's stuff that should be obvious to you. Things that don't make any sense.'

'Such as?'

'All right. Two purported attacks in the space of a week-end. The old woman in Hampton Wick and Adam Strauss at Richmond station.'

'You say "purported". Do you think Adam Strauss falling down the stairs could have just been an accident?'

'Whatever happened at the station had to be a part of it . . .'

'That's why you wanted to see the CCTV footage.'

'Exactly – although it didn't help in the end. Anyway, that's not so important. What you should really be focusing on are the two meetings.'

'What two meetings?'

He paused, then continued patiently. 'There were two meetings in Riverview Close. The first one happened six weeks before the murder.'

'Yes. I've described that one. They all got together at The Stables, but the Kenworthys didn't show up.'

'That's right. But what's interesting is to look at the events before that meeting and then compare them with what hap-pened afterwards.' I still didn't know what he was talking about. 'There was an escalation,' he explained. 'Andrew Pennington's flowers got torn to shreds. The dog got put in the well.'

189

'Adam Strauss's best chess set got smashed. And a man died.'

Hawthorne nodded. 'Three deaths. Giles Kenworthy. Ellery the French bulldog. And Raymond Shaw, a patient of Dr Beresford.'

I couldn't tell if he was joking or not, listing them like that. 'Was Raymond Shaw deliberately killed? I don't know anything about him. I don't even know who he is.'

'He had a heart attack in Dr Beresford's surgery. It was a natural death.'

I gave up. 'So when was the second meeting?' I asked. 'How do you even know it happened?'

He looked at me a little sadly. 'You wrote it. Didn't you see it?'

'No!'

He looked at me like a teacher with a difficult child. 'When I was with Roderick Browne, he mentioned that there had been a meeting and the moment he said it, he looked scared. You described it perfectly. "*Something close to panic flitted across his eyes . . .*" He thought he'd given away too much and he quickly added that this was a meeting that had happened a long time ago. Six weeks.' Hawthorne waited for me to react. 'He wanted us to know it had happened a long time ago. It was obvious to me that he was deliberately steering us away from a more recent meeting to one that had happened earlier.

'The same thing happened with Gemma Beresford, the doctor's wife. Dudley asked her if she and the neighbours had ever talked about killing Giles Kenworthy and straight away, she went on the defensive. "No. Of course not. When would anyone ever say something like that? I never heard anything!" Too much denial! She went on to say I couldn't turn her against her friends. She was protecting them. They'd met and they'd talked about murder.

'And then there was the clincher. I asked Andrew Pennington about the meeting when the Kenworthys didn't show up and he said: "You're referring to the meeting we had six weeks ago." Not *a* meeting. *The* meeting. Because there was more than one.'

'Surely that's just semantics.'

'The trouble with you, Tony, is that you're great with long words, but you never think them through. The semantics! It's the small things that matter. That's how criminals give themselves away.'

'So what happened at this second meeting?'

'You can find out for yourself . . .'

He produced another sheaf of interviews and hand-written notes and handed them to me. 'You take a look at all this and put something together – maybe without the parakeets and the climbing roses – and we can meet in a couple of weeks and see where we are.'

'And that's it?'

'What else do you need?'

'I told you. I'd like to meet John Dudley.'

'That's not going to happen.'

2

I wasn't going to let it go.

Hawthorne's remark had annoyed me. It was unfair to say that I'd never noticed anything when I'd followed him on his investigations. I noticed and described lots of things; it's just that I wasn't always aware of their significance. Yes, I did make mistakes. Getting a senior police officer to arrest the wrong person was certainly one of them. My questions did sometimes have unintended consequences: an old man's house got burned down, for example. And I'd been stabbed twice. Even so, I'd say that I was often quite helpful, especially considering that, unlike Dudley, I had never been in the police force.

I had very little to go on. I had heard Dudley's voice on the recordings he had made throughout the day, but he had no discernible accent and although he had travelled in and out of London with Hawthorne, I couldn't be sure he even lived in the city. He had mentioned working in Bristol. I thought briefly of using a computer search engine to track him down, but there seemed little point: I couldn't even be sure I'd been given his real name.

That gave me another idea.

I've already mentioned the book I was working on, *Murder at the Vaudeville Theatre*. In it, I had described how I had been forced into hiding in Hawthorne's flat, fearing that I was about to be arrested for the murder of theatre critic Harriet Throsby. While I was there, I had been discovered by a man who had called in, using his own key. This was Roland Hawthorne, who turned out to be Hawthorne's adoptive brother. It had always infuriated me that I knew so little about the man I was supposed to be writing about, so of course I had used the chance meeting to get some information out of him. It wasn't easy. Roland knew who I was and he was careful not to give too much away.

However, he had confirmed that his father – another policeman – had adopted Hawthorne, whose own parents had died in a place called Reeth. The two of them worked for an organisation that Roland described as 'a creative and business development service', but which sounded like a high-end security firm, employing private detectives and investigators. They also seemed to own several flats in the same block where Hawthorne lived.

Roland had told me very little more, but he had been

carrying an envelope with him: it contained details of Hawthorne's next case. I had seen the name BARRACLOUGH written on the outside and Roland had mentioned that it concerned a husband who had run off with another woman and who was now holed up in Grand Cayman. That was all he had said. But it was enough.

If I could find Barraclough's wife, I might be able to track down the organisation she had hired to help her. It might be an opportunity to find out more about Hawthorne, and there was a good chance that John Dudley was working for this organisation too. I should have thought of all this sooner. It was time to get out from behind my desk.

I went back to my computer.

With the information I already had, tracking down Mrs Barraclough wouldn't be too difficult. For a start, her husband must have worked in the world of finance. There are over six hundred banks and trust companies in Grand Cayman, even though the entire island only stretches some twenty miles. Fraud and white-collar crime are as much part of the landscape as coral reefs and cocktails at sunset. I could easily see Mr Barraclough as a crooked financier, cheating on his wife. She would live in Mayfair or Belgravia. She would have a little black book with the names of several discreet detective agencies. She could lead me to the one that had employed Hawthorne.

It helped that she had a fairly uncommon surname. I opened a search engine and found it almost at once, on the

second page. There was a report published in the *Daily Mail*
with the headline: BARRACLOUGH 'FISH & CHIPS'
DIVORCE. It referred to a hearing that had taken place just
a few months before and the timeline fitted exactly with my
visit to Hawthorne's flat. I read:

> The American wife of a well-known international financier
> has been awarded a remarkable £230 million in a High
> Court **divorce** case which the judge described as 'one of
> the most acrimonious I have ever heard'.
>
> Sir Jack **Barraclough** and his wife, Greta, 59, were argu-
> ing over assets believed to be worth more than £500
> million, including properties in New York, London and **Grand
> Cayman**. Their nineteen-year marriage came to an end
> earlier this year after Lady **Barraclough** discovered her
> husband was having an affair, but he made headlines when
> he publicly announced that she deserved 'the price of a
> fish and chip supper and nothing more'.
>
> Greta **Barraclough** remains in the family home in
> Knightsbridge, London. The couple have four children.

Hawthorne was wrong. I wouldn't have made a bad detective
after all. I was fairly sure I had found the right name and after
several more searches I came across an article in *Hello!*
Magazine, that well-known shop window for the wealthy and
famous, dated August 2009. The Barracloughs ('socialites,
philanthropists and entrepreneurs') were showing off the

house they had just bought and redecorated. Sir Jack was solid and pugnacious. His wife tended more to the glamorous and artistic. Were they already unhappy in each other's company? It was hard to tell. They had been photographed together and apart in several of the rooms, surrounded by vast stretches of marble, gilt-edged mirrors, chandeliers and a grand piano that didn't look as if it had ever been played. Everything, including them, had been airbrushed to perfection. There was no dust or dirty laundry anywhere to be seen. Their four sons – the youngest six months, the oldest eight years – had been arranged like stuffed toys on a velvet sofa, collector's items, with even the baby displaying that easy self-confidence that comes when you know Daddy has millions in the bank.

Lady Barraclough loved the house. '*It's so marvellous being just a minute's walk from Harrods,*' she told the magazine, which provided me with the next piece of the puzzle. I launched Zoopla, the property website, and – street by street – searched for houses in the immediate vicinity of Harrods department store in Knightsbridge. This took a bit longer, but eventually I came across a property in Trevor Square, just the other side of Brompton Road. It had sold for £18 million in 2008, and comparing it with the pictures of the Barracloughs' home in *Hello!*, I could see that they were one and the same.

I went over there straight away.

3

'You wrote this?' Greta Barraclough asked.

She was holding a copy of *The Word is Murder*, the first book I had written about Hawthorne.

'Yes. I thought you might like a copy.'

'That's very kind of you.' She set it down beside her in a way that somehow told me she would never open it. Like the piano. It didn't matter. The book had been the calling card that had got me in.

I'd been very lucky.

Lady Barraclough could have been in her second home in Barbados. She could have been in any one of the five-star hotels she frequented all over the world or cruising with friends in the Mediterranean or out riding in the countryside. But that same afternoon, I'd tracked her down to the five-bedroom, £18 million house that she had bought close to Harrods and which she had wrestled from her ex-husband.

Not only that, I'd managed to talk my way past her unsmiling butler and even less amicable personal assistant and into one of her half-dozen living rooms, where we were sitting now, perched on velvet sofas, facing each other and separated by a monstrous Indonesian coffee table with an assortment of quite unappetising biscuits and small cups of tea laid out in front of us. But then she knew my books. Her children were all boys, now aged nine to seventeen, and at least one of them had read Alex Rider. It's one of the things I've found throughout my career. Being a children's author opens doors.

For a woman who had ended her marriage with £230 million in her pocket, she seemed extraordinarily damaged. Had Sir Jack's betrayal really been that bad? The different parts of her body didn't seem to fit together properly, her knees barely carrying her across the room and her hands swivelling unnecessarily as she sat down. She had the sort of self-awareness that suggested she might once have been beautiful, that heads would have turned as she entered the room – but that had been another room and a long time ago. What remained were sad, empty eyes, thin strands of colourless hair hanging down to her shoulders, a long neck and a hollowed-out throat. She looked as if she hadn't eaten in days. Expensive jewellery clung to every possible part of her body – ears, wrists, fingers, neck – but only put me in mind of an Aztec mummy. Something in her had died.

At the door, I had given my name – and my book – to a severe young woman who was either Spanish or Portuguese.

This was Maria, Lady Barraclough's personal assistant. I had explained who I was and asked to speak to Lady Barraclough on an important personal matter, assuring her that it would take no more than ten minutes and that the book was a gift to show my appreciation for her time. Maria had made me wait while she disappeared into the inner recesses of the house. I was quite surprised when, fifteen minutes later, I was invited up to the first floor. We took the stairs, although I noticed what looked like an antique French lift to one side.

'Why have you come here?' Lady Barraclough asked me now. She had a throaty voice and when she spoke, something in her throat rippled like a miniature keyboard. 'What is it you wish to know?'

'Did you ever meet a man called Daniel Hawthorne?' I asked her.

She nodded. 'Of course I met him. I hired him.'

I was surprised she was so matter-of-fact. From the day Hawthorne had walked into my life, he had shrouded himself in mystery, but to her he was just another employee. I wondered what the relationship between them had been like. 'He investigated your husband,' I said.

'Do you really expect me to talk about this with you?'

'I'm sorry. I don't mean to intrude—'

'You are intruding. This is still extremely painful for me. It's all public knowledge. I've had my whole life eviscerated in the tabloid press. Did you read what they wrote?'

'Some of it.'

'They are beasts. They have no humanity.'

She closed her eyes, took a deep breath, then slowly opened them.

'My husband had an affair with my son's Russian tutor. Can you imagine that? This woman came into our house. She sat at our table and she ate our food. She taught our son! I call her a woman, but she was only a girl, twenty years younger than my husband. He took her to Grand Cayman. I did not know this, but I suspected it. Men are like schoolboys. Their whole life, they are schoolboys. He lied to me, but I knew he was lying and I was determined to discover the truth.'

She paused and I saw a shroud of puzzlement cross her face and for a brief moment she had forgotten who I was.

'Why are you asking about him?' she demanded. 'What has it got to do with you?'

'I'm not here about your husband,' I assured her. 'I need to contact the agency that you used . . . the one that employed Mr Hawthorne. It's difficult to explain, but I'd be very grateful if you could give me their address.'

'What do you need them for?'

'I'm looking for someone. I'm hoping they may be able to help.'

'Someone you know?'

'Someone I want to know.'

She thought for a moment. 'Marcus always liked your books,' she said. 'So did Harry, my youngest son. I don't see the two of them very much. Marcus went to Montenegro with his father, and Harry . . .' She tried to summon up a memory of where Harry had gone. It didn't come. She reached forward and pressed a remote control resting on the table.

'I think you are making a mistake,' she said. 'The company that I used was extremely efficient. They tracked my husband down. They managed to hack into his telephone, although I thought it was meant to be impossible.' I had an idea who might have done that for them. It had to be Kevin Chakraborty. But I said nothing. 'They gave me a printout of every single message he had sent his mistress. They even provided me with filmed footage of the two of them in bed together, first in a hotel in London, later in Grand Cayman. When we divorced, they tracked down all his assets, including properties I didn't even know we had. There was nothing he could hide from them. They delivered him to me, signed and sealed, tied with a red ribbon.

'But this is what I want you to know. They enjoyed what they did. I asked them for the truth, but they didn't need to rub my face in it. They spared me no details of my husband's infidelity—'

'Are you talking about Hawthorne?' I interrupted.

'Not Hawthorne. No. I liked him. He's a good man, a kind man – not at all like the people he was working for. I sometimes got the feeling that I wasn't so much their client as their victim. They belong to a different world to you and me and if you employ them, you will understand what I'm saying. My advice to you would be to stay well away. They will cost you a great deal. How many of these books have you sold? You will have to be very wealthy indeed to afford them, but it is not just your money that they will take from you. They're like vampires. They'll suck you dry.'

A door opened at the back of the room and the personal assistant appeared.

'My guest is leaving,' Lady Barraclough announced. Then, just as I thought she wasn't going to give me the information I needed . . . 'The company is called Fenchurch International. Maria will give you their contact details and their address.'

I got to my feet. 'Thank you, Lady Barraclough.'

She shuddered. 'Don't call me that! I lost the title along with everything else.' She took one last look at me. 'Thank you for the book. I would ask you not to return here. I really want nothing more to do with you. Now, I'll wish you a good day.'

Maria showed me out of the house. When I got to the end of the street, I turned round and looked back. She was still there, watching me, making sure I wasn't going to come back.

4

I'm not sure what I was expecting from Fenchurch International, but I walked past the drab three-storey building twice before I noticed it was there and even then I wasn't sure I was right: it didn't have any signage and one of the numbers had fallen off. The area was prestigious enough – this was, after all, the financial district of the City of London – but the office had all the charm of a civic building put up on the cheap back in the seventies. The architecture was strikingly utilitarian, all concrete and glass, with four rows of identical windows and a nasty revolving door. This led into a cramped reception area with a single woman working on her nails, a headset connecting her to an old-fashioned console on a faux-marble desk.

'Hello. Can I help you?' She brightened up when she saw me. I got the impression that despite her job description, this was a receptionist who didn't have that many guests to receive.

'I'm here to see Mr Morton.'

'And you are?'

'Anthony Green.' It was probably stupid of me to use my wife's name. I'd be found out eventually. But it had occurred to me that if I had gone in as myself, they would almost certainly have known my connection with Hawthorne and might have refused to see me.

'Fourth floor. Room five. You can use the lift.'

The lift was as out of date as the rest of the building, with solid aluminium doors and chunky buttons that sprang back when they were pushed. It moved slowly. The fourth-floor corridor was equally disappointing: not shabby or cheap – despite everything, the rent on this place must have been astronomical – but almost deliberately unimpressive. It must have been years since I had last walked on parquet flooring. A woman with spectacles and her hair tied in a bun hurried past me, nervous and unsmiling, clutching a bundle of papers. I walked past Rooms 1 to 4 and knocked at the one at the end of the corridor.

'Come!'

Why do some people use that construction? Why do they drop the 'in'? The voice had come from the other side of the door and I opened it to find myself in a small, square room with a window looking out over railway lines branching out from Fenchurch Street Station, which was about five minutes' walk away. A man was sitting behind the sort of desk a child or a cartoonist might draw. He had been typing on a laptop computer, but he closed the lid as I came in and looked up affably.

'Mr Green?'

'Mr Morton?'

'Alastair Morton. Please . . .' He gestured me towards the two identical armchairs that faced each other across an ugly glass coffee table with a couple of files on top.

I examined him as we sat down. He was not an attractive man; somewhere in his forties, out of shape, with a sprouting of hair on his chin that was too scrappy to be a beard, but which nonetheless must have been grown by design. His eyes were tired and his skin was not good. He was wearing a dark jacket and jeans with an open-neck shirt – the same uniform as those Californian tech entrepreneurs who are worth billions and are brilliant enough to have invented some new algorithm or sent tourists into space, but who work on their appearance to suggest the opposite. He had difficulty breathing. Even the short journey from the desk to the chair had tired him. I wondered if he was ill.

Certainly, it was hard to believe that this was the man who employed Hawthorne, his adoptive brother, Roland, and quite possibly John Dudley too. Nothing about him fitted what Lady Barraclough had told me – her sense of being victimised and humiliated. Perhaps she'd met someone else.

'So you're looking for a missing person,' he began. His voice was throaty. He licked his lips at the end of the sentence.

'Yes.'

'And you were recommended to us by Lady Barraclough.'

'That's right. She spoke very highly of you.'

'That's very good of her. How is she?'

'Not terribly well, I'm afraid.'

'Well, it was an unpleasant business.' He sniffed apologetically, took out a paper tissue and wiped his nose. 'Who is it you want to find?'

'His name is John Dudley. He used to be a police officer. I know very little about him. He may have worked in Bristol. When I met him, he was working as a private detective and it occurred to me that he might be employed by you.'

'There's no John Dudley working here as far as I know. Why do you need to find him?'

'I can't really explain. There's something I want to ask him.'

Morton considered this. 'What else can you tell me?'

'I have his photograph.' I took out the picture I had been given by Hawthorne. It showed the two of them together. 'This was taken five years ago. John Dudley is standing on the left. The man who's with him is called Daniel Hawthorne.'

'Mr Hawthorne can't help you?'

'He won't help me. He doesn't want me to meet Dudley.' Morton had only glanced at the photograph. He didn't seem to have recognised Hawthorne and hadn't reacted at all to his name.

'Where was this taken?' he asked.

'Riverview Close. It's a private street in Richmond.'

He laid the picture down. 'I'd have thought it would be a simple matter to find him,' he said.

'For you, perhaps. But I'm certain that Hawthorne works for you. Lady Barraclough told me that she met him. I'd be interested to know anything you can tell me about him.'

'What, exactly?'

'I want to know how his parents died and what happened in Reeth.'

That was the moment when the pretence ended. I saw it in his eyes: a flash of intelligence, even cruelty. Alistair Morton had known who I was before I even walked into the room. All along, he'd been toying with me, seeing where this was going to lead. We looked at each other like two actors who have come to the end of a rehearsal and can now put down their lines.

'Hawthorne isn't going to be pleased that you came here,' he said.

'You know who I am.'

'You think we'd just let anyone walk in here?' Now he was having less trouble with his breathing. 'Who do you think we are? The second you emailed us from your wife's computer, we knew everything about her – who she was married to and therefore, obviously, who and what you were. For what it's worth, you also gave us access to the financial accounts of her film production company for the last seven years, her per-sonal bank details, all her email correspondence and seven thousand, two hundred and thirty family snaps. If I were you, I'd think twice before doing that again.'

'Does Kevin Chakraborty work for you?' I asked.

He ignored this. 'We know all about you too. Born in Stanmore in 1955. Unhappy schooldays – you seem to have talked about that at quite worrisome length. Both parents dead of cancer. You ought to have regular scans.'

'How do you know I don't?'

'Your wife, your sons, your Labrador . . . everything. Did you really think it was a good idea walking in here, pretending to be a client?'

'Well, it seems to have worked,' I said. 'I've managed to meet you.'

'You needn't have bothered. I was going to call you anyway. I was thinking we might have a drink.'

'You've read my books about Hawthorne?'

'I've read all four of them. I can't say I enjoyed them.'

'I'm sorry to hear it.' Then I remembered. 'The last one hasn't been published yet!'

'I want you to understand that I'm not at all happy about this project of yours: you and Hawthorne. I was very annoyed that he came to you with the idea in the first place. I don't want to be part of your narrative. In my business, we like to keep a low profile. In fact, no profile at all is preferable.'

'What exactly is your business?' I asked.

'Security.' He made it sound obvious. 'I've also read some of the book you're writing at the moment. Do you have a title yet?'

'I'm thinking about *Death Comes to a Close*.'

He frowned. 'I don't get it.'

'It's a play on words.'

'I see that. But it doesn't really make any sense. It's life that normally comes to a close. How about *Close to Death*? That's a little more direct.' He shrugged. 'Not that it really matters.

I'd much rather this book didn't appear. Don't you have other fish to fry?'

'What are you talking about?' I asked.

'You're a busy man. The Ian Fleming estate wants a new Bond novel. You have television projects. You could find yourself doing something more constructive – and safer – than writing about Hawthorne.'

'Are you threatening me?'

He looked at me blankly. 'I haven't said a single word that anyone could say was threatening – and you might as well know that this conversation is being recorded to protect both our interests. Anyway, you've missed the point. I'm thinking of what's best for you. I know what happened at Riverview Close five years ago and let me assure you that the story doesn't end well. Not for Hawthorne. Not for you. Your readers aren't going to like it one little bit.'

'Perhaps I should be the judge of that, Mr Morton.'

'Do you know who killed Giles Kenworthy?'

That threw me. 'I have my suspicions,' I said.

He smiled at that. 'If you'll forgive me for saying so, you don't ever get it right. You don't even come close.'

'Do you know?'

'Of course I do. It's one of the first rules in my line of business: never ask a question unless you already have the answer.' He paused. 'Would you like me to tell you?'

I sat and stared.

It was the most perplexing, the most difficult question I

had ever been asked and I didn't have any idea how to reply. Did I want to know who had killed Giles Kenworthy? Of course I did. It was the whole point of the book and it would be wonderful, just for once, to be ahead of the game – by which I mean, ahead of Hawthorne. I had spent hours and hours raking through the documents he had given me, trying to decipher the information that might be useful and setting aside anything that was not. If I knew the answer, it would save me hours of time – reading, researching, reimagining.

But did I want Morton to tell me? I wasn't so sure. This felt like the wrong time. The solution comes at the end of a murder mystery, not halfway through. It would be like cheating. It would take away the reason for finishing the book, a bit like being given the bill before the end of a meal. Everything that followed would be an anticlimax. And did I really want to be in debt to a man like this? I understood exactly what Lady Barraclough had said. He had made the offer quite deliberately. He was taunting me with it. And if I accepted, I would make the book his.

And yet I had to know. I couldn't stop myself.

'All right,' I said. 'Tell me.'

He smiled. A vampire smile.

'It was Roderick Browne, the dentist. He would have done anything to protect his wife and he killed Giles Kenworthy to stop the swimming pool being built. That was the end of the matter. Detective Superintendent Khan was given the credit for a successful investigation. Hawthorne was quietly removed from the case.'

I sat back, reeling. Could it really be so simple? I couldn't believe it. All the questions, all the clues, all the dissimulations, all the different smokescreens added up to that? The killer was one of the most obvious suspects with a motive he hadn't even bothered to hide? I'd almost have preferred Sarah, the gardener. At the same time, I knew that Morton had enjoyed telling me. He had just committed the cardinal crime in crime fiction, the one thing that no critic, however vituperative, has ever done. He had told me the ending before I had got to the end.

'Why should I believe you . . . ?' I stammered.

He had been ready for this. 'Why would I lie?' he asked. He opened one of the files and took out a clipping from a tabloid newspaper. He turned it round for me to read. I saw that it had been published on 21 July 2014.

CELEBRITY DENTIST FOUND DEAD

Police have today revealed the identity of the man they believe was responsible for the death of Giles Kenworthy, the hedge fund manager found dead in his Richmond home on Tuesday morning. Roderick Browne, 49, who took his own life following the event, was once called a 'dentist to the stars' due to the number of well-known personalities who visited his clinic in Cadogan Square, London.

Mr Browne had written a detailed note confessing to the murder of his neighbour, which followed a lengthy dispute. His wife is being looked after by relatives.

Speaking at a press conference held at the scene of the original crime, Detective Superintendent Tariq Khan said: 'This is a case of a neighbourhood feud spiralling out of control. Mr Browne objected to Mr Kenworthy's plans for a new Jacuzzi and swimming pool in his garden and this led to a double tragedy. I can confirm that there are no other suspects in this investigation and to all intents and purposes, the case is closed.'

Giles Kenworthy will be cremated at Kingston Crematorium. He leaves behind a wife and two sons.

'He killed himself!' It was all I managed to say. In a way, the second death – the suicide of the dentist – was as big a shock as the revelation that he was the one who had killed Giles Kenworthy.

'That's right.' Morton smiled at me. 'There was a lot of news that week, but still, you'd have thought they'd squeeze out a few more paragraphs. Celebrity dentists. They don't gas themselves every day.'

'Is that how he did it? Gas?'

'Nitrous oxide. Laughing gas. I don't think he can have found it too amusing, though.'

I sat there, reeling. Part of me was wondering if Morton was tricking me, if he'd produced a fake newspaper report to throw me off the track. But that made no sense. The article felt real and he knew perfectly well that I could cross-check it with other stories on the net. No. This was the solution. I could see it in his eyes, his cold assurance.

'Can I get you a glass of water?' Morton asked. 'You look a bit shocked.'

'I am shocked,' I said. 'I wasn't expecting you to blurt it out like that.'

'It's too bad. But I'm sure you understand. I needed to prove to you that it's time to move on. There's no point writing the book.'

Of course that was why he had done it. He simply wanted me to stop.

'I don't agree,' I said. From shock to dismay to anger and now to recovery, I was running rapidly through the emotions. 'Just because I know the ending, it doesn't mean I have to tell the reader. Once the book is finished, I may be able to twist it all round.' I was already thinking of ways to rewrite the pages I'd done.

'You don't know what you're doing.'

'I know exactly what I'm doing. Why don't you want me to write it, Mr Morton? Who exactly are you trying to protect?'

'I already told you . . .'

'Is it Hawthorne? You said the story didn't end well for him. What happened? What did he do?'

'I think I've said enough.' Morton's eyes had narrowed. Right then I saw past the appearance and knew that this was one man I wouldn't want as an enemy. 'I suggest you think very carefully,' he went on. 'The story doesn't end the way you think it's going to. You may discover things about Hawthorne that you wish you hadn't known and once you uncover them, there'll be no going back. It may end your friendship with him. Hawthorne is clever. He's very useful to us. But you know as well as I do that there's a darker side to his nature. You remember how and why he left the police force. Trust me, Anthony. There are plenty of other stories you can tell. Leave this one alone.'

The interview was over. Alastair Morton stood up.

'It was nice to meet you,' he said.

I stood up. We did not shake hands. I walked back to the lift, which seemed to take even longer to return to the ground floor. I was totally confused. Roderick Browne was the killer. Roderick Browne was dead. How was I going to write my way around that? And what had Morton meant by those parting words, *'The story doesn't end the way you think it's going to'*? What else was going to happen? Suddenly I needed to get back to my office, to break open the next raft of documents. What had started as a simple act of vengeance in a quiet suburban setting had already turned into something much darker – and I couldn't help wondering . . .

Was there worse still to come?

FIVE

ANOTHER DEATH

1

Hawthorne and Dudley knew something was wrong the moment they got back to Riverview Close the next morning. The ambulance had returned, along with a fleet of police cars. The number of officers on the scene had increased. The gaggle of journalists who had attended the murder of Giles Kenworthy was back too, more of them this time. There was also a constable standing guard at the archway. He had been friendly enough the day before, but this time he blocked their path.

'DS Khan wants to talk to you,' he explained.

'Well, we can find him . . .' Dudley replied.

'He says you're to wait here.'

The policeman spoke briefly into his radio, but it was another ten minutes before Khan wandered over, smartly dressed in a navy blue suit and brown shoes, with his silver hair neatly brushed. As the cameras clicked, snatching another dozen photographs for the next day's news, he seemed not to have noticed them and it must have been no more than a coincidence that he had presented the reporters with his best profile and his most serious, businesslike face. This changed as he approached Hawthorne and Dudley. He seemed irritated that they had arrived.

'Nice of you to show up,' he began, glancing at his watch. It was after ten o'clock.

'Seven-hour shift,' Dudley replied, cheerfully.

'Well, I'm afraid you've wasted your time.'

'You've made an arrest?'

'Not exactly. But as far as I'm concerned, the case is closed.' He lowered his voice, keeping his back to the press pack. 'Roderick Browne. He's written a letter confessing to the crime and I'm afraid he's taken his own life.'

'How?' Hawthorne asked.

Khan shook his head. 'That's not the first question I would have asked, but it makes no difference because there's nothing more for you to do. I would have called you to tell you not to show up, but as you can imagine, I've been busy. You're off the case. I'm sorry I wasted your time, but I don't need you any more.'

'You owe us for two days,' Dudley said.

'One day. But I'm a reasonable man. I'll throw in the tube fare.'

'We came by taxi.'

'That's your lookout.'

It was remarkable how quickly Khan had turned against them. He had been reluctant to employ them in the first place, but it was almost as if he was blaming them for the way things had turned out. A crime that had effectively solved itself and a killer who had escaped justice – neither of these would provide the publicity and promotion he had hoped for. Worse still, his use of Hawthorne would have sent a signal to his superior officers. He had shown a lack of confidence in his own abilities when if he'd just waited a couple of days the whole thing would have gone away.

'I don't believe Roderick Browne killed anyone,' Hawthorne said. 'And that includes himself.'

'You don't? Really? And why is that?'

'I met him. He didn't have it in him.'

'That's right, Hawthorne. You knew him for – what? – all of half an hour? I bow to your superior instincts. But you're wrong. Roderick Browne gassed himself in his garage with a cylinder of nitrous oxide, used by dentists as a sedative. He's sitting in there right now with a plastic bag over his head.'

'What sort of bag?'

'Tesco. From the middle of Richmond.'

'Did he shop at Tesco?' Dudley sounded surprised. 'I had him down as more of a Waitrose sort of guy.'

Khan snapped back: 'I very much doubt that he thought about which supermarket he planned to advertise in his last moments! He was found this morning by Sarah Baines, the gardener. You might like to know that the garage was locked from the inside. The key was in the door.'

'So how did Sarah get in?'

'Browne's neighbour, May Winslow, was a keyholder in case of emergencies. Sarah needed to enter the garage to get her tools and start work, but there was no answer from anyone in the house, so she went next door. Mrs Winslow found her key and the two of them opened the front door, walked through the kitchen and went into the garage that way. Except they couldn't open the door because the key was in the lock – on the other side. Sarah did that old trick with a piece of wire and a sheet of newspaper. Wiggled the key out and pulled it underneath the door. Then they went in and discovered the body.'

'Are they on your suspect list?'

'There are no suspects, Hawthorne, so there is no list. Browne was in his car, which was also locked, windows and doors, with the ignition key – the only ignition key that we've been able to find – in his left trouser pocket. A locked car in a locked garage. And on his lap, right in front of him, we found a letter. It was written in his own hand and signed, setting out his intentions in plain English.' Khan smiled mirthlessly. 'I'd say that adds up to an open-and-shut case.'

'No such thing,' Hawthorne replied. 'Let us take a look. I'd say you owe it to us, Khan. You've dragged us halfway across London. Where's the harm?'

'I don't see . . .'

'And I'd like to talk to Roderick Browne's wife.'

'She's not here. Browne took her to her sister yesterday morning. He explains in the letter. He didn't want her to see what he was going to do.'

'I'd like to see the letter too.' Hawthorne took a step closer, standing right next to Khan so that there was no chance of anyone overhearing. 'Just suppose you're wrong,' he said quietly. 'Suppose there's something you've missed. If there's a killer still out there, you might even have a third death on your hands and maybe it'll be Strauss or Pennington next. How do you think that will look on your CV?'

Khan hesitated. For all his dislike of Hawthorne, he had to admit that he might have a point. Chief superintendent in two years, then commander, then all the way up to commissioner . . . He and his wife had his future all planned. From the day he'd joined the police force, he'd had more than his share of luck, but he knew that even one miscalculation could do incalculable damage to his image and, subsequently, his career. That was the trouble with being a high-flyer. There were too many bastards waiting for you to fall, and this Richmond business – two deaths in a nice, upmarket community – could all too easily go sour.

He came to a decision.

'Well, since you're here, you might as well stay. Just for today. But you're now in an unofficial capacity, as observers. You're not getting paid.'

221

It was a mean little victory. Khan had found a way of capitulating whilst still showing he was the one who pulled the strings.

He walked with them, back into Riverview Close. As they continued towards the dead man's house, Teri Strauss suddenly appeared, coming out of The Stables, clutching the edges of the silk kimono she had wrapped around herself. 'What's happened?' she demanded.

'Please go back into your home, Mrs Strauss,' Khan said.

'Is it true that Roderick is dead?'

'We'll talk to you shortly.'

They went round the side of the house, Khan leading the way. The garage was too small for the number of forensic officers who needed to get in, so they'd raised the up-and-over door to provide access from the drive. DC Goodwin was inside, in charge of a slimmed-down team.

The Skoda Octavia Mark 3 took up almost all the available space and the body was still inside it, sitting in the front seat, behind the steering wheel. The police photographers had struggled to get a good angle, and bagging the hands and feet had required unusual contortions, the procedure made all the more grotesque by the fact that Roderick had already done the same for his head. The forensic team had left much of their equipment outside. Standing in the driveway, looking into the garage, Hawthorne could see very little – a vague shape on the other side of the back window. The driver's window had been smashed. There were fragments of tinted glass scattered over the concrete floor.

Without waiting for permission, Hawthorne moved forward, avoiding a puddle on the floor, and eased himself down the side of the car. A couple of men in white protective overalls glanced at him curiously but didn't try to challenge him. Now he could see the body, the supermarket bag, the gas cylinder sitting on the passenger seat, the rubber tube stretching across.

'That's a nine-hundred-litre cylinder of medical-grade nitrous oxide, one hundred per cent pure.' Khan had followed him. 'We've already confirmed that it's the same manufacturer and supplier that Mr Browne used at his Cadogan Square clinic, and he seems to have kept spares in the basement of his house. I'll say one thing for him. He didn't do things by halves. As well as the gas, he'd taken an overdose of zolpidem, a well-known sleeping pill, and there was about a quarter of a bottle of Scotch in his bloodstream. Put them together, though, and they still wouldn't have been enough to kill him. My guess is that he was already half-asleep when he turned on the gas. He arranged things so he slept through his own death.'

'Who broke the window?' Hawthorne asked.

'That was Sarah Baines. It was the right thing to do. When she and Mrs Winslow entered the garage, the car's windows and doors were all locked. Mr Browne wasn't moving, but there was always a chance he could have still been alive. She smashed the window, which set off the alarm and woke up all the neighbours, if they weren't already up and about. The moment she leaned in, she saw it was too late. He was a goner.'

'You're aware of her prison record?'

'Burglary and a pub brawl where someone got glassed. Of course I know. But this is a different league. Roderick Browne liked her. When I spoke to him, he only had good things to say.'

'When was the time of death?' Dudley asked, standing at the entrance.

'Just before midnight.'

'The same as Giles Kenworthy. The middle of the night seems a popular time to get yourself done in if you're living in Riverview Close.'

'He wasn't done in.' Khan glowered at Dudley. 'Mrs Winslow and Sarah Baines came in, as I explained. The up-and-over door was bolted from the inside and they entered through the house. Mrs Winslow was the first to see the body and as you can imagine, she was deeply shocked. If you talk to her, it would be nice if you could try and hold back on that sense of humour of yours.'

They were preparing to lever the body out. Roderick Browne's head was still concealed.

'Has anyone taken that bag off yet?' Dudley asked.

'No. Why do you ask?'

'It'll just come as a bit of a surprise if you discover that it's not the dentist sitting in the car.'

Khan felt a brief moment of unease, then remembered that the dead man was wearing some of the same clothes he'd had on the day before: white shirt, linen trousers, moccasins – along with a pale blue jacket that was very much in Roderick Browne's style. It was him all right. It had to be.

Meanwhile, Hawthorne had turned his attention to the rest of the garage. He mentally ticked off the gardening tools, the paint pots and brushes, the golf clubs, the tap with its plastic bucket . . . all the items that had been there when he had visited the day before. There were a few additions and he looked at these with particular interest. A box of electrical bits and pieces – plugs, cables, connectors – had been dumped on one side of the door. A Dyson hoover with a cracked plastic casing was propped up next to it. A dustbin bag revealed a collection of old DVDs. 'Where did these come from?' he asked Khan.

Khan was standing on the other side of the car. He was aware that everyone in the garage could hear what was being said. 'Maybe he was having a clear-out,' he suggested.

'Having a spring clean before he topped himself?'

'Leaving things nice and tidy behind him. You don't know what was in his mind. What are you doing now . . . ?'

Hawthorne was being careful not to touch anything, but he was craning his neck, examining the skylight above the

225

car. It projected above the flat roof, but it hadn't been constructed in a way that allowed it to open.

'You're thinking that someone could have got in or out via the roof,' Khan said. 'Well, DC Goodwin went up there just before you arrived. The whole thing is screwed in and it looks as if the screws have rusted solid. She got a screwdriver and tried to undo them. They wouldn't budge.'

'What's happened to the suicide note?'

'It's in the house. Now, if you don't mind, I'd ask you to leave the crime scene. We need to get the body out.'

'Whatever you say, Detective Superintendent.'

The three men went back into the house and sat down at the kitchen table.

'It's not suicide,' Hawthorne said.

'It can't be anything else,' Khan replied, sourly.

'A dead man in a locked car in a locked garage. That's a new definition of a riddle wrapped in a mystery locked in an enigma,' Dudley misquoted.

'Where's this suicide note?' Hawthorne asked.

'It's been taken away for examination, but I've got a picture.' Khan had left his laptop on the table and he opened it, then swung it round to show them a set of photographs on the screen. The note had been written on both sides of a single sheet of paper in a loose, flowery scrawl. Roderick Browne had used turquoise ink. Hawthorne and Dudley read it together.

My dearest Fee,

I am so, so sorry. I did something very stupid and I have sent you away because I cannot bear you to see the consequences. I know what I must do. I have to pay the price. I told you that you might feel better staying at your sister and this is the first time I ever lied to you. The truth is that I do not want you to see this, my love. You are better out of it.

Be strong. I know you have had to put up with so much on account of your illness. I wish I could have done more for you, but at least you are financially secure and will be able to stay in the house you love. The Kenworthys will go, I am sure of it. The swimming pool will never be built. You will be left in peace.

Goodbye, my dearest. We will see each other again on the other side.

All my love,
Roderick

'I'd say that's pretty conclusive,' Khan muttered. 'All that's missing is a selfie taken when he was getting in the car with the gas cylinder and the plastic bag. Wouldn't you agree?'

Hawthorne said nothing. He tapped a keyboard and another image appeared, a second evidence bag.

227

'Do you mind?' Khan was offended.

'What's this?' Hawthorne asked.

He was looking at a photograph of a slim white paper tube, about an inch long, with a swirly red pattern.

'I'm not sure that's relevant to what happened,' Khan said. 'It was in the breast pocket of the deceased's jacket. It's a drinking straw.'

'You mean part of one.'

'Yes.' Khan sniffed. 'It's too early to say, but there's no indication that Mr Browne ever used illegal substances.'

'That's a good point, Detective Superintendent,' Hawthorne said. It was true that cocaine users often used a piece cut off a drinking straw to inhale the drug. Wealthier addicts were quite likely to have a personalised tube made out of silver or gold.

'Mind you, we can't be sure,' Khan went on. 'He had a lot of celebrity clients.'

They were interrupted by the sound of raised voices out in the hall. Someone was arguing with one of the policemen. 'What now?' Khan asked. He walked out of the kitchen. Hawthorne and Dudley followed.

A young man had arrived, casually dressed, with a Whole Foods bag over his shoulder. He was thin and delicate, not someone who might be expected to push his way in. He looked upset. A uniformed policeman was trying to stop him coming any further.

'Leave this to me,' Khan said, taking over. The policeman

stepped away and he went up to the man. 'Who are you?' he asked.

'I'm Mrs Browne's carer.' Damien Shaw had clearly been taken aback to find so many policemen at Riverview Close. Had he so quickly forgotten about the murder that had taken place just a few days before? Or had no one told him?

'Mrs Browne isn't here.'

'I know. But I wanted to make the house nice for her when she got back from her sister's. I was going to change the sheets and maybe do a bit of dusting.' Damien looked around him. 'Why are there so many policemen here? Has this got something to do with Giles Kenworthy? Mr Browne called me. He told me about it. He sounded very upset.'

'Stop there!' Hawthorne had taken charge. 'Let's talk in the kitchen. It may be more comfortable.'

Khan nodded as if it had been his suggestion in the first place.

'How did you get into the close?' he asked, once they were sitting round the table in the kitchen with the laptop closed and pushed aside.

'The constable there tried to stop me. He was very rude, even though I told them I worked here.'

'Do you have a set of keys to this house?'

'Yes. Of course.' Damien took out a ring and held up a single key. 'This opens the front door.'

Hawthorne took over. 'You said you spoke to Mr Browne,' he said. 'When was that?'

'Yesterday morning.'

'What time exactly?'

'Ten o'clock.' That was before Hawthorne had met Browne and interviewed him in this same room. The dentist had been a bundle of nerves, still in shock after the murder of his neighbour. 'He called me at home. I don't come in Wednesdays, but he wanted to tell me what had happened, that someone had killed Mr Kenworthy . . . with a crossbow! He told me that it was his crossbow that had been used. The one in the garage.'

'Did you know it was there?'

'Oh, yes. He never made any secret of it. Everyone knew.' Damien paused. 'I imagine that's why he was so upset. He was in a real state, if you want the truth. I was quite worried about him and I offered to come over, but he said he'd be OK.'

'Did he have any thoughts? Any suspicions as to who might have done it?' Khan asked.

'No. Not that he said.'

'So you left him on his own,' Khan said, accusingly.

'That's not fair. It wasn't like that at all!' Now Damien was indignant. 'What was I meant to do? It wasn't as if I was *his* carer! My job was to look after Felicity, and anyway, he had plenty of friends he could turn to. As a matter of fact, he mentioned he was going to talk to Adam Strauss. "Adam will help. Adam will know what to do." That's what he said to me. Those were his very words.'

'Why Adam Strauss?' Dudley asked.

'The two of them were close. Adam gave Roderick a lot of support in the early days when Felicity got ill, and in fact it was Adam who gave him the name of the agency that I work for, so I'm grateful to him for that. But it wasn't just him. The other neighbours were very kind too. Tom Beresford was always asking after Felicity, and the old ladies next door are sweethearts. But Adam knew Roderick even before they both ended up living in Riverview Close. Adam was a patient of his — did you know that? The others may have talked the talk, but he was the one who came round and offered proper advice and sympathy. I'm sure Roderick was grateful.'

There was a short silence.

'So Roderick Browne told you that Giles Kenworthy had been killed,' Hawthorne said. 'How did you react to that news, Damien?'

'How do you think? I was horrified! I know he wasn't very popular, but I'd never even met Mr Kenworthy . . . not properly. I saw him quite a few times going in and out and he struck me as a bit high and mighty. I knew how much trouble he was causing everyone. Felicity was very upset that he was going to build this swimming pool and ruin her view. She even said they might have to move.'

'What else did Roderick tell you?'

Damien thought back. He shrugged. 'Nothing very much. He did say that he was taking Felicity to her sister in Woking. He didn't want her here with all this police activity going on.'

231

Hawthorne knew this already. 'So her sister was going to look after her.'

'Yes. It worked very well. As I said, I don't work Wednesdays. I only come in three times a week. So I said I'd see him today and we rang off—'

'Mr Browne was expecting you today?' Hawthorne cut in.

'Yes. That's why I'm here.' Damien stopped. An awful thought had occurred to him. 'Where is he?'

'I'm afraid Mr Browne is dead,' Khan said.

'What?' In an instant, all the colour had left Damien's face. He looked as if he was about to faint. 'How?' he whispered. 'What happened?'

'Get him a glass of water,' Hawthorne muttered. Dudley went over to the sink. 'The police believe he may have taken his own life,' he said.

'But that's impossible! There's no way he'd do that.'

'He'd been under a lot of strain.' Khan was doing his best to keep the situation under control. 'How long had you been looking after his wife?' he asked.

'Two years . . .' Damien's eyes were filled with tears. Dudley returned with a glass of water and Damien drank it all in one go. When he put the glass down, his hands were shaking. 'I come in Mondays, Thursdays and Fridays . . .' he went on. 'Felicity's a lovely lady. We get on together brilliantly. I had to take a week off just a short while ago and she hated it. She said she couldn't manage without me.' He wiped his eyes with the back of his hand. 'Does she know?'

'She has been informed,' Khan said.

'I should go to her! She must be in shock. This is terrible. I can't even think how she'll manage without him.'

'I think you should stay away for the time being,' Khan warned him.

'But Roderick was everything to her. He adored Felicity. He'd never leave her on her own.'

Khan didn't look happy with Damien's assessment and moved on quickly. 'I do have one more question for you, Mr Shaw,' he said. 'I don't suppose you can tell me where Mr Browne kept his mobile phone?'

Damien nodded. 'It'll be on the chest of drawers in the hall. Roderick was always losing things, so he was quite religious about it. He always left it there.'

'I didn't see it.' Khan glanced at Hawthorne. 'We'd obviously like to look at any messages he may have sent prior to his death,' he said defensively. 'It's standard procedure.' He turned back to Damien. 'Would you like one of my officers to drive you home?'

'No. I live in Richmond. I can walk.'

'You live with your parents?' Hawthorne asked.

'With my mum.'

Hawthorne waited until Damien had left. Then he turned to Khan. 'It's interesting,' he said. 'Roderick Browne is going to kill himself. But first of all he does a bit of spring-cleaning. And you'd have thought he'd have warned his wife's carer not to come in.'

'You heard what he said, Hawthorne,' Khan returned. 'Damien spoke to him after Giles Kenworthy died. He was frightened. He wasn't making any sense. That was because he knew what he'd done and he'd decided to take the easy way out.'

'When did you interview Roderick Browne?' Hawthorne asked. 'You told us he was your prime suspect.' A thought occurred to him. 'Did you take him into the station?'

'I interviewed him the morning after Giles Kenworthy's body had been discovered.' Khan looked guilty. 'That was here – in his own home. Based on what he said, I decided to interrogate him more formally the next day, so I had him taken to Shepherd's Bush.'

'Was that before or after he dropped his wife in Woking?'

'It was in the afternoon, when he got back.'

'How long did you keep him?'

'Two hours.'

'Under caution?'

Khan was becoming increasingly uncomfortable as the consequences of what he had done became apparent to him. 'Yes.'

'Poor bastard,' Dudley said. 'He must have been terrified. If he did kill himself, at least we know why.' He shook his head reproachfully. 'You scared the living daylights out of him, Detective Superintendent. It may be that you didn't give him any other choice.'

2

'I cannot tell you how upset I am,' May Winslow said.

'He was a lovely man,' Phyllis agreed. She pulled a tissue out of her sleeve and touched it to her cheek.

'Always friendly, always ready to lend a helping hand. We moved into the close at the same time as him and we hit it off straight away. He helped us move some of the furniture and he always asked us if we needed anything when he went to the shops. He never minded us knocking on his door if something went wrong.'

'The oven,' Phyllis reminded her. 'Do you remember that?'

'It was so embarrassing.' May sighed. 'It was only the timer. Phyllis had turned it on accidentally. I'm not blaming you, dear! Why do they have to make these things so complicated? But we ate salads and cold food for a week before he came and sorted it for us. Nothing was ever too much trouble.'

The sitting room of The Gables had not been designed for

five people. It was too small, with too many ornaments, too many pictures on the wall, and furniture that was a little too big for the area in which it stood. An old-fashioned television set took up rather too much space in one corner and the only empty space in the room told its own sad story: it was where a wicker dog basket had once been placed. A wooden cross stood on the mantelpiece and a Bible sat prominently on an otherwise unnecessary side table. There was no other indication of the ladies' religious past.

May and Phyllis each had an armchair that was most definitely theirs, moulded to their exact shape over the fourteen years they had lived there. Hawthorne and Dudley were pressed together on a floral-patterned sofa while Khan perched on a stool brought in from the kitchen. The front windows looked out onto the close, but May had drawn the curtains to blot out the sight of the police cars and all the activity taking place next door. As a result, the air in the room was warm and stale. It still smelled of Ellery.

'Did Mr Browne ever talk to you about his animosity towards Giles Kenworthy?' Khan asked, shifting uncomfortably on his stool. He didn't want to be here – he had already interviewed both women and he was sure that they had nothing more to say – but he hadn't been keen to let Hawthorne continue on his own. If any further information presented itself regarding the death of Roderick Browne, he wanted to be the first to hear it.

'I'm not sure that "animosity" is the right word, Detective Superintendent,' May replied. 'He didn't really have feelings

236

towards Mr Kenworthy. Of course he was upset about the pool. Mrs Browne hardly ever leaves her bed these days and it mattered to her, the view from the window.'

'A view is important,' Phyllis agreed.

'I'm sure we all know that, dear.' May gave her friend a pinched smile. 'All I'm saying is that Mr Browne was a very kind and very gentle man who didn't harbour grudges and I find it impossible to believe that he killed anyone.'

'Then why do you think he committed suicide?' Khan asked.

'You should never use the word "committed" in that context, Detective Superintendent. Suicide may be a sin, but it is not a crime! As to your question, I'm afraid I have no answer. I saw him with my own eyes, sitting in that car with a bag over his head. I wish I hadn't. It's something I will take with me to the grave. All I can say is, he was questioned yesterday at Shepherd's Bush Police Station for two whole hours and he was terribly upset.'

Khan squirmed, avoiding Hawthorne's eye. 'He told you this?'

'Not me. Phyllis. She spoke to him over the garden hedge.'

'He wasn't himself,' Phyllis said. She seemed to be too nervous of May to utter more than three words.

'What did he say to you?' Dudley asked. He had his notebook poised. 'And how do you spell your name, by the way?'

'Moore. Phyllis Moore.'

'Is that with two o's? Or like St Thomas?'

'Two o's.'

Dudley wrote this down.

Phyllis glanced at May for permission, then continued. 'It was late in the afternoon. He'd just come back in a police car! We didn't speak very much. He said that he'd been asked a lot of questions and that he was relieved he had taken his wife to her sister's.'

'Did he think he was about to be arrested?' Hawthorne asked.

'He didn't say. But the police wouldn't have arrested him for something he hadn't done.'

'I'm sure that's never happened,' Dudley agreed.

'He told me he was going to call Adam Strauss and ask him for advice.'

Hawthorne frowned. 'Why not Andrew Pennington? He was a barrister. He'd know a lot more.'

'That's a very good point. I would have thought Mr Pennington would be exactly the right person to go to. I can't imagine why he didn't.'

Dudley wrote something down in his notebook. He added a question mark and circled it.

'How did the two of you come to be living in Richmond?' Khan asked.

'You were nuns.' Hawthorne made it sound improbable, like the first line of a joke.

'We met at the Franciscan Convent of St Clare in Osmond-thorpe, near Leeds,' May said.

'We were cellies,' Phyllis added.

'That's what we called the sisters who shared rooms. There

was very little space. I arrived two years before Phyllis – and we left at the same time.'

'How long were you there for?'

'Almost three decades. I went in when I was in my forties.'

'Why?' Hawthorne sounded almost hostile.

'It's rather personal, Mr Hawthorne. And I don't see that it has anything to do with what's happened here, but I suppose this is a murder investigation so I'll tell you what you want to know.

'I had a very unhappy marriage. I was living in Chester at the time and I was in an abusive relationship. My husband was an alcoholic and hurt me quite badly on many occasions. Once, he even put me in hospital. And yet I found myself unable to leave him. I'm told this is not uncommon in cases like mine. It was a bit like Stockholm syndrome. Is that the one I mean? We had a son and I did my best to protect him until he turned eighteen and left home. I thank the Lord that he had no idea what his father was like. David had a hold over me that I cannot explain to this day. He destroyed my self-confidence, my inner resolve. He controlled my every waking moment until the day he died of a heart attack . . . and I'm ashamed to say I didn't mourn him for a single minute. The bigger question was – what was I going to do? I was forty. I had a house, a little money and no income.

'It's funny, really. I had always been a regular churchgoer, although I didn't think of myself as a religious person. It was more of a respite from David. He would drink on Saturday night and sleep it off on Sunday, so church was somewhere for me to go. The vicar was a friend of mine and after David died, she talked to me about St Clare's. At first, the idea was that I might go there for a month or two while I thought about what I might do next, but from the moment I arrived, I felt happy and didn't want to leave. It was a safe space. I liked the simplicity . . . Not so much the prayers and the meditation but the friendship and the sense that I was doing something useful. We ran soup kitchens and food pantries in Bradford and Leeds. We visited families in their homes. It was the first time in my life that I actually felt wanted.'

Dudley turned to Phyllis. 'Were you ever married?' he asked.

Phyllis seemed reluctant to answer. She lowered her head. 'My husband passed away.' That was all she would say.

'So why did you leave the convent?' Hawthorne continued.

May answered. 'It was time. Almost thirty years. Phyllis and I often spoke at night about what we might do after St Clare's. As she just told you, we shared a room.'

'We weren't meant to speak to each other after vespers,' Phyllis added. 'But we'd whisper to each other in the darkness.'

'It's true. There was no talking after night prayer. Maybe that little disobedience should have told me something.' May paused. 'And then an aunt of mine died and left me money. It was like something out of a fairy story! I'd already given everything I had to the convent and the mother superior expected me to do the same with my inheritance. But I didn't agree, I'm afraid. I saw it as a sign that it was time to move on – a sign from God, if you like. So I talked to Phyllis and we left together the same day.'

'Why Richmond?'

'This is where I grew up. I saw the house on the internet and I thought it looked perfect.'

'It is perfect,' Phyllis agreed. 'We've been very happy here.'

'Until all this business started, anyway.'

'You run a bookshop selling crime fiction,' Dudley said. 'That seems like a strange occupation after all those years in a convent.'

'Well, we had to do something to keep ourselves busy,' May replied. 'I used to like Gladys Mitchell when I was a girl. She wrote over sixty novels, you know. But they were never violent. They were never horrible like so much modern fiction. And lovely Dorothy, too. And Agatha. All this modern interest in dead bodies and women being killed – and children too! Why would anyone want to read stories like that? That was what gave me the idea for The Tea Cosy. We never stock books with bad language, and I'm afraid there are a lot of writers we simply won't touch. The truth is, we don't make a lot of money out of it, but that isn't the point.'

'We used to love walking up there with Ellery,' Phyllis said sadly.

Khan turned to Hawthorne. 'Is there anything else you want to ask?'

'One thing.' He turned to May. 'You had a spare key to the Brownes' home.'

'That's right.'

'Who else knew you had it?'

'Nobody . . . apart from Sarah. Mr Browne told her I had it so she could get into the house if a pipe burst or something. But she didn't know where it was kept. I had it in my medicine box in the bathroom cabinet. Nobody knew it was there.'

'Sarah told us that she only got employed here thanks to you,' Hawthorne said.

'It's true.' May pulled a face, as if she had just sniffed sour milk. 'She was knocking on doors, looking for work, and we took her on. You have to give young people a chance these days. Once she started working for us, we recommended her to other people in the close.'

'We wouldn't have gone anywhere near her if we'd known what she was going to do,' Phyllis said, fresh tears welling in her eyes.

'You blame her for the death of your dog.'

'How could anyone do anything as horrible as that – and to an animal that had never done any harm to anyone? I wouldn't have believed it – but she had scratches on her arms. I asked her about that. She said she'd been clearing a dead rose bush for Mr Strauss, but that's not what it looks like to me.'

'Does she still look after your garden?'

May paused. 'We have no choice. It's not so easy to find help around here.'

Hawthorne smiled at Khan. 'No further questions,' he said.

242

3

No tea or butter cookies were served at The Stables this time. Adam Strauss was slumped in an armchair, his hands clasped between his knees, a look of utter defeat on his face. For a man who guarded his emotions, who had learned to do so professionally, he had clearly taken a beating. He barely looked up as his wife showed Detective Superintendent Khan, Hawthorne and Dudley into the room.

'Mr Strauss . . .' Khan tried to get hold of his attention.

Strauss looked up dully. He was wearing a loose bottle-green velvet jacket and a wide-collared shirt, as if he had just come back from a late-night party, albeit one that had taken place in the nineties. 'I thought I'd see you again,' he said eventually.

'I'm sorry, sir. I know you were close to Roderick Browne.'

'He was my dentist.'

'He was more than that, as I understand it.'

'Oh, yes. We were friends. He was the one who introduced us to Riverview Close in the first place. He was thinking of buying Woodlands and he showed me the brochure. That's how I came to acquire the Lodge. I saw him last night, you know. I suppose I must have been the last person to see him alive – unless Sarah Baines came in this morning?'

'She arrived too late, sir.'

'Well, it's all down to me, then.' Strauss fell silent.

'He called you and asked you to come round,' Khan said.

'That's right. That was just after he came back from the police station.' Suddenly, Adam was angry. He looked at Khan accusingly. 'You really put him through the wringer, didn't you! Did you have to interview him at such length?'

'He was a suspect in a murder investigation, sir, and he was treated with the utmost courtesy . . .'

'We were all suspects, Detective Superintendent. God knows, I had as much reason to kill Giles Kenworthy as anyone.'

'His children did thousands of pounds' worth of damage,' Teri cut in. She had taken a seat next to her husband. Now she reached out and took his hand. 'They smashed my husband's beautiful chess set. And their father didn't give a damn.'

'But it was Roderick Browne's crossbow.'

Strauss shook his head. 'Anyone could have taken it . . . including me! I was in and out of his house all the time. There's a corridor at the back, next to the kitchen. It leads straight in. Roderick would be upstairs half the time, fetching and carrying for Felicity. It would have been easy to walk in and take it.' He stared at Khan. 'You picked on him and you browbeat him and although it pains me to say it, you may have been responsible for his suicide, Detective Superintendent. He was a middle-aged man with the worry of a very sick wife and then you come barging in, making false accusations. I think you should be ashamed of yourself.'

'I didn't accuse him of anything, sir.'

'So what did you talk about for over two hours? The weather?'

If Hawthorne had been enjoying the sight of Khan being put in his place, he was careful not to show it. 'You said you saw Mr Browne,' he said. 'Can you tell us what happened?'

Strauss nodded. 'Teri, can you get me a glass of mineral water?'

Teri got up and went over to the fridge without saying a word.

'I got the call from him at about six o'clock yesterday evening,' Strauss continued. 'He asked me if I'd come over. He said he wanted my advice.'

'It would be helpful if I could see your mobile,' Khan said. 'We'll need to verify all the timings.'

'Of course. But I'd have thought you could get that off Roderick's.'

Khan looked embarrassed. 'Mr Browne seems to have misplaced his phone. We're still looking for it.'

245

'Are you saying someone's stolen it?'

'No, sir. We just can't find it.'

'It seems to me that so far you haven't helped solve anything at all.'

'Mr Browne confessed to the murder of Giles Kenworthy.' Khan did his best to hold his ground. 'We have every reason to believe that he killed himself to escape justice.'

'That's impossible. I don't believe it.'

'He left behind a letter. He couldn't have been clearer. Everything about the manner of his death suggests that he committed . . . that he decided on suicide. It would help us a great deal if you could tell me what happened when you saw him last night. What did you talk about? What was his state of mind?'

Adam Strauss calmed down a little, as if acknowledging the need to cooperate. His wife brought over a glass of fizzy water with a lemon slice and ice cubes. He didn't thank her but emptied it in one gulp and set the glass down. She took her place next to him.

'I went over to Woodlands at about half past eight, after we finished eating,' he explained. 'Roderick was on his own, of course. He'd dropped his wife off with her sister and at least it comforted him to know that she was being looked after. I got the feeling that he was nervous about being on his own. He'd had a bit to drink. There was an open bottle of Scotch on the table when I arrived.'

This accorded with what the police pathologist had found in his blood.

'Did he offer you some?' Dudley asked.

'Yes. He might have. I don't really remember. I didn't drink any.'

'Go on,' Khan said.

'We sat down and we talked. He told me that he'd had a dreadful time at the police station in Shepherd's Bush, that he'd been treated like a common criminal and even threatened.'

'Nobody threatened him,' Khan said.

'I can only tell you what he told me. He was quite sure that the police had made up their minds, that he was the one who had killed Giles Kenworthy. It was his weapon. He had a motive. He was going to be arrested and it would be the end of his practice, his marriage, his life. He might have to go to prison! If you knew Roderick, you'd know he wouldn't have lasted a week there. The thought filled him with horror.

'I tried to reassure him. I told him that everyone in the close was behind him and we knew that he hadn't shot anyone. We'd all been interviewed – first by you and then by Mr Hawthorne. Any one of us could have done it or – and I still believe this is the most likely possibility – it could have been someone from outside. I said this to you the last time you were here. Kenworthy was a hedge fund manager. Hedge fund managers have enemies.'

'How long were you with him?' Hawthorne asked.

'A couple of hours, give or take. I left about ten o'clock.'

'Was there anything in Mr Browne's manner that caused you alarm?'

'Everything in his manner caused me alarm, but if you're asking me if I thought he might kill himself, the answer's obviously no. I told Roderick to go to bed and I assured him that everything would seem better in the morning. I thought I'd helped him. By the time I left, he seemed quieter and more relaxed.' He glanced down into his empty glass. 'Now you're making me worry that I was wrong. I shouldn't have left him on his own. I should have stayed longer or maybe invited him over here.'

'You did everything you could,' Teri assured him.

'I don't know. I really don't.'

'I don't suppose anyone saw you leave?' Dudley asked.

'Why are you even asking my husband that question?' Teri cut in. 'Are you suggesting that he's lying to you? You think that he killed his friend?'

'I can assure you that such a thought never crossed my mind, Mrs Strauss,' Dudley said.

Adam held up a conciliatory hand. 'You don't need to worry yourself, my dear. They have to ask these questions. It's part of the game.' He glanced at Dudley. 'As it happens, there was someone. I heard the electric gate open and Andrew Pennington came in just as I was saying goodbye. I didn't speak to him, but I saw him and I'm sure he saw me.'

'Was he in a car or on foot?'

'On foot.'

'Adam was very upset when he arrived home,' Teri volunteered. 'His leg hurt him very much. He was tired. But if you say he had anything to do with the death of Roderick Browne, that's disgusting. You have no right to come here and say these things!'

There was a tone of dismissal in her voice. The three men stood up and made their goodbyes and Teri escorted them out of the house. Strauss stayed where he was, too exhausted to move. His wife stood there on the doorstep for a moment, glaring at Hawthorne as if all this was his fault. 'My husband has to prepare for Chennai,' she said. 'This business – murder, suicide, policemen, all these questions. We've had enough. You have to make it stop.'

She closed the door.

4

Andrew Pennington confirmed Strauss's story.

'I was playing bridge,' he said. 'My Wednesday-night game. I'll be honest and say that it was a relief to take my mind off what's happening here. There are two groups I like to play with, but that evening I was in Richmond.'

'Can you provide an address?' Khan asked.

'Of course. The Leggatts in Friars Lane. A very pleasant couple. We always meet at seven, have a quick supper and then play a few rubbers . . . usually three or four. I try to be home by ten and read for an hour before bed. You must think me a very dull old stick, but I'm afraid that's what happens when you live alone. Everything falls into a pattern. Radio 4 in the morning. A stroll before lunch. A quick nap in the afternoon. That sort of thing.

'I heard the two of them as I came through the gate. Adam Strauss was standing in the doorway. I didn't see Roderick, but I heard him speak. He was thanking Adam. "You've always been so kind to me. I'm very grateful to you." Or words to that effect. I wasn't close enough to hear them exactly. The lights went out, the front door closed and Adam walked away. I assume Roderick must have turned in. As for Adam, he went round the other side of the driveway, past Gardener's Cottage, so we didn't talk to each other. I stood outside in the fresh air for a moment, looking at the stars. I saw him go into The Stables and that was that.'

'Did you see anyone else?' Dudley asked.

Pennington stiffened. 'Why are you asking me that? I understood that Roderick's death was self-inflicted.'

'It almost certainly was,' Khan said. 'But this is still a murder investigation.'

'You're treating Roderick's death as murder?'

'No, sir. I'm referring to the murder of Giles Kenworthy – to which, I'm sorry to say, your friend Mr Browne confessed.'

Andrew shook his head. 'It's terrible. Just terrible. I never thought he would take it this far.'

For an experienced barrister, Andrew Pennington had made an elementary mistake. He had offered up more information than he had intended and Hawthorne jumped straight in. 'Are you saying you knew what Roderick Browne was going to do?' he asked.

'No, no. Not at all. I had absolutely no idea.' Andrew searched for the right words, desperately trying to find a way to escape the implications of what he had just said. 'Obviously, if I had known anything of his intentions, I would have con-tacted the appropriate authorities.'

'You must have known something. That's the only way you might have been able to stop him.' Hawthorne sounded completely reasonable but at the same time he was merciless. 'And what exactly was the "it" that you didn't think would go so far?'

'He did, on one occasion, express a very strong – indeed, a violent – dislike of his neighbour. He even went so far as to say that . . .'

'What?'

'. . . that he wanted to kill him.'

'What occasion was this?' Khan demanded. 'And why didn't you tell me any of this when I spoke to you yesterday?'

'Because I'd forgotten all about it! It was just an evening we'd had together a while ago . . . over a drink. You know how it is. You have a couple of glasses of wine, you say stupid things. Everyone does it!'

'I've never threatened to shoot a crossbow bolt through somebody's throat,' Dudley remarked.

'I'll ignore that comment, if you don't mind, Mr Dudley. What Roderick said wasn't a serious death threat and at the time I thought nothing of it. Obviously, in light of recent developments, it's only now that I find myself forced to reconsider.'

'I'm frankly amazed that a man with your experience would keep this sort of information to yourself, Mr Pennington,'

Khan said. 'I may have to ask you to come in and make another statement.'

'Of course. I'll help you any way I can. But as I've already explained, Roderick had drunk a bit too much wine and he made an off-colour remark. That's all there was to it.'

Khan stood up. The four of them had met in Pennington's sitting room and he had heard enough. But Dudley hadn't finished. 'You never answered my question,' he said.

'What question was that?' Pennington was also on his feet.

'If you saw anyone else in the close when you got back from bridge.'

'I don't feel comfortable implicating my neighbours.'

'If Mr Browne really committed suicide, you're not implicating anyone.'

'These aren't just my neighbours. They're my friends.'

'So which one of your friends did you see?'

Andrew realised he had no way of escape. 'I saw Tom Beresford,' he said, speaking the words heavily. 'He didn't go anywhere near Roderick's house. He appeared at the front door of his own place and walked round the side. He might have been going into his garage.'

'At ten o'clock at night? Did you hear him drive off?'

'I didn't hear a car. No.'

'You didn't see him head towards Mr Browne's house?'

'Definitely not. He disappeared into the shadows.'

'Like he didn't want to be seen?'

'No. It was ten o'clock at night and it was dark. He was

there one moment and gone the next.' Pennington walked to the front door and opened it. 'Maybe Tom had left something in the car,' he continued. 'It could have been as simple as that.' He turned to Khan. 'I know you have a job to do, Detective Superintendent, but you must understand that we've all known each other for years. This is our home. You're suggesting that Roderick committed the murder and killed himself out of remorse, and I have to say I'm inclined to agree with you. There seems to be no alternative explanation. So why are you continuing with this investigation? Can't you just move on and leave us all in peace?'

They left Well House and stood outside, near the gate. It was early afternoon and once again the police presence was thinning out. Khan seemed to come to a decision. 'All right,' he said. 'Are you satisfied, Hawthorne? I'd say we've come to the end of the road.'

'What road's that, Detective Superintendent?' Hawthorne asked.

'We now know that Roderick Browne threatened to kill Giles Kenworthy. It was his crossbow and he had the most obvious motive. He was under a lot of pressure, having to deal with his wife's illness, and it seems fair to say that he was acting on her behalf. If Kenworthy was dead, the pool wouldn't be built, her view would be protected and they wouldn't have to move.

'So let's move on to the suicide itself. It may well be that my interview with him upset him more than I thought, but I was not alone in the interrogation room. The whole thing was recorded. I observed all the correct procedures and Mr Browne was absolutely fine when he was taken home. We've now learned that he became distressed later in the evening and called Adam Strauss for help. He drank whisky and took an overdose of sleeping pills. He used nitrous oxide and other apparatus consistent with his work as a dentist. He wrote a suicide letter. The garage door was double-locked, the skylight was securely fastened and there was no other way in or out.

'So when I say we've come to the end of the road, I mean that I am going to recommend that we close this inquiry or, at least, that we do not interview any other witnesses. Mr Browne killed Mr Kenworthy and, out of remorse, took his own life. It's as simple as that.'

'Can I just say one thing?' Hawthorne asked.

'What?'

'If Browne's suicide is so cut and dried, why didn't he cancel the carer? If he was going to kill himself, wouldn't he have told Damien Shaw not to come in? And while we're on the subject of Damien, he doesn't believe the suicide theory either. He agreed that Browne would never have left his wife on her own. He was devoted to her! May Winslow and Phyllis Moore said much the same thing.

'But according to you, that's just what he did, and although there are a lot of unanswered questions, you seem to be ignoring them. What happened to his missing phone? And the missing car key? For someone about to top himself, Mr Browne seems to have been missing a lot. And here's something else that may not have crossed your mind. You told us that one set of keys to the Skoda were found in Browne's trouser pocket. But doesn't that strike you as odd? For a start, he didn't need the key. He wasn't going anywhere. And if he'd used it to open and shut the doors, wouldn't it have been in his hand or on the seat next to him? No one ever puts car keys in their trouser pockets – and nor do they carry a one-inch drinking straw with them, not even if they fancy a quick sniff of cocaine. Anyway, as far as I can see, Browne wasn't into that. Lots and lots of questions, but for some reason you don't seem to want to do your job.'

Khan was about to argue, but he'd had enough. 'I don't need to take this from you,' he said. 'Your work here is over and I want you to leave. I've heard a lot about you, Hawthorne, and to be honest, none of it is good. I had misgivings about inviting you here in the first place and now I see why. You meet a police officer who's making good in his career and all you want to do is stir things up. But it's not going to work with me. I'll wish you a good day.'

Khan turned on his heel and walked off.

SIX

A LOCKED-ROOM
MYSTERY

1

I have never been a huge fan of so-called 'locked-room' mysteries.

There's a very specific subgenre in the murder mystery/crime arena that has its own rules and effectively presents the reader with a seemingly impossible puzzle. It's not enough for the characters to be isolated (*The Mousetrap*, *Orient Express*). Everything has to be so fiendishly arranged that the detective has no chance of solving the puzzle . . . until he or she does.

The first and still the most famous locked-room mystery is said to be *The Murders in the Rue Morgue*, written in 1841 by Edgar Allan Poe, the man who inspired Sherlock Holmes. Here, a mother and a daughter are brutally murdered in their flat, the daughter stuffed up a chimney, but the door and the shutters are securely fastened from inside and the flat is four floors up from the street, with no way to climb in. The story has a great ending, but one that doesn't really play fair. I'm not sure a modern writer would get away with it.

The real problem of the locked-room mystery is that the mechanics are often so complicated and even contorted that it's hard to believe the murderer could go to so much trouble, and the emotions of the story can disappear in a Heath Robinson construction of cogs and wheels, mirrors, sliding doors and body doubles. As much as you may admire the solution, you are forced to suspend disbelief. The killers are so clever that they seem positively inhuman, literally so in Poe's story. It's difficult to avoid a sense of contrivance.

Try reading *The Hollow Man*, written by the 'king of crime', John Dickson Carr, in 1935. It's unquestionably brilliant, often cited as the best locked-room mystery ever written. Here a man is seen entering a professor's study, a shot rings out and the professor is found dead. There is a window, but the ground outside is covered in snow, there are no footprints and the killer has disappeared. The explanation is interminable and eventually blots out the actual reason for the murder — another crime committed long ago, blackmail and betrayal. The solution relies on chance and coincidence. The clock had broken. The snow wasn't forecast. It left me cold.

It's my belief that, these days, the best locked-room mysteries come from Japan. Try *Murder in the Crooked House* by Soji Shimada, or *The Honjin Murders* by Seishi Yokomizo, a true master of the art and the author of almost eighty books. They are both fiendish and elegant. In the first, the entire setting becomes an accomplice to the crime. As for the second, the gurgle of the waterwheel and the music played on the koto (a sort of zither), both integral to the plot, will always stay with me. Sheer genius. But far removed from real life.

I only mention all this to explain why my immediate reaction to the last batch of material I had received had been one of dismay. Hawthorne was insisting that Roderick Browne had not committed suicide and all the ingredients of the locked-room mystery were set out in front of me. Nobody could have got into the garage. There was only one key fob, which Roderick must have used to lock the car doors *after* he got inside. He couldn't have been carried there. And he had written a suicide note! It was always possible that Hawthorne was wrong. After all, he had said that the case hadn't worked out the way he wanted and Alastair Morton, the CEO of Fenchurch International, had also warned me that I shouldn't write the book because it would show Hawthorne in a bad light.

Of course, that would be even worse. It would mean that Morton was right and that the story wasn't worth writing. Hawthorne hadn't solved anything and the killer had simply confessed. The end.

I'd been depressed enough when I left the offices of Fenchurch International. Morton had ruined everything for me by revealing the solution . . . which I'm sure was exactly what he'd intended. And so far, he'd been spot on. Khan had said the case was closed. Roderick Browne had been named as the killer and he had then taken his own life. Where did that leave me? With a very short book, for a start, more a novella than a novel. And I couldn't see my editor jumping up and down with excitement when the manuscript was delivered.

So, on reflection, I realised that a locked-room mystery might be exactly what I needed. If it turned out that Roderick Browne's entire garage swivelled round to reveal a hidden staircase which had allowed someone to gain access through an underground passage that connected with the medieval well, I'd just have to grit my teeth and get on with it. At least it would mean that Roderick Browne hadn't committed suicide after all and that someone had indeed murdered him; presumably the same person who had shot Giles Kenworthy.

But who?

I'd sent Hawthorne the next section ('Another Death') and was waiting for him to show up. He was coming to the flat again at eleven o'clock. That gave me thirty minutes to get myself into his mindset. I went to my desk and sat there, thinking about the possibilities, trying to work it out for myself. It should have been simple. After all, there weren't that many suspects.

Who had killed Giles Kenworthy?

The way I saw it, May Winslow and Phyllis Moore had replaced Sarah Baines as the most likely suspects . . . even if it seemed almost impossible to believe. Isn't that how it always works? The killer is the last person you expect and these two were ex-nuns with such a hatred of violence that they wouldn't even stock Jo Nesbø in their 'cosy crime' bookshop. I would have been surprised if, at eighty-one and seventy-nine, they even had the strength to lift the crossbow and take aim, but maybe one of them had held it while the other pulled the trigger?

They certainly had a motive. They had been shattered by the death of their dog, and although Sarah Baines was almost certainly responsible, it was Giles Kenworthy who had given the order. They had a key to Roderick's house. They could have slipped into the garage at any time. That would also have helped them to engineer his death. I wondered how they'd raised the money to buy both their house and the shop in Richmond. That story about the surprise inheritance hadn't rung true. It's the sort of thing that only happens in children's books. And an aunt, of all things!

I reached for a sheet of paper and scribbled their names at the top.

Who next?

Sarah Baines had slipped down to number two. She was an ex-prisoner who had somehow talked her way into Riverview Close, taking advantage of May Winslow's good nature. She certainly had a reason to kill Giles Kenworthy. He had found her snooping around in his office and had fired her, threatening to report her to the police, which would have been the last thing she needed. There was also an interesting link between her and Roderick Browne. She had called him while he was in the garage with Hawthorne and Dudley. Was it possible that she was sharing something she had found on Kenworthy's computer? Roderick was certainly an enthusiastic supporter. *'She's a fine young woman, very hard-working and always helpful . . . '* – although his untidy garden told a different story. Did she have some hold over him? Why had his phone gone missing at around the same time as his death? Did he know something that had got him killed?

And then there was Dr Tom Beresford and his wife. Hawthorne had described Dr Beresford as an alcoholic, addicted to sleeping pills, stressed and miserable, locked into an endless row with his neighbour about a narrow driveway and who had the right to park there. But it was more likely to have been the death of his patient, Raymond Shaw, that had tipped the balance and turned him into a potential murderer. Was there some link between Shaw and Beresford that I hadn't yet discovered? Suppose he had stolen the crossbow and Roderick had seen him? That might have been a motive for a second murder . . . although I still had no idea how he could have done it.

Unless he was assisted by his wife!

Gemma Beresford would surely do anything to protect her husband. I opened a drawer and took out one of the photographs that Hawthorne had sent me. It was a printout from her website showing her Rare Poison collection of jewellery: snakes, scorpions, spiders and doll's eyes (a toxic plant from North America). There was definitely something sinister about her and I wondered how far she would go to keep her family together. Far enough to kill?

She reminded me a bit of Teri Strauss, Adam's second wife. Of the two of them, I found it easier to imagine Teri creeping around Riverview Close in the middle of the night with a crossbow, and there was definitely something sinister about her, even the fact that she was a blood relative of Strauss's first wife, Wendy. She had a reason to kill Giles Kenworthy, although not a very good one. It was his children who had smashed her husband's prize chess set, a gift from Sheikh Mohammed bin Rashid Al Maktoum, no less. She was certainly ferocious in her devotion to Adam. She thought he was a genius. She accompanied him to all his chess tournaments. But would she really murder someone on account of a broken chess set? I wasn't sure.

A chess grandmaster might have the intelligence required to plan a murder – I've always thought of chess as a rather cold-blooded game – and it was true that Adam Strauss had always been the spider at the heart of the web that was Riverview Close. One way or another, he was connected to everyone who lived there and he had hosted the meeting that Kenworthy had failed to show up for. It was also his fault that the new family had arrived in the first place. Even so, I could see no serious reason why he would have murdered either of the two men. Roderick Browne was a close friend. When Roderick was at his lowest, it was Adam he had called, and he had certainly been alive when Adam left his home.

Or had Andrew Pennington got that wrong? He was the only witness (he had also seen Tom Beresford sneaking out of his front door at ten o'clock at night). Pennington had accused Giles Kenworthy of racial prejudice, and there was a vague link with the attack on the old lady in Hampton Wick. A leaflet advertising the UK Independence Party had been found at the scene of the crime. And Marsha Clarke had a connection with the Beresford household. Their nanny had been looking after her.

It was all very confusing. The more I thought about it, the more I regretted ever taking on the book. Despite what I'd hoped when I set out, it was much easier following Hawthorne round, writing down what I saw. Trying to piece a solution together from a mountain of information, not all of which might be reliable, was like trying to construct a jigsaw puzzle without ever having been shown the picture it was supposed to form.

The doorbell rang. It had to be Hawthorne with the next batch of documents he had promised to bring.

But when I went downstairs, it was not Hawthorne standing at the door. It took me a few seconds to recognise the pink-faced, plump-cheeked man in the baggy suit, with his untidy hair and apologetic smile.

'Roland! I exclaimed.

Hawthorne's adoptive brother was carrying a large manila envelope, just as he had the first time we met, although on this occasion he was holding it out for me. 'I was asked to give you this,' he said.

'By Hawthorne?'

'Yes.'

'I was expecting to see him.'

'He asked me to apologise on his behalf. He's not able to come.'

This was almost certainly untrue. Hawthorne had never apologised to me in his life. 'Would you like to come in?' I asked.

'No, thank you.' He thrust the packet into my hands. 'I'm just passing. I need to be on my way.'

'Is this more stuff about Richmond?' I asked.

'Yes.'

He was already turning back towards Farringdon station, but I stopped him. 'He knows I saw Morton, doesn't he.'

Roland and Hawthorne couldn't have been more different. Whereas Hawthorne would never have let anyone – or anything – stand in his way, his adoptive brother was more diffident, more unwilling to cause offence. Hawthorne, for that matter, would simply have lied. Roland blurted out the truth. 'Yes,' he admitted. 'I have to tell you, he's not happy about it.'

'Well, tell him I'm sorry.'

His cheeks reddened and I realised that this was probably as angry as he ever got. 'And you might as well know, I'm not happy either. I'm the one who got the blame. I was foolish enough to trust you when we met at the flat. I told you about the Barracloughs and I'm never going to hear the end of it. You don't just walk in on a man like Morton! Do you have any idea who he is, what you're dealing with? You've certainly landed me in it.'

'So tell me!' I snapped. I was becoming exasperated with the loss of control, of having my own book revealed to me before I'd written it. 'Who is Morton? And what is Fenchurch International? Why are you so scared of them?'

Roland hesitated. He looked around him, as if afraid of being overheard. 'They are the biggest security company in the UK and quite possibly the world,' he said. 'Cyber security, protection, risk assessment, personal and financial investigation. They provide specialised services to government and to industry. They work in the military. You have no idea how much power they have, how much they know.'

'You work for them.'

'I'm nothing.' He glanced at the package he'd brought with him. 'A postboy.'

'Morton told me not to write the book,' I said.

'Then if you've got any sense, you'll stop.' He glanced at me one last time. 'But you won't listen to me. You're like every writer I've ever met. You only think of yourself and you don't care how much damage you might do.'

He stepped round me and walked off. I watched him, feeling guilty. Roland was clearly a decent man and it was true that I'd taken advantage of him. But then what was I to do when Hawthorne was so endlessly uncooperative? I must have stood there for a couple of minutes, the commuters walking past me on both sides of the pavement. Should I be nervous? Could there be someone watching me even now? I went back into my flat, closing the door behind me.

As soon as I reached my office, I sat down and tore open the envelope, leafing through the notes and transcripts that poured onto my desk. What I was looking for wasn't there. There was no personal note from Hawthorne, no explanation as to why he had cancelled our meeting at the last minute, not even something about Fenchurch International and the mistake I'd made going there. I tried to focus. All I saw was words, thousands more words to add to the tens of thousands I'd already written.

I couldn't connect with them. Riverview Close, Hawthorne and John Dudley, Khan, the doctor, the dentist, the dog, the dear old ladies . . . they'd all somehow fused into each other. The sun was glaring at me through the window. I was suffocating.

I knew what I had to do.

I got up, left my own locked room behind me and took a train to Richmond.

2

Richmond station was only an hour away, although all the time I'd been writing, it could have been on the other side of the planet. A flight of steps led up from the platform and I realised that this must have been where Adam Strauss had fallen. Or had he been pushed? The steps were quite wide and empty at this time of the day, but I could imagine that in the rush hour they would present a very different prospect. I wondered if Dudley had managed to look at the CCTV camera footage yet. The answer to that question might be sitting on my desk even now.

I emerged into sunlight and looked around me. The station was on the edge of the town and had an attractive façade and, unusually, a clock that worked. I was intending to walk straight down to Riverview Close, but since I was on the High Street and surrounded by shops, it made sense to start with The Tea Cosy, always assuming it was still in business. Five years had passed since the events I have been describing; it was one of the reasons why I'd never made it a priority to come out here. May Winslow and Phyllis Moore could both be dead by now. The other neighbours might well have left. I wasn't returning to the scene of the crime so much as to a distant memory of it.

I found a Waterstones on a corner and knew I must be getting near. This was where the two ladies had sent any customers looking for books they considered violent or profane. I continued past an incredibly tatty Odeon cinema ('Fanatical about film', it said, with the first F falling off) and up the hill. After that, I passed an estate agent, two coffee bars, a fireplace shop and a health centre – but there was no sign of anyone selling golden age crime or humorous tea towels. I retraced my steps and went into what looked like a well-established flower shop. A woman with frizzy fair hair was standing behind a counter, surrounded by an abundance of exotic plants. I asked her about The Tea Cosy.

'That was two doors away,' she told me. 'May Winslow was the owner. I used to see her – and was it her sister? – from to time. They were quite sweet, although no business sense at all! They didn't carry any of the new bestsellers.'

'Do you know where they went?'

'I heard a rumour they'd gone back north. The story was that they'd spent years in a convent and maybe they went back there.' She sighed. 'The rates are too high. It's just not fair. If they're not careful, the whole High Street will turn into telephones and tat.'

It was a disappointing start. I'd been looking forward to meeting May and Phyllis, browsing through their bookshelves and finding out if they stocked me. I put all that behind me and set off back down the hill, then followed the road in the direction of Petersham, with a quite extraordinary view of the River Thames and the fields beyond that could have inspired Constable or Turner: a huge azure sky and a ribbon of glinting water twisting all the way to the horizon. The Italian Gothic towers of the Petersham Hotel rose up in front of me – the building had been there since the nineteenth century – and for the first time I understood something of what it must have meant to live in Riverview Close. Richmond was exclusive in the true sense of the word. It excluded much of the worst of modern life.

I recognised the archway before I saw the road sign that named it and walked through with a sense of unreality, even though this was the first 'real' thing I had done. And there I was. Standing in my own book! Well House was on my right. I could see Riverview Lodge in front of me and noticed at once that the swimming pool had not been built after all. I walked forward, taking in the roundabout, which looked neat and tidy with a blaze of bright colours. There was Gardener's Cottage, where the Beresfords had lived, over to the left. Were they still here? Was anyone? It was only now that I realised how odd it would be to meet some of the characters I had been writing about.

Everything looked very much as I had imagined it,

although it was a touch smaller than I had thought, the houses closer together. It was easy to see why too many parked cars would have been an issue. The driveways heading left and right, with the Beresfords' garage on one side and Roderick Browne's on the other, were particularly narrow and poorly designed, as if the architects had intended there to be trouble.

I was feeling increasingly uncomfortable, just standing there. It dawned on me that I was effectively trespassing – I wondered how many tourists and ghouls strolled in here every month. After all, this was the site of two unnatural deaths and there are parts of London where murder walks are very much an attraction. Follow in the footsteps of Jack the Ripper or the Kray brothers or Sherlock Holmes. I didn't want to draw attention to myself, so I headed meaningfully for The Stables – as if I was expected and had every right to be there. Adam Strauss was low on my list of suspects, but he would probably know more than anyone else. I rang the front doorbell. There was no answer. I looked through a gap in the net curtains (Hawthorne hadn't mentioned these) and saw that the room had changed. There were no chessboards, no refectory table. Adam and his wife must have moved.

I glanced across at Gardener's Cottage, but there was no sign of any movement. Dr Beresford was probably at his surgery, his wife in town, his children – nine years old now – at school. That really only left me with one option. I walked over to Well House and rang the bell. This time I was in luck. The door opened. Andrew Pennington stood in front of me.

'Yes?'

It was so odd to be seeing him in the flesh that it took me a few moments to find a way to introduce myself. Up until now, he had been little more than a figment of my imagination. When I was writing, I'd felt that I owned him. I'd used the photographs and the transcripts I'd been sent and had tried to be as accurate as possible, but I'd invented lots of things too. Neither Hawthorne nor Dudley had been there, for example, when Ellery was found in the well and I'd had to recreate the entire scene. I didn't know if he drank gin and tonic. It was almost like meeting a penfriend for the first time. I had formed a picture of him that might turn out to be far from the truth.

Well, at least he looked more or less the same, though he had aged considerably in the last five years. The white edges of his hair were more pronounced than I had described. He looked thinner, too, as if he was recovering from an illness. There was a pinched quality to his face, with its sunken cheeks and hollow eyes. He was dressed in a tracksuit, a pair of spectacles hanging on a chain around his neck. His eyesight must have got worse as I was sure I had never mentioned them.

'Andrew Pennington,' I said.

'Yes.'

'I wonder if I could have a word.' I told him my name. 'I'm a writer,' I said.

'A journalist?'

'No. Not at all. I'm a children's author.' I don't know why

I said that. I suppose it wouldn't have done me any favours, turning up at a crime scene and announcing I wrote murder mysteries. 'I think you met a friend of mine once, a while ago. Daniel Hawthorne. He came here when Giles Kenworthy was killed.'

'Oh, yes.' His face gave nothing away. 'He spoke to me a few times.'

'I'm writing a book about him. Not a children's book. A sort of biography. I was wondering if I could talk to you about the time you spent with him . . . how it was to meet him.'

Pennington considered. 'You know my name,' he said. 'Did he talk to you about me?'

'A little.'

'You know what happened here?'

'I know some of it.'

He surprised me. 'Come in,' he said. 'Let me make you a cup of coffee.'

He led me into the kitchen and, for what it's worth, I'd got his house exactly right. We chatted about the many attractions of Richmond while he went through the business of grinding the beans, percolating the coffee, warming the milk. He seemed pleased to see me and I guessed that he didn't have many visitors. At last he came over and sat opposite me.

'It's not the same here,' he said. 'Almost everyone's gone. May and Phyllis were the first to leave.'

I had told him about the bookshop that had closed. 'Did they leave a forwarding address?' I asked.

275

'They didn't need to. They never received any mail and I don't think I saw anyone visit them either. They only had each other, and although it saddens me to say it, I'm not sure they were all that close. I got the sense it was more that they needed the company and tolerated each other.'

'The flower-shop lady said they went back to their convent.'

'They may well have. They came out of nowhere and that's where they went. They didn't even say goodbye. They dropped a note through my door and that was it. The next day, they had gone. We'd been neighbours for fourteen years and we'd been on friendly terms, but perhaps that terrible night when their dog fell into my well changed things. They were never the same after that.'

'They blamed you?'

'No. I obviously had nothing to do with it. But I suppose my house, even its name, had bad associations for them. They didn't like coming here after that and we drifted apart.'

'You say the dog fell in. Is that what you believe?'

'They had it in their heads that the Kenworthys might been involved, but they had absolutely no evidence and I'd prefer to give them the benefit of the doubt.'

'Who lives at The Gables now?'

'A retired couple. An artist and his wife. They're very pleasant, but I don't see a lot of them. Felicity Browne never came back, by the way. She's still with her sister in Woking, I believe. It's ironic because the swimming pool was never built in the end. But there was nothing for her here.'

'Who else went?' I asked.

'Dr Beresford and his wife were the next to go. They left shortly afterwards. It had nothing to do with the murder or anything like that. I don't think Tom had ever been that comfortable here. It was too far out of London for him. He and Gemma went back to Notting Hill Gate with their girls and they're all much happier. They send me a Christmas card every year, which is nice. Gemma Beresford is doing very well. There was a piece about her in *Vogue* magazine. Her new range of jewellery is inspired by bacteria and viruses. According to what she said in the article, they have very beautiful shapes. I can't see it myself, and I can imagine what my wife would have said. They sold their house to a Bangladeshi family, the Hossains. Three children ... and cats! That makes a change from Ellery. Is the coffee all right?'

'It's fine, thank you.' It wasn't. He had made it too strong and I could feel the grounds sticking to my tongue.

'You wanted to talk to me about Daniel Hawthorne,' he reminded me. 'I have to say, I think he'd make an interesting subject for a book. You said he's a friend of yours?'

'Yes.' I wasn't ready to talk about him yet. 'What about Adam Strauss and his wife?' I asked. 'Have they gone too?'

'Yes.' He paused. 'I can't say I particularly miss them.'

'Why is that?'

'Well, I sometimes think that Adam was responsible for much of what happened. It was he who sold Riverview Lodge, which allowed the Kenworthys to move in. Of course, it's not fair to blame him — but he did have a way of being in control, of placing himself centre stage, so to speak. And I always thought that he could have done more to help poor Roderick. He was there that last night. I saw them together. He just walked away and a few hours later, Roderick went into the garage and . . .' He shook his head. 'Mind you, Adam was just as upset as the rest of us. He wasn't to know what was going to happen. And anyway, I shouldn't speak ill of the dead.'

I had to play back what he had just said. 'Adam died?' I asked.

'Yes. It was a terrible business, especially after everything that had happened. He fell off a hotel balcony in London. The first I heard of it was when I saw it reported in the papers.'

'When was this?' I was shocked.

'I can't remember exactly. It would have been about six months after the business here . . . a few weeks after he put his house on the market. He and Teri had also planned to move on. They were thinking of moving to Thailand, believe it or not. Quite a change from Richmond upon Thames! There were interested buyers, but the accident happened before a sale could be agreed. I went to his funeral at Mortlake Cemetery. That was the last time I saw Tom and Gemma Beresford. They were there too. None of us could believe it.'

Nor could I.

I remembered that Strauss had been pushed down the stairs

at Richmond station just a couple of days before the death of Giles Kenworthy. And now he might have been pushed again – this time with a fatal result. Andrew Pennington had spoken of an accident, but the two incidents had to be related in some way. Could it be that whoever had attacked him the first time had returned to finish the job – and if so, why? Giles Kenworthy was dead. Roderick Browne had taken the blame. What could possibly be gained by murdering the chess grandmaster?

'Did the police investigate?' I asked.

'Oh, yes. They were definitely suspicious. But I'm afraid the investigation came to nothing. Adam was alone in his room. Teri had gone out for a walk. Nobody saw anything. The railing was quite low and they assumed that he slipped and fell.'

I wondered if Hawthorne knew about this. He had never mentioned that Adam Strauss was dead and there had been nothing in the pages he'd sent me so far. I would have to ask him when I next saw him.

'So what happened to Teri?' I asked.

'She went through with the sale and left. I'm afraid I don't have a contact for her.'

All of them, one after another. Giles Kenworthy and Roderick Browne. Felicity Browne, May Winslow and Phyllis Moore. Dr Beresford and his wife. Adam Strauss dead. His widow gone. I remembered the title Morton had given me. *Close to Death*. That was what this place had become.

'Mr Pennington, can I ask you something about the death of Giles Kenworthy?'

'Andrew, please. And of course you can. It's all far behind me now. Water under Richmond Bridge, you might say.'

'Do you think Roderick Browne killed him? Hawthorne had his doubts – that's what he told me, and he wasn't sure about Mr Browne's suicide either.'

Andrew Pennington took off his glasses and wiped them with a tissue. Then he put them back on again. He had given himself time to think. 'My opinion hasn't changed since I spoke to Mr Hawthorne all those years ago. I am quite sure that Roderick did indeed shoot Giles Kenworthy with the crossbow that he kept in his garage. He would have done anything for Felicity and it may be that she was much stronger than she seemed. I wouldn't have been surprised if she had suggested it to him.

'It's also a fact that he threatened to commit the crime. I heard him. So it's a natural assumption that he took his own life out of guilt and remorse and fear of being arrested. The note he left behind said as much. I hope you're not trying to reopen old wounds, Anthony. What's to be gained? I'm still living in Riverview Close. It's not the place it used to be, but you have to accept change as part of life. At least some sort of peace has returned.'

'You never thought of leaving?' I asked.

He smiled sadly. 'Where would I go? I bought this house

with my wife, Iris. We were very happy together and, living here, I still feel close to her. I have friends in Richmond. When everyone else departed, I did think briefly about putting the place on the market, but at the end of the day I couldn't see any point.'

Andrew Pennington stirred his coffee with a spoon. He had hardly drunk any of it.

'It's a strange thing, isn't it,' he mused. 'Living in a place like this, being surrounded by the same people, day in, day out. What are they exactly? They're your neighbours. They're not quite your friends, although they're closer to you than anyone in the world. You live in and out of each other's pockets and you know everything about them. It was no secret that Adam used to have shouting matches with his first wife or that Gemma Beresford was worried to death about Tom's drinking. Lynda Kenworthy was cheating on her husband. There were strange men in and out of that house all the time when he was away. May bullied Phyllis and often made her life a misery. And not a single person in the close liked their dog. It really was a terrible nuisance.

'But that's human life, isn't it. We all have our upsets and disagreements, but when we come together as friends and neighbours, they don't matter so much. It's a wonderful word . . . a close. Because that was what we all were. Closeness was what we had and I miss it now that it's gone. I miss the people who lived here. I won't pretend otherwise.' He got to

281

his feet. 'I'm sorry. The older I get, the more maudlin I seem to become. That's what happens when you live alone. Where are you based?'

'I'm in a flat. In Clerkenwell.'

'I couldn't bear that. You should move to Richmond!'

I had finished as much of my coffee as I could manage. I stood up and we shook hands. 'Thank you for seeing me.'

'It was a pleasure. I shall look out for your book.'

He walked with me to the door and I paused for a moment before I went out. 'I forgot to ask – who bought Riverview Lodge?' I said.

Pennington looked surprised. 'Oh. Didn't I tell you? Lynda Kenworthy and her children are still there! The house is on the market, but she hasn't managed to sell it yet. She only put it on in the spring. The funny thing is, she's told me how much she likes Riverview Close. It's hard to believe, looking back. Maybe it suits her more now that she's on her own.' He glanced at his watch. 'If you're lucky, you might find her in.'

'Do you ever talk to her?'

'Now and then. If we happen to be passing . . .'

We shook hands and he closed the door.

So Lynda Kenworthy was still at Riverview Lodge. I walked up the drive, past The Gables and Woodlands. I rang the bell.

3

I hadn't written very much about Lynda Kenworthy and that
was just as well. She was quite different to the woman I'd
described.

She was remarkably attractive . . . much warmer and more
welcoming than I'd expected, with a relaxed, easy-going
quality that made her easy to like. In my defence, I'd been
relying on the descriptions given to me by Hawthorne, who
had interrogated her, and her neighbours, who'd disliked her.
The police photographers had simply snapped her for the
records. It hadn't been their job to flatter her.

Maybe her changed circumstances, everything that had
happened since the death of her husband, had softened her,
but she met me at the door and invited me in as if we were old
friends. It helped that her children had read my books.
'Tristram is crazy about Alex Rider,' she said. 'He's seen the
film three times and he'll be furious he missed you – but both

283

the boys are at school. We're going to have to take a selfie together.'

How could I dislike her after that?

There had been many changes made to the house since the time of the murder. I had written about abstract art, pale carpets and a neatness that was almost oppressive. The artwork had been replaced by original posters in frames – mainly French films by Truffaut and Tati. The carpets were modern and bright (the one in the hall would have had to have been replaced, for obvious reasons) and everywhere I looked I saw evidence of a carefree family life: trainers left by the stairs, jerseys hanging off the bannisters, a basket of laundry on a chair, the dreaded skateboards leaning against the wall by the front door.

'Are Hugo and Tristram at Eton?' I asked her.

She laughed. 'No. Hugo didn't want to go there, and anyway, it suited me to put them both in the local comprehensive. For someone who spent his whole life dealing with money, Giles left his affairs in a terrible mess and I wasn't even sure I had enough in the bank to get them through private education. They're much happier growing up with normal kids. I didn't want them ending up like their dad.'

That surprised me. I thought she'd adored him.

We were sitting at the far end of the kitchen, which had a conservatory area looking out over the garden. Just round the corner, I could see the famous magnolia tree that Adam Strauss had planted and which Giles had intended to cut down. The blossoms had faded as autumn drew in, but there were still a few hints of dark red and white, memories of its summer glory. I asked her about the swimming pool.

'I couldn't afford it now if I wanted it,' she told me. 'But to be honest with you, I was never that keen. That was another of Giles's ideas. I like the garden the way it is and looking at the magnolia. Who would want to lose that? I'll miss it when we go.'

'I see you've taken down the Union Jack.'

'That came down even before the funeral,' she replied with a sniff of laughter. 'I hated it. Giles was always banging on about politics, Brexit . . . that's why he had the flag.'

I wanted to ask her if he had been a racist but couldn't find a polite way of putting it. So instead I said: 'Have you found a buyer for the house yet?'

'Are you interested?'

I shook my head. 'I don't think so.'

She nodded sadly. 'Even after everything that happened, I'd still like to stay. The boys like it and they've got lots of friends in the area. But the house is far too big for the three of us. We had to let Jasmine go. We just have a daily now. She comes in twice a week and she's not here until tomorrow, so apologies for the mess. It turns out that Giles wasn't quite as clever with the finances as he thought he was. The banks wrote to me after he died and it was all just one debt after another. He'd even sold his life insurance . . . the prat. He never told me that and it came as quite a shock. I'll still be all right. This place is on the market for four million and there's no mortgage or anything. I sold all the art and my jewellery. I don't need it now.'

'How do you feel about what happened here?' I asked her.

'Well, I'm not overjoyed, if that's what you mean. You don't mind if I smoke?' She reached for a packet of cigarettes and lit one. 'I did love Giles . . . when we first met. It was a dream, the sort of thing you read about in a book. Not one of yours. You don't do romance, do you?'

'I haven't yet.'

'I was cabin crew. He was travelling first class. He invited me out and I knew from the very start that we were kindred spirits. We were made for each other. Things only started going wrong when we moved here.'

'The neighbours, you mean . . .'

'Not really. They weren't such a bad lot. I mean, Adam Strauss never really forgave us for moving into his precious home. He didn't like the fact that we'd taken his place as lord of the manor. And there were all those stupid rows with Dr Beresford . . .'

'Why did you keep blocking the driveway?'

'We had to put the cars somewhere! And he only had access. The right of way belonged to us.' She sighed. 'I don't know why I'm still discussing it. Talk about mountains and molehills! We've never had a single complaint from the Hossains, and their cats are no trouble either.'

'Do you like your new neighbours?'

'They're fine. There's nothing special about Riverview Close, you know. I'd say there isn't a street in England where the neighbours don't have disputes. I was brought up in Frinton and it was just the same.'

'People don't usually get killed.'

'I think Roderick Browne was ill. He was so worried and upset about his wife, and he was a pervert too . . . Sometimes I saw him staring into my bedroom window. He had a view from his second floor. I made a point of always getting changed for bed round the back.'

'You're certain he was the one who murdered your husband?'

'Detective Superintendent Khan had no doubt at all. I've spoken to him a few times since then. He's a very nice man. He gave me his card and he said I could call him any time I wanted.'

That was something I hadn't considered. 'Could you give me his number?' I asked.

'No problem. I'll give it to you before you go.'

'What about May and Phyllis?' I asked. 'You fell out with them pretty badly.'

Her mouth fell. She shook her head. 'Hand on heart, Giles and I never touched their dog and I never told Sarah to go anywhere near it. Do I look like the sort of person who'd do something like that? I'm the mother of two boys! I'm not a monster.' She blew a great plume of grey smoke into the air. 'We argued about Hilary. Was that its name? They should

287

have controlled it. It was always coming into our garden, sniffing around the magnolia and leaving its business on the grass. I used to pick up after it and deliver the bags to their front door. I wasn't trying to be mean. I could see how old they were. But they never listened to me. What else was I supposed to do?'

'It must have been awful for you, the whole experience . . .'

'You have no idea! Nobody should have to go through what I went through. Being questioned by the police – as if I had anything to do with it. And your friend, Mr Hawthorne, he was the worst. Prying into my private life and making jokes about me in that sneery way of his. When I was with British Airways, there were always passengers you knew you had to avoid, the ones who were going to make trouble when you were thirty-five thousand feet up. He was just like them.

'But it wasn't only the investigation. Mercifully, that didn't last very long. It was afterwards! I couldn't even go shopping without people staring at me. I could hear them whispering behind my back. The children missed weeks of school. Tristram still has nightmares about it and he wasn't even here when it happened. You write murder stories, don't you? Well, perhaps you should think a little more about the people who have to live through them and what it does to them. To this day, there are still people who believe I had something to do with what happened. It never goes away.'

'You suggested that things went wrong between you and Giles when you moved to Richmond.'

'Yes. It was such a mistake! We were never meant to live in a cul-de-sac with lawnmowers and Sunday lunches, cocktail parties and school plays. Growing old together! It was the last thing I wanted. This is a big house, but we both felt trapped in it. It's hardly surprising we grew apart. Giles had his work, his head was always buried in his computers. He had his cars and his clubs. He gambled . . . and he always lost. But he never really cared about me. Not after we were married.'

'Were you sorry he died?'

I hadn't meant to be so blunt.

Lynda wasn't offended. 'It was horrible, finding him in the hallway. I'll never forget that for as long as I live. But it's like I say . . . we weren't together by the end. I knew he was being unfaithful to me, but I was doing the same to him. Ours was an open marriage and it would have ended sooner or later anyway. I'd have preferred a divorce, but I suppose I can't complain. This way I got everything.'

We were interrupted by the arrival of a man who must have been in the house the whole time. He strutted in, dressed like a male model in a T-shirt and skinny jeans and looking like one too: perfect teeth and moustache, chest hair and a medallion, chiselled features and dark brown eyes. He was in his mid-thirties and he was surprised to find me there.

'I did not know you had company,' he said to Lynda. He spoke with a French accent.

'This is Jean-François,' Lynda said. 'Anthony is asking me about the murder,' she explained.

'Why?'

'He's writing about it.'

'I don't think you should talk about it.'

Jean-François. I remembered the name. 'You were with Lynda the night her husband was killed,' I said.

He shrugged . . . Very Gallic. 'Maybe.'

'You're a French teacher.'

'I was. Not any more.'

'Jean-François writes about sport for lots of French magazines,' Lynda told me. 'He's an Olympic champion. He won a bronze medal in 2012 – at the London Olympics.'

I was impressed. 'What sport?' I asked.

He had already lost interest in me. '*Tir à l'arc,*' he said.

My French is good, but I didn't know that one. I looked blank.

'Archery,' Lynda said. Smiling, she took hold of his hand.

4

Lynda Kenworthy had given me the telephone number of Detective Superintendent Khan and I rang him on my way back to Richmond station.

I felt depressed after my visit to Riverview Close. Thinking about it, I saw that both Lynda Kenworthy and Andrew Pennington were casualties. It had never occurred to me before, but murder is in many ways like a fatal car crash, a coming together of people from different walks of life who will all be damaged by the experience. At least one of them will die. One or more will take the blame. But none of them will be glad that they were involved.

And what did that make me? I had come to Riverview Close like the worst rubbernecker . . . and a foolish one too. I had arrived far too late to pick up anything very much in the way of debris. I had nothing to take back home.

I didn't know it then, but both Andrew and Lynda had

provided me with clues that, if I'd only been a little more alert, would have taken me to the very heart of what had really happened at Riverview Close. I just wasn't thinking — or, at least, my thoughts were still focused on Hawthorne and John Dudley.

In one of our earlier meetings, Hawthorne had vigorously praised the assistant who had come before me. *'I'd never have solved the case without him.'* But even then, he'd been reluctant to tell me very much about John Dudley. He'd been a policeman. He'd been ill. And something had happened to end the relationship between the two men. That was where I had come in. Was it any wonder that I wanted to find out more?

It was the principal reason I was calling DS Khan. Once again, those words of Morton's were echoing in my head. *'The story doesn't end the way you think it's going to.'* I had to know what he'd meant and I figured that Khan might be the one person who could tell me.

He answered on the third ring.

'Khan.'

'Detective Superintendent Khan? I hope you'll forgive me ringing you on your private number. It was given to me by Lynda Kenworthy.'

'Who is this speaking?'

I told him my name. There was a pause at the other end.

'I know who you are,' he said.

'I'm working with Hawthorne.'

'Yes. I've read one of your books.'

I waited for him to say he'd enjoyed it. He didn't.

'I was wondering if it would be possible to meet you.'

'Why?'

'I'm writing about Riverview Close.'

There was a lengthy silence as he considered. 'That's all done and dusted,' he said. 'It was a long time ago and I'd like to think we've moved on. It's not a good idea.'

'Meeting you? Or writing about the murder?'

'Both.'

'I was hoping you could help me. I'm planning a book about the murder. I know a lot about what happened, but it would be very useful to get your point of view. How you enjoyed working with Hawthorne . . .'

'I didn't enjoy it at all. And he was only on the case for two days.'

'I'm also trying to find John Dudley. Do you have a phone number or an email address for him?'

'I have neither.'

He was about to hang up. I could hear it in his voice.

'Detective Superintendent, would you at least consider meeting me for ten or fifteen minutes? I'll come to any-where in London. The book is going to be published either way and you're going to be a central character. Obviously, I'm not going to write anything that will cause you embarrassment.'

'I hope not.' That was a warning.

'The death of Giles Kenworthy and everything that followed is in the public domain. All I'm saying is that I'd like to
get your side of the story.'

There was a second, longer silence.

He hung up.

SEVEN

THE SECOND MEETING

1

Alison Munds and her husband, Gareth, lived in a street on the edge of Woking where every home was a variation on the same theme. Each one had a hedge running along the pavement, bay windows, faux-Tudor beams above the second floor, a portico, a garage and a small front garden with a parking area separating the front door from the road. Behind each house, a garden of exactly the same size and proportions ran down to a wire fence and a row of trees partly concealing a railway line.

The doorbell of number 16 played a tune: the opening bars of Beethoven's 'Für Elise'. Gareth liked classical music. Alison said it drove her mad, but they recognised and tolerated each other's fads. It was the secret of a long and successful marriage. The two of them heard the familiar phrase now.

'They're here,' Gareth called out.

'You get it!' Alison's voice came from the kitchen.

He opened the door.

'Mr Munds?' Hawthorne was standing on the other side with Dudley behind him. The car that had brought them here was just pulling away. 'I'm Hawthorne. My colleague, John Dudley. How is your sister-in-law getting on?'

'Well, it's not easy . . .' Hawthorne had called the day before and Gareth had been expecting them, but he was still reluctant to let them in. 'The police were here last week,' he said.

'Detective Superintendent Khan . . .'

'Yes.'

'This is a follow-up. We need to be sure that everything is as it should be. I hope you understand.'

Gareth didn't – but he felt he had no choice in the matter and showed them into the small, square living room that looked out onto the main road. The room had a fake gas fire and a mantelpiece crowded with swans made of crystal, porcelain, painted wood and plastic. Alison collected swans. A tropical fish tank stood in one corner, brightly coloured species swimming back and forth behind the glass in endless exploration of their tiny world.

Felicity Browne had come down from the bedroom and was sitting on the sofa next to her sister. She was wearing a dressing gown and slippers and her hair was bedraggled, but apart from that, she didn't look much worse than she had done when her husband was still alive. That was the cruelty of her illness. It had dragged her down to such a low level

Company Reg No. 12663459

DN Roofing
& Building Ltd

In Partnership with DN Building Services

Our family-run business specialises in restoring and installing pitched and flat roofs, soffits, fascias and guttering for domestic and commercial properties in London and surrounding areas. Our in-depth knowledge, craftsmanship, care and professionalism guarantee a bespoke solution for every need.

OUR VALUES

RELIABILITY
We are incredibly proud of our reputation and will happily provide references for you to inspect our craftsmanship

HONESTY
We believe in integrity and quality. We never oversell our services and are always honest about the best approach for your roof.

RELATABILITY
We are a family-run business that values roofing repairs and installations. You can trust our care and craftsmanship.

COMMUNICATION
We believe good communication is key. Our customers receive verbal and photographic updates throughout the project.

Check✓atrade.com
Where reputation matters

Freephone: 0800 696 5478
Mobile: 07765 577 705
dnroofingandbuildingltd@outlook.com

www.dnroofingandbuildingltd.co.uk

FEDERATION OF
MASTER BUILDERS
fmb.org.uk

that there wasn't anywhere further to go. Hawthorne and Dudley sat on a second sofa, facing her. Gareth had already taken the only armchair.

'I know how difficult this is for you,' Hawthorne said. 'But there are still unanswered questions relating to the deaths of both your husband and Giles Kenworthy.'

Felicity said nothing.

'You don't have to talk to them,' Alison said quietly.

'Actually, I think she does,' Hawthorne contradicted her. 'We believe there's a good chance that Mr Browne did not kill himself . . .'

'Mr Khan never said anything about that.'

'Fresh information has come to light over the weekend which may have altered the picture.' Hawthorne was deliberately trying to sound as official as possible. In fact, had Khan known they were there, they might well have ended up under arrest.

His strategy worked. 'What do you want to know?' Felicity asked.

Dudley took out his notebook. His iPhone was already recording everything that was said.

'Do you think your husband killed Giles Kenworthy?' Hawthorne asked.

'What sort of question is that?' Alison cut in, appalled.

'A reasonable one,' Hawthorne returned.

'Maybe we should call the Detective Superintendent . . .' Alison took hold of her sister's hand.

But Felicity pulled away. Hawthorne had roused something within her, an anger that until now she hadn't been allowed to express. Khan had told her that her husband was dead. He had explained that he had confessed to the murder. He had destroyed her world. But he had never listened to her. 'Of course he didn't kill anyone,' she said. 'Roderick didn't have it in him. He was the gentlest, kindest of men. The police don't know what they're talking about.'

'So you don't believe he committed suicide either,' Dudley said.

'He would never have left me on my own. We'd been together for twenty-six years and we were happy until this illness came and turned me into what I am. Nobody wants to be married to an invalid, but he stuck by me because that was the sort of man he was. Ask any of his patients. They'll tell you the same thing. He worried about every single one of them. If he was going to do something complicated – root canal surgery, or an extraction – he would go over and over the X-rays. Everything had to be perfect.'

Alison and Gareth exchanged glances. It had been a long time since they had heard Felicity say so much in one breath.

'So how do you explain the letter he sent you?' Hawthorne asked.

'I can't.'

'Why do you think he wanted you out of the house?'

'He was worried about me.'

'Roderick called us,' Alison said. 'He told us that Felicity's neighbour had been found dead. He said there were police everywhere, a lot of noise and activity, and it would be better for Fee to be away for twenty-four hours. He asked to bring her round.'

'Of course we agreed,' Gareth said. He was a large, bearded man, sitting with legs splayed and his hands on his knees. 'Ever since Felicity got poorly, we've taken her in from time to time. We've got both our kids at college now and it's not as if we don't have the room.'

Hawthorne turned back to Felicity. 'In the car, when he drove you over here, did he say anything that struck you as strange? Did he give you any indication of what he was thinking about?'

'He said he'd done something stupid.'

'Like . . . killing his neighbour with a crossbow?' Dudley suggested.

'No. That's not what he meant. He was angry with himself. But he told me not to worry. He brought me in and he kissed me goodbye in this very room and I can tell you – just from the way he looked at me – he was expecting to see me again.' She closed her eyes, remembering the moment. 'It wasn't a final goodbye. I'd have known.'

A Siamese fighting fish swam lazily across the aquarium, a multicoloured tail rippling behind it. Bubbles were rising from a pump concealed in a plastic pirate's galleon. The hum of the motor was constant, insinuating itself into every silence.

'So what do you think happened?' Hawthorne asked. 'If he didn't take his own life, why do you think he was killed?'

'I think he saw something and somebody silenced him.'

'Who?' Dudley asked.

'The same person who killed Giles Kenworthy.' Felicity made it sound as if she was explaining the obvious. 'I don't know who that was – but when they took the crossbow from our garage, Roderick might have seen them. There's a sky-light on the roof and you can look through it from the bathroom. He could have seen them while he was cleaning his teeth.'

'But he didn't say anything to you.'

'He wouldn't have wanted to worry me.'

'Do you have any more questions, Mr Hawthorne?' Gareth cut in. 'I think Felicity should get back to bed. This has been a terrible time for her.'

'Yes. I do.' Hawthorne ignored the brother-in-law and turned back to Felicity. 'Adam Strauss was the last person to see your husband.'

'I know. The police told me.'

'They were friends?'

'Very much so. Adam was always helping us, finding ways to do small kindnesses. All our neighbours were lovely. May and Phyllis next door. Andrew Pennington, giving us advice about the planning permission. Tom Beresford prescribing temazepam for me . . .'

'Roderick couldn't do that?'

'It's against the guidelines set down by the General Dental Council.' She struggled for breath. 'How can I help you, Mr Hawthorne? I will do anything . . . anything to find out what really happened.'

'I want to revisit the house,' Hawthorne said. 'Can I borrow your keys?'

'Well, I don't know——' Alison began.

'Let him have them,' Felicity said. 'The police have given up on us. They don't care about Roderick.' She pointed towards the floor. 'They're in my handbag.'

Gareth looked doubtful but fished them out: two Yale keys attached to a silver ring with a mortice key next to them. Hawthorne showed Felicity the third key. 'This opens the door into the garage,' he said.

She nodded. 'Yes.'

'And you've had it on you all the time? There's no chance someone else might have used it?'

'No. It always stays with me.' Felicity had answered enough questions. She was exhausted. 'If there's nothing more you want to know, I think I'll go back to bed now,' she said.

'I'm sorry, but there are still a few things, Mrs Browne. The police were only able to find one set of car keys. It was in your husband's pocket.'

She nodded. 'There is only one set. He lost the other one while we were on holiday in Torquay and he hadn't got round to ordering a replacement. Why? Is it important?'

'Probably not. Also, they weren't able to find his mobile.'

'That's very strange.'

'He had it when he came here,' Alison cut in. 'He checked his messages. That was about midday. I saw him.'

'And then he went straight back home?'

'He kept his phone on the chest of drawers in the hallway,' Felicity said. 'He was quite religious about that. He could hear it from everywhere in the house if it rang and he always knew where to find it.'

'We'll look for it,' Hawthorne said. 'I don't suppose you happen to know the PIN?' Felicity looked unsure, so he added: 'If we do find it, it might give us valuable information. We'll need to open it.'

She nodded. 'One nine six five. It was his birthday.'

She reached out and Gareth helped her to her feet. She had expended all her strength on the conversation. Gareth started to lead her out of the room, but before she reached the door, Hawthorne stopped her.

'There was a second meeting,' he said.

'I'm sorry?' Felicity turned.

'I'd imagine they were all there – probably at The Stables. That was where the first one happened. It was probably sometime over the weekend. Giles Kenworthy died on Monday, so just before that.'

She stood there, clinging on to Gareth. It took her a long time to find the strength to reply. 'It was Sunday evening,' she said. 'How did you know about it? Who told you?'

'Nobody told me,' Hawthorne said. 'Not in so many words. Were you there?'

'No.' She shook her head. 'I was too tired and I couldn't see any point in talking any more.'

'And . . . ?'

'I can't tell you anything, Mr Hawthorne. I didn't see Roderick on Sunday evening, but I could tell he must have drunk a lot because I could smell the alcohol the next morning. He went into work on Monday like he always did. He brought in my breakfast before he left. I could see he wasn't himself. He said that he had been at The Stables the night before and I could see that something had upset him, but when I asked him about it, he refused to tell me. He said I wasn't to mention it to anyone.

'I didn't ask him again. He was so wrapped up in his own thoughts that I didn't like to, but maybe I should have – because two days later he was gone. Two days later, he was taken from me.'

She was desperate to leave the room, but there was one last thing she had to say.

'They did meet a second time. I don't know what happened, but I hope you'll find out, because whatever it was, that was the reason my Roderick had to die.'

2

Hawthorne and Dudley took a taxi back from Woking to Richmond. Not a black cab. The distance was almost twenty miles. They had wedged themselves into the back of a car provided by a local company: sticky plastic seats, half-inflated tyres and a driver who was too cheerful by half. Hawthorne seldom used public transport. He didn't like being close to people he didn't know. But in many ways, this ponderous journey along the M3 was even worse.

'A question . . .' Dudley said, as they overtook the one vehicle on the road that happened to be slower than them. There was no risk of the two of them being overheard by the driver. The engine was barely up to the journey and it was howling in protest. They were having difficulty even hearing each other.

'Go on.'

'Just wondering what we're doing. We're not on Khan's

payroll any more. He's closed the investigation, wrapped it up and filed it under P for promotion. Which means we're not getting paid.'

'I'll sort that out for you, mate.'

'Out of your own pocket?' Dudley looked doubtful. 'That's not like you, Danny . . . going in for charity.'

'Not charity. I need you to help me get to the end of this.'

'You don't need anyone.'

'Khan will pay when we deliver a result. And if he won't, Morton will cough up.'

'Why would he do that?'

'To keep me happy. And it's good for business to keep in with the police. It's company policy.'

They drove along in silence . . . at least, without talking. The car was still an echo chamber of distress and the driver had turned on the radio, to Pharrell Williams singing 'Happy', which had gone viral across the country. The motorway slipped past as all motorways do, without the slightest interest.

'Don't you want to know?' Hawthorne asked.

'Who did it? Of course I do. Have you worked it out yet?'

'Most of it. I don't know how Roderick Browne was killed. We need to get into that garage and have a proper look around. But I think I know why.'

'The straw.'

'Yeah. The straw . . .'

'. . . in the top pocket of his jacket . . .'

'. . . and the keys in his trouser pocket.'

'Yeah. That was wrong too. I thought you'd pick up on that.'

The driver changed gear with a nasty grinding sound.

'Khan's an idiot,' Dudley said.

Hawthorne nodded. 'That's the only part of this case that's been obvious from the start.' He looked out of the window. On the radio, Pharrell Williams had reached the reprise.

'*Happiness is the truth* . . .'

'He's got a point,' Hawthorne said.

Dudley shook his head. 'Happiness isn't the truth, Danny. It's making sure the bastards pay for it.' A bitterness that Hawthorne hadn't seen before had crept into his eyes. 'Kenworthy was a prat. Money, old Etonian, neighbour from hell. But he didn't deserve a crossbow bolt in his throat. And Roderick Browne was a decent man, looking after his sick wife. He was tricked, wasn't he? Tricked and then got rid of. You're right: we can't walk away from this. We've got to get to the end.'

The driver swerved to get past an articulated lorry, cutting in front of a delivery van that blasted its horn in protest. For a moment, he wobbled in the central lane, then veered back towards the hard shoulder.

'If we live that long,' Hawthorne said.

The Richmond turn-off was signposted. Six miles ahead. They shuddered towards it.

3

The Tea Cosy was unusually busy. There were two customers browsing through the shelves, and a third sitting at a table, tucking into red velvet cake and Earl Grey tea. May Winslow knew her well. Mrs Simpson came into the shop at least once a week and very seldom bought anything.

May was sitting opposite her, holding a book. The cover showed the silhouette of a village with the title in red letters above: *The Inverted Jenny: An Amelia Strange Mystery*. 'It's a wonderful story,' she was saying. 'Of course, you've read *The Murder of Roger Ackroyd* – this was written in 1924, the same year. It starts with a summer fête in the village of Blossombury in Wiltshire. The vicar, who is running the coconut shy, is poisoned and it turns out his uncle is Sir Henry Fellowes, the local squire and a well-known philatelist. The mystery starts when a very valuable stamp is found inside one of the coconuts.'

'I'm not sure,' Mrs Simpson said. 'Who's Jenny?'

'It's the name of the stamp. This is the third Amelia Strange story. There were forty-two of them in total. She's one of my favourite detectives. She sings in the choir and she has an incredibly clever Siamese cat and they solve the mysteries together—'

The door of the shop opened and two men came in. May's heart sank. They had already visited her once at The Gables. She thought she'd seen the last of them.

'Mrs Winslow.' Hawthorne nodded at her. 'I wonder if we could have a word with you in private?'

'I don't understand.' May forced a smile to her lips. 'I understood that the investigation was over.'

'Far from it, I'm afraid. We need to ask you some questions.'

'About Mr Browne? I've already said—'

'No. About the Franciscan Convent of St Clare in Leeds.'

Hawthorne stood where he was, daring her to pick a fight. John Dudley looked almost embarrassed to be with him and was shuffling his feet. May understood. In a way, she had been expecting it. She got to her feet. 'I'm afraid we're going to have to close early,' she announced so that everyone could hear.

'I was going to buy that book!' Mrs Simpson muttered.

May remembered she was still holding it and thrust it into her hands. 'You can have it, my dear,' she said. 'Just let me know if you enjoy it.'

Phyllis had been standing in the kitchen area of the shop all this time and watched, discomfited, as the three customers trailed out into the street. May went over and locked the door.

310

Hawthorne and Dudley sat down at the table. 'Would you like some tea?' Phyllis asked.

'You'd better come and join us, Phyllis,' May instructed her friend. 'They don't need tea.'

Phyllis did as she was told.

'We've just seen Felicity Browne,' Hawthorne began.

'Oh. How is she?'

'You mean, apart from the incurable disease and the suicide of her husband?' Dudley chipped in. 'She's not doing too badly.'

May flushed. 'What do you want, Mr Hawthorne?'

'We were just on our way back to Riverview Close and we were passing the shop, so we thought we might have a word, if that's all right.'

'And it would be nice if – this time – you told us the truth,' Dudley added.

'I think you're a very rude young man.'

'I'm not that young.'

'We know your real names,' Hawthorne said.

Phyllis looked shocked. May tried not to show any emotion.

Hawthorne continued. 'Two old ladies move into a house in Richmond. They've come from nowhere. Nobody knows anything about them. Nobody visits them. They don't get any letters or parcels. I try to find out more about them, but nothing turns up and I ask myself if they're even using their own names. Or maybe they've changed them.

'It's quite easy to do it without anyone noticing. If your

name is More, for example, spelled like Sir Thomas, you just add a second o. Or you can go back to your maiden name. May Winslow, for example, instead of May Brenner. In this country it's also dead easy to use the deed poll system. Criminals do it all the time. And if you're not applying for a passport or a driving licence, who's even going to notice?'

May had gone white. She was breathing heavily, little gasps that made her shoulders rise and fall.

'You gave yourselves away a few times, love,' Hawthorne went on. 'You want to know how?'

May nodded.

'Well, to start with, you said you were at the convent for almost thirty years, but your friend Phyllis here seems to think that the last service before bed is vespers, when she really ought to have worked out that it's compline or night prayer, which is followed by the great silence, when nobody is meant to talk. Also, she said that you and she were "cellies" and you were quick to explain this meant you shared a room, but quite apart from the fact that I'm not sure nuns ever have to share, it's prisoners who call themselves cellies, women prisoners in particular.

'Let's work this out. St Clare was supposedly in Osmondthorpe, near Leeds. By an amazing coincidence, that's just half an hour away from HMP New Hall in Wakefield, which is where Sarah Baines did her time, and you recommended Sarah for a job here. "You have to give young people a chance". That's what you said. It's a lovely thought and I suppose it's doubly true if she's threatening to expose who you really are. It's also why you couldn't fire her, even though she's a useless gardener and she may have killed your dog. She had you by the short and curlies.'

'Do nuns have short and curlies?' Dudley asked.

May glared at Phyllis. 'I was always warning you,' she said. 'But you never could keep your mouth shut.'

'I didn't mean to . . .' Phyllis began miserably.

May looked across the table at Hawthorne, the half-eaten cake and the cold tea between them. 'I've done my time,' she said. 'I've done nothing wrong. All I wanted was to get on with the rest of my life in peace. Sarah knew that. And you're right, the little cow blackmailed us. She knew who we were and she was going to tell everyone.'

'What was she going to say?' Hawthorne asked.

'That we'd been in prison.'

'Rather more than that, I think.'

'You murdered your husband,' Dudley said. 'His name was David Brenner.'

'He deserved it.'

'Well, you certainly made your point. You hit him thirty times with a meat cleaver. There was so much blood in the house that even the police dogs threw up. You piled up the pieces in the bath and put his head in a dustbin for the Thursday-morning collection.'

'I told you the truth about him. David was a monster. I was seventeen when I met him. I didn't know anything about the world. I was just a child. And once I was in his hands . . . you have no idea. The things he did to me! He beat me and he brutalised me and he destroyed any confidence I had in myself until the day I finally snapped.' She paused. 'I'll have one of your snouts, Phyllis, if you don't mind.'

'Snouts,' Dudley muttered. 'More prison slang.'

'You can never get it completely out of your system.' May had got rid of the fear and anger when the accusations had been made. Now she was regaining her composure. Phyllis handed her a pouch of tobacco and she rolled a cigarette for herself with expert fingers and lit it. 'The judge agreed with me,' she said. 'He said I had a submissive personality and that David had tormented me. Those were his exact words. He said it was because of David's appalling behaviour throughout our entire married life that I'd been driven to such extremes and that I wasn't entirely responsible for what I did.'

'He still sent you to prison.'

'That was because I'd planned the crime.' Despite herself, she half smiled. 'I planned it for ten years. The judge had no choice. But he felt sorry for me and he let me keep the money.'

'You mean, your husband's money.'

'Yes.'

'The Forfeiture Act of 1982,' Dudley said.

'You know your law! In normal circumstances, you're not allowed to keep your partner's cash if you kill them. You lose everything. But judges can make exceptions – and he did that for me.'

'I never did believe your story about the rich aunt,'

314

Hawthorne said. 'That sort of thing might happen in one of the books you sell here but never in real life.'

'And let's not forget Phyllis More with one o . . .' Dudley said.

Phyllis squirmed. 'Do we have to?' she asked, feebly.

'It's best to have it all on the table, love.' Dudley sighed. 'You didn't much like your husband either, did you! You smashed a whisky bottle over his head, doused him in petrol and set fire to him. They heard his screams a mile away.' He shook his head. 'If either of you two ever write your auto-biographies, I rather doubt you'd be able to stock them here.'

'I lost my temper,' Phyllis said. Her eyes were downcast. 'But you'd have done the same if you'd been married to him. He was a dreadful man.'

'How did Sarah Baines find you?' Hawthorne asked.

'It was just bad luck. She saw us on the street in Richmond and followed us home.' May glared at Hawthorne. 'I'm not proud of what I did, but I'm not ashamed either,' she declared. 'Nobody understands murder . . . not real murder.' She waved a dismissive hand, drawing in the entire bookshop. 'All of this is entertainment. It doesn't mean anything. But Phyllis and me, we've been to a terrible place.'

'New Hall,' Phyllis said.

'No, dear. Not prison. Before that.' May drew on her cig-arette. 'You have no idea what it's like to commit murder, the darkness that destroys everything inside you and consumes you. To take a human life. Not in a battlefield or a place of

315

war but in your kitchen, your living room, in the home where you felt safe. In that single moment, it's two lives, not one, that are finished.

'You sit there and you feel euphoria. It's over! All the anger and the rage has finally burst out of you. But then comes the recognition of what you've done, the knowledge that there's no going back, the terrible fear of being found out, and, of course, regret. How you wish . . . how you wish it hadn't happened. Have you read *Thérèse Raquin*? We have a copy here somewhere. You should take it with you.' She paused. 'All murderers regret their deeds . . . unless they're completely insane. When I was in New Hall, and in Holloway before that, I never met a single woman who still celebrated what she'd done. There were some who pretended, but you could see it eating at them, day after day. I spent twenty-four years behind bars for what I did. Look at me now! I'm a shadow. Everything has gone. I have a son who won't even speak to me, who lives in California and who probably regrets he ever came out of my womb. I have grandchildren I've never seen.'

She hadn't finished the cigarette, but she stubbed it out anyway.

'So now you know the truth, Mr Hawthorne. What else do you want?'

'I want to know what Sarah Baines was doing with Roderick Browne.' May looked blank so he went on. 'The two of them had a relationship. He was protecting her . . . just like you were. She texted him while we were with him.'

316

'I don't know. She's a devil. She was always taking money from us. She'd steal anything she could get her hands on.' She gave a sniff of laughter. 'Giles Kenworthy and his precious Rolex. I could have told him where to look on eBay.'

'Is that why you went with her when she found the body?'

'I wasn't going to leave her alone with Roderick's keys! He'd have come back to an empty house. I followed her there and we went into the garage together. I managed to wiggle the key out and open the door and there he was in his car. A horrible sight with the bag over his head.'

'Sarah broke the car window.'

'I told her to. Roderick wasn't moving, but there was always a chance he was still alive.'

'What happened then?'

'I opened the car door and felt for a pulse. There wasn't one. We went back into the house and called the police.'

'You did or she did?'

'She did.'

'She had her own phone?'

'Yes.'

'You're sure she didn't see Roderick's?'

'I think I saw Roderick's phone on the chest of drawers in the hall. She definitely used her own.'

'Can we go home now?' Phyllis asked.

'We may not have a home any more, dear. But you're right. There's no point staying here. Why don't you start clearing up?' May waited until Phyllis had moved away, then spoke quietly. 'We'll have to sell the house after all this – and The Tea Cosy. You know who we are. So does Detective Superintendent Khan. It won't be long before the whole of Richmond finds out.'

'You may find people are more forgiving than you think,' Dudley said.

'I don't want their forgiveness. I just want to be left alone.'

Hawthorne hadn't finished yet. 'There's one thing more I want you to tell me,' he said. 'On the Sunday night – Sunday, July the sixteenth – you went to a meeting at The Stables. That was one night before Giles Kenworthy was killed. Who was there?'

'I didn't go to the meeting.'

'Yes, you did. If you're going to lie to me, Mrs Brenner, your face is going to be all over the *Richmond and Twickenham Times* – and every other newspaper in the country. To be honest with you, I'm getting a tiny bit tired of being led up the garden path by the residents of Riverview Close. Who was there?'

May was stone-faced. 'Almost everyone. Mrs Beresford came with her husband. They had a babysitter looking after the children because their nanny was away. Mrs Browne wasn't well enough to come over, but otherwise we were all there.'

'So what happened?'

'I can't tell you, Mr Hawthorne. Not on my own. I'm sure we all have different memories anyway. I'm not going to say anything to you unless the others are there.'

4

There was room for all nine of them around the table in the garden of Well House. The well itself was just out of sight, but May and Phyllis still made sure they sat with their backs to it. They had called the others from the bookshop. Gemma Beresford had driven back from her jewellery shop in Mayfair and was sitting next to her husband, who had left the surgery early. Adam and Teri Strauss had walked across from The Stables after Andrew Pennington had offered his home for this third and final congregation. Hawthorne had taken his place at the head of the table. Dudley was next to him, his notebook poised.

It could have been a summer luncheon that had stretched on into afternoon tea. Andrew had even provided a jug of iced lemonade. But the atmosphere was far from convivial as they finally revealed the shadows that they had been living under all along.

May Winslow

The worst of it was that we'd all been so happy here. Phyllis and I knew we'd love The Gables the moment we saw a picture of it online. It was secluded, but it was in its own community and it was all so picturesque. I was born in Richmond. I made the decision without a second thought and we moved into The Gables in the spring of 2000. And for twelve years or more, everything was perfect. Phyllis and I aren't the most sociable people. We tend to keep ourselves to ourselves. But I'd like to think we were all friends in Riverview Close. Nobody complained about anything. Not until the Kenworthys moved in.

We do need a sense of perspective. They weren't the most unpleasant people in the world and I really did try to give them the benefit of the doubt. But they were causing so much upset and discord that when Mr Strauss invited us to that first meeting, six or seven weeks ago, we didn't hesitate. It really mattered that we got things sorted out – and even Felicity Browne left her sickbed to be there. Dear Mr Strauss and his wife provided lovely hospitality and wouldn't hear of any one of us contributing. We were all there – and then, at the last minute, the Kenworthys didn't show up. That really was a slap in the face and quite unnecessary!

Adam Strauss

I agree. It was a serious disappointment. It sent a signal to us that they just didn't care. Andrew would be the first to say that the best way to solve a neighbourhood dispute is through conciliation – but what's the point of talking if your neighbours refuse to listen? And May is right, incidentally. Giles Kenworthy wasn't a monster. He was arrogant and he was insensitive. But I can't say he ever did me any harm. Well, apart from my chess set – I was sorry about that.

What I think is interesting is how much worse things got after that first meeting. It was almost as if the Kenworthys were telling us that they didn't care any more. They could park their cars and make as much noise as they wanted and there was nothing we could do about it. That carelessness led to the death of one of Tom's patients. Looking back, I'd say that was the critical position, if you'll forgive a piece of chess terminology. After that, everything had a sort of inevitability.

Teri Strauss

It wasn't just the parking. What about the swimming pool and Jacuzzi? That was what mattered most to Roderick. We didn't care about it . . . Adam and me. We live on the other side of the close and we wouldn't hear all the noise or smell the chlorine. But poor Felicity! She had nothing left in her life except for peace and quiet and the view, and that was all going to be wiped away. How could Richmond Council do that to her? Don't they have any sense? I have a friend on Richmond Hill – she couldn't even put in new windows. But the Kenworthys could do anything they liked.

Tom Beresford

In my view, Giles Kenworthy took a petty delight in punishing us, in making life difficult any way he could. That camper van of his. The Union Jack that only went up after he met Andrew. The smoke from the barbecue – it's funny how he only ever lit it when the wind was blowing our way. And yes, I have to live with the fact that if I had been in my surgery instead of arguing with him about his bloody parked car, Raymond Shaw would still be alive.

But I'm not sure I entirely agree with Adam. The real turning point in all this was the moment when Giles Kenworthy chose not to come to the first meeting – and didn't even bother telling us until after we'd all arrived. That was when he showed his true colours and after that he seemed to think he could get away with anything he wanted.

Gemma Beresford

Like having poor Ellery killed. How could he do that? That was disgusting!

It was Andrew's idea to have the second meeting and he was absolutely right. Tom had put up with more than enough. We all had! We had to get together and work something out. That man was going to drive us all mad if we didn't take some sort of action. None of us could have known what was going to happen. I still don't quite understand how things turned out the way they did, but we didn't have any ill intentions. That's what we have to remember. We were there to look after each other. That's all. We were just being good neighbours.

Andrew Pennington

Was the meeting my idea? I'm not sure. It came up in conversation with Adam and Teri. Does it really matter? I'm not trying to evade responsibility. Far from it!

There must be a word for it when a group of people, normally quite sane and sensible, have a sort of collective breakdown – that's how I see it. I'm not for a moment suggesting that Giles Kenworthy deserved what happened to him, but it's unarguable that he pushed us all over the edge. Some of us were beginning to think that we would have to sell our homes and leave Riverview Close – although that in itself might be problematic because, as I pointed out several times, we would have been obliged to fill in a Property Information Form highlighting our relationship with the Kenworthys and that would have been enough to put any buyer off.

The second meeting took place at The Stables on a Sunday evening – eight days ago. The aim was to explore possibilities, to see if we could find a way out of the situation in which we found ourselves. I was the first to speak once everyone had arrived and I must confess that I didn't have a great deal to offer. Property law isn't my speciality and as far as I could see we had limited options.

Riverview Close is controlled by a management company, Riverview Close Ltd, of which I am currently the chair-person. We all have shares and the idea is that, together, we take responsibility for supervision and maintenance, insurance, repairs and antisocial behaviour – although it's never an easy matter, defining what antisocial behaviour is. The Kenworthys had parties. Their children did a certain amount of damage. There were parking problems. But what could we do? At the end of the day, threatening Giles Kenworthy with legal action might only have exacerbated the issues and could have led to ruinous expenses. Who had the bigger pockets? It was probably him.

And then there was the overarching question of the swimming pool – but this was a matter between the Kenworthys and the local council. Unfortunately, there was a limit to what we could do as we were no more than third parties. The management company had little room for manoeuvre. We could suggest to the council that they had failed to consider the impact of a swimming pool on neighbouring properties, especially given Felicity Browne's illness. But once planning permission has been given, it's always very difficult to turn it around.

That's really what we wanted to talk about, but at the same time I have to admit that we all had rather too much to drink. That's down to Adam's generosity, although I also brought wine and so, I think, did May . . .

May Winslow

I brought vodka. I didn't think for a minute that it was going to be a knees-up. Nor would I have wanted such a thing. But after what had happened with Ellery, I needed something to keep up my spirits. We were all upset. And if I may say so, without wishing to be rude to Mrs Strauss, I did think there would be a little more food.

Anyway, we all sat down and we talked about Giles Kenworthy and what we were going to do and somehow the conversation turned to murder.

Adam Strauss

We didn't mean it seriously! We were just letting off steam! I can't even remember who started it, but I'm pretty sure it was Roderick. Or Phyllis, talking about the bookshop. It's hardly surprising when you've got two ladies with a whole library of golden age crime. *'Why don't we just kill him?'* I'm sure it was Phyllis who started it.

Phyllis Moore

That's not true.

Adam Strauss

I'm not making accusations. It might have been Roderick. But whoever it was, they didn't mean it. We'd all had a bit too much to drink, that's all. He was joking!

Tom Beresford

Roderick didn't say it. I did.

It was stupid and for what it's worth, Gemma did try to stop me. Looking after me has become a full-time job for her and don't think I don't know it. I said we should kill him and then we all took it in turns suggesting different ways. I started. My idea was to inject a couple of mill of air into his pulmonary veins and hope it would find a way into his cerebral circulation. May suggested cyanide. Do you remember? She said it turns up in lots of crime novels. Teri said she could buy a herb called heartbreak grass in a Hong Kong market. Even Gemma joined in. She talked about doll's eyes, another poisonous plant. And Andrew was all for pushing him off the roof of a tall building. Oh yes, it was a jolly little evening.

Roderick didn't hold back. If anything he was more enthusiastic than anyone else, and I'm sure every one of us here remembers what he said. How could we forget? He reminded us that he had a crossbow in his garage. Do you remember what he said? *'It would be easy. Just ring the front doorbell and put a bolt in him when he answers.'*

Teri Strauss

And then Phyllis said – why don't we all do it together!

Phyllis Moore

It was me. Yes. Of course, it was Agatha Christie who gave me the idea. It was that book where all the suspects do the murder and then afterwards they look after each other. They give each other alibis and things like that. You know the one I mean! It's been filmed twice and David Suchet did it on television. I do love David Suchet! I don't think anyone did Poirot better than him. And here's the funny thing. By coincidence, we'd sold two copies of that very same book that week. Two different people! That probably explains why it was on my mind.

I said we should shoot a bolt into him, each and every one of us. Turn him into a pincushion! That's what I said.

Andrew Pennington

In retrospect, there was something very strange and psychological going on in that room. Almost a mass hysteria. The idea took hold of us. We were laughing, but at the same time we were saying the most dreadful things. How would we do it? When would we do it? How would we get away with it? I think the situation we were facing – the anger we all felt – had no solution in reality and so we moved into the world of fantasy to hold ourselves together.

327

Do you understand what I'm saying? Nobody in the room was *seriously considering* murder. But we were finding some sort of *psychological* release by expressing it.

Gemma Beresford

There's not a single person in the world who hasn't dreamed of killing an unpleasant boss, an irritating husband, a mean teacher, a lying politician. We were just doing the same. But we were doing it out loud.

We all agreed to kill him. And then someone asked the obvious question. Who was going to do it?

Hawthorne

So you drew straws.

May Winslow

You really are very clever, Mr Hawthorne. I don't know how you worked that out. But you're right. We talked about playing cards — making the ace of spades the death card. Or throwing a dice. Party games! I used to play something similar with my parents when I was a little girl. We'd sit around the table and we'd choose a killer by drawing matchsticks — and then whoever was the killer had to wink at you, but he had to do it without being seen and the idea was that he'd go on until either someone guessed who it was or there was no one left.

But in this case, Mr Strauss remembered that he had some straws left over from a party and it just seemed so appropriate – so biblical, almost. We would draw straws and whoever picked the shortest would have to kill Giles Kenworthy. Of course, sitting here in the light of day, it may seem very silly and irresponsible to you. But that's what we did.

Phyllis Moore

We cut eight pieces of straw, each one of them a different size. There were eight of us there. And so there could be no cheating, Mr Strauss held them behind his back so he couldn't see which straw was being taken. I went first. It was quite exciting. We all entered into the spirit of the thing . . . the game.

Andrew Pennington

It's true. We were all very caught up in the spirit of the moment, and I might add that Roderick was probably keener than anyone. Mrs Winslow drew a straw that was about two or three inches long. I was next and mine was shorter, but I knew there was an even shorter one somewhere in there. There was quite a bit of nervous laughter as Adam shuffled from person to person until there was only him and Roderick left.

And then it was Roderick's turn. He looked at the two straws that were sticking out of Adam's hand and he milked the moment for all it was worth. Then he made his choice and drew the shortest straw, holding it up for us all to see. He wasn't upset. He was almost triumphant. *'Well, that's it,'* he said. *'I suppose I'd better go round and get it over with!'*

Adam Strauss

It's funny how quickly the mood changed after that. The whole thing was a joke, of course, but we'd reached the punchline and I suppose it wasn't as funny as we'd thought it was going to be. The conversation turned quite serious again – the letters we were going to write, the actions that we might take. Andrew repeated some of the advice he had already given us. By now it was about half past nine and we were all tired and a little drunk. Nothing had been resolved. Things went downhill pretty quickly and everyone went home to bed.

Roderick was the last to leave and I was very worried about him. Not because I thought he'd go through with it and take it upon himself to kill Giles Kenworthy. That thought never crossed my mind. But he was desperately worried about Felicity. The meeting had achieved nothing. And I could see that he was depressed. I told him to call me the next day if he wanted to talk, but as things turned out, I didn't speak to him again properly until the day he died. As you know, he called me and asked me to come round.

That was Wednesday evening. By then, Giles Kenworthy was dead. Three days after Roderick had told everyone he was going to do it. And Kenworthy had been killed in exactly the way that he had described – a crossbow bolt through the neck. Everything I told you, the last time we spoke about this, was true. The only thing I omitted to mention was the context, what had happened at that second meeting. It was the reason why Roderick was so upset.

In fact, he was terrified. He told me over and over again that he hadn't done it, that it wasn't him, and although I did my best to calm him down, I'm not sure if I believed him or not. It just seemed like too much of a coincidence – unless someone else in the room had heard what he'd said and had decided to do it themselves. But, hand on heart, I can't say I suspect anyone here. And anyway, how would they have got into the garage with both Roderick and Felicity in the house? As far as I know, the up-and-over door was kept locked and they could hardly have sneaked in through the kitchen.

He had already been interrogated – twice – and he said he could feel the net closing in on him, that Detective Superintendent Khan was going to arrest him at any moment. And then there was the added worry that one of us would tell the police about the second meeting, drawing straws, everything you now know. If that happened, he'd be finished. He'd confessed to the murder before it had even happened!

Andrew Pennington

That second meeting has cast a very long shadow. None of us could be completely honest with you, Mr Hawthorne. We also had to conceal what we knew from the police. I'm sure you can imagine how difficult that was for me. It went against everything in my nature.

The basic fact of the matter is this. We had taken part in what we have described as a fantasy, a party game. But everything had changed when Giles Kenworthy was killed. We were guilty of conspiracy to commit murder as defined by the Criminal Law Act of 1977. Looking back, I can't believe I allowed it to continue. We had selected the victim and discussed various weapons. We had drawn straws to decide who was going to do it, for heaven's sake! Even if Giles Kenworthy hadn't been touched, we had still committed a crime – technically speaking. But if any of it had come out during the police investigation, we could all of us have been facing a life sentence.

May Winslow

The moment I left the garage, I telephoned Mr Pennington. I told him what had happened and he came straight round to my house. He couldn't believe it. Nor could I. He warned me that we might all be in serious trouble. We couldn't lie to the police. That would be an offence in itself. We couldn't obstruct their investigation. But nor could we tell them about the meeting we'd had on Sunday night. That was what he told me. We had to keep absolutely quiet about that.

Andrew Pennington

I telephoned everyone on the Thursday morning when Roderick's body was discovered. We could not lie. But the law does not compel a witness to provide information to the police. Our silence was not itself illegal and there was no reason why anyone should have asked us what we were doing on Sunday evening. I'm afraid this has also coloured our dealings with you, Mr Hawthorne, and for that I must apologise. I suppose there's nothing to prevent you passing on what you know to Detective Superintendent Khan.

Tom Beresford

What's the point? We all know the truth. Roderick Browne was a decent enough man. I liked him. We all did. And we're all desperately sorry for Felicity. But what we said and what we did that evening have got nothing to do with the end result. Roderick was the one who had the most to lose if Giles Kenworthy went on living. It was his crossbow. I have never doubted, not for a minute, that he was the one who committed the crime.

And then he got scared. The police knew it was him: Detective Superintendent Khan had made that clear. He was going to be arrested. So he sent his wife off to Woking, wrote a suicide note and killed himself. A dead man in a locked car in a locked garage with a suicide note in his lap. What other explanation can there be?

333

5

Hawthorne and Dudley let themselves into Woodlands with the keys that Felicity Browne had given them. There were cameras in Gardener's Cottage and burglar alarms in both The Stables and the Lodge, but otherwise the houses in Riverview Close were surprisingly lacking in electronic security. It was part of the charm of the place that it existed in the world as it had been fifty years ago, when neighbours left their doors open or their keys under the mat and burglaries were rare enough to be news.

The house was still in pain. Both Hawthorne and Dudley sensed it the moment they crossed the threshold, the strange atmosphere, almost an awareness, that always lingers after a sudden death, as if the bricks and the plasterwork that have embraced so much day-to-day activity somehow know. Roderick Browne's absence was everywhere. The police had been and gone, taking with them their photographic markers and crime-scene tape. But they had been unable to erase the memories.

It was late afternoon and still bright, but Hawthorne reached out and flicked on the light switch beside the door. The lights in the hallway, above the stairs and on the upper floor came on. He looked around him as if he had just proved a point. Andrew Pennington had described the last thing he had seen before Roderick took his own life. The light going out, in every sense.

Hawthorne went back through the kitchen and into the garage where Roderick had been found. The door had not been locked. The space on the other side was empty. The Skoda Octavia Mark 3 had been removed by the police and would be thoroughly examined for the coroner's report, even if the conclusions had already been reached. In its absence, a drain with a cast-iron gully grid had been revealed, set in the concrete floor. Dudley knelt down and tried to move the cover. It was stuck fast.

The up-and-over door was locked in place. The various bits and pieces that Hawthorne had seen when he had last been here hadn't moved. The crossbow had been taken, but it too had left its ghost behind, an empty space on the shelf. The interior was lit by the sun, not quite overhead, streaming diagonally through the skylight and picking out a thousand motes of dust.

'If I was going to kill myself, I'm not sure this is the place I'd choose.' Dudley had followed Hawthorne in and was looking around him with a sour expression on his face.

'People who kill themselves don't usually care,' Hawthorne said.

'They might do if they have the right self-image. Dentist to the stars. I see Roderick in a comfy chair with a bottle of champagne. And definitely Waitrose, not Tesco.'

'You may be right, mate. But you know what the real puzzle is? Roderick Browne going to all this trouble to make it one hundred per cent clear that he's offing himself because he killed Giles Kenworthy and all his neighbours know he did.'

'But he still leaves the straw in his top pocket.'

'Exactly. It leads us directly to them.'

'It's almost like he's trying to implicate them.'

Hawthorne went over to the cardboard box filled with electrical bits and pieces that had been added to the garage after his first visit. He pulled out different plugs and cables and plastic boxes, some of them smashed. They hardly seemed to merit examination, but he still rummaged through them. Meanwhile, Dudley was examining the Dyson hoover.

'Is it working?' Hawthorne asked.

'Are you kidding? I had one of these once. It never did the job.' He showed Hawthorne a plastic cylinder. 'The dust collector's cracked and the trigger's missing. It doesn't even look that old.' He put the piece down. 'What you need is a bigger Dyson to scoop up this one.'

Hawthorne had already moved on to the box of DVDs, the various gardening tools and the golf clubs. One of the putting irons seemed to be missing. He examined the bolts that held the up-and-over door in place. They were solid steel, as thick as his finger.

'Let's take this step by step,' he said. 'We know that Roderick Browne died around midnight.'

'That's what Khan said.'

'And we know he was alive and conscious at ten o'clock because that was when he was heard saying goodbye to Adam Strauss. He turned off the light. What does that say to you?'

'It says something's wrong.' Dudley had brought a chair in with him from the kitchen. He placed it in the middle of the floor – approximately where the driver's seat would have been. He sat down. 'He took sleeping pills and then he gassed himself with nitrous oxide. Why would he turn the light off? He wasn't going to bed and I somehow doubt he wanted to save electricity!'

'I agree. Let's say he goes into the kitchen, swallows the pills and then, when he's feeling sleepy, enters the garage for the final act. He climbs into the car, locks the doors and closes the windows from inside . . .'

'. . . slips the key fob into his trouser pocket . . .'

'. . . and dies.'

'But if it wasn't suicide, if it's murder, the big question is – how did the killer get out?'

They both looked up at the same moment.

'The skylight,' Dudley said. 'It's the only way.'

'We need a ladder.'

They found one outside, lying flat on the grass beside the garage. It was exactly the right length too. They leaned it against the wall and Dudley held it while Hawthorne climbed up, then followed.

They found themselves on a flat surface lined with asphalt, securely nailed down. The skylight was in the middle. From where they were standing, they could see the window of Roderick Browne's bathroom a short distance above them and all three gardens stretching out behind. The view of the close was largely blocked by the roof of the house, but they could make out a window in the eaves of Gardener's Cottage and the figure of a young woman, framed behind the glass. This had to be Kylie, the Beresfords' nanny.

'We're being watched,' Dudley said. He knelt beside the skylight and examined the eight stainless-steel screws that held the frame in place. He took a screwdriver out of his pocket and tried to turn one of them, then another. They didn't move.

'Khan said they'd rusted into place,' Hawthorne said.

'They're certainly stuck fast.'

He tried two more, then gave up.

Hawthorne took out a cigarette and lit it. 'Let's imagine the glass wasn't here,' he said. 'How easy would it be to climb onto the roof of the car and pull yourself up here and then go back down the ladder if, say, you had a sprained ankle?'

'Not easy.'

'That's what I was thinking.'

'It wouldn't be easy if you were seventy-nine or eighty-one either.'

Hawthorne nodded. Smoke trickled up from between his fingers. The two men stood where they were, watching the shadows stretch themselves across the lawns.

'You should go back into the police,' Hawthorne said.

'You giving me the elbow?'

'You can do better than working with me.'

'I thought you enjoyed it.'

'I'm not thinking of myself. I'm thinking of you. You should go back to Bristol and pick up where you left off. What happened, happened. You can't let it grind you down.'

'That's what Suzmann says.' Dudley looked at Hawthorne with eyes that were almost mournful. 'Seems a strange time to be mentioning it.'

'I've just got a bad feeling about this business – Riverview Close. I can't explain it. I've worked out who killed Giles Kenworthy and Roderick Browne. I can tell you how they did it and why. There are still one or two loose ends, but otherwise it's in the bag.'

'You worrying about Khan? Getting him to see the light?'

'He's already made up his mind. You and me are off the case. He's not going to want to lose face.' Hawthorne smoked. 'But that's not the worst of it.'

'Go on.'

'There are killers and there are killers. This one is different. Maybe you should back out now and leave this to me.'

'I'd prefer to see it to the end.'

'That's your choice, John. Just don't say you weren't warned.'

Hawthorne glanced up. He had spotted movements in Gardener's Cottage. The nanny was still at the window, watching them. Even at this distance, they could tell she was uneasy. Two strange men on a roof, one of them smoking. Hang around much longer and she might report them to the police.

Hawthorne flicked his cigarette into the gutter. 'All right. Kylie. Let's see what she's got to say.'

6

'I'm sorry. This isn't a very good time.'

Tom Beresford looked surprised to find Hawthorne and Dudley standing outside his door so soon after the meeting in Andrew Pennington's garden. He was reluctant to let them in.

'Not a good time for who, exactly?' Hawthorne asked. 'Not for Lynda Kenworthy or Felicity Browne, obviously. Not for that woman in Hampton Wick. Is she out of hospital yet? Not for Raymond Shaw, who dropped dead in your clinic while you were having a row about parking, and not for his wife and son. Not really a good time for anyone in Riverview Close when you think about it, what with blackmail, theft, racism and all the other activities that have been going on around here.'

'Nice neighbourhood,' Dudley agreed.

'I don't understand,' Beresford said. 'I thought you'd have gone by now. We've already told you everything we know. What are you doing here?'

'You're still telling me that Roderick Browne murdered his neighbour and killed himself?'

'Have you got another explanation?'

'If you let us in, you might find out. But meanwhile, let's start with a little anomaly that I've noticed, Dr Beresford. Roderick took an overdose of sleeping pills. You had given his wife a prescription for temazepam.'

'That's right. But if you're suggesting—'

'I'm not suggesting anything. I'm just telling you that according to the police report, Roderick Browne swallowed thirty milligrams of zolpidem – which is the medication you prescribed to yourself. Doesn't that strike you as a bit odd?'

Standing there, filling the doorway, Tom Beresford was suddenly looking less sure of himself. 'I didn't give Roderick my sleeping pills, if that's what you're thinking.'

'Then how did he get them?'

'He came to my house now and then. He could have taken them.' A thought occurred to him. 'Who told you what pills I was taking? That's confidential information.'

'Nothing is confidential in a murder investigation,' Hawthorne replied with a smile of innocence. 'By the way, when did you start smoking again?'

'That's none of your business.'

'You ever sneak round and have a puff in your garage?'

'Occasionally.'

'Andrew Pennington saw you on the night of Roderick's death. I just thought you might like to know.'

Hawthorne wasn't moving. Tom Beresford realised he had no choice. 'You'd better come in,' he said.

He led them towards the kitchen. The sound of children shouting came from somewhere upstairs and then the voice of a young woman with an Australian accent.

'Lucy! Claire! Will you both pipe down?'

'Through here . . .' Tom said.

Gemma Beresford was sitting at the table. She was not alone. She was deep in conversation with a young man who turned round as Hawthorne and Dudley came in. Neither of them looked surprised to see Felicity's carer, Damien Shaw. For his part, he sat there squirming, obviously unhappy to see them.

'I couldn't stop them coming in.' Tom's words fell heavily. 'They're still investigating the two deaths. They think the police have got it wrong.'

'Any reason you wouldn't want us to find the three of you together?' Hawthorne asked.

'None at all!' Gemma glared at him. 'We've been seeing a lot of Damien since——'

'Since the death of his father . . . Raymond Shaw.'

'Yes, Mr Hawthorne. We feel we owe him a duty of care.'

Damien had already told Hawthorne that he'd recently been forced to take a week off and that he was living with his mother, who was on her own. Given his surname, it hadn't taken a great leap of imagination to put things together.

'I don't blame Tom for what happened,' Damien said, leaping to the defence.

'Dr Beresford couldn't get to your dad in time because he was held up by his neighbour.' Hawthorne seemed to consider the matter for the first time. 'Did you blame Giles Kenworthy?'

Damien blushed an angry red. 'What if I did?'

'Well, you might have been tempted to put a crossbow bolt through his neck.'

'That's ridiculous.'

'It doesn't seem ridiculous to me,' Dudley said. 'You knew about the crossbow. You were home alone with Felicity. You had access to the garage.'

'Leave him alone!' Gemma reached out and took hold of Damien's arm. 'Damien wouldn't hurt anyone. And anyway, we know who killed Giles Kenworthy.'

'He says it wasn't Roderick,' Tom muttered.

'Roderick Browne and Giles Kenworthy were both killed by the same person,' Hawthorne said. 'That's been clear from the start.'

'Well, it wasn't Damien,' Gemma insisted, still clinging on to him.

'Why are you here?' Dudley asked.

'I've come to say goodbye,' Damien faltered. He withdrew his arm. 'I've handed in my notice at the agency. I've spoken to Felicity and she's not coming back to Richmond anytime soon. She was my main client and I need a break anyway. This is all so horrible! I'm going travelling in Europe.'

'Alone?'

'With a friend.'

As if on cue, there was a movement at the door and the girl from the window appeared. She was in her twenties, fair-haired, wearing cut-off jeans and a shirt tied at the waist. 'Claire and Lucy are watching *Horrid Henry* on TV,' she said. 'I'm trying to get them to quieten down before—'

She stopped, recognising Hawthorne and Dudley from the roof.

'Those are the guys I saw,' she said.

Gemma nodded. 'It's all right, Kylie. We know them.'

'We haven't met,' Hawthorne said.

'I'm Kylie Jane.' She looked wary, keeping her distance.

'Kylie's coming with me,' Damien said.

In fact, it had been obvious that they were together the moment Kylie had walked in. Hawthorne could tell from the way they looked at each other. They made an attractive couple.

'You're leaving Richmond?' Hawthorne asked.

Kylie nodded. 'I handed in my notice last week.'

'We're going to miss her terribly,' Gemma said. 'We still haven't broken it to the girls. But it's hardly surprising, given everything that's happened. They're both better off out of it.' She glared at Hawthorne as if it was all his fault.

'Well, before you go, I'd like to ask you a couple of things,' Hawthorne said.

'I don't know anything about Giles Kenworthy,' Kylie protested.

345

'But you know a lady called Marsha Clarke who lives in Hampton Wick.'

Kylie stared. 'What's she got to do with anything?'

'How is she?'

Kylie looked from Gemma to Tom, as if asking permission to speak. They were as puzzled as she was. 'She's better,' she said. 'They've allowed her to go home now. She was very worried about her cats.'

'I'm sure she'll miss you when you're in Europe.'

If there was an implied accusation, Kylie ignored it. 'I won't be away for ever. And I've spoken to the charity. They're going to make sure another volunteer goes round.'

'What exactly are you on about?' Tom asked.

Hawthorne ignored him. 'Can you tell us what happened to her?'

'She was attacked.'

'You must know more than that, love.'

'Sure.' Kylie was annoyed by the way she'd been addressed but went on anyway. 'I've been visiting Marsha for three years . . . ever since her husband died. She's well into her eighties and she's on her own. She's a sweet old lady and she's never done anyone any harm.

'Every evening, during the summer, she walks down to the river and feeds the ducks. I used to take her lots of stale bread from the close when I went to visit her. She's not the sort of person to ask for anything, but that's something that gives her real pleasure.

'So, a week ago, at around seven thirty, she was walking back to her house. She has a little terraced cottage at the end of Milton Gardens, which is near the park. She let herself in through the gate and someone hit her on the back of the head. They must have been waiting for her. The police say she was lucky her skull wasn't fractured. She could have been killed!'

'Do they know why she was attacked?'

'It wasn't a mugging. She had her handbag with her and the keys to her front door were inside, so it wasn't a burglary either. They found a flyer from a political party stuffed through her letter box – the UK Independence Party. The strange thing is that nobody else in Milton Gardens got one and the party hasn't been campaigning in Hampton Wick. And Marsha just happens to be the only black woman in Milton Gardens.'

'It was a racist attack,' Dudley said.

'This happened the night before Giles Kenworthy was killed,' Hawthorne added. 'And he was a member of the same party.'

'I don't know anything about that, Mr Hawthorne,' Kylie said. 'The police called me and I spent half the night in the hospital. After that, I stayed in her home to look after the cats.'

'It's funny,' Dudley muttered, almost to himself. 'But why do I get the feeling that everyone in this room had a good reason to hate Giles Kenworthy?'

Damien stood up and went over to Kylie. He put an arm

around her shoulders. 'We don't hate anyone,' he said. 'And Tom and Gemma have been nothing but kind to us. You're the one who seems to know a lot about hate, Mr Hawthorne.'

Hawthorne smiled. 'Well, I've met a lot of murderers,' he said.

7

The taxi took them across Richmond Bridge and into St Margaret's. Then it looped round, following the river back towards Petersham but on the other side. Dudley watched the scenery go past, but Hawthorne's attention was fixed on his iPhone, which he was holding in both hands, watching a pulsating blue dot in the centre of the screen.

'Turn left on Orleans Road,' he instructed.

The driver obeyed, cutting down the edge of Marble Hill Park, the river now ahead of them. They came to a sharp right turn. Hawthorne had seen it on the screen. 'Stop here!'

They paid and got out, then followed a narrow footpath that brought them to the water's edge. There were a couple of old barges moored here, tied to the riverbank a short distance apart. Hawthorne checked the screen one last time. 'That one!' he said, pointing towards the nearest of the two.

It was called *Bella*, perhaps not the most appropriate name for such an ancient and unattractive vessel. It was sitting low in the water, which only added to its sense of dejection, along with its rotting wooden planks, algae-covered ropes and dusty windows. Much of the deck space was taken up with rubbish: plastic bins, cables, a rusting bike, a roll of tarpaulin, bits of machinery, a barbecue missing a leg. Surrounded by water and willow trees, with geese and swans flapping past and no roads or buildings in sight, this would be an extraordinary place to wake up, so it was all the more surprising that *Bella* should have been so neglected, barely able to keep afloat.

A rickety gangplank led down to the one clear space in front of the entrance, but as Hawthorne took his first step, his weight caused the boat to rock slightly and at once the door flew open and Sarah Baines emerged, furious even before she knew who was visiting her. She recognised Hawthorne and her face didn't change.

'This is private property. What are you doing here?'

'Nice place you've got,' Hawthorne said. 'Is it yours?'

'I rent it. What do you want?'

'We've come to see you.'

'How did you know I was here?'

'We didn't. Can we come in?' Hawthorne dared her to refuse.

Sarah examined him grumpily. 'I'll give you five minutes,' she said.

The inside of the barge was a little more homely than the

decks with all the rubbish had suggested. There was a tiny galley, a table that folded down from the wall, three stools, a sitting area and a cast-iron stove at the back. A sofa doubled as a bed. Clothes lines stretched the entire length of the cabin with an assortment of faded but multicoloured T-shirts, scarves, trousers and socks, giving the place the feel of a Dickens novel. It would have been no surprise if Fagin had appeared from behind the stove, holding a piece of burnt toast on a fork.

'So why are you here?' Sarah asked as they sat down on the stools. There was to be no offer of tea . . . or hot gin and sugar.

'You asked how we found you,' Hawthorne reminded her.

'All right. Surprise me.'

'You know the app Find My iPhone? I used that to track down Roderick Browne's phone.'

Sarah considered what he had just said. 'How is that even possible?'

'I have a friend who made it easy.'

'The phone disappeared after he got home and died in the garage,' Dudley cut in. 'You and May Winslow were alone in the house and it seems pretty obvious that one of you must have taken it.' He smiled. 'And speaking personally, I don't believe that nice Mrs Winslow would go around nicking things.'

'She not as nice as you think,' Sarah growled.

'We know all about Mrs Winslow, just like we know all about you.' Hawthorne held out a hand. 'Where is it?'

Sarah could see that there was no point pretending. She went over to one of the galley drawers, pulled it open and took out Roderick's phone. 'It's useless anyway,' she said. 'I don't have the passcode.'

'Is that why you took it? To sell it?'

'Maybe.'

'I wonder . . .' Hawthorne turned the phone on, then entered the code that Felicity had given him.

'It's his date of birth,' Dudley said.

'Aren't you the clever ones!'

'We try to be.'

It took Hawthorne only a few seconds to find what he was looking for. He had opened Roderick's text messages and turned the phone round to show Sarah an image he had expanded to fill the screen. She glanced at it as briefly as she could, then turned her head away, embarrassed.

The image showed her posing naked. It was one of several she had sent Roderick Browne. Hawthorne quickly scrolled through the others. The poses were raw and explicit. Dudley closed his eyes. Hawthorne showed no emotion at all. 'Paid you for these, did he?' he asked.

'What if he did?'

'Just answer the question, love. It's late. I want to get home for tea . . .'

'Turn it off!'

Hawthorne did as she had asked.

'All right,' Sarah admitted. 'Roderick was paying me twenty quid a shot, but I was doing him a favour, poor sod. With his wife locked in the bedroom, he hadn't seen a naked woman for ten years. I made him happy.'

'So between blackmailing May Winslow, stealing from the Kenworthys, putting Ellery down the well and selling dirty pictures to Roderick, you were pretty busy in Riverview Close,' Hawthorne said.

'No wonder you didn't have much time for gardening,' Dudley remarked.

'I told you, I never touched that dog. I know Lynda was complaining about him, but if there was anyone who was cruel enough to do something like that, it was Giles Kenworthy, and maybe that was what got him killed. As for me, I've done nothing wrong.'

'You've done quite a lot wrong, darling.' Hawthorne slipped the phone into his pocket. 'You got any idea who killed Roderick Browne?'

'He killed himself.'

'You really think that? You seem a smart girl . . . in and out of everyone's houses. I was just wondering if you'd seen anything and maybe worked it out.'

'I'll tell you one thing if it will get you off my back.' Hawthorne looked at her enquiringly. 'Those flowers of Mr Pennington. The ones in the roundabout. They were trashed deliberately – and it wasn't the kids.'

This time, Hawthorne smiled. 'How do you know?'

'Wheel marks in the soil. But no mud tracks on the drive. How is that possible?'

'I'd worked that one out, too, Sarah. But you're right, and I'm grateful.' Hawthorne stood up, being careful not to hit his head on the ceiling. 'If you'll take my advice, you'll move on. Maybe it's time to find another river.'

'Me and *Bella* have got nowhere to go.'

Hawthorne opened the door.

'Do me a favour, Mr Hawthorne. Don't show anyone those photos. People like me don't get a lot of choice in what we do. I wasn't brought up in no Riverview Close. My whole life has been just one thing after another, but I've still got some pride.'

Hawthorne didn't answer. He and Dudley returned to the bank and walked away from the barge, watching as a couple of late canoeists slid past. It was going to be one of those perfect evenings with the light soft and painted and a stillness in the air. The sort of evening that's unique to the Thames in the summer months.

Hawthorne suddenly stopped, took Roderick's iPhone and weighed it in his hand. Then he threw it into the air and watched it splash down, leaving just a few ripples behind.

EIGHT

THE SOLUTION

1

Detective Superintendent Tariq Khan wasn't happy to find himself driving back to Richmond.

For a start, the traffic was terrible on Kew Bridge, which had been built in 1903 when horse-drawn omnibuses and hansom cabs would have been carrying pleasure-seekers to Kew Gardens and Richmond Green, but was now, over a hundred years later, completely unfit for purpose. More to the point, though, he had finished with the business at Riverview Close. He had briefed the press. He had, once again, been on TV and his wife and parents-in-law had all said how handsome he looked. Going back could be seen as an acceptance of defeat, or at least an acknowledgement that it was just possible there was something he had missed. The worst of it was, he couldn't resist it. He had to know.

DC Goodwin was behind the wheel. Khan liked to check

the messages and social media on his phone (he had set up a Google Alert for his name), to scroll through the news and generally keep his mind off the road. This was the start of another week, but neither of them had discussed what they had done over the weekend. They had a good relationship at work but none at all out of it.

Half an hour later, they had reached the centre of Richmond and the annoying one-way system that would take them literally round the houses before allowing them to strike out for Petersham. Ruth Goodwin spoke for almost the first time.

'Why are we doing this, sir?' she asked.

'Good question.' Khan tapped a few last words into his iPhone and put it away.

'You know Hawthorne is dangerous,' Goodwin continued. 'He committed a violent assault on a suspect . . .'

'As I recall, you were the one who suggested using him in the first place.'

'I thought he might be useful to us. But the whole thing turned out to be a whole lot easier than we first thought. You did a very good job, sir.'

Khan sniffed but made no answer to that.

'It's just that it might be trouble bringing him back.'

'He says he has new information.'

'And if everything changes, what are we going to tell the *Daily Mail*?'

The back seat of the car was covered with old newspaper

and magazine articles relating to the case and the *Daily Mail* had indeed made it to the top, open at a double-page spread with the headline: CELEBRITY DENTIST FOUND DEAD. There was a photograph of Roderick Browne, another of the actor Ewan McGregor and – above a caption reading 'THE CASE IS CLOSED' SAYS POLICE HOTSHOT DS TARIQ KHAN – a picture of the detective superintendent too.

'If he really does know something, it's better that he talks to us than to the press,' he said now.

'And if he says we've got it all wrong?'

'We've got nothing wrong, Ruth. Nothing at all.'

They drove down Richmond Hill and into Riverview Close. Hawthorne and Dudley were already there, waiting for them on the other side of the archway and the gate. Khan noticed that Hawthorne was dressed in the same clothes he'd worn the last two times they had met. Goodwin parked outside Woodlands and they both got out.

'I hope you're not wasting my time,' Khan said. There were no greetings, no handshakes.

'If you thought I was wasting your time, you wouldn't have come,' Hawthorne said reasonably.

'So what do you want to tell me?'

'Well, the first thing to mention is that Dudley and I haven't been paid, since you ask. And as we've done your job for you, it would be nice if you'd see your way to giving us the whole week plus bonus.'

'It's in the contract,' Dudley said.

'You tell us what you know and I'll be the judge of that,' Khan said. He looked around him. 'It seems very quiet here.'

'The killer's in. Don't worry. We wouldn't drag you all the way over here without making sure of that.'

Khan looked for movement behind the windows. Woodlands was empty, obviously, but Gardener's Cottage? The Stables? Well House? There was no sign of anyone.

'I thought we might start out here,' Hawthorne said. 'It's a nice day and we need to get back to the beginning.'

'And when was that?' Goodwin asked.

'A long time ago, as a matter of fact. Much longer than any of us thought.'

Hawthorne took a few steps forward so that he was on the edge of the roundabout, surrounded by the six houses. Dudley stayed where he was. He had nothing more to do, but he was quietly pleased to be here. Khan and Goodwin stood, a little self-consciously, waiting for Hawthorne to begin.

'Most murderers don't really think about what they're going to do,' he said. 'You get the fantasists, the husbands who hate their wives, the kids who hate their stepdads, and they may think about murder for years . . . but they're never going to do it. Planning it is enough. You know as well as I do that most murders are acts of passion – spur-of-the-moment things. One drink too many. A fight that gets out of control. But then, just now and again, you get the genius, the killer who's not going to get caught, who sits down and works it all out. These are what you call the stickers, the crimes that are like no others because there's an intelligence behind them. That's where I come in. That's sort of my speciality.

'You knew from the start that something was wrong, but what was it exactly that worried you about this one? Well, the crossbow and bolt screamed out that something weird was going on. It's not a weapon of choice for your average killer. And then there was the setting: a smart close in Richmond. Do you know how many people get killed in a place like this? You could probably count them on the fingers of one posh lady's hand. Finally, everyone had the same motive. That doesn't even seem fair! How do you choose between the neighbour who's pissed off about the smoke coming off the barbecue and the one who can't park his car?

'So you decided to get me involved. To be honest with you, the first day I came here, I thought you were wasting my time. It all seemed pretty straightforward to me. Nightmare neighbour. Crossbow in the garage. Who's going to fire it? They draw straws and . . . bang!'

'What are you talking about – drawing straws?' Khan asked.

'Oh yeah. You never found out about that.' Quickly, Hawthorne described his meetings with Felicity Browne and then May Winslow and Phyllis Moore and where they had taken him.

'So the piece of straw in the dead man's pocket . . . ?' Goodwin began.

'Got it in one, Detective Constable. Roderick drew the short straw and took it with him to his death.'

Hawthorne paused.

'Except it wasn't like that. What I've realised, since I arrived at Riverview Close, is that nothing here is what it seems. Nothing! Every clue, every suspect, every question, every answer . . . it's all been carefully worked out. Everyone who lives here has been manipulated. So have you. So have I. Something happens and you think that it somehow connects with the murder – but you're wrong. It's been designed to trick you. Smoke and bloody mirrors. I've never seen anything like it.

'I mean . . . take all the coincidences. What is a coincidence? It's the most random thing in the world. It's like when you go to the supermarket and bump into your mum. And it never occurs to you that it might have been carefully arranged—'

'Hawthorne, where is this taking us?' Khan was losing his patience.

'To the solution, Detective Superintendent. I'm just trying to explain what we've been up against.'

'What coincidences?' Goodwin asked.

'Well, three attacks. One was an old lady living a couple of miles away in Hampton Wick. This happened the night before Giles Kenworthy was killed. Nothing to do with it, you'd think. Except the old lady, Marsha Clarke, was being looked after by Kylie Jane, who was the Beresfords' nanny.

And a couple of days before that, on Friday morning, some-one pushed Adam Strauss down a flight of stairs.'

'Well, you'd know about that,' Goodwin muttered and immediately wished she hadn't.

Hawthorne didn't care. 'We've checked out the CCTV,' he said.

'There's definitely someone behind Mr Strauss,' Dudley said. 'Wearing a hoodie and filmed from behind. Looks like a kid. CCTV wasn't a lot of help.'

'Again, these things happen. You'd think it had nothing to do with a murder that was being planned in Riverview Close. But you'd be wrong. It was all part of the same thing.'

'What was the third attack?' Ruth Goodwin asked.

'That happened six weeks earlier. Someone hacked into Giles Kenworthy's computer system. It was the reason he couldn't come to The Stables the first time he was invited. Again, it hardly seems likely that it was part of the plot, but I've got every reason to think it was.'

'Why don't you just cut to the chase and tell us who did it?' Khan asked. He didn't like the feeling of being strung along.

'There are more coincidences,' Hawthorne said. 'We now know there were two meetings where the neighbours tried to work out what to do about Giles Kenworthy. I think it's fair to say that the first time they met, they were divided fifty-fifty. Roderick and Felicity Browne would do anything to get rid of Giles Kenworthy. They hated him and they were des-perate not to lose their view. The same goes for Tom and

Gemma Beresford. Mrs Beresford in particular was worried sick about her husband and the stress he was feeling from this parking thing. But, on the other side of the coin, Andrew Pennington wasn't going to step out of line. His solution to the whole situation was to write letters, to stop things escalating – exactly what you'd expect from a criminal barrister. May Winslow and Phyllis Moore agreed. They had their own reasons for avoiding anything that might look like criminal activity. And Adam Strauss and his wife were neutral, happy to see how things developed.

'What happened in the next six weeks? Everyone who didn't already hate Giles Kenworthy was given a good reason to. May Winslow and Phyllis Moore lost their pet dog in a particularly cruel way, and they were led to believe that this was down to Kenworthy. Adam Strauss had his most expensive and precious chessboard smashed by a cricket ball. As it happens, cricket had been mentioned at the meeting – along with skateboards. And guess what! Andrew Pennington's flower arrangement, a tribute to his dead wife which he'd spent years looking after, was crushed by a skateboard. And not just that. It happened on the fifth anniversary of her death. That's terrible luck.

'But was it luck? Or was everyone being tricked into thinking things they didn't actually think?

'Let's take the whole premise of what was going on in Riverview Close. The "Nightmare Neighbours" scenario. I agree that Giles Kenworthy doesn't sound like the nicest of guys, but was he really such a monster? You know the most sensible thing anyone said when I was asking questions? It was Lynda Kenworthy – "There's nothing special about Riverview Close . . . There isn't a street in England where the neighbours don't have disputes. I was brought up in Frinton and it was just the same." Everyone argues with their neighbours. They've been doing it since the Middle Ages, and maybe there have been odd instances where it's led to murder. But hen's teeth, I'd say. Even in tower blocks and housing associations, where a thoughtless neighbour can make life a complete misery, people somehow manage to put up with it. Are we really going to believe that selfish parking could be a motive for murder? Or kids on skateboards? Or flying a Union Jack in a back garden? It's ridiculous!'

'What about the swimming pool?' Khan asked.

'Oh, yes. That was the one big thing that happened between the first meeting and the second meeting. The Kenworthys got permission to build their pool. And we've heard lots of things about that, haven't we. The loss of Felicity Browne's view was the big one. It's strange how nobody has considered that Felicity could have crawled out of bed and shot Giles Kenworthy with her husband's crossbow or that Roderick might have killed himself to protect her, taking the blame. I wondered about that for a while. There were plenty of other reasons to stop the swimming pool being built: the noise, the chlorine, the disruption, the extra traffic. But do any of those sound like a motive for murder, or was there something else that no one had mentioned that might have had more serious consequences?'

'You've been talking for a long time, Hawthorne,' Khan interrupted. 'And you haven't said anything yet that's made me think it was worth coming here.'

'Then maybe you haven't been listening, Detective Superintendent. But everything will make sense soon. We just need to talk a little bit about the so-called suicide of Roderick Browne.'

'There was nothing so-called about it,' Ruth Goodwin cut in. 'This second meeting you just told us about. It proves we were right. Roderick Browne drew the short straw. He killed Giles Kenworthy and then he was worried sick he was going to be found out, so he did himself in.'

'Oh, come on, love. Why don't you go back and read that letter of his? There isn't a single word that admits to his having killed anyone! "*I did something very stupid*". You really think he would use the word stupid to describe murdering his neighbour? "*I cannot bear you to see the consequences.*" Is that him killing himself? "*I do not want you to see this*". That must be his body in the garage?'

'Exactly,' Goodwin said.

'Rubbish. What he did that was stupid was to announce, in front of everyone, that he was going to murder Kenworthy. The consequences were that everyone would assume he had done it and he would be arrested. And that was what he didn't want her to see – him being led away in handcuffs.'

'A bit convenient that he should have framed it that way,' Khan muttered.

'Not convenient. All part of the plan!'

Hawthorne slowed down. He was trying to make it as simple as he could.

'Let's look at yet another coincidence. The whole idea of killing Giles Kenworthy starts with Phyllis Moore because – guess what – two people have gone into her bookshop and bought the same Agatha Christie novel just days apart and that novel has a plot in which all the suspects have joined together to kill a man they hate! What do you reckon the chances of that happening are?'

'People *like* Agatha Christie.'

'Yes. But once again, you don't seem to appreciate what was going on here, how every detail was being thought out in advance.

'If you believe for a single minute that Roderick Browne killed himself because of what happened at that second meeting, ask yourself this. First, why was the suicide so bloody complicated? A locked car in a locked garage. The only keys inside the one pocket you don't normally use to store them. You try getting them in when you're sitting down! Stainless-steel screws which don't rust have somehow gone rusty, making it impossible to open the skylight. And here are two more questions. Why is there a puddle on the floor when it hasn't rained for weeks, and what is a piece of drinking straw doing in his top pocket?'

'You've already told us where the straw came from,' Goodwin said.

'So when Roderick Browne killed himself, he made sure that it was somewhere we'd find it because he wanted us to know what had happened? You really think he even kept the straw, took it with him from The Stables? That clue was more planted than any of the flowers in Andrew Pennington's roundabout. The aim was to manipulate us, to steer us to the second meeting, which would shine a light on the suicide-that-had-to-be-suicide and couldn't possibly be murder!'

Hawthorne had said enough. He came to a halt, turning his soft brown eyes on the two police officers, daring them to challenge him.

There was a long silence.

'What you're saying,' Khan began at last, 'is that someone else killed Giles Kenworthy. They set up Roderick Browne and then killed him too, making it look like suicide. And that from start to finish, they've been dangling everyone on a string – a series of strings – and have been in complete control?'

'You've finally got there, Detective Superintendent. Even now they're laughing at us. They think it's all gone their way.'

'So who are you talking about?' Khan looked around him, at the six houses that made up the close: Riverview Lodge, Woodlands, The Gables, Well House, The Stables, Gardener's Cottage. Hawthorne had said that the killer was at home. 'Which door do we knock on?'

Hawthorne smiled. 'I'll show you,' he said.

2

The six of them were sitting quite formally in the living room, facing each other on two sofas and two chairs. Hawthorne and Dudley had taken the chairs.

'What sort of person would always be ten moves ahead?' Hawthorne was saying. 'That was the question I asked myself. Who might see the whole world as a game where you could manoeuvre people left and right, this way and that, making them do almost anything you wanted? Who would remember every last detail about everyone around them so that they could use it to their own advantage? Who could plan against any eventuality so that no matter what happened, they'd be able to come back with the right response?'

'A chess player,' Adam Strauss said. 'I have to admit, it's an interesting idea, Mr Hawthorne.'

'Why are you here?' Teri demanded. 'Are you accusing my husband of murdering Giles Kenworthy?'

'And Roderick Browne,' Hawthorne remarked amicably.

'It's lies! You are telling lies! You should get out of my house.'

Adam smiled and laid a hand on his wife's thigh. 'Don't worry, darling,' he said. 'I've got nothing to be afraid of and I'd be quite interested to hear what Mr Hawthorne has got to say.'

'You're denying it?' Detective Superintendent Khan asked.

'I'm not quite sure yet what it is I'm being asked to deny. Murder, obviously. But how, why and when? I've never been a great shot with a bow and arrow and right now –' he lifted the walking stick '– I'm in no fit state to have broken into Roderick's house and killed him. In fact, I was the last person to see him alive. Alive being the operative word. We were also good friends, although I don't suppose that counts for anything in Mr Hawthorne's mind. Do go ahead, Mr Hawthorne. So far, you've made complete sense, even if you're barking up entirely the wrong tree.'

'Unlike Mrs Winslow's dog,' Dudley said. 'He had a thing about that magnolia in the Kenworthys' garden.'

'We'll come to that in a minute,' Hawthorne said. He hadn't been put off by Strauss's denials. He was quite relaxed.

'We already know everything about the first meeting,' he continued. 'All the neighbours get together to air their complaints and at the last moment Giles Kenworthy pulls out – because someone's tried to hack into his computer system. I'd guess you had a hand in that, Mr Strauss. It's a smart move. It makes him look bad, worse than he is. It helps turn him into the target that he'll eventually become. And that's just the start of it. In the weeks that follow, the weaker chess pieces – May Winslow and Andrew Pennington – will be advanced across the board. Horrible things will happen to them to bring them onside. May's pet dog will be killed. Andrew's flower display will be spoiled – and in both cases the Kenworthys will get the blame.'

'My chess set was also smashed,' Adam reminded him.

'Yeah . . . you and your precious chess set, Mr Strauss! You had to be one of the team. You had to suffer too. That's part of the reason everyone trusted you. They thought you were with them. But it wasn't a cricket ball that came through your window. You did it – just like you cold-bloodedly crept out and killed that poor bloody dog, and cut down the flowers on the anniversary of Andrew Pennington's wife's death. Only, here's the funny thing, you were too vain to destroy any-thing that was truly valuable. So you chose a piece of posh merchandise made under licence from a film that came out thirteen years ago. You may have tried to big it up, but even when it was in a hundred pieces rather than thirty-two, I could tell it wasn't up to much, and my friend Dudley thought it was rubbish too. A king that looks like Ian McKellen? A knight based on Orlando Bloom? The whole idea of hobbits against orcs? Fifty quid on eBay even if it was given to you by some major sheikh, which, incidentally, I doubt. Pull the other one!

'The first meeting assembled the pieces that really mattered – your neighbours. The second moved them into position. By the way, Andrew Pennington thought it might have been his idea for all of you to get together again, but he also mentioned that it came out of a conversation with you two lovebirds. So you probably found a way to suggest it to him, the same way you hired two people to buy the same book at The Tea Cosy so that Phyllis or May would bring up the idea about everyone committing the same murder. The way you see the world, everyone's a pawn.

'So now they're all pissed off with the Kenworthys and this time you make sure there's lots of alcohol but no food so that things get a bit out of hand and there will be no inhibitions. When someone brings up the idea of murder, it's all a bit of a laugh. To start with, you're all going to do it – just like in the book. But then you remember that you've got a packet of drinking straws in the kitchen. You know, the very first time I heard that, it struck me as weird. You don't have kids but you've got drinking straws left over from some party? It's rubbish, of course. You'd bought them specially for that night. More manipulation.

'And there was something else about the drawing of the straws that didn't add up. Phyllis Moore told me that you were the one who held them – no surprises there – but she added that they were behind your back "so there could be no cheating". But that makes no sense at all. It's exactly the reason why you hold them in front of you, so everyone can see. If they're behind your back, it's easy to conceal the shortest straw in the waistband of your trousers or somewhere and force it on the person you've chosen by leaving them until last. That person was Roderick Browne. All along, you'd decided that he was going to be your patsy. But then, like every opponent you've ever come across, you had him psychologically pinned down like a butterfly. He was perfect for what you wanted.

'He and his wife, Felicity, had been the most vocal opponents of Giles Kenworthy – along with Dr Beresford, of course. The death of his patient, Raymond Shaw, was a bonus . . . I doubt even a chess grandmaster could arrange a heart attack, so we'll put that one down to real coincidence. Tom Beresford was onside anyway. Roderick Browne was the actual target. He and Felicity were hopping mad about the pool. For them it was almost a matter of life and death. And they had the murder weapon, right where they needed it. Everything was set up.

'My guess is that you'd taken the crossbow before the trick with the drinking straws. That was always your method. Ten moves ahead. You knew that the Kenworthy kids would be boarding. You probably even knew about Lynda Kenworthy and her French teacher. You slipped round to the house when Giles Kenworthy was on his own, shot him and generously left the crossbow complete with Roderick Browne's fingerprints, even making sure it was pointing at the right house for the police to find. As for that chess game you told us about, the one you were playing online with your Polish friend and which provided your alibi – my guess is that you were doing it on your phone at the same time. Talk about multitasking!

'What's the end result of all this? You've created the perfect conspiracy. What was a joke, a drunken game of "let's pretend", has suddenly become a reality. Roderick Browne has told everyone he's going to kill Giles Kenworthy and he's even been generous enough to name the murder weapon. How you must have laughed! Because the following morning, Kenworthy is found with a bolt in his throat and of course everybody assumes that Roderick went through with it, that it must have been him.

'At the same time, they're terrified. Like it or not, they were all part of it. Andrew Pennington is quick to warn them. It's a classic "conspiracy to commit murder" and Roderick won't be the only one to go down. They all will! Nice, respectable people: a doctor, his posh jewellery-designer wife, a retired barrister, two old ladies . . . they were all there. Before the police even arrive, they've all taken a vow of omertà. Nobody can say anything that might incriminate them. Don't mention the second meeting! Everyone has to lie. What was the first thing Roderick said to me when I met him? "Has anyone said anything?" He was terrified that one of his neighbours would land him in it.

'And things only got worse for Roderick. You talked to him once on Tuesday, Detective Superintendent, and then on Wednesday, after he'd taken his wife to Woking, you pulled him into Shepherd's Bush. By the end of a heavy session, he was convinced he was going to be arrested and charged – and that was why he ended up writing that letter. Read it again! It's not a confession! All he meant was the public humiliation of being taken away in handcuffs. "*We will see each other again on the other side.*" Did you think he was talking about the Pearly Gates? He meant the other side of the arrest, the trial, or even the prison sentence. But once the letter was sitting on his lap and he had a bag over his head and a tank of nitrous oxide, it wasn't surprising that you should think otherwise.'

'So he killed himself because he was afraid of going to jail,' Goodwin said.

'You haven't been listening, love. Adam Strauss killed Roderick Browne just like he'd always planned.'

'This is all lies,' Teri hissed.

Adam Strauss squeezed her hand. 'We'll have our chance to respond,' he said, speaking quietly.

'I examined that garage,' Khan said. 'It was impossible to get in or out. Are you going to explain that?'

'Of course. But let's start with the set-up. Strauss deliberately made it look like suicide. In fact, it screamed suicide. You're right! Two locked doors. A skylight securely fastened. The only set of car keys in his trouser pocket. Suicide note in his lap. Nobody in their right mind goes to so much trouble unless they really, really want you to accept the obvious. And surely by now you understand that, all along, Strauss was playing with your mind. He even left the supposed reason for the suicide sitting there for you to find. There's no reason on earth why Roderick Browne would have slipped the cut-off piece of drinking straw in his top pocket. He didn't mention it in his letter. Right to the end, he was protecting his neighbours. No. Strauss put a new straw in there. And if Detective Superintendent Khan had stuck with the idea that Roderick was taking cocaine – as he suggested – I'm sure Strauss would have found a way to drop another clue to lead us all back to the second meeting, which was what he wanted all along.

'We know that Strauss was the last person to see Roderick Browne alive and that Browne invited him over. Strauss knew that Andrew Pennington played bridge every Wednesday evening, so it's easy enough to time everything for the exact moment Pennington gets home. And what does Pennington see? Strauss says goodbye to Browne, who replies, "You've been very kind . . ." Words to that effect. The door closes and the light goes off. The time of death is two hours away. So, at this moment, Browne is very much alive.

'That's what we're meant to think. But Strauss has been with Browne, by his own admission, for at least an hour and a half. What really happened was that he slipped a whole lot of sleeping pills into Browne's whisky. One little mistake there. He couldn't get hold of Felicity's temazepam, so he used pills he must have stolen from Dr Beresford . . . which were the next best thing. Always good to point suspicion in the wrong direction. When he leaves at ten o'clock, Browne is already unconscious. How to fake the conversation on the doorstep? Easy with an iPhone and a portable speaker. Dudley here has been recording every conversation I've had, including this one! That's what Pennington hears.

'As for the lights, he said something very interesting to me. "The front door closed, the light went out and Adam walked away." But that's strange for all sorts of reasons. Firstly, Roderick clearly wasn't going to bed. More to the point, think about what he said. A single light going off. The light switch by the door turns off the lights in the hallway, the stairs and the first landing. If Roderick had flicked the switch by the door, that's what Pennington would have seen. But if it was a single light, Roderick would have had to close the door and then cross the hallway to turn off the antique lamp on the chest of drawers.'

'So are you saying that it was Strauss who turned it off?' Goodwin asked. She was finally entertaining the possibility that some sort of trick had been involved.

'Exactly.'

'How?' Khan demanded.

'Easy. He could have used a piece of string and pulled the plug out of the wall. But there were all sorts of electrical bits and pieces that suddenly turned up inside the garage and I think what he used was a cheap remote control he'd brought with him. In reality, Roderick Browne is sound asleep in the kitchen because of the zolpidem. Strauss plays the recording. He closes the door. He turns off the lights with the remote control, which he dumps in the garage later. No point risking the police finding it in his home. Anyway, that's the illusion. Roderick Browne is alive and all is well. Except it isn't.

'Adam Strauss returns to the house. He's left the garage open so he can get in without any trouble. First, though, he uses the ladder to climb onto the roof and remove the screws that hold down the skylight. And that, incidentally, is where Marsha Clarke enters the equation. The dear old lady in Hampton Wick! When Dudley and I stood on the garage roof, we could see just one window in the close: the room belonging to Kylie Jane, the Beresfords' nanny. But that meant if she'd been there, she would have had a view of the garage and there was always a chance that she would look out and see what was happening. So she had to go. It was Strauss who attacked Marsha Clarke. He must have seen Kylie leaving the close with her breadcrumbs for the birds . . . he knew what was going on. He bashed the old lady, knowing Kylie would stay there and look after the cats. As for the political leaflet, that was more misdirection. It was another lie.

'Anyway, as I was just saying, Strauss goes back into the house. My guess is that he's already helped his old friend write the letter to his wife, maybe suggesting a phrase or two. He's got to be sure it'll work for him. Now he drags the unconscious man into the garage. Puts a bag over his head – making another small mistake. Roderick doesn't shop at Tesco's. But it's a suicide. Who's going to notice? He turns on the gas. And now comes the clever part. How is he going to leave Roderick in the car, with the only key fob in his pocket and with all the windows and doors locked from inside?

'In fact, it couldn't be easier. When I visited the garage, I had to step over a pool of water on the concrete floor and I did wonder what it was doing there. After all, it hasn't rained for weeks – you can tell that from the state of the gardens. The answer's built into the car that Roderick Browne drove, the Skoda Octavia. It comes with a range of accessories, but one of them is a rain sensor, located in front of the windscreen. If you're driving and it rains, the wipers come on automatically. And if you've left the car parked, the windows close themselves.

'There was a tap and a bucket in the garage. All Strauss had to do was pour a certain amount of water in the right place to complete the illusion that Browne had locked himself in. Most of the water drained away, but unfortunately for him a little puddle was left and I noticed it the moment I went in.

'So. Back to the night of the crime.

'The up-and-over garage door is locked. The door into the house likewise. Now Strauss climbs onto the Skoda and exits through the skylight. Of course, it would have been hard work doing that with a badly sprained ankle, but he'd faked that ahead of the game too, pretending to fall down the stairs at Richmond station. He pulls himself onto the roof, with no Kylie Jane to spot him, and fastens the screws using glue, which he's brought with him. It was never rust. Stainless steel doesn't rust. Then he climbs down the ladder and goes home to bed.

'That's pretty much it. The one question you might like to ask, Detective Superintendent, is how much Teri Strauss knew about all this. I'm surprised she wasn't woken up when her husband tiptoed in sometime around midnight – and there was definitely someone behind him at Richmond station wearing a hoodie when he was "pushed" down those stairs. She seems quite a feisty little number. Maybe her oriental brain even came up with some of the plot.'

'You are a racist!' Teri snapped.

'Better a racist than a murderer,' Hawthorne retorted.

'Wait a minute!' Khan cut in. 'You've said all this and I suppose it makes some sort of sense, even if it's hardly very likely. But there's one thing you haven't explained. Why would Mr Strauss have wanted to kill Giles Kenworthy in the first place? If it wasn't his chess set and it wasn't any of the other complaints, why go to all this trouble?'

'That's the biggest misdirection of them all,' Hawthorne replied. 'The whole "Nightmare Neighbour" thing – it had nothing to do with it. You've got to ask, what was the one big change that happened at the time of the first meeting?'

'The swimming pool,' Dudley said.

'Exactly. Kenworthy was going to dig up the garden to build a pool. Now, the evidence is a bit circumstantial, but let's put it all together. First, there's the magnolia tree with its amazing blossoms. Even Lynda Kenworthy was impressed by that. And Mrs Winslow's dog was always sniffing around it . . . so it must have been attracted by something. Then we come to Wendy Strauss, Adam's first wife, who divorced him and disappeared from the scene. What do we know about her? Only that she didn't like chess. She wasn't happy in the close. And she and Adam didn't get on. We also know that Adam was having financial difficulties, so it probably wouldn't have helped him to lose half his savings in a divorce.'

'What are you suggesting?' Strauss asked. He seemed completely relaxed, half smiling.

'That she's under the magnolia tree,' Hawthorne said. 'If Kenworthy had gone ahead and built his pool, her skeleton would have been the first thing they discovered. The moment he got planning permission, that was when he had to die.'

There was a lengthy silence in the room. It was broken, at last, by Detective Superintendent Khan.

'So, Mr Strauss,' he said. 'What have you got to say?'

3

'I don't even know where to begin,' Adam Strauss said. 'It's one of the most extraordinary things I've ever heard. It's quite brilliant in its own way – and I ought to congratulate you, Mr Hawthorne – but it's also fantastical, conjectural and full of holes. It wishes on me almost supernatural powers and it would be wonderful if I possessed them, but, unfortunately, I do not.'

He turned his attention to Detective Superintendent Khan.

'I have to say, I'm a little surprised that the police have taken to hiring . . . what? Private detectives? I even wonder if it's legal.'

'We haven't hired anyone,' Khan said. 'Right now, Mr Hawthorne is working under his own aegis, but we have a responsibility to respond to information provided by any member of the public.'

It was half a lie, wrapped in police officialese to make it more palatable.

'What part of it did he get wrong?' Ruth Goodwin asked. This drew an ugly glance from Khan.

By way of an answer, Strauss turned to his wife. 'Can you get the postcards?' he said. 'One of them came in April or May. The other's more recent.'

Teri rose out of the sofa, transported by rage. 'Everything he says is a lie,' she insisted. 'Why do you let him come here to tell these lies?'

She went into the kitchen.

'And the Chinese New Year card,' he called after her.

'We don't have it.'

'Yes, we do. It's in the letters drawer.'

While she was looking, he turned back to Hawthorne, examining him with something close to sadness.

'My first wife is not dead,' he said. 'She left England five years ago, on October the seventeenth, 2009. I remember the date because it's the day after my birthday. She didn't go straight to Hong Kong. She took a flight from Heathrow to New York because she had friends there she wanted to see. I'm sure the records are still available. You only need to check them out. I drove her to the airport. Our marriage wasn't a great success, but that was largely my fault. Chess has been my life. At least you correctly described that part of my character. It's my obsession. Wendy had no interest in it whatsoever and I should have known that this would be a recipe for disaster. It seems that I don't quite have the fore-sight you ascribe to me. She felt left out and that led to our separation.

'But you're wrong to suggest that it was acrimonious. Wendy and Teri are cousins. They speak regularly. She and I have stayed in touch too. We're more friendly now that we're apart.'

'I have them!' Teri called out from the kitchen.

She came back to the sofa, carrying three pieces of mail, which she handed to Khan. The first was a postcard from Macau showing an extraordinary skyscraper shaped like a flower with the words GRAND LISBOA shining out at the top. Each floor was swathed in different-coloured neon lights. Khan turned it over and saw a message, written in blue ink.

This place is crazy. I'm scared I'm going to lose all my money so I haven't even put a ten-avo coin in a slot machine. Liu says hello. Will call when I'm home.

Wendy x

'Who is Liu?' Khan asked.

'It's Wendy's friend,' Teri replied. 'He works in Macau. She often goes to see him.'

'Why has she written this in English?'

'If you look, Detective Superintendent, you will see it's addressed to both of us. Adam can't read traditional Chinese.'

'You may be able to see the postmark,' Strauss added. 'It was sent four months ago, I think. Not from beyond the grave. The second one was just for Teri, so it's in Chinese.'

The second card showed Hong Kong harbour. Because of the Chinese characters, it was difficult to see if it had been written by the same hand, but it was certainly the same colour ink.

'There's a PS,' Teri said. 'It's in English.'

Tell Roderick I said hello. Will write again soon. W.

'Roderick was her dentist,' Teri explained. 'They were friends when she was here.'

Meanwhile, Adam had taken out his iPhone and was scrolling through it as he talked. 'The other card came in February . . .'

Khan was already examining it. There was a picture of a jade horse on the front. The message inside, written in the same hand, was short:

Be happy. Love, Wendy

'She always sent us a card at Chinese New Year,' Strauss explained. 'This is the Year of the Horse.' He found what he was looking for on his phone and handed it over to Goodwin, who was seated nearest to him. 'Here's a photograph she sent at the same time . . .'

There was a photograph of a smiling young woman –
Hong Kong Chinese – holding up a hand and waving.

'You can see the date it was taken,' Strauss continued. 'I'm
not quite sure where it is, but I think it's Hong Kong.'

Goodwin turned the phone towards Teri. Hawthorne and
Dudley both saw the image too.

'Is this your cousin?' she asked.

'Yes. It's my cousin!' Teri agreed.

'This is ridiculous,' Strauss exclaimed. He snatched the
phone, scrolled through it a second time and touched the
screen. 'It's early evening in Hong Kong,' he explained.
'Wendy works at the Maritime Museum, next to the Star
Ferry. You can check that out too if you want.'

'What are you doing?' Khan asked.

'I'm FaceTiming her.' Adam passed his phone across. 'She
should have got home by now. I won't say anything. You
speak to her.'

The phone was making the warbling sound of a FaceTime
call. It rang for about ten seconds before a woman appeared
in her own little box, which then expanded to cover the entire
screen. It was the same woman Strauss had just shown them
in the photograph. She was in a kitchen with a window
behind her.

She said something in Chinese.

'Excuse me,' Khan interrupted her. 'My name is Detective
Superintendent Tariq Khan. I'm calling you from Richmond
in England.'

The woman looked concerned. 'Has something happened to Adam?' she asked, speaking now in English.

'No. Mr and Mrs Strauss are fine. May I ask who I'm speaking to?'

'I'm Wendy Yeung.'

Khan frowned. 'I'm not speaking to Wendy Strauss?'

'Yes! Yes! I am Wendy Strauss, but that is not the name I use any more. My husband and I divorce.' Her English was excellent but not perfect. 'Why are you calling?'

'Ms Yeung, can you confirm that you left the UK about five years ago?'

'Yes. I went back to Hong Kong.'

'Did you go straight to Hong Kong?'

'I'm sorry?'

Khan repeated the question.

'No. I went first to America. I stayed with friends.'

'And where are you now?'

She seemed puzzled by the question. 'I will show you!' There was a blur as she moved across the kitchen and turned the camera round to show a street that was distinctly Asian. Khan could see trams, crowds of people passing in front of shops, banners with Chinese characters. 'This is Hong Kong!' She turned the phone round again. 'Why are you asking? Why do you want to know?'

'We were just checking something, Ms Yeung. I'm sorry to disturb you.'

Khan handed the phone back to Strauss, who spoke briefly.

'I'll explain later, Wendy. It's nothing to worry about.' He clicked it off, then looked at Khan defiantly. 'There is one other thing I would like to mention as I found it personally offensive,' he said. 'Mr Hawthorne suggested that I killed Wendy because I didn't want to pay her alimony. It's true that I've had financial difficulties. It's the reason I downsized. But if you like, I can arrange for my bank manager to send you details of a standing order that I've been paying every month for several years now. It's one thousand pounds, paid directly to an account in Hong Kong. You may not think twelve thousand pounds a year is overgenerous, but it's all I can afford and it's all Wendy needs. She gets plenty of support from the family, and since Teri is part of that same family, it's an arrangement that suits everyone. Is there anything more you want to know?'

There was a long silence. Khan turned to Hawthorne with a look of utter contempt.

'Detective Superintendent . . .' Hawthorne began.

Khan held up a hand for silence.

'I think we've heard enough, thank you, Hawthorne.' He stood up. 'I owe you an apology, Mr Strauss.'

'You don't need to apologise, Detective Superintendent. You weren't the one making the accusations. And if there's any further information you require – bank details, whatever – please let me know.'

'Ten moves ahead . . .' Hawthorne muttered.

'We'll show ourselves out,' Khan said.

NINE

ENDGAME

1

Was this the ending that Hawthorne had warned me against?

Hawthorne hadn't wanted me to write the book. He'd said he wasn't happy about the way it had turned out – both the case and his relationship with John Dudley. Dudley was part of the fallout. I already knew that because, of course, I'd taken his place. Roland Hawthorne had also tried to get me to stop. And when I was at Fenchurch International, Morton had described the whole exercise as a mistake I would come to regret. He must have known that Hawthorne's conclusions would be thrown out by the police and that Adam Strauss would never be arrested or brought to trial. In which case, all the work I'd done so far had been a complete waste of time. It was the one thing I'd always feared. That I'd get to the end of the book and realise that I didn't have one.

I called Hawthorne three times once I'd listened to Dudley's recording, but got no reply, not even a voice message. He must have deactivated his phone because he knew how I'd feel and didn't want to talk to me. I sat at my desk, unable to concentrate on Riverview Close, James Bond or anything else. All I could think about was how much time I'd wasted on a book that was never going to be published. It was incredible to think that when I'd set out, I'd thought it was going to be easy!

Was it possible that I'd missed something, that there was some clue I'd overlooked? I went through everything I'd been given and everything I'd written so far. In particular, I examined what Hawthorne had said in front of Detective Superintendent Khan at The Stables. It had all sounded so credible – until the letters and New Year's card had been produced. And then that FaceTime call! Could it be that Adam Strauss *had* committed the two murders, but for a different reason, that if Wendy Strauss wasn't buried under the magnolia tree, something else was concealed there?

But then I had to remind myself that Strauss had never been brought to trial. He was a chess grandmaster and a television celebrity of sorts: it would have been a huge story if he had been. Instead, he had died in an accident, falling off a hotel balcony. I shuddered. Giles Kenworthy, Roderick Browne, Raymond Shaw, Ellery the dog, and then Adam Strauss . . . How could a quiet residential close in a nice part of London have been responsible for so much death?

Had it been an accident?

Adam Strauss, accused of murder, somehow plunging to his death. I tried to convince myself otherwise, but I knew it was too much of a coincidence. He had been murdered. There was no escaping it. And that led me to an inescapable thought.

I've often mentioned Derek Abbott, the suspect manhandled and badly injured by Hawthorne. I'm not sure if it was a criminal offence, but there could be no doubt that he had eventually talked Abbott into killing himself. Could he have gone one step further with Adam Strauss? I remembered something that Morton had said to me and searched through my own manuscript to find it. Yes. There it was: '*You may discover things about Hawthorne that you wish you hadn't known and once you uncover them, there'll be no going back. It may end your friendship with him.*'

No. Hawthorne was many things. He could be cruel. Many of his attitudes were seriously questionable. He was damaged. But he was basically decent.

He was not a killer. I refused to believe it.

And then my telephone rang.

I snatched it up without even looking at the caller ID. I was certain it would be Hawthorne. But when I put the phone to my ear, there was a voice I didn't recognise.

'Is that Anthony?'

'Yes.'

'This is Detective Superintendent Khan.' He was the last person I had expected to call. 'I'm in London . . . at

New Scotland Yard. I can give you ten minutes if you come over now.'

'I'm on my way.'

'There's a pub round the corner. The Red Lion in Parliament Street. I'll be there at twelve.'

I looked at my watch. That gave me half an hour to get across town.

'I'll see you there,' I said. 'Thank you.'

But he had cut me off before I'd reached those last two words.

2

The Red Lion was about as traditional as a pub can be: brass lamps and window boxes on the outside, polished wood and mirrored shelves within. It stood on a corner, a few minutes' walk from New Scotland Yard, with Downing Street just across the road. I arrived there exactly on time and found the detective sitting at a table with a glass of Coke.

I recognised him at once, although he was older than I'd imagined and a little less of the film star. Once again, I had to remind myself that quite a few years had passed since the murders at Riverview Close. He was wearing a nondescript suit with his tie pulled down and his collar open. I had rather hoped that Ruth Goodwin would be with him – the more characters I met, the better – but he was alone. He looked tired and not particularly pleased to see me, even though he was the one who had rung.

I introduced myself and sat down. It was only now that I realised I had absolutely no idea why he had invited me here.

'So, how's the book going?' he began.

'It's finished,' I said and I didn't mean I'd finished writing it.

'Am I in it?'

'Of course.'

'My son seems to think that's pretty cool. His words, not mine.' He had an eleven-year-old son, who'd been mentioned in one of his many newspaper profiles. 'You should be careful,' he went on. 'You write crap about me, you won't hear the end of it.'

His language surprised me. He'd sounded more polite on the tapes I'd listened to, but then, I suppose, he'd been presenting himself in a more official capacity. A couple of phrases I'd used to describe him flashed through my mind. *Slow and unimaginative. Too pleased with himself.* I made a mental note to take them out.

I was carrying a backpack and I opened it and took out a book . . . the latest Alex Rider. 'I brought this for your son,' I said. 'I thought he might enjoy it.'

Khan glanced at it. 'He's already got that one.' He took it anyway. 'But thanks. You can sign it for him.'

'So why did you call me?' I asked.

'I thought you might like to know that I've just been interviewed. I'm up for chief superintendent.'

'Congratulations.'

'I don't need your support, thanks all the same. I'm only

telling you that because it would be very unhelpful to have you writing about me at the moment, particularly if Hawthorne is your first source of information. I want you to understand that my lawyers will be looking very closely at anything you publish, particularly with respect to how it ends.'

'I'm not sure about that part myself,' I admitted. 'What happened at The Stables, what Hawthorne said – it all seemed so sensible.' Khan said nothing, so I added: 'Did you ever dig up the garden?'

'Of course I didn't dig up the bloody garden. It all checked out. There is a Wendy Yeung working at the Maritime Museum in Hong Kong. She did leave Heathrow on the date Strauss said. I spoke to her! You think I was going to get the bulldozers in after that?'

'It's unusual for Hawthorne to get things wrong.'

'We all make mistakes.'

'Including you?'

He shook his head. 'Not this time – and it would be a mistake to suggest otherwise. The case is closed. It's been closed a long time. You start raking up the past, you're going to cause a lot of grief, and I should warn you that wasting police time is an offence that can land you in jail.'

This wasn't the first time I'd been threatened by a detective.

'What happened to Adam Strauss?' I asked.

That threw him. 'The official story is that he was staying at a hotel in Park Lane, taking part in a chess tournament. He went to his room between games and somehow fell off the balcony. His wife wasn't with him at the time. There was evidence that he'd been drinking.'

'Do you believe that?'

He smiled, but not pleasantly. 'According to Teri Strauss, he never drank when he was playing chess. He needed to keep a clear mind. On the other hand, he wasn't doing well. He was losing. That might have had a part to play.'

'Presumably, you investigated.'

'As a matter of fact, I was called in – because of my prior acquaintance with Mr Strauss. It wasn't my investigation, though.'

'And?'

'Do you want to know because of your concern for the deceased?' He paused. 'Or is it because you think your friend ex-Detective Inspector Hawthorne might have had something to do with it?'

'Of course not,' I said. 'That thought never crossed my mind.'

'Well, it crossed mine. He's got a bit of a reputation for this sort of thing.'

'He would never kill anyone.'

'We looked at CCTV footage, but that was a waste of time. Lots of people going in and out of the reception area, but these days it's all baseball caps, sunglasses and hoodies. Anyway, if someone did want to sneak into the room, they could have got in through the service area and up the backstairs. Security at the hotel was pathetic. You might like to know that we pulled Hawthorne in and we talked to him at length. Of course he played wide-eyed and innocent. But there was no one who could tell us where he was when the supposed accident happened. Home alone, he said. Strange that he didn't make or receive any calls either. Total radio silence. He said he was assembling an Airfix Supermarine Spitfire Mark One. Makes you wonder what sort of man spends an entire day on his own with a model kit.'

'I refuse to believe he went anywhere near Adam Strauss.'

'You can believe what you like. But he'd still concluded, against all the evidence, that Adam Strauss was a killer, and given his past record, it's hardly a surprise that he decided to take things into his own hands . . .'

'I think you should leave him alone.'

'You leave me alone and that'll make us quits.'

He opened the book I had given him and twisted it round for me to sign. 'My boy's name is Nadeem,' he said.

I dedicated the book and he closed it without looking at what I'd written.

'Are you still interested in John Dudley?' he asked, almost as an afterthought.

'Very much so. Can you tell me anything about him?'

Khan nodded. 'In a way, he and Hawthorne were made for each other. He's a sad act – a bright, up-and-coming DC down in Bristol. A lot of people spoke very highly of him. But it all went wrong when his fiancée was killed in an accident. It happened just before Christmas. The driver was a man called Terence Stagg. He was the bar manager at a hotel in Cardiff and not a nice piece of work. He knocked her down on the way to work. The thing is, though, he was on his mobile at the time.'

'Is he in jail?'

'He should have got ten to twelve years, but he had smart lawyers and they managed to get him off scot-free. They couldn't prove he was speeding. He was seen holding the phone, but he claimed he was using it hands-free. And one of the street lights was broken – that was the key to the defence. Anyway, it was enough. He walked away without even paying a fine.

'These things happen from time to time and you have to live with them, but it didn't work out that way. Stagg had some mates meet him outside the court and they were all having a laugh, celebrating his release. One of them had even brought a bottle of champagne. Dudley came out and saw them and went berserk. Punched the lights out of one of them and put Stagg in hospital with a broken jaw. He was lucky not to get prosecuted himself, but his work went to pieces after that. He started drinking. There were a couple of other incidents and he was out of the force within a year. He's spent the last four years working as a security guard . . . something like that. Bit pathetic, really.'

Khan took a folded piece of paper out of his pocket. He laid it on the table in front of me.

'Anyway, I managed to track him down for you. This is where he lives – not so far from here. If you visit him, don't say you got this from me.'

He walked away. I opened the piece of paper and glanced at the address. I recognised it immediately. I knew exactly where it was. I should have known all along.

3

Nineteen B, River Court.

Another address with a river in the name – but this was a building I had been to many times. Hawthorne lived here on the twelfth floor and now it turned out that Dudley had a flat on the first. Had Hawthorne arranged it for him or did he have Morton to thank for his accommodation? I would have been really interested to know just how many of the flats belonged to Fenchurch International and what other refugees, criminals or aliens of one sort or another they had hiding out here.

As I arrived at the front door, I was in two minds. Who should I call on: Hawthorne or his former assistant? It was a decision easily made. Neither of them wanted to see me, but there was more chance that Dudley would open the door. What did he have to lose?

I rang the bell.

Silence.

Then . . .

'Hello?' It was quite something to hear his voice. A lot of writers say that their characters talk to them but very few of them mean it literally.

'John Dudley?'

'Yes.'

I told him who I was. 'I work with Hawthorne,' I explained. 'Can I come in?'

There was another long pause and I wondered whether he was going to ignore me. He might be calling Hawthorne. He might have gone out a back way. Then I heard a buzzing sound. I pushed the door and it opened. He had let me in.

I walked up to the first floor. Dudley was waiting for me outside an open door, about halfway down a corridor that was identical to Hawthorne's: the same neutral colours and discreet lights. Everything was very quiet. I walked up to him.

'Does Hawthorne know you're here?' he asked.

It was interesting that this should be his first question. 'No,' I said.

'Probably just as well. Did Detective Superintendent Khan give you my address?'

How did he even know we'd met? I decided to tell him the truth. 'Yes. I gave him a signed book.'

'I'm surprised he's so cheap.' He examined me for a few moments. Then he came to a decision. 'Well, since you're here, you might as well come in.'

I walked into a flat that was as empty as Hawthorne's – but

for a different reason. There were three suitcases by the door, a pile of cardboard boxes over by the window, the sort removal men use to pack up your life. A single plate, a knife and a fork sat beside the sink in the open-plan kitchen. The furniture had been reduced to the bare necessities. This wasn't how he always lived. He was leaving.

'You've just caught me,' he said.

'Where are you going?'

'The Cayman Islands. Tomorrow.'

That made me think of Lady Barraclough. 'Will you be gone for long?' I asked.

'It may be a one-way ticket.' I felt him examining me, although his face gave nothing away. 'Would you like a coffee?' he asked.

'That would be nice. Thank you.'

He opened a cupboard that contained a jar of instant coffee, two mugs, a bag of sugar. He put the kettle on and took a carton of milk out of the fridge. And all the time I watched him with the uncanny feeling that in a strange way I was watching myself. I had taken his place! And looking at his brown eyes, his dark – definitely lank – hair, it occurred to me that in some ways he looked rather like me, although I was older and perhaps more smartly dressed. Neither of us spoke while he made the coffee. Maybe he was waiting for me to go first.

'You know I'm writing about Hawthorne,' I said as he sat down.

404

'I've read the first two books,' he said. 'I hear they've done quite well.'

I got a faint sense of disapproval. 'I feel I've stepped into your shoes,' I suggested.

'I don't agree.' Dudley added three teaspoons of sugar to his coffee. 'You're writing about him. I worked for him. I'd say we had very different roles.'

'Did he tell you that I'm writing about Riverview Close?'

Dudley paused, mid-stir. 'No. I heard about that – but not from him.'

'Then who?'

'From Alastair Morton.' He looked around him at the empty flat. 'In case you're wondering, it's no coincidence that I'm packing up and I'm on my way. It's thanks to you.'

'How come?'

'You talked to Khan.' That made no sense to me so he continued. 'You've been asking questions about me. You've found your way to my home. Did you know that Fenchurch International owns half the flats in this building? It's meant to be a safe space – but not any more. Morton wants me out of the way. And so I've got to go.'

He had spoken without malice but I still felt terrible. 'Does he really have such a hold over you?' I asked.

'He employs me. Hawthorne got me the job, but Morton signs the cheques.'

'I'm very sorry . . .' I didn't know what to say.

'Don't be. I don't mind a bit of sunshine and I've always

fancied trying my hand at fraud – white-collar crime. It'll be an experience.'

There was a brief silence.

'You must see quite a lot of Hawthorne,' I said. 'Living in the same building.'

'I used to – but you could say we had a difference of opinion. Sometimes we see each other coming in, going out. But we tend to keep our distance.'

'Where did the two of you meet?'

I hadn't expected him to answer and I was surprised when he did.

'In Reeth.'

'You grew up there?'

'We were at school together.' Dudley smiled. 'We knew each other when we were eight years old. We were best friends in the way that only eight-year-olds can be. He was like a brother to me.'

'I don't suppose you're going to tell me what happened in Reeth?'

He shook his head. 'It's not my story to tell.' He deliberately changed the subject. 'You know, he speaks very highly of you.'

'Does he?'

'That's why I let you in. I've wanted to meet you for quite a while now, although if you'll do me a favour, I wouldn't mention any of this to Hawthorne.'

'Or Morton.'

'He already knows. He knows everyone who comes in and out of this building.'

'I hope I'm not going to get you into more trouble.'

I meant it. It was strange, but I felt completely relaxed with John Dudley, as if I'd known him a long time. There was some sort of affinity between us. Despite what he'd said about our different roles, we had both come into Hawthorne's orbit and that connected us.

He shook his head. 'It's too late now. Anyway, I'll be gone by tomorrow evening, so we can just pretend it never happened.'

'That's fine by me,' I said.

'He's not an easy man. I know that. But it's good that you're helping him. I think you're what he needs.'

We lifted our coffee cups at the same moment. Again, I got that weird sense of reflection.

'There's one thing I really want to know,' I said. 'It's the one thing that's been really bothering me and I hope you can tell me. Why did the two of you part company?' He didn't answer, so I leapt in. 'Was it because you discovered that he'd pushed Adam Strauss off a hotel balcony?'

He smiled at me. 'That's very direct.'

'Well, as you say, you're about to leave for the other side of the world. You might as well tell me the truth.'

'It was something like that,' he admitted.

He didn't need to say any more. Khan had known Hawthorne was responsible, although he hadn't been able to prove it. Morton was afraid of the truth coming out. Dudley must have worked it out for himself and that was why the two of them had gone their separate ways.

'I was sorry the investigation didn't have a better outcome,' I said.

He shrugged. 'It ended the way it ended. I'm not sure it's going to be very helpful for your book.'

'Who do you think killed Roderick Browne?'

He gazed at me and I saw the puzzlement in his eyes. 'I know who killed him. It was Adam Strauss.'

'But you never found out why?'

'I know exactly why. Hawthorne got it all right. Everything he said was correct!'

I was puzzled. 'That last meeting at The Stables . . .'

'That's what I'm talking about. The last meeting: Hawthorne and me, the Strausses. Have you heard the recording?'

'I've heard all your recordings. I'm grateful to you for making them. I couldn't have written the book without them.'

'Everything that Hawthorne said that day was bang on the money. I knew it before we went in. Adam Strauss murdered his first wife when he was living at Riverview Lodge and buried her in his back garden. If Detective Superintendent Khan was too stupid to see it or too up his own arse to accept it, that was his problem. I will admit, though, that Strauss played a blinder. But that was what was so brilliant about him. He was a chess grandmaster and he was always ten moves ahead.'

I'd heard that quite a few times.

'He'd boasted about it when we first met him,' Dudley went on. 'But the act he put on in that room . . . that was something else.'

'What do you mean?'

Just for a moment, Dudley looked irritated. 'He'd planned it all a long time ago, exactly the same way he'd planned the murder and the so-called suicide. He'd left nothing to chance. What was he going to do if a police officer walked into his house and tried to arrest him? He'd thought of that before he even killed his wife and he always made sure he had post-cards, stashed away, ready to be brought out if anyone started asking awkward questions. Plus, every year a New Year's card sent from Hong Kong: 2013, the Year of the Snake; 2014, the Year of the Horse. Photos of Wendy that he could show off on his phone. Don't make any mistake. She was rotting away underneath that magnolia tree, but he'd built up a whole legend to keep her alive.

'I have no doubt that it was Teri and not Wendy who took that flight to New York after the divorce. Planning ahead! They must have looked quite similar, even without the racial stereotypes. They were family! And anyway, a single woman travelling business class to New York would barely have got a second glance from a border control guard at either end of the journey. Strauss could probably have done it in drag!'

'He told you there was a Wendy Yeung working at the Maritime Museum in Hong Kong.'

'If DS Khan had bothered to check, which he didn't, he would have found that there is — but not the same Wendy Yeung. It's a common name. It would have been easy enough for Strauss to find someone who shared it.' He paused. 'It's like when a magician tells you to pick a card and then says you can change your mind. You very seldom do. Just the fact that he gives you the opportunity is enough. It makes you believe he's playing fair and square.'

'You called her from the room.'

He sighed.

'No. Adam Strauss dialled the number and passed the phone across. He made a point of announcing that he wasn't going to say a word. Again, the magician! Khan was the one who did the talking and what was the first thing he said? "My name is Detective Superintendent Khan." That was the stupidest thing he could have done. That was the trigger! Whoever it was in Hong Kong, it wasn't Wendy. It was a friend, a relation, an actress, someone who had been paid to play a part years ago. And he'd tipped them off. There was no hesitation, no need for any explanation. When the woman heard who she was speaking to, she simply did what she and Strauss had rehearsed.'

'He said he was paying her money. Was that a lie too?'

'It's probably true. One thousand pounds a month into an account in Hong Kong would be easy enough to arrange. He pays it in. It gets passed across to a second account and then it gets paid back again.' He drank his coffee. 'You've got to understand, Anthony. Nobody has ever planned a murder so far in advance. That was what made Strauss so unique. And why he was so dangerous. In a way, he was the most obvious suspect from the start. Only a chess grandmaster could have dreamt up anything as elaborate.'

I took this all in.

'Thank you,' I said.

'You needed to know.'

'Yes. And you didn't call me Tony.'

I wondered at what point he'd worked out the truth – before or after Hawthorne? But I didn't ask him that. Hawthorne had mocked me once, telling me how much smarter Dudley was out of the two of us. Well, he was right. For what it's worth, I'd come to the conclusion that the killer was Damien Shaw, possibly working with Tom Beresford. I didn't tell him that either.

'What did you think when you heard that Adam Strauss was dead?' I asked.

Dudley smiled, but for a brief moment all the sadness in the world caught up with him: the loss of his fiancée, his lone-liness and alcoholism, sessions with a therapist called Dr Suzmann, his broken friendship with Hawthorne, his exile to the Cayman Islands. I saw his whole history flicker through his eyes.

'I suppose there are some people who might say that he deserved it, but I can't celebrate anyone's death. Not even his. Hawthorne saw things differently to me and maybe that

411

was what drove us apart. I'll miss him when I go, but I think it's for the best. As for your book, you know the truth now and I'm sure you'll agree that the world is a better place without Adam Strauss, so that gives you a happy ending of sorts. I'm not sure what happened to his wife. She was in it all along, of course . . .'

'How can you be so sure?'

He put down his coffee cup. 'I saw it, just as we were leaving The Stables. DS Khan and DC Goodwin went out first. Then Hawthorne. But as I approached the door, I happened to notice their reflections in a mirror in a gold frame on the wall. Strauss and his wife were holding hands, and their faces . . . it was extraordinary to see. The triumph! They were celebrating. They had got away with it. And in that one brief glance, I realised they were monsters. They were evil. And if Hawthorne was the one who pushed Strauss off that balcony, I'm not the one to pass judgement.'

He looked at his watch.

'Despite everything, I'm glad I met you, Anthony. Do you sell many books in Grand Cayman?'

'I don't know . . .'

'Well, I'll look out for the new one.'

He stood up. It was time for me to go.

'No need to come with me,' I said. 'I'll find my way out.'

4

All along, while I'd been talking to Dudley, I'd been thinking that once we'd finished, I'd head up to the twelfth floor. I wouldn't repeat what he'd said to me. I wouldn't even say we'd met. That would have been like betraying myself! But I would knock on Hawthorne's door and go in and see him. I'd explain why I'd gone to Fenchurch International and I'd apologise – to him and to Roland. I was afraid that the damage had already been done, but I couldn't bear the thought that I'd let him down and that I might not work with him again.

Something stopped me. I was thinking about what Dudley had said. I went back downstairs and let myself out into the autumn sunshine. Eight weeks had passed since Hawthorne and I had first discussed the book that I was now calling *Close to Death* and the new season had crept up on me, as it does for so many writers, without being noticed. There were leaves blowing in the street and a metallic quality to the sky:

all too soon the Christmas lights would be going up. I found a bench on the other side of the road with a good view of River Court and sat down, half hoping that I might catch sight of Hawthorne going in or out. I didn't want to speak to him. There was no need. I knew now that we did, after all, have a book. I knew how it ended.

Dudley had turned out to be central to everything that had happened. I hadn't realised quite what part he'd play when I'd first introduced him, arriving with Hawthorne at Riverview Close. When I was writing those pages, I'd thought he was just the sidekick. Like me.

But now I remembered the way he had looked at me when I asked him about the death of Adam Strauss, the story he'd told me about the reflections he'd glimpsed in the mirror, Strauss and his wife. Monsters. Evil. That was how he had described them.

I know that I'm not much of a detective. Time after time, I've followed in Hawthorne's footsteps, getting everything wrong. I've made stupid mistakes and even put my own life in danger. I'll be the first to admit that Hawthorne was right and that Dudley was in every way sharper than me. But this time, just for once, I'd guessed the truth all on my own and I knew that I was right.

The triumph. They were celebrating. They had got away with it.
Just like Terence Stagg.

Even before I'd walked out of the flat, I'd realised that it wasn't Dudley who had found out what Hawthorne had done and who had chosen to walk away from him, but the other way round. It wasn't Hawthorne who had pushed Adam Strauss off that balcony. It was Dudley — and Morton had known it all along. The moment I had started asking questions, Morton had decided to send Dudley as far away as possible. As for Hawthorne, he knew it too, but he had kept silent even when he had become the subject of a police investigation and still remained the number-one suspect in Adam Strauss's murder. Even I had thought the worst of him, but Hawthorne would go on protecting Dudley because they had been eight-years-olds together, sharing a life about which I still knew almost nothing. Because they were friends.

I sat there for perhaps an hour before a taxi pulled up opposite me. I saw Hawthorne get out. He paid the driver and walked slowly towards the front door of River Court, found his keys and let himself in. I didn't call out to him. I waited until he had disappeared.

Then I got up and walked away.

Acknowledgements

This was quite a complicated novel to write . . . mainly because of the different timelines.

The events at Riverview Close take place during the months of June and July 2014 – but it wasn't until 2019 that Hawthorne and I sat down and he told me about the death of Giles Kenworthy and what had followed. We had a series of meetings over a period of eight weeks and I didn't actually finish writing the book until April 2020, missing the Christmas deadline that my agent, Hilda Starke, had demanded.

It didn't matter anyway. For one reason and another, *Close to Death* has only been published in 2024 – so there was no need for all that pressure in the first place.

I only mention this because I want to pay a special tribute to my copy editor, Caroline Johnson, who has had to pull together all the separate strands, work out what was happening and when, where I was at the time, what Hawthorne was doing and how it all fitted together. Without her, the book wouldn't have made any sense at all, although, conversely, if there are any mistakes, it's entirely her fault.

By coincidence, I actually moved to Richmond shortly after I finished the book and I want to thank the writer Michael Frayn, who provided me with further details about Riverview Close and its residents. He happens to live near the close and I was very fortunate to meet him. I was also given some very useful insights by Harry Matovu, KC, a senior Silk at the Commercial Bar who has been recognised four times running by Powerlist as one of the most influential black professionals in the UK. I had, of course, spoken to Andrew Pennington, but Harry told me a great deal more.

A word of thanks to Jon Emin, who had briefly resided in Riverview Close. He was so pleased to be mentioned in the book that he gave a generous donation to Home-Start in Suffolk, a brilliant charity working in the community. I'm a patron. I'm also grateful to Jeffrey Hunter White, my online stress counsellor (based in Palm Springs), who was always ready with advice and support.

As always, my wife, Jill Green, was the first person to read the manuscript and gave me some excellent notes. I do wonder how I'd cope without her. With my sons, Nicholas and Cassian, my two daughters-in-law, Iona and Sophia, and now a new arrival – Leander Horowitz – I am extremely lucky to have a close family around me and one that fills the vacuum in which all writers live. My assistant, Tess Cutler, continues to organise my life and to stop me making commitments I can't possibly fulfil. My agent, Hilda Starke, is often too busy to take my calls, but her assistant, Jonathan Lloyd, is always there for me.

The team at Penguin Random House is listed separately, but I want to extend a special thank you to Darren Bennett for the terrific map at the front of the book (I do like maps in murder mysteries) and to Glenn O'Neill for working tirelessly to create the new style for all the covers. My editor, Selina Walker, is the spider at the heart of the web, but not a poisonous one like Gemma Beresford's jewellery. You wouldn't be reading this without her.

Writers often feel isolated and alone but the truth is that producing a book is a huge team effort.

It's my pleasure to acknowledge the fantastic support I've been given in the long journey from idea to manuscript to finished publication.

PUBLISHER
Selina Walker

EDITORIAL
Joanna Taylor
Charlotte Osment
Caroline Johnson

DESIGN
Glenn O'Neill

PRODUCTION
Helen Wynn-Smith

UK SALES
Alice Gomer
Olivia Allen
Kirsten Greenwood
Jade Unwin
Evie Kettlewell

INTERNATIONAL SALES
Anna Curvis
Linda Viberg

PUBLICITY
Sarah Harwood
Klara Zak

MARKETING
Sam Rees-Williams

AUDIO
James Keyte
Meredith Benson